THE
CRUE
ME

To Pattie, who minded two generations of our family in Kilbride and Trim and was my childhood connection to the ancient world. Also to all who were incarcerated in the Magdalene Laundries, Industrial Schools, and mental institutions in Ireland; their endurance and bravery inspired this book.

THE CRUELTY MEN

EMER MARTIN

THE LILLIPUT PRESS
DUBLIN

First published 2018 by
THE LILLIPUT PRESS
62–63 Sitric Road, Arbour Hill
Dublin 7, Ireland
www.lilliputpress.ie

ISBN 978 1 84351 739 9

A CIP record for this title is available
from The British Library.

1 3 5 7 9 10 8 6 4 2

Front cover: photograph by Brendan Walsh incorporating
image of police and civilians in Dublin, 1933 (Independent
Newspapers, courtesy National Library of Ireland).

Set in 10 pt on 15 pt Hoefler by Marsha Swan
Printed in Spain by GraphyCems

Prologue

As a spider, I pluck off my long legs one by one until, reaching the last two, I hesitate and become human.

I am the hag. I am Ireland. I was here before you. And I was already old when you came. I was lonely and I let you come into me.

My hair is a long, strong, ropey grey. My skin is crumpled and cracked. From my anus, I dropped the rocks that form the shore. I pinched the hills into small shapes. I sat into the mountains buckling with ferocious cramps, letting rivers spring from my monthly blood and, as they ran clear, the last traces of this blood turned the hook-jawed silver salmon red. By the time you arrived my sisters were already dead.

One of them killed by the bull.

By the sea alone, I was a shaper. I spat out hawks and scald crows as I danced to keep warm. The moon was wider then. Easier to jump onto. I don't make those moon landings anymore. A bird whose eggs have been touched by human hands, I never return to that nest.

I'm not ashamed to say I was lonely here; waiting for no one by the edge of a long frozen world. A second freezing. I scraped my nails along the edge of the land and made cliffs. Giant deer got tangled in my guts. My tears pollinated the island's thawing interior. I screamed out wolves who darted, predatory grey in forests, then, sleeping, I whimpered foxes who left sea onion outside their dens to keep the wolves away.

From the moment I saw you rowing down the horizon I put my fingers out to still the sea for your tiny vessels. The crags of my fingers left a granite trace.

You left your boats behind and entered my forests. The trees accepted you. You felt you were home. My world had been a verb world. The trees were treeing. The birds were birding. The rivers were rivering. The pink salmon, sacred always with the knowledge of return, were salmoning.

Everything was in dance.

You came and marked it all out with those static, false nouns. You were wrong about that too. You didn't fathom how it was all flowing back and forth and swapping. You didn't know it never belonged to you; it never even belonged to me.

A time of great change is coming.

I have my end too. But it comes with the last swell of the sun. My time is not fettered by yours. This is the circle that spirals down and down and down and round and round and round. That's why it was so familiar when you stepped from your boats. It's why you recognized Ireland at first landing.

For so long you didn't want me. For so long you created and adopted gods to suit you but they're all melting away. What did you end up saying about me?

Is fuar cumann cailleach. The affection of a hag is a cold thing. And that's the truth.

Did you know before I was this, I was something else? Unlike you, I did not shift my shape from noisy ape. I was quiet as a spider – look at all I wove.

I am spider no longer.

You turned away from me, and you've said things about me and told stories full of lies. Over a teardrop of time, you did what I thought you couldn't. In the end, within a mere ten thousand years, you had broken my insect heart.

The change is coming.

Your eyes are dead starlight.

Your souls are sorrowing. You are shining – already gone.

To hell with you! I'll still be here on the grey edge of the Atlantic when you are done.

PART I

DISPLACEMENT AND RESETTLEMENT

No one went ever to Bolus but in the hope of getting something there.

Proverb from Iveragh, County Kerry

Connaire O Mac Tire

Wolfland
(1653)

An English captain of General Ireton's regiment who was present at a battle in 1647 reported, to king and country, that several of the slaughtered native Irish garrison of Cashel were found to have wolves' tails.

This came as no surprise. English people referred to Ireland as Wolfland. Wolves were long gone in England and they were horrified to find them rampant in Ireland.

There was a long list of things that they wanted to rid their neighbouring island of: wolves, forests, rebels, the Irish language, harps, priests.

I am Connaire O Mac Tire. I am the last of my line. I lived in the forests among the wolves for the last three years or so. They called us the Tories, 'pursued men'. I grew up on a farm and there had been a war against the new English settlers since I was a wee boy. These settlers caused much bitterness. But nothing prepared us for what was to come. I was the only boy, and my mother quickly gave me a long knife. In all the confusion, she told me that I was the last of the line in Ireland and to run and hide while my father and all my uncles stood to fight Cromwell's armies. I hid in a narrow space behind the sheds and covered myself with firewood. I could not see anything, but I heard the ugly screams of battle. When I finally emerged shivering I found my father and his brothers dead in the yard. They took my four sisters and my mother as slaves and sent them off to the tobacco lands. With my heart heavily burdened I slipped away from the Parliamentarian soldiers and I came to the forest. In the dark forest I chanted a prayer my mother had taught me.

May the spectres not harm me during my journey.

They had hunted the few of us who escaped their big guns into the thickest part of the forest. All the townlands were cleared of people, and the crops laid waste. There was nothing to eat. There were children hiding all along the roads, and if the wolves didn't get them, they joined us rather than be captured. The black plague had broken out. They said the towns were full of it, and one by one all the towns fell to the invaders in a great tide of blood. The wolves grew in numbers, thriving on the chaos and death. All this I saw from the forest.

May old age be mine
And death not come to me until I reach it.

Cromwell had warnings of an invasion of England from Scotland so he went back to England, leaving General Ireton in command. We were hoping our friends the Scots would give trouble and then come help us. We knew it was hopeless by ourselves. The enemy was formidable. In the end, even Black Hugh, son of Hugh Mac Neil, had to creep out of Clonmel and flee. All the news that got to us as we hid among the trees was mighty bad and we were sore tired to hear it.

May my tomb not be prepared,
May I not die on my journey.

In these dense forests we lived close to the wolf. The settlers spoke of us in the same breath as the wolf. They hated the forests that sheltered us. We ran from drumlins, to freezing bogs, to dark forest, causing whatever trouble we could to settlers and soldiers. We picked up those hiding to join us. I was half starved, and my clothes fallen to rags. I killed wolves with my long knife and ate their flesh and wore their skin. We had a tailor among us who had lost all his family to the soldiers; he fashioned the wolfskins into clothes. We only ate wolf meat, and the abandoned pups we took with us, until we became a close pack, wolves and men wearing wolves.

We looked out from the forest; the very branches trembled on the trees. The land lay empty and burnt. Everything we had ever known was dead.

May my return be granted!
May the headless serpent not catch me.

Sometimes the chaos in my head could be stilled by lying against a tree and letting its rooted peace pass into my skull. I began to think tree thoughts. The trees could tell what was happening. I could promise them nothing. I would have died for them. But I wasn't even sure I could save myself or my pack. And the forest could hardly move with us.

We few who had survived gave as much resistance as we could to the settlers and the army, but they began to set the woods on fire and the hunters were closing in, their barking wolfhounds as big as colts. We could continue no longer like this, and as we lost our terrain we began to make our way west under the cover of night. There was no time I was not frightened for my pack's life. I hunched hungry in the trees, rattling with the cold. Most of our kind didn't make it. Some talked of getting to the ports and sneaking off to France and Spain. I wished them well. But I could not leave the land. I remembered my mother's words. I was the last of the O Mac Tires in Ireland.

Before Cromwell came we had once lived with the wolf. We prayed to the wolves and wished them well so they wouldn't harm us. We used their ground-down dung to soothe our colicky babies. We ate wolf meat to protect us from seeing ghosts. If you were plagued with nightmares, a wolf's head under the pillow would chase any demons away. There was an entrance to the underworld in Co. Roscommon. Three women emerged every year from this cave in the shape of wolves.

The foreigners knew nothing of all this. They only knew that the land and people were too wild for them.

The Parliament in England was broke after the War of Three Kingdoms, as they called it, and they were using our land to pay their debts and placate their exhausted armies. Regiment after regiment, troop after troop, were being given our land as they conquered. Their New Model Army was vast, and as efficient in settling as in slaughter.

There was no stopping them.

May no robber harm me,
Nor troop of women,
Nor troop of warriors!

Only the five counties of Connacht were reserved for the 'home of the Irish race'. The Irish were forbidden to stay within ten miles of the Shannon River.

'We'll not go there. It's too congested and Galway reeks of the plague. We're going south,' I said to my pack. We hunted only at night. By day we dug dens, huddled, and told each other stories to keep our spirits. Before he died of a fever, a young boy in my pack told me the story of the Bull Bhalbhae and that became my story to tell.

'Where are we going?' my pack asked me. I heard tell of a cave in Connacht that was an entrance to the other world. A wolf man called Old Ai came out of this cave. The wolves could use the caves to travel into other worlds. I thought of leading my pack there. If I could find another world I would surely go into it.

One by one my pack was dying off. We found a terrified priest hiding by a riverbank and he joined us. At first he kept looking at me sideways, afraid. He was educated abroad and much travelled. He told us that Cromwell himself despaired of it all, and wrote:

> *For if the priest had not been in Ireland, the trouble would not have arisen, nor the English have come, nor have made the country almost a ruinous heap, nor would the wolves have so increased.*

He was the one who told us that we were called Tories, and some called us Woodkern, since we dwelt in the woods. There was a generous bounty on every wolf, priest and Woodkern in the land. The adult male wolf got its killer five pounds, the same price as a priest. He said they were cutting off the balls of the priests. They found all the harps in the land and built a big pyre with them in Dublin, within the Pale, and destroyed them in flames. We were in grave danger so, for to subdue this land the forests would have to go, and so too the wolves. We knew this. The trees knew this. The wolves knew this. Though their numbers had increased since the land was laid waste, they were now as cursed as we were. Cromwell brought out a bill to destroy the wolves in 1653. I wondered where to lead my pack.

When the new moon came out I would hunker down and try to gather strength. The priest shook his head and got on his knees. He ordered the men to pray. I recited my own prayers taught to me by my mother's mother.

> *May the King of Everything*
> *Cast more time my way.*

The men were caught between the two of us. I told them to get strength from the moon but to pray with the priest if they saw fit, and it benefited them. I told them they did not have to choose, but the priest warned they would be damned. I thought of killing the priest, but I had never killed any innocent man. In the end everyone followed me, though I didn't know where I was taking them.

'You are a born leader,' he said, one grey day as we sheltered from the rain. 'You should become a priest.'

'I cannot, mister,' I replied. 'I am the last O Mac Tire in Ireland and I must carry on my name.'

'Names are of little importance in these dire days,' he said. 'You are strange and wild. You are a wolf. But you have a great head for stories. Your memory is like a trap. We could smuggle you out to France, Italy or Spain and get you ordained and you could return and be a greater influence on your people.'

'I'll not leave Ireland. I'm looking for an entrance to the world underneath. It's there I have to go.'

'But you can't go there alive.' He frowned.

'There are those who can live between two worlds,' I told him.

'I pity you.' He shook his head.

The priest and I vied for the souls of our pack. He told them to renounce violence and pray to God, to stay loyal to the Roman religion St Patrick brought to us. I told them to keep fighting the settlers, and beware of all things foreign. They were weary and sick for the past, before the world turned inside out and they had to become wolves among the trees. The stench of the plague was everywhere so we avoided the few ragged settlements that were left. There in the forest I saw the foxes lay sea onion at the mouths of their dens to keep the wolves away. I could not abide the stuff. We crept west through the forest, moving only at night guided by the stars. One dawn, as we were walking, there was a new bird in the sky. I pointed it out to the priest. Big and bold and black and white. It seemed to have been brought in on a great storm with Cromwell's armies. The priest said it was called the magpie. It brought us no luck. I hurled stones as I cursed it.

Magpie invader bird
One for certain sorrow,
Swept in with Cromwell
We'll never rid of you.

The truth is we had been defeated, the land had been cleared and settled with those foreign-tongued, for them the land was not storied, it was just wealth. The woods were now gone, even our music, the mountain of harps in Dublin burnt to a cinder. We ran with the wolves to higher ground. To the great mountains. To the end of the world, looking for another.

On we travelled to the southwest, to the kingless Kingdom of Kerry. We were ambushed by the English soldiers on the bogs. My pack scattered. The wolves made it to higher ground but I feared I was the only man left alive, the priest was badly wounded and I carried him on my back. For miles and miles I bore him, leaving a trail of blood in our wake. He was taken in, at great risk, and hidden in a smallholding. Though it was dangerous, the native Irish felt honoured to have him, and I stayed till he got some strength back. News went round that there was a priest among us. He said Mass in the strange Latin language out on a secret rock and the local people gathered with their heads bowed. I finally got down on my knees and prayed with all my heart and soul. I let his Latin inside me. No one knew what it all meant. But belief was something else.

The priest said he'd stay a little there, disguised as a peasant, as the people were hungry for the Mass. We were sad to part as we had great respect for each other. Though our aims were different, we shared much, and he had many stories of saints and wolves. The last night he urged me to tell the story of the Bull Bhalbhae to all gathered.

This was my last hiding place. Now all the forests were cut and burned. Solitary, I walked for aeons at night and slept in ditches at day, until I reached Bolus Head, the very end of Ireland. An old old hag, agile as a goat, found me wandering lost and lone, she brought me to her cave in a cliff overlooking the jagged Skellig Islands and fed me some broth. I had strange dreams that night. I woke up somewhere entirely different, on the side of a mountain among five stones standing. I saw a drove of hares on this mountain and they signalled for me to follow. They brought me to a family in the village of Cill Rialaig, called the O Conaills. One of the daughters invited me into her bed and I was welcomed. This was the strangest of times, where wolf and hare lay together. My name would live on.

I had stories for them. They had stories for me. For though our English neighbours had gathered all the harps and burned them, the stories could not be burned, or cut down, or hunted. The stories were an unconquered place.

I usually didn't make anything up in the stories. But there was something in my head that came unbidden and I could not rid myself of it. A chant of words that I knew not its origins. Some kind of prophecy.

Cormac Mac Airt,
Son of a wolf,
A thief took my eyes from my head.
They said if I ate wolf meat it would protect me from seeing ghosts,
But a wolf has eaten the moon,
A wolf devoured the sun,
Now it has turned wide-jawed
To the ice cold frozen,
Tide-wild earth.
A wolf has eaten the world.

Mary

We Lived in a Dream at the Edge of the World (1935)

A man came up the mountain on a bicycle. We lived in Cill Rialaig village on Bolus Head by the township of Ballinskelligs in the Barony of Iveragh in Co. Kerry. Ten houses all in a row at the side of the road. As it was, the road was barely cut out from the mountain. There were no houses on the other side of this road because they would have fallen straight into the sea. There was no facing each other or gathering around each other. There was just a procession of us. Sometimes I felt the houses were the people. With their window eyes and their door mouths, and the wind came in through slate, stone skin and lashed about the insides. Often the hens were blown up onto the rocks that hung over us. There was no shortage of water coming down from the mountains: brown, soft, boggy and cold. We licked it off the mossy rocks.

The Great Hunger was over when I was born but the living memory of it was still strong, and roads around us were jittery with ruins of houses. These ruins were just like the dead. Part of our world, we accepted their sadness, their crowded, blacker past; for this hillside had once been a busier place. Many had fallen from the hunger before they could get away. The ditches we played in as children were full of their bones. Some of them would have survived and settled elsewhere. And if you had family in America sending home remittances, you were on the pig's back. But the majority who survived ran out of here and never looked back.

We had heard that the English were finally gone after 800 years. Indeed they were gone about four years before I was born, but this had not made much difference for those of us on the last road in Ireland. We existed in a dream at the edge of the world. We spoke only Irish. We lived on the mountain and the mountain lived in us. Empires had fallen on the continent and wars had been fought, lost, won, epidemics had raged, but little mind we paid to it. I can recall the bony cattle standing in the deserted cabins looking with their blank faces out of the windows and the ragged curtains still hanging there. Not only were the houses ruined, but we were forgotten too, remember?

That is until the man came up the road on his bicycle.

He was pushing it up the steep hill and he had a big book strapped to the back. The sun was swollen up that day and the sea was hard and sparkling. The islands that lay just out from us were luminous in the water. Dinnish, Scarriff, and the long finger of the Beara Peninsula with three distant islands, the Bull, the Cow and the Calf. They looked like great floating whales. They were our family too. When you see them every one of your born days it becomes that way. Those islands and the mountains were as much part of me as my limbs.

We children ran to him. It was our hill. We swarmed around him and asked him lots of questions. He was sweating and mopped his brow with a large, white, initialled hanky, the likes of which I'd never seen. He spoke mostly English and a different kind of Irish that didn't flow, but we could understand. He sat most of the day on a stool outside the O Conaill's house and instructed us to go fetch all the grown-ups. We ran into the hills and told everyone to gather that evening.

It was the brightest day of the year and the longest, still light when we sat in front of the small fire. We didn't need it for heat but we did all our cooking in a big black pot over it. There were about thirty people in the house and we ran in and out of the two doors at either side. We'd hare round the cabin and through it again.

We all thought the man was from the Folklore Commission. There was a few of them who went around the country on bicycles and got the stories from the old people before they disappeared into their graves, and all their knowledge with them. For nothing was written down, all was kept in our heads. We welcomed folks from the Folklore Commission. Things were changing so fast, that every time an old person died they took centuries of knowledge with them.

This man was not looking for our stories. He had come for us, body and soul.

'I'm from the Land Commission,' he announced.

When the man laid maps on the table before us he explained that we could have land elsewhere, really good land. County Meath, the best land in the country. County Meath was the Royal County; the land had always been good and fertile. The kings of Tara were the high kings of Ireland. The most sacred river in Ireland was the Boyne where the Salmon of Knowledge had once dwelt. For these reasons it was the seat of the ancient kings and queens of Ireland. He told us, it was the part of Ireland where there were the most sacred places.

The new government of Ireland would give it to us, just like that. A fierce excitement merged with deep suspicion, for why would anybody give land for free? The man drank his cup of tea and stood to give a speech. We sat on the floor in front of him and the women sat behind us and the men stood looking in the windows or at the doors.

'Now that we are an independent country for over a decade, we want to decolonize the country. The Irish language, once outlawed in our very schools, has disappeared so quickly. From the time they hung a tally stick around your children's neck and marked it everytime they spoke. And beat them for as many marks they had. Is it no wonder it has been so willingly surrendered by a broken self-loathing people? But we are free now and everything will be better. We must take pride in ourselves again, and our language is our pride. We want to revive the Irish language in the East and the Midlands. Everyone has forgotten how to speak there. Vast estates of absentee landlords are being redistributed as small farm holdings to poor farmers from the overcrowded Gaeltacht areas of Connemara, Mayo and Kerry.'

'Why would ye do that for us? Why not just give us land around here,' my mother, who was always a talker and afraid of no one, shouted up to him.

'Look. There's still too many here for this bad rocky land to support, and the aim is to redress a centuries-old imbalance. The English under Oliver Cromwell forcibly removed your ancestors from the land, shouting "to Hell or Connacht". How do you think so many of ye got over here to this part of the country? Do ye not remember that? That was in 1649.'

'Sure they didn't want this land,' a man said. The others nodded.

'Precisely,' the man continued, mopping his bright red brow with his white hanky. He could see he was winning people over and visibly relaxed. 'Connemara has been designated as a congested district, and these parts of Kerry; they are overpopulated and the holdings are too small. Sure even in the time of famine the British were passing laws to clear people out from here and thinking the famine would just do the work for them. Am I right? Or am I right?'

This got a hearty, rueful laugh and the man laughed with us. We were beginning to see the sense of what he was saying. The men were looking at each other and the women were wringing their hands to think that life might be changed utterly, as of this moment. As kids we just thought of the night that was in it and picked up on the thrill from our families around us. There were some of the old people who closed their eyes for they knew that they would be left behind. After all they'd seen, they trusted no man from any government, even if it was our own. Dublin felt as distant to these mountains as London once had.

'This is the genuine article. There won't be another chance the likes of this in your lifetimes. How many times do we have revolutions that clear the land for people who have suffered such as ye?' He began to run his pencil around a big map of far-off Meath and draw lines from the west and the south going to it. 'The Ráth Chairn Gaeltacht is to be established this year. We are offering about twenty-seven families from Connemara, mostly from Ceantar Na nOileán, to be settled on land previously acquired by the Land Commission.'

'Who did they push off that land? If they've been there since 1649 they might have thought of it as home,' my mother said, and the others looked at her and bit their lips. The man looked down at her and continued without answering.

'The good news is that your district is designated too, as a congested district, so you are eligible under the scheme.'

We couldn't quite believe this. The adults wanted all the information. Free land was not something you came by in an ancient fought-over country like ours. The men said they had plenty to think about and the man on the bicycle was offered poitín, which he declined. But he knew well enough not to leave now, but to join in the gathering. Many came up to talk to him personally. He told them at one point that it was their patriotic duty to bring their lovely language back to the people who had lost it and were only left with the enemy tongue in their mouths. That won many a soul over, as we all like to pretend we're doing somebody good when we're helping ourselves.

Though I was only a child of ten they pushed me out into the front and I told some stories. I had no voice for singing so that was what I did. My father and mother were proud that I had committed a whole welter of stories to memory by age five and I never missed a word. That was my small gift. Not that it would bring me fortune or even luck but it did shorten the nights for all who gathered. But that night, as the stories were told by the fire and the songs were sung, many of the grown-ups were thinking of other things. They were thinking that leaving those islands out at sea was akin to hacking of their own limbs. They were thinking of going where the people were mute. Where they wandered around their own land unable to utter sounds. Where they encountered one another and could not speak.

I would have loved to be a teacher. That was my dream when I was very young. But even in Bolus Head I had not gone to school; like most of the girls as soon as I was old enough to fend for myself I would be sent off to work as a servant in a town. I was ten now and already my father was making inquiries on my behalf at the market. There was a storyteller in one of the cabins and I listened to all his stories and kept them in my head. He knew as he was telling them that I was remembering. Sometimes I thought it was only me he was telling them to even though there would be a full room.

The old storyteller's greatest fear was that he would forget his stories, so he used to tell them to himself. While bringing the cattle home, he would come down the road with his arms flying and gesticulating, telling himself the stories out loud, lest they all just dissolved into the back of his brain. Like a fairy child I was only four when I would pad softly behind him listening, and he would brighten when he saw me.

'Now that the old age pension came in, you don't see the old people wandering the roads with their stories,' he would sigh.

The old storyteller died at a great old age and, before he went away from us, I came in and sat by him in front of the fire. He couldn't speak but I told him one of his stories back to him and in his watery eyes I saw a glimmer. He couldn't read nor write, nor could he speak English. Neither could I. But I would learn to do both.

We were eligible as a family for relocation, everything was offered us and my parents decided to pack up and go. Mammy was only a girl and the cabin, and field near it, would belong to her eldest brother not her. She was some woman. Once a chick was in our house and a pot fell on it and split its stomach open. Mammy scooped it out of my hands and sewed it back up then and there, and sure enough didn't the chick become a fine hen. Mammy was tough but I don't know how tough my father was. He was a man of few words, who did not suffer fools, but he looked to her for everything and he did her bidding. He followed her as night followed day.

My very body started to grieve as soon as I heard. Sure I knew I'd never come back. I walked up to the standing stones on the hill. I howled and raged and it echoed through the surrounding marshes. I stumbled down the mountain onto the road.

We left in a pony and trap. Mammy said she would stay on until she had her baby. She was seven and half months pregnant and didn't want to make the journey. My father kissed her outside the house. He kissed her on the lips like I'd never seen him do before. We turned away embarrassed. There were six of us childer then.

'Don't look so sad, Mary,' Mammy said to me as I got down out of the cart and ran to her for a last hug. I had never been away from her for even a night. She grabbed my shoulders. 'You are ten years old now. We'd have had to send you away into service in the town anyway. This way we can keep you for a few more years. That's one of the reasons I've decided. I couldn't bear to be losing you now but we couldn't have kept you. You be their mammy until I have the baby and come to you. You are in charge of all the wee ones, do ye hear?'

I nodded, crying now.

'Whisht your crying girl. You take care of them for me? Promise?'

'I promise.'

'They're in your hands now, Mary. Understand? I'm relying on you.'

My father whooshed me back into the trap. I felt important and scared.

Suddenly Mammy's face changed as if a cloud had come over her mind, she ran to us all in the trap and we held onto her and embraced her. All of us together. My father turned to the sea and shook his head. Like my mother, he had been born and bred on Bolus Head and him leaving the mountain would be the pain of having the mountain wrenched out of him. He looked away from us at the silver sea and the slate-grey sky with bursts of light like God's fingers.

She told him, 'Look at me now. You'll see the sea again. I saw on the maps there's a biteen of sea at one end of Meath and I'll take you to it. Now mind you take good care of all my chicks.' I thought of her sure hand scooping the wee chick up and stitching it.

Padraig was like a wild hare and had to be secured into the cart for he never could stop moving. Mammy hugged him even as he wriggled away from her, and Maeve and Bridget reached over and threw their arms around her. None of us had ever spent so much as a night away from each other. Seamus was a child with little patience and looked like he wanted to get on with it, he shook her hand curtly. She grabbed Seán, the baby, once more and raised him above her head until he squealed with laughter. 'My beautiful wee Seán. This one will take care of us all someday.' She handed me Seán and nodded to me. I knew she was entrusting him especially to me, for he was one of those lit babies, a light inside him that anyone could see. 'I'll take care of them all, Mammy.' By God I tried to keep that promise.

Daddy hoisted himself to the front and gave the horse a lash. We all looked back.

That's how I remember my mother, Grainne. At the door of the cabin. Her hand shielding her eyes from the sun. Her other hand resting on her giant belly.

We expected to see the man on the bicycle in Co. Meath when we arrived but we never saw him again. There was a barn where they were organizing the arriving families. Each family was provided with a three-room Land Commission house and a farm of approximately twenty-two acres, a sow, piglets and basic implements. That was all they did with us and we were left to fend for ourselves. My father slept with the deeds to his new lands on his chest and his hands over them. Being the youngest of sixteen children, he had never owned land before. To some of the adults it was a triumph, they told us that the defeat of the Boyne was the beginning of our sorrow; it is that which left the stranger and the enemy directing and mastering us. Sure weren't we pleased as punch that we had avenged the Devil, Cromwell.

So that is how we were given land in Co. Meath and told to work it and speak the Irish. But no one outside the settlement wanted to talk to us. They were angry with us for getting local land for nothing. In their eyes, the government had seized it and given it to strangers, not the local Catholic families who had laboured for the Protestant settlers for centuries. Where was their retribution? We were viewed as colonizers, invaders.

Daddy started to hate it. He had not wanted to go and it was my mother who insisted that life would be better if we did. It was herself that had been excited about the adventure. She was livelier than he was, quicker and funnier and more resilient. He knew it, and he pined for her. She was to have her wee one and join us. But she never appeared as the months went on. Daddy could not leave as there were six of us among strangers and we had to get a crop into the land so we'd have something to eat when it came round to harvest. The fear of starvation was strong in him. Daddy thought it might be too late already. He was given a few pigs and had a bit of money for three or four cattle. We had taken our chickens and they gave us eggs. But we were constantly hungry and missed my mother something awful.

It wasn't long before Daddy seemed to be leaving us also. He sank further and further into his own self. I asked him, as we worked in the field, what was wrong when I found him hunkered down just pushing the soil with his fingers.

He said, 'Mary, you tell me what this life is about.'

I thought about an old rhyme.

'Twenty years a child,' I recited, 'Twenty years going mad. Twenty years a sane person. And after that offering up your prayers.'

With that he stood up and stroked my face with his rough farmer's hand. 'You've listened well to the old man's stories. I just can't get used to it here. It's all so flat.' He groaned and pulled his trousers up under him. He was getting thinner and thinner.

'I miss her too,' I said. 'She's our mammy. We don't like being without her. When is she coming?'

'No word,' Daddy growled. 'If there was only a mountain here to walk up against. Sure I can't think straight at all, at all, my thoughts do be flying out over the land before I can think them.'

When there were clouds in the evening, rested blue on the horizon line, I'd squint my eyes and pretend they were mountains and it gave me some comfort and I could breathe again. In this grassy, fertile land we dreamt about the rough sea and the cold rocks on the hills. My younger brothers and sisters were put into the local Irish-speaking school set up for us, but I never went. Daddy said I could go as soon as Mammy came but until then I helped my father by running the house. A year and a half later he asked me to look after them all so he could go back to Bolus Head to get Mammy. He said he'd leave me with the pony and trap and he'd take the bicycle. 'How are you going to go on a bicycle to the other side of the world,' I asked him. He didn't laugh. I remembered the journey to get here.

'I'm a mountain man, Mary. I'll never settle here.'

'I do miss being in the mountains. And I miss the sea. Do you, Daddy? Sometimes I close my eyes and pretend I can hear it.'

'And that priest, Fr Gilligan, always sniffing around. The good thing about the mountain we lived on was the priest in the parish was too fat to make it up the roads to us. We were left in peace.'

I was shocked to hear him talk of a priest like that, but my father was his own man. Though we went to Mass he always told us to give the clergy their own side of the road.

'Where is she?' He was tearing at his own head with his fingernails.

'Maybe the baby is sick and she can't travel yet. She'll come. Then maybe if there's time I can do a year of school before it finishes. I'm eleven now, I want to learn to read. The others have picked it up fast.'

'I have to find Grainne,' he said. Using her name and not referring to her as 'your mother' like he usually did made me feel suddenly distant from them both. As if I had nothing to do with their lives. As if it was only the two of them. Dessie and Grainne.

'Remember to leave the grass untopped, so come summer the fields have short green grass and taller brown hay. It looks patchy but that's how the birds and hares like it.'

'When will you be back?' I asked.

He didn't answer me.

He left when I was outside milking and the only way I knew he was gone was that his pipe wasn't over the fire and the bicycle was gone and he didn't come back that night. The house had two tiny bedrooms, one for the men and one for myself and my two sisters, Bridget and Maeve, but all of us children slept in the same one that night.

Padraig was three. He was wild and not talking, so Daddy just let him run around the fields and paid little mind to him. Daddy always did prefer us girls. Bridget and Maeve used to wait on him at the table and he'd always chat to us in the kitchen. In them days the girls had to stand up and give the boys their seats when they came in but my father never asked us to do it for Seamus and Padraig so we stopped doing it. Seamus protested that one too and my father just waved a hand at him and said, 'Whisht now, Seamus, sure you can find your own seat.' Then he was gone.

The morning after Daddy left I got all the little ones out to school. They walked down the lane and I watched them. Spring was coming in and the wild flowers were growing in the hedges. I picked some primroses and took my ease that morning because I didn't have my father around to snarl if the work wasn't done on time and perfectly. That was something I could depend on, the work was endless. When Daddy was out in the fields he came in hungry, wolfing the food down. I had boiled him potatoes and made stews and baked bread. 'When your mother comes it'll be easier on you' he had said, without looking at me.

That day, I put the primroses into a small inkpot that I found in the field when we first came and filled it with a bit of water. My hands shook so much at first I couldn't put the flowers in. I took a deep breath and steadied myself.

The neighbour, Patsey, became a constant visitor and he told us about the Cruelty Men.

'They usually are retired guards or teachers and they wear brown shirts. If you see them get out of their sight. They answer to no one and I've heard tell that they take bribes from the local industrial school to get more kids in there and put them to work. They're shovelling childer in there and they never get out.'

'What kind of schools?' I asked, terrified at the thought.

'If they got their hands on you in one of them schools you'd be a slave for the rest of your childhood. The priests are always looking for more children. You know them schools, you see the children out on the road being marched to work.'

'They looked starved and ragged,' I said. 'A bit like us.'

'Not like ye. Ye don't have the look in yer eyes like them childer have. And the state makes sure you don't escape until you're sixteen.' Patsey sighed and got up from the fire. 'Fr Gilligan arranges to have some of them boys released and put to work on farms. I've seen what state they're in. You wouldn't be up to all the shenanigans that go on in the name of God and country, I'm not codding ye.'

'Why do they take them?' I asked.

'They're raking it in, girleen, raking it in.'

Patsey was really the only neighbour who helped us to be sure. The others wanted to buy our little farm. Most felt they had to grow bigger than the twenty-two acres to survive. Patsey was different though. A soft Connemara man always with his cap on his head and a gentle way about him. His tummy was swollen with spuds and butter but his arms and legs were thin. He never entered our house without a blessing; he had a hundred different blessings up his sleeve.

'Here's to a wet night and a dry morning!' he proclaimed this time. 'There's a certain class of people who are rabid against the poor because they are so close to it themselves. Look after each other. Ye have your land here and each other. That's more than many a poor craytur has. Don't go looking to them priests to help ye. You'll never see each other or this land again.'

After a cup of tea, Patsey turned and went out into the summer night. The crows in the trees lifted as he swung onto his bicycle.

'That's it,' I said to the little ones. 'Not a word about yer father going when ye are up at the school. Patsey doesn't seem like a man to tell a lie. And his land is next to ours so it would be in his interests to have us off it and have it for himself. I think he's a fair man to give us that warning.'

Seamus sniffed and spat on the kitchen floor where Patsey had stood. 'Pity he's he such a dullamaloo.'

Seán came up and put his small hand in mine and led me back to the chair by the fire. We all piled onto the chair and hugged each other tightly. Even Seamus joined in the hug. I vowed I'd lose none of them. I promised them.

I began to work the fields as my father had taught me. The little ones helped when they came home from school but I wouldn't let the boys give up school until they were twelve. I wanted them to read and write. I wished I could have. There was a fairy ring in the field and a little mound that I was sure was fairy too. It rose out of the field like a hillock all by itself and didn't look as if it was natural to the land. I was careful with this. I left offerings that we couldn't afford. I hoped they knew we too were ancient people, and we too had been driven away. We too needed protection.

I sat on the hill and talked to them fairies. I told them that we weren't land-grabbers, that I didn't know how right it was that we were farming this new land but that we had been offered it back because Ireland was now free and perhaps our people had once been here and been driven off. The way the land works is that within a few years and a few harvests you feel it inside yourself.

Looking back on it I don't know if we were happy, but we were all together. Maeve was great at doing imitations of people and we had a good laugh in the evenings. It was our own little world and we were all the people in it. As a child every moment is swollen. Though those years of your life are short, they are the ones that stay with you the longest.

Padraig

My Little White Darling

Remember mother, singing the song, knees thin and strong. She held tightly to the middle. Shh! *A stór. A Mhuirnín Ban.* My little white darling.

Wide water blue green, dancing sky, writhing clouds, tumbling mountains, long grasses, the rocks on the hill.

The old hag would come, carried to her cave. The wet inside the dark. Soothing ocean curling into the land with white foamy hands beckoning, but no. Drowning would feel nice but no more.

Brown shirt, brown shirt, brown shirt. The Cruelty Men are coming. Hide, burrow underground

Mary

The Graveyard Growth

When I was fifteen Patsey came around and took off his cap when he saw me. He gestured for me to go into the house. There was no blessing this time. 'Child we've got word from Kerry that both your parents are dead.'

I didn't believe it. Patsey guided me to the armchair by the fire. 'I know it's hard and you were always hoping, but you need to get on with things and we need to take care of your land. It's in your father's name. We should put in into Seamus's name. He's the eldest boy.'

I made Patsey promise that he would not report to the state or the church about this because we were all under age. Patsey nodded. 'I'll say nothing and when the lad is eighteen he can take over and ye'll all be safe then. He can be your guardian.'

Patsey's eyes were moist but I couldn't cry. He patted me on the head. He handed me a basket of eggs and some gooseberries. 'I see you out working all day, Mary. You're a good girl. Without you they'd have been all sent off a few years ago. If ever you need anything just ask me. I'm getting a new plough and I'll do your fields for you. You've fed me enough dinners.'

The next week there was a man in uniform with a brown shirt that came around looking for us children. He came down the lane on a bike.

Padraig saw him from the field and whistled to me, and I ran into the house before he made it down the garden path. He was a big, grey-haired man who filled the doorway when he entered, he had a round face and his eyes were watery and shrewd. He looked around the house as I offered him tea.

'Mary, isn't it? I've been sent by people who are very concerned for you. You can't take care of the little ones. They're in rags in the school, and as wild as March hares. We're all concerned for your welfare. You must understand you are too young to have these children in your care.'

'I'm eighteen,' I lied. My English wasn't good and none of these people who came looking for us over the years spoke Irish.

'Can you prove that, Mary?' he said sharply.

'No,' I said. Seán was terrified and I scooped him up in my arms.

'Fr Gilligan tells me you sometimes don't even have the turf to give the children to take to school.'

'It's Patsey that gives us the turf, sir. Sometimes I don't, but when I have they bring it in. I swear to God.'

'Please child don't use God's name in vain. I can arrange to take you to places where none of ye will be hungry ever again, and all of the children under twelve will receive a sound education. What age are you anyhow? Do you have enough to keep the kids warm here?'

It wasn't help he was offering so I lied. 'Yes, sir. We're fine here. We have Patsey here to look in on us. He takes care of us.' More lies.

Patsey must have seen his bike too, and he burst into the house in an awful hurry through the back door. His big red face almost made me laugh. He ran a wide clay-marked hand over his sprouting black hair, smoothing it over a shiny bald patch.

'May you always have walls for the wind.'

The Cruelty Man didn't look happy to see him.

With Patsey there I felt my courage come back. I remembered the promise I'd made to my mother to keep us all safe.

'You're the neighbour?' the Cruelty Man said. 'Fr Gilligan told me about the situation. I believe it's between myself and the girl.'

'I've only come to translate, like.' Patsey said. 'She speaks mostly the Irish.'

'I've work to do, sir.' I was emboldened by Patsey's presence. 'I'm eighteen years old, so I am. You're not taking the wee ones. Not until the last cow is gone!'

'You are a brazen girl. You need to think of your sisters and brothers and what's best for them.'

'Mary is well able to look after them.' Patsey escorted him to the door.

'What about the feral one? I've heard stories they have a brother who sleeps in the shed like an animal. Is this a decent Christian household? I don't even see a cross up, or a statue.'

I pointed to the St Bridget's cross we'd made from rushes, he narrowed his eyes at it, as if it were a pagan object.

'To be sure you're looking for a shop-bought one with a man dying on it,' Patsey said. 'But that's a real cross where we come from.'

Patsey's voice was raised. 'Mary is the most decent person in this whole country. She's at Mass every Sunday with all her brothers and sisters and she works from before dawn to after dusk to keep the farm and keep them chislers fed. Their mother and father are down in Kerry and will be up any day now. You can tell Fr Gilligan that from me as well.'

The Cruelty Man must have been a retired guard, because he stood right in front of Patsey and towered over him. 'The boy in the shed should be in an asylum. It'll be no expense for them and he'd get the care he needs. I'm only doing my job here. This was reported to me.'

Patsey looked back at myself in the door holding Seán in my arms. 'We'll talk about that, won't we Mary?'

I nodded, feeling my knees shake with terror.

Patsey came into the kitchen and I gave him tea and a slice of bread and butter.

'You might think of your brother, Padraig. The poor craytur never sits still, he's like a snot on a hot shovel. If you gave him up to them maybe they'd get off your back. You don't want a fight with Fr Gilligan if he's sending around the likes of them.'

'I can't give Padraig to them. What would I say if Mammy and Daddy came back? I promised Mammy to keep everyone safe. Why do they want him?'

'Arra, I don't know Mary,' Patsey said. 'Did you not believe me when I told you your parents are dead?'

'They can't put Padraig to work like the other children.'

'You've been a great girl, Mary. You have the land, that'll protect you. If you didn't have that, you'd have all been in the industrial school by now. These are hard times for many. Them industrial schools have mushroomed all over the country. He has a quota to fill and he'll fill it without you. I'll have a word in Fr Gilligan's ear. See if I can get him to call them off now that they have ye in their sights. Am I doing the right thing? Are ye really fine here, Mary?'

'Thanks to God and to Mary, if I did not get enough, I got as much as anyone else.'

'Isn't that the God's honest truth, Mary!'

He belched some tea in acknowledgment and scratched his arse by the fire. It was with reluctance he got up and walked out the back door. I gave him some jam to take home.

I watched as he walked back through our field into his. Seamus came in and sensed something had gone on.

'The Cruelty Man came, he wants to take us all to schools,' I said. I was still shaking, but I wouldn't let on.

'What did Patsey want?' Seamus sat down and waited for me to serve him his tea.

'He got him out of the house for us. If it wasn't for him they might come and get us.'

'I don't trust that bollix. Why wouldn't he want us gone?' Seamus glowered. 'Not like he's in here doing anything for us. The old codger is always getting free jam and butter from you. What does he give us in return? He walks over our fields like they're his. He thinks we're all childer and he can have the run of the place.'

I said nothing. Patsey was our only outside contact that I trusted.

'There must be something wrong with him, he keeps buying more fields but he never gets married.'

'He brings us meat,' Seán piped up. 'It's the only meat we get besides chicken.'

Seamus shivered. 'He came up to me in the potato field the other day with his awful blessings, and then told me I had the graveyard growth in me. What in the jaysus was that about? I almost hit him. Except he's so stupid I feel sorry for him half the time.'

I laughed and little Seán laughed with me.

'Why are we laughing?' Seán then asked.

'Well back home when young people grew up very tall, and very quickly it often happened they'd get sick and die.'

'Why?' Seán asked.

'Sure wasn't it the terrible demand made on them. Food was awful scant and poor, this was so certain almost, that the sudden growth was itself a disease.'

Seán looked at Seamus and went to hug him. 'Seamus isn't going to die? Sure you're feeding him, Mary.'

Seamus pushed Seán away roughly. 'You're making this one as soft as you.'

Seamus was thirteen years old and knew he would get the farm in a few years. As the eldest boy he was the only one of us with a future secured and you'd think this would have been enough to soothe him but he had a heart full of nettles ever since Daddy left and he only a wee lad.

Patsey tried to talk to Seamus about our situation but Seamus couldn't stand him. Regardless, Patsey began to plough our fields and help out with big jobs. Seamus thought he was making a claim on our land but I knew better. After working a bit for us, he would come into the kitchen, always with some good meat wrapped in paper for my stew. I'd feed him my sloe wine and gooseberry jam on brown bread and the homemade butter I made in the sheds. Some nights he'd stay and we'd tell stories by the fire and Maeve would do her impressions. She was a tonic. She'd even do the stern walk of Fr Gilligan and his pinched-up face always looking horrified. We'd fall about laughing. Seamus would sit away from us all at the table but he'd still smirk at Maeve. Poor Padraig was so wild he'd lie under the chair and make bird noises, but he'd stay all the same, especially if there were stories. He never took to the talking so we never could tell what he was thinking.

Padraig

Found by the Hag

Found by the hag by the stream, fallen and was wet – drinking face first. Taken to the edge. In her cave there was a hole in the floor – down into it. Travelled groping in the dark, hands bleeding against the narrow tunnel walls, slipping head first under the earth, passing layers and layers of rock, heat ahead – burst into blazing wet liquid heat but became hardened with searing pain – faster until at the very centre rolled in fire – orange were eyes – red the skin the yellow breath.

Came up swimming under the flat bogs, brown was the world – entangled in oak and wood – some of the wood was leather – the leather was men, the bog men were whispering telling tales excited to be heard chanting the same story

Where you found us
We were put
Promises of afterlife
Promises of great light
But not this wet long time

Under this lonely bog
Star stolen night robbed
Is this your idea of beauty?

Sighed kinship with these boundary beings. Border bog men let slide away, intestinal earth travel – float back to the cave loud with sea noise. Popped out of the gut hole in the floor of the cave by the sea in Bolus Head. The hag – waiting.

Mary

Bridget Is the First to Leave

When Bridget finished primary school, I could not keep her fed and she couldn't continue school. I tried to keep her local but instead she went to Dublin to be a servant for a stranger family. She was all of twelve. She cried the whole night before she left and Maeve, whom she was very close to, cried with her. They were like two banshees tearing at their hair and wailing. Maeve brushed Bridget's long dark hair in the morning and set it up in a bun on her head. When she finished she leaned forward from behind and put her arms around her sister. Bridget clasped Maeve's arms and breathed in and out deeply. It was the way things were.

I felt very bad. Mammy had moved the family here in part to keep me, but I couldn't keep them.

Happy-go-lucky, easy-going, pragmatic Bridget was gone one grey morning. She wrote one or two letters from Dublin, but she was never one for the writing. I assumed she just got busy with her life and wanted to forget the times when she was half starved with no shoes on her feet, and who would blame her? I didn't know much about getting money out of the land. Patsey helped me from time to time and did some hard work for us. His farm was growing bigger and bigger and he had a good few lads working for him.

Little Seán was the baby of the family. Always the pet. He was still in school and loved it. His teachers at Scoil Uí Ghrámhnaigh said he was special and ahead of all the other children in his learning.

'We could have a priest in the family,' I said to Seamus one night. 'Wouldn't that be grand?'

'When has the priest ever been around here except to try and take away the farm?' Seamus scowled.

'Imagine if Mammy and Daddy came back and found wee Seán a priest,' I sighed.

'I don't remember us having any truck with the priests until we came here.'

Seamus was no fool, in fact he was right. As far as I remember, my mother never thought much of the priests or any of that. She used to think of any reason not to go to Mass. But I had kept us all going every Sunday since we arrived in this strange place. We sat in a back row and didn't draw attention to ourselves on account of our missing father and the terror in us that we'd be stolen and scattered.

Wee Seán was not physically strong, he was a dreamer, and he was a bright and funny wee gossin. The farm work did not interest him. It was too drudgerous, and he wasn't quite connected with this world but very in tune with the underworld. He had a great sense for the unseen, always stopping in his tracks in the fields and standing still and after telling me what world he went to. I worried about him and all his sensitivities, for I knew that those who get to live in many worlds could be taken from this one more easily.

What could I do for him? To be a worker on your big brother's farm would not get you a wife. He'd be doomed. I knew Bridget was tough and she'd make it. Maeve was the prettiest of us all, she was tall with a beautiful head of yellow hair; she mesmerized any man who saw her. I didn't know what to do with Seán.

When Dessie went to get Grainne he was two and a half. Seán was one of the shining ones from the beginning, lit from within. He tiptoed around the farm like a little fairy wearing a cap and swinging a stick, his blond hair catching the sunlight. He would disappear into the fields for hours by himself. I had told him all about the fairies and he would tell me the ones he had seen, and report the conversations he was having with them. He knew we were a family who could turn into hares. He told me that the fairies had recognized us from the moment we came to these fields.

Another eleven families from Connemara were resettled near us in 1937. There were a few of us from Kerry but our Irish was different. Within that division the Kerry families looked at us as the poorest of all, orphans and needy and ragged. Though they never offered us any assistance we were grateful to them that they never reported us in order to get our land. Their neglect of us was their kindness. Our separateness kept us at a distance from all around. We were our own world. We had our own sun that rose for us and our own moon that glowed through the cottage window. Maeve would still get up on the kitchen table and dance and sing. God but we missed Bridget and her tin whistle. I would tell stories and Seamus would sit staring into the fire, and telling us all we were eejits, which only encouraged our nightly shenanigans. I think we never stopped doing it even when Bridget left because it was the only time Padraig would come near us. He'd always slip under my chair by the fire, sometimes his feet would be all we'd see. We knew he was listening.

Padraig

This Can Happen

Loud hooves clip-clopping, whip cracking, carriage rocking – new taste, new milk watery. She is as kind – smells new. She tells stories. But no touch, nor pick up, nor put on her knee. The skin creeps – crawls pushing away. New mother and the fairy hill. Follows. The shapes gather on the hill – all the noise stops – only here soft touch, pick up, soft warm knee. Stories told on the fairy hill.

Choosing broken wood – a knife in hand – whistles whittled into mirrors of birds' songs. The sound of the whistle like a call, finding a needle to puncture into the other world beside – another world beside that – another beside that, all worlds – the blind dark rock world beneath – the vast world around everything, pulled so heavy the dark light cannot be. Squeezed into a tiny space. This can happen. Invisible. Act differently. Made when the centre falls in.

Fire from the centre and the needle ties them all together – the whistle moves the needle – sewing the mirror worlds together with sound.

The sun is not big enough to be in danger now. Stays in the small woods – listens to the trees talking. Always in low voices, they never stop until winter. Then they lose their chattering leaves – sleep, long frost closed sleep. Cold chattering burning. New mother tells stories inside the walls – small fire she makes like a spit from the sun, is warm now, lie down – listen to her voice.

Mary

My Hair Turns Grey and Maeve Leaves Home

To Seán it was the only home he knew and he was happy with County Meath. I would see him on a summer's day stretch into the grass like a star, his limbs spread out in every direction. My black hair turned completely grey at sixteen. I woke up one morning and the others screamed laughing. And there I was old.

'Was it a fright that did that to you?' Maeve put her hand to her own head in fear it might be contagious.

'No. I can't even remember my dream,' I told her. There was no mirror in the house so it didn't bother me. I made Maeve cut it short so I wouldn't see the grey falling about my shoulders. She cried as she did it but I didn't pay much mind. If I looked older they might leave us alone for good. I liked the feel of my head without hair weighing me down.

Seamus was two years younger than me. Seamus always said our parents took their little baby and got a boat to America to start a new life. I did not see how my quiet, dutiful father, who had not a cruel bone in his body, would fail to come back. Even if he had grown very dark and sad when we left Bolus Head.

I was close to Maeve, who was seven years younger than me. She was feisty and sure of herself. She loved my stories as much as any soul on Earth, and made me tell 'The Children of Lir' till we were all sick of it. When she was eleven, I went to Fr Gilligan and asked that she be placed close to us. He was not a warm man but he was obliging, and she would go to work in a shop in Trim. That meant she was close enough that she could come back and see us a few times a year. Maeve, with her long golden hair and blue and grey eyes, would not be long in meeting someone and having a family of her own. I had great hope for Maeve, as much as it hurt me to see her set out walking for Trim with only a small bundle at eleven years old. I had intended to walk with her but that night Seán came down with a terrible fever and I thought I'd seen a fairy face at the window just before dawn so I was in a terrible state of worry. Maeve told me to stay and mind him. She waved at me and Seamus as we stood out on the lane and watched her walk out of our world, she kept turning her head to look back, and then she was out of our sight.

She had miles ahead of her. It was a chilly, overcast day. Seamus and I stood awhile after she disappeared, in silence. Then I went to feed the two pigs. It began to rain and I stood in the shed and looked at the huge deluge framed by the door. The drops were so big they were bouncing off the ground and back up into the sky to fall again, as if there were two rains falling. I couldn't bear it any longer so I walked out into the yard and just stood out there, very still, so I would get as wet as I knew she was getting on the long walk to Trim. I felt every drop come down the inside of my blouse. My hair stuck to my head as the water poured down me. My bare feet as bare as her bare feet in muddy puddles. I stood in that rain for her. So that, though she would not know it, she would not be alone.

Padraig

With Little Boy a Thaw

Little boy follows around. His hair is gold. They play with their things in the woods. Little boy lies on the fairy ring – look at the blue membrane sky – all the spirits filter in – out. Little boy is good at talking to the trees. They stop chattering – listen to his stories. Little boy never shouts and never gets angry. Little boy combs dark hair – cuts it. With little boy a thaw – new mother and little boy take the purple black colour from the bush – eat it – fill tins. Whistles for them – birds made from the trees who gave their wood falling onto ground.

Little boy brings out clothes – new mother watches,

'Mind you do what your brother Seán says, Padraig, he'll look out for you.'

So who's coming? Understands their language but it is only one of the many languages that come all day long. Little boy too understands many of these languages. More birds for little boy – one bird has leaves for wings. The flying tree, tree bird, winter flightless but spring new budding – off off leaves the green ground – flies into the air, legs trailing, great swoops of joy.

Mary

Little Padraig the Fairy Child

There was little Padraig, the handsomest of all the boys, who was almost three when we left and was a wild thing altogether. He had been a regular happy gossin, my mother said, and then all of a sudden, before he was two years, he had pulled away from everything. My mother had taken him to local healers, and even to the priest to do an exorcism. But the old people said the fairies had switched him with one of their own and she might never get him back.

She told the story of how he was wandering the mountainside on his own and fell into the stream face first. He came back soaking wet and was never the same. He could have drowned, she said, but this change was a kind of drowning. He just sank away from us. Stopped playing, stopped calling us by name, stopped answering to his own.

He never sat on a chair in his life. He was always jumping and tearing things up. By the time he was five our school wouldn't take him anymore because he was stone mad. I could hardly use him on the farm so I let him run through the fields. He never learnt to talk and sometimes he didn't come home.

I would go out to tell him the stories and he would sit a few feet away from me and run off if he didn't like them. I could tell he loved the early stories about Balor the one-eyed Fomorian. He was part of another world. I wondered if he was kin at all.

There was no badness in him, but as Padraig got older Seamus said we'd have to commit him because no one could take care of him. But I wouldn't let that happen. Seán had a way with him and it was him who cut his hair and changed his clothes.

Padraig had a small knife and made whistles out of fallen wood. Sometimes these whistles would be in the shape of birds and they were lovely things. When we saw his little creations we knew he had a human soul somewhere in him hidden. He would blow them, sharp loud shrieking whistles as if calling someone to him or to us. We got used to his whistles; they were part of the air to us, the music of our quiet world. Another sound in the trees at night. Along with the owls: the strange lonely sound of the curlews, the coarse grating of the pheasants, the corncrakes, the cuckoos. As he used to imitate birds all the time, I could never tell if it was him calling or they. But we couldn't help him.

Padraig

Makes a Whistle for Patsey

In fields down by the woods, by the woods, the woods.

New mother says, 'The Cruelty Men come round and they're paid to find children like you and take them away.' Hide. The Cruelty Men are looking to pluck from trees – take it to theirs. What is their place? Rubber tyres from twenty miles away spinning – slicing the bockety roads – swerving to avoid the big holes – the creak of the gate, brown uniform, blue watery eyes, no light at the centre – new mother sending little boy to run – tell hide. Patsey from next world comes – stands by their door making sure the Cruelty Men never stay too long. Patsey doesn't come near woods. Waves from a distance. Patsey can be seen from the top field. At night on his own Pastey is in a dress and high shoes – stands in his yard with a bucket – runs inside. The prettiest wood bird tree spirit special for Patsey. Patsey comes from the house – whiskey breath,

'Padraig, is that you, you poor craytur? What's it you want?'

Patsey in dress – shoes that tip him forward with their heel. Bird whistle. Patsey takes it in big rough hand – smiles – cries. His lips are painted purple, they shimmer.

Patsey rains from his eyes, 'Poor innocent boy. You know you are so beautiful. The most beautiful of all of them. My cousin has one blessed just like you, a boy; he's a fine-looking boy too. Isn't that always the way with fellahs like you, your strange beauty a poor compensation for a torn-up head?'

The needle punctures the side of the world.

Patsey takes the whistle – puts it into his own sparkle-dark mouth – blows. But he's crying – back to the trees. Patsey's world at night – never seen. Floating to the window. Patsey, always on his own staring into the orange embers till the wee morning hours, holding the golden water of life. Patsey sips sighs – rubs his eyes. But the wooden bird is inside the kitchen window; the bird on the sill with the kindred wooden statue of a man with night dark skin. Patsey is a friend – though he is lone lone lonely his house laughs because his heart is open – his fields are soft and the hag allows an abundance to grow there. The world keeps giving to Patsey – but Patsey can't take as much as it gives.

Mary

You Never Knew What He Was Thinking

Sometimes I rubbed my eyes while facing the sun and I could get an image imprinted on my eyelids of the group of islands from our home in Kerry in the shining sea. Dinnish, Scarriff, so close, and the Bull, the Cow and the Calf farther out. These empty islands would hover in front of me and I would stop my work for a minute to re-summon them. Not for strength because it made me sad and weaker. Not for anything. I never lost my homesickness for Kerry. If I had stood amid the pigs and cried, my tears would have not been water, I would have wept wild, stony, empty islands.

As soon as Seán went to school he was determined to have me read and write and do sums. I told him I didn't have time. I was secretly afraid it would be beyond me. Seán followed me around in my chores and wrote letters in the muck outside the house. He drew numbers in the condensation on the windows. He scratched words in the ice on the wall. He made sentences out of crumbs on his plate. It was his mission and he was a born teacher. Maeve joined in with him and the two of them taught me to read and write without ever wasting a pencil or paper. Maeve would say, 'You're quicker than all of us. You should have gone to school.' But she fell silent as soon as she knew what she had said. Because it really did hurt me that I never did.

Seamus, was two years younger than me and a different kettle of fish altogether, he was a small wiry scut of a man. The poor craytur was afflicted by fierce bad skin for a while but that went away when he was sixteen. I'll grant that he was a hard worker and tried to help me out on the farm as much as he could. He was nine when our father left. Though he went to school he didn't have much interest in it. Seamus was quieter than the rest of us. You never knew what he was thinking. He was angry too. Angry with the neighbours for ignoring us, angry with Mammy and Daddy for leaving us, angry with the little ones when they ran wild, angry that he had an idiot brother, angry with his teachers for giving him the belt when he hadn't done his work because he was out helping me in the fields and with the pigs and cows. Angry at me for needing his help.

I understood all the places his anger came from and it washed over me like the soft rain I collected from the rain barrels.

The farm frustrated him and bored him, but it was his all along and we all knew it. Except maybe me. I thought it was all of ours. I hadn't thought of one or the other of us owning it. It was a gift this farm. We who had been dispossessed by Cromwell, and starved over centuries out West were now back and sowing seeds in the flat fertile fields. But sure we only kept ourselves barely alive with it.

To be sure Seamus was a dark horse but what came was still an awful shock. When my brother Seamus was seventeen he announced that he was to take a wife. I nearly fell out of me standing when I got wind of it. Her name was Sheila. She spoke English but was as poor as we were, though she still managed to look down on us. I fought with him over her. Patsey our neighbour had two nieces. I told him he should have made a match with someone who had a bit of adjoining land and we could have extended our holding. This one came with nothing but a suitcase and a face on her like a boiled shite. I pitied my brother waking to that in the morning. There were only the three of us left and Seán was just over ten. From her entry into our house when they were courting we gradually began to speak English, because she was liable to fly into a rage if she heard the Irish. She was convinced that it was a secret language we used to exclude her. So it was the end of the old language in our house.

Seamus

As Bold as a Pig in the Peas

If my father had shown up at this stage I would have run him off my fields with my spade.

'To the hole of Liaban's house with you,' I'd shout in my daydreams and chase him all the way back to Bolus Head.

I wanted to see him run from me in terror. I wanted to hurt him. But Patsey's nieces, I suppose one of them came to me after Mass and walked me home and I should have paid a bit of attention to her but I didn't know women that well except my sisters and I couldn't even look her in the eye. Now that I think of it she was a bit flat-footed for my liking. Though he would have given me a few fields for it. But then I thought of his satisfaction when he saw his grand-nephews have this farm and I couldn't bear to give him that.

I met Sheila through a man in the pub. He said she was new around these parts and could do sewing and mending. I caught a glimpse of her once at Mass. She wiggled her backside when she walked and she kept flinging her long hair back over her shoulder. She wore white gloves. I never thought she would look at me, but we were introduced in the graveyard outside the church and it was she who asked me to walk her home to her digs. She was staying with a family at the time. She wore high heels and I'd a good mind to pull her into the field and mount her. She did something to me like that. Something that Patsey's daughters never did to me. Maybe they both looked too much like Patsey and I couldn't imagine climbing up on top of them and seeing his big self-satisfied face with all his old guff, blessings, and plamaus and words of advice and wise-old-man shite. I'd enough of his auld rawmeash. The way he wore his trousers all the way up under his chest, the way he held his braces and gave me queer looks. I tried to kiss Sheila the next day after the Mass and she wouldn't have any of it, so I asked her to marry me. She was shocked. She said she'd ask around about me. I told her not to ask Patsey on any account but ask who she liked. Except him.

Of course he was the first she went to. That was Sheila. She never listened to me anyhow.

What did that gobshite tell her?

That I was a good man and a hard worker. Yes, he did tell her that. That I had a fine twenty-two acres for myself and set to inherit it all. But that my sister Mary was the light in the house. She kept it going. He told her I was a dark soul that never smiled. That never laughed except for a sneer. We had a brother who was mad and ran about the place as wild as one of the animals but we refused to do anything about him. But that the family were good and Mary had kept us from the Cruelty Men and made sure we got through school till age eleven.

Sure he wasn't going to like the land going to any other than his own; I told her when she relayed all this back to me the next week after Mass. I tried to kiss her again and this time she opened her mouth and we touched tongues. I felt myself get hard and my hands raised up to grab her tits but she pushed them down again.

'Seamus O Conaill, when do we get married?'

'What about my dark soul?' I asked, looking away from her, feeling a rage build inside me.

'I'm not frightened of your dark soul Seamus O Conaill,' she shrugged, 'but I don't like the sound of Mary. You have some idiot brother and a little brother who's in school? You've a lot depending on you and that small farm. Twenty-two acres won't keep us all.'

'I do, they're my family to be sure. I'd be lost without Mary. She's a great worker and knows how to get food on the table in any circumstances. And it tastes good and all. Seán is the family pet. But I'll need him to work with me. He might as well slave for his family than in a school. He'll not own anything though, you need not worry about that.'

'Mary can stay if she serves me in the house before she helps you on the farm. And are you forgetting the other one? The idiot.'

'Sure that's only Padraig, he's harmless. He barely comes inside, he sleeps with the two pigs in winter or under the trees in the summer. What about him?'

'I never want to see him.' She poked me in the chest and it hurt. 'He's to be gone when I arrive.'

'So you'll be my wife?' I could feel myself hard again. Imagining all the times I could get into her and see her without that print dress and those gloves and those black stockings.

Patsey, of course, came over to me that evening in the field, and that's when he put his hand on my shovel and said Sheila was a hard case.

'She's desperate, Seamus. You're a young man and you have land. She's no people and no skills. There's nothing for her but to be a servant and she doesn't look like she's fond of the work. Be careful there, boy, you know what she is?'

'What is she Patsey? I'm sure you'll tell me, like.' I spat on the ground.

'A bold woman,' and he roared with laughter.

'What do ye mean?' I rose to punch him in the face but he waved me down still chuckling to himself.

Don't marry a bold woman on any account,
For she'll be as bold as a pig in the peas;
She will beat the children before they do wrong,
And she will raise a noise without any cause at all.

And the eejit did a little jig after that and curtsied. God, but I was surrounded by fools and madmen.

'Go away with yourself Patsey, yer only jealous that I'd get a woman of education and distinction.'

'I'm not sure what school this Sheila is schooled in. Sure aren't my two nieces educated?' Patsey said. 'In the same wee school as yerself. You know their people. You know where they're buried. And my brother sent them on further, like to the convent school. But I'm not sure I'd wish you on them. You're a moody hoor at times, Seamus. Arra sure, maybe it's better off they'd be without you. One is soft on you, but. Just watch out boy, yer fierce young to be rushing into it like that. Wait and court her and see what she really wants. She's come from nowhere and no one knows a thing about her people. Rumour is they were all in the workhouse.'

When he said that, I almost wanted his niece. But maybe he was tricking me. The fat old bastard was a cute hoor, up for anything.

'She's not local, like,' Patsey sighed.

'She's from Oldcastle, it's still in County Meath. We'll still be cheering for the same team.'

Patsey scratched himself and hoisted up his trousers.

'Oldcastle, sure that's practically Cavan. I think you're not seeing the rough edge to her, boy. You're dazzled by her perfume, her tight dresses and scarlet lipstick.'

'Maybe you want her for yerself, Patsey.' I smirked.

'I know nawthing about women and I lived with five sisters most of me life, boy.' Patsey shrugged. 'It's your life I just don't want to see you make a hames of it.'

Anyhow I got Sheila.

I remember the day of my wedding. I was just turned eighteen years old and my wife was twenty-eight. I only found that out on the day when we had to fill in the papers. She had said she was eighteen. I knew nothing about women and I still don't.

On the day of the wedding Mary didn't know about what I done to Padraig on account of the deal I'd made with Sheila.

Padraig

Should Not Have Gone Near Him

The big brother was beckoning. Light dragged in a thin line around him, shadow stuck. Messy. Impatient. He stood at the border of the tree world, the trees leaned and tried to protect. Big brother snap shouted. A shriek surge wolf pushed through the woods, concealed predatory force – because the brother never came near – a change in the world. Thought to orbit – not get too close. Should not have gone near him.

Seamus

There's a Wild Look on Him

On the day before the wedding, I went down the fields to find him. There was a small wood at the end of our farm, and he was usually there. I followed his whistles. I stood at the trees' boundary and I beckoned him. Mad as a coot he'd always been. Though he was a grand baby and if he was just in a photo you would think he was an angel he was so beautiful. All the women prattling on about the fairies swapping him. He was twelve years old now and as tall as I was. The priest, Fr Gilligan, had arranged to bring him to the big house in Mullingar and the state were willing to pay for it. So it was the best solution. I knew the Cruelty Men would have liked to get their hands on all of us who could work, to send to them schools. They were shovelling children into them places. Fr Gilligan said he'd keep them off our backs if we gave him one for the asylum. So Padraig was to be our sacrifice. I told Mary this but she wouldn't have it. Mary seemed to think it was perfectly alright to have a complete ludramaun running wild about the farm and sleeping in the animal sheds. She said he was harmless. She took care of his needs. Washed him and fed him and said she could talk to him. Said she'd bring him to the fairy fort and he'd be at peace there. Sitting on top of his people. That's the sort of nonsense I had to listen to. I might have put Mary into the big house as well except she was too useful to me.

Padraig walked out to me. I never could look at him even though he was my brother. He reminded me of everything wrong with our family. We weren't like the others, even at home in Kerry, because of him.

The only reliable person in my life was Mary. But in the end she was talking of leaving me with a whole farm to keep by myself so she could send Seán to the Christian Brothers and keep him there. She knew I had no money to do any hiring. Someone had to be the man in the family.

Padraig stood before me stock still. He handed me something, as if I had asked him for it. It was a small bird he'd carved from wood and he put it into my hand. I threw it to the side, not taking my eyes off of him, thought I'd stare him down like a bull.

'Come on now, Padraig,' I said in a low voice, taking him by the arm and leading him. 'I've someone you have to meet.'

He walked beside me to the pony and trap that the priest had brought. When he saw the priest he tried to bolt. He never had been to Mass with us. He ran into Patsey's yard and I chased after him. Patsey was there holding a bucket and he followed us. Padraig was fast, boy. But I got him. Leapt and tackled him in the field. I was the faster.

Patsey would not help me but he followed me and did not stop me as I dragged Padraig back to the trap, and the priest had a man with him in a brown shirt. He must have been a Cruelty Man. I didn't know he'd be involved. We tied him up.

'Hurry, Father, or Mary will be home,' I panted.

'Where is she?' Fr Gilligan snapped. 'Did ye not tell her about the court order?'

'We're not hiding anything here, Seamus.' Patsey started looking worried. 'I wouldn't want to do that to Mary.'

'She's off at the market. I'll tell her when she gets home. She'd never do it.'

'Mary doesn't know what's best,' Fr Gilligan said to Patsey. 'She's too young. She's too much on her hands. Seamus is the man of the house.'

'I thought ye only wanted them that could work?' I said to the Cruelty Man. He never even looked at me.

'You've another boy here you can't feed who could benefit from an education. I can take him off yer hands too.'

The Cruelty Man glanced at the priest. Patsey was scratching his head but he was a cute hoor and could tell there was something going on.

The Cruelty Man shrugged. 'Yer new wife needs a fresh start in the house, just saying. How many burdens can one man take?'

When he said it like that I almost went in and got Seán out here too. But I was afraid of Mary. 'We're only bringing one to market today,' I sneered. 'We'll talk about that wee fellah another time.'

Fr Gilligan, the Cruelty Man and I made sure Padraig was buckled with ropes. He might have only been a child but he was as fit and strong as a young bull. I got into the trap with him and waved thanks to Patsey. Patsey stared at us and turned to go back into his yard.

Then he stopped and came back to the priest.

'Make sure the poor crayter gets the help he needs.'

'Oh I will Patsey. He needs treatment. They have all sorts of cures up there in the big house. It's a new world, Patsey.'

'It is indeed, Father, it is indeed.' Patsey leaned his red blotchy face in to me. 'Don't you worry Seamus, I'll tell Mary for you when she comes home.'

I looked down at Padraig lying on the floor of the trap; they had gagged him to stop him screaming.

'Not till after the wedding. Don't let on about how he's tied up and all,' I warned him.

'Arra, I won't, of course. Maybe, he'll be better off.' Patsey hiked his trousers even further up.

It was then I saw Seán looking over the gatepost as we pulled away. Fair play to the little sod, but he never ever told Mary how we took him.

The Cruelty Man stared at Seán too. Seán stood without moving. His fists were clenched. I swung up into the trap.

'You don't have to come,' Fr Gilligan said. 'You must have preparations for the wedding.'

'Mary's taking care of things, Father,' I said. When we put out down the road Padraig pissed in his trousers. I had my feet up on him, as there was not a lot of room in the trap. Why didn't Fr Gilligan have a car? He had said he was going to pick us up in a car. You can't trust no one. Fr Gilligan tried to make room for me and he pushed my legs down so they wouldn't be standing on Padraig.

'It's a strange thing, Seamus,' he sighed. 'How you could have two brothers, one like this and one like yon wee Seán who's the pride of the school. God works in mysterious ways, to be sure.'

After a few miles I jumped out of the trap without a word.

Padraig

The Trap

Little boy by the gate and little boy's eyes were wide – swallowing. The horse swung its head to signal danger. Patsey did not help. Little boy did not help. The horse did not help. The brown-shirted Cruelty Man pulled arms then body – folded on the floor. In the trap bound to the floor – the stinging of the wet piss running hot then creeping cold – the stink – the bump bump like a punch punch all the way to the belly button of the world.

The King of the Cruelty Men wore black – his neck had a square of white, an empty space into which stuff poured out of him all the way, awful stuff that the world couldn't do anything with so it stuck to everything and stained it – big brother kept his mucky boots on top of the folded-up stolen child all the way down the lane. Then big brother turned into a hare – jumped away home.

Seamus

It Is You Killed my Mother

Mary's eyes were red with the crying the next day when I married in the church. Not because I had told her about Padraig, because I'd have to work up my nerve to do that, but because she had been out around the trees and calling him. As she and Seán were the only ones who he came out for, she wanted Seán to help but he avoided her. Wee Seán was smart but he was a bit of a coward and wouldn't tell her. She got very upset at us all and then I told her to pull herself together and she did. No one was there except what was left of our family and Patsey. Maeve did come back for the day. She was full of town airs and though they were polite to Sheila, all of them were shocked I'd decided so quickly and that was that. Sheila was tall and had worldliness about her and wore a white dress tight around her tiny waist. I was eighteen, what did I know? Patsey followed us to the house and he'd brought some whiskey and we got Mary to tell her stories. She made the best of it. She might have even known, as Padraig became a man, there was nothing to do with him. I didn't want him in there with the animals anymore. I wanted to become normal like the rest of the world.

As he poured a glass of whiskey Patsey lifted it up and spoke to the glass, 'You thief? It is you killed my mother: I'll put an end to you now.' And with that he downed it in one gulp and I had to fill up another one for him.

It was funny, I admit, the first time, and even Sheila smiled, which might have been the last time both of us were smiling at the same time.

But Patsey being the eejit he was, impressed with the rise he got out of us, went and said it to every glass he had. Sheila and the others slipped off to bed.

Patsey was singing songs and we were both drunk. It was just him and me at the end of the night. I said I had to go into my wife now. I had to pull him out of the chair, Patsey could drink Lough Sheelin. He tried to clear his throat but it didn't clear fully.

In a gravelly voice he slurred, 'Seamus, you're to be a man now. I've know ye since ye were knee-high to a grasshopper.'

He put his hand on my knee for a moment and I jumped like a scalded cat.

He stood quickly and looked around as if he barely recognized the place and cleared his throat, hacking into our fire. We watched the bile fizz there on the turf. I had enough of him. I was hoping to God he wasn't going to start giving me advice about my wedding night. I had been around animals all my life. I didn't need anything from him. I wanted to go in now and get what was mine from my new wife, and I couldn't figure out why I was here by the fire with feckin Patsey.

But all he said was, 'If you wish to be reviled, marry. If you wish to be praised, die.' And with that he took his hat from the hook and stumbled out into the pitch of night, and me stumbling into my marital bed.

Mary

A Living Dread
(1945)

Sheila was a living dread. She was the farmer's wife and what was I? When she first came, the neighbours said she was a Sunday girl – she would be of no use except for putting on Sunday finery. Shocking altogether to see Seamus with a woman like that. She was an English speaker and not from the land but the far-off town of Oldcastle at the other side of Meath. She was not one to give out much information and I was not one to seek it. I believed in minding my own, that was all. She made it understood that she had no kin of her own. Her mother had died of TB and she did not know her father. She was the youngest it seemed of a large brood, none of who she talked about or who ever came near her. She had no understanding of what it really meant to be a farmer's wife. She didn't want to do any work and there wasn't much time for rest once you started. Seamus caught his breath looking at her stockings hanging outside on the line. Them black yokes were the most exotic things we had seen in our lives. I spotted him stroking them between his fingers and feeling their dark seam. At first she was seductive and coy but she soon tired of him. Seamus was a taciturn, sullen boy still and wouldn't talk from one end of the day to the other. He wasn't going to be whispering things to her and cherishing her. He was a young man though and I heard him every night try to mount her. Horrified by her fate, after one month in the house she took to the bed.

I did feel some pity, and I could have been more sisterly to her, but I had neither patience nor time. Suddenly, as if a spell had been cast, I was no more than a servant and drudge on the land and in the house. I did the work of ten men and five women, so Seamus was eager I stay on because it soon became apparent that Sheila was not only sour as buttermilk but lazy to boot. We argued into the nights. I wanted Seán to go on to secondary school and that would cost money, even if he could land himself a scholarship. I reminded him of the time we all sat in the trap and our mother grabbed us and embraced us and she would have expected that we all look out for one another.

'But sure she never came. She was well rid of us. And him too. They've gone to America,' Seamus said.

The teachers at the school wanted to get a scholarship for Seán. They said he could put his hand to anything. He had a way with languages, a knack for maths problems. He could write beautifully. I knew all this.

'He knows everything before we tell him,' the master said.

To my great relief the Christian Brothers were going school to school recruiting for their order. All secondary schools in the country cost an arm and a leg, but since Seán had the vocation he was to be sent full-time up to the training college at Baldoyle in Dublin. But we would still need to get him his books and other expenses.

Seamus would hear none of it. Sheila was even more adamant that Seán give up school and begin to help on the farm.

'What's in it for him?' I pleaded with them one afternoon.

'The same that's in it for you,' Seamus snapped.

'And what is that?' I put my hands out that were calloused and hard as an Egyptian crocodile. Sheila looked at my grey cropped head of hair and actually glanced nervously at Seamus in case he would push me too far.

'A roof over yer head, Mary,' Sheila said. 'Where else would ye go?'

'That's me,' I said. 'But wee Seán has what none of us girls had. He has a chance. And he's not like me. He's special. He has gifts and second sight and he could be anything he wanted to be.'

'So you send him off with those baby-snatchers? Making little priests out of them at twelve. We don't have the money. Even with the Brothers paying for most of it we can't afford the other stuff. I need him here. I can't afford to hire farm hands and I can't do it all on me own. If he needs an education the Cruelty Man can send him off to one of them schools for a bit of training and he'd be done at eighteen. It's not a life sentence like the Brothers.'

'You made some deal with the Cruelty Man, didn't you?' I said. 'It was her wanting to get rid of Padraig, but you'll not take my Seán. And is she worth it? She's not worth a horse's nit on the farm, or in the house, and you know it.'

I regretted I said that. I was just tired and scared. Sheila lunged at me, and hit me a wallop. I tried to get her off me but she kept landing punches. Seamus laughed and laughed until Seán came out of his bedroom and tried to pull us apart. I think she might have killed me if he hadn't.

We were out of breath, glaring at each other. The two of us were standing in the small cottage as if about to kill each other. Seán was upset.

'I don't need to go,' Seán said. 'I like it here on the farm. I love this land. I don't mind, Mary, I don't mind. I want to stay with you. We'll work together here and everything will be alright Mary as long as I'm with you.'

For a moment that's what I would have wanted too. 'Come on, let's go blackberry picking and I'll make some jam and tarts.'

'Are you sure ye have time for that today?' Seamus growled. 'There's other stuff to be done.'

'I'll do that too, Seamus. You know I will.'

Seamus almost smiled at me. A rare sight. 'I know you will, Mary,' he relented. 'And yer jam and tarts are the only sweetness any of us have in our lives, or ever had.' He glanced at his wife and she marched into the bedroom and shut the door for the day. She complained about everything and handed me clothes to wash and iron and didn't like the food I put before her. I was, at that time, making gooseberry jam and blackberry jam. Seán and I would go up the lanes to pick the berries. That was the happiest time of my life so there was always lots of jam. Nothing would please Sheila though.

Poor Seamus went out the back and got his spade to go digging.

Seán ran about the house to get all the tins he could find. The hedges hung lush over the road and the bushes were weighed down with big succulent blackberries that oozed purple juice when you squeezed them. We always ate more than we picked.

To rest with all our bounty, we went to the fairy fort.

The fairy fort was a mound in the middle of the field. The local Meath people wouldn't go near it but we were from the edge of the world, and had lived with the spirits at such close quarters that I felt they were my kin at times. Hadn't they taken Padraig and given us one of their own?

But what had I let happen to that fairy child? And would they hold it against me? I couldn't bear to think of Padraig.

It was here where I told Seán all my stories. He was a good listener. Sometimes he told them back to me word for word and I was happy to pass them down. It's always the duty of a storyteller to find the next person to keep them going on and on. Seán was eleven years old. Around the age I had been when I left Kerry.

I told him the story of what the stranger said to Columcille when Columcille asked him what this land looked like in the old time. The stranger answered:

It was yellow. It was blossoming. It was green. It was hilly. It was a place of drinking. It had silver in it and chariots. I went through it when I was a deer. When I was a salmon. When I was a wild dog. When I was a man I bathed in it. I carried a yellow sail and a green sail. I know neither father nor mother. I speak with the living and the dead.

'Mary, do you know what you are made of?' he asked me suddenly. 'My schoolmaster has told us, and given me a book on it.'

'What are you on about?'

'Atoms, Mary. They are the tiniest things in the world and anything smaller than that is just energy. Everything, this piece of grass, the air, you, me, that rock. It's all atoms. Everything in the universe. The stars. The moon.'

'We are made of the same stuff as the moon?'

Seán nodded. 'And part of the atom is the electron and the electron spins about the centre of the atom so fast you never see it.'

I nodded, trying to grasp this.

'That bomb the Americans just dropped. Have you heard of it?'

'Patsey was telling me.'

'It's the biggest bomb in the world. It can wipe out a whole city in a second. Splitting the centre of a bunch of atoms made that. They discovered how to do this. Before the electrons moved and jump all the time but the centre held tight. Everything is made of atoms, Mary. In the centre of every atom is a nucleus with protons and neutrons. Humans learning to crack open the centre can create the biggest bomb. The master told us that this is the greatest bomb ever made. Now that we have learnt to tear apart the centre we can kill the whole world. Before only God could do that. We had to learn a Yeats poem.

The falcon cannot hear the falconer;
Things fall apart; the centre cannot hold;
Mere anarchy is loosed upon the world.'

He talked more and told me that nothing was still, everything was moving all the time. Everything that existed, including the chairs, the stones, the iron gates were alive. I wasn't surprised to learn this. It seemed natural to me. As if I had known it all along. I had come from Bolus Head. We sat in silence for a long time.

'There is a place inside me, Mary,' Seán said. 'The one still place in this world. A place when I can stop thinking for a moment.'

'You'll be a good priest. I know from this moment.'

He smiled at me. 'You'll be a teacher.'

'Ach, I won't. I won't. Too late for me now. But not for you, Seán.'

It was getting chilly. We sat at the fairy fort as the sun went down and the sky became a deep, longing blue. Seán's hair was so blond by the sun. And I thought I heard Padraig's whistles. This was Padraig's land too.

'This fairy mound was the only place where Padraig would allow me hold him,' I said. Seán put his head in his hands. I couldn't see his face. I rubbed his back. 'I know you were there. Patsey told me. I know you couldn't tell me. It's not your fault. You're only a wee gossin.'

'Teach me a poem now, Mary,' Seán said. He was so solemn. Though it was the height of summer I told him an old poem about the coming winter for I knew I had to get him off this farm he seemed to love so much. It would never be his, just as it would never be mine. Only the fairy mound was ours. He shivered as the evening lost heat and as I recited it to him, his mouth stained purple with the fraughans. And I was so glad to have my wee Seán with me that evening; a child doesn't have to come through you for them to be your own; a child just has to listen to you for you to love them, through raising him I learnt what love was.

I have news for you: the stag bells, winter snows, summer has gone,
Wind high and cold, the sun low, short its course, the sea running high.
Deep red the bracken, its shape is lost; the wild goose has raised its accustomed cry.
Cold has seized the birds' wings; season of ice, this is my news.

Seán put his dry little hand in mine and squeezed it for a moment. We took all our tins and headed back to the house. It didn't matter what Seamus and Sheila said to us now. We had had our lovely hours.

So summer ended and I put all my resources and plans into action. My actions might seem extreme but they were in response to the bad thing that Seamus and Sheila had done to Padraig.

I couldn't protect Padraig. I couldn't save him. But I wanted to make sure Seán would escape the land, and use his cleverness to rise up above us all. Above this flat farm, full of fairies and spirits and trees, full of Cromwell's magpies, full of the ghosts of the people who had it taken away from them for us, and wild hares appearing and disappearing, and lonely owls scaring the rats through the grasses.

Padraig

Captured by Balor

Dream of the land under waves. The one the new mother had told about. The King of the Cruelty Men untied the burning ropes that had dug in and cut. Small blood stains on the ropes. Sun eye in the sky watching. Stood straight – the Cruelty Man's fingers like iron spider legs clutching one arm, and dragged inside a dark, dreary, death-looking country without grass or trees. Sick green walls locked around. Frosted glass doors. This is not the land under wave but the country of Balor of the Evil Eye, the King of the Formorians.

A knife in pocket to carve the birds with – they took that – stripped piss clothes – scrubbed over rash – dressed in heavy linen cloths. Two big doors, one for males, one for females. Through the door for men. An attendant took a paper out – the King of the Cruelty Men signed. They took one look about this land – fled back to the shores of their own. Through the panes of glass on the half doors a woman being sucked into the other door. She was screaming. Quiet. Nothing to scream, no one to hear.

PART II

INSTITUTIONALIZATION

Every child has a madman on their street:
The only trouble about our madman is that he's our father.
Paul Durcan

Batt

He Was a Great Man for the Stories, It Was Said (1799)

I was born in 1786 the same year they killed the last wolf in Ireland. My grandfather on my mother's side was said to be a Connaire O Mac Tire. He had come to Kerry as a very young man after Cromwell had killed the men in his family and sent the women to Barbados as slaves. He was a great man for the stories, people would come from miles to listen, he knew many cures, and he had passed them onto my father who had married my mother. He had only daughters so his name died with him. Reputedly, he was fierce bitter about this since he was the last O Mac Tire in Ireland. But though his name died out with him, to be sure, his stories didn't.

He knew so many stories that the master from the hedge schools would have him along to regale the students with tales of old Ireland. They would sit at the side of a hill in the shelter and learn Latin, Greek and mathematics. A boy or girl would take it in turns to keep watch for the Redcoats. For in those days if you were caught educating Irish children you would be shot. They said my grandfather was able to turn into a wolf when he needed to know something he couldn't know as a man.

I had the gift too. If I heard a tale I could take it up and store it in my head word by word by word. This gave me a strong wish for them, to be sure. I'd follow the old people around and get everything from them. If they were salting the fish by the fire, I would be at their feet addling their heads and asking for all they knew. The old and the landless used to be wandering the land as beggars, and would stop and spend a night in the hay beds and eat a dinner in exchange for a story. To be sure I got a power of stories from the likes of them poor crayturs. I was only a lad of thirteen years old and the people would hush each other and gather around in our cabin while I told them of all sorts. It shortened the long, wet, dark, windy nights for us.

There was nothing I liked better; we were a conquered people so it gave us some power. The fact we could remember who we were. And I knew for sure that who we were was kept in the stories. This was all that was left to us after being pushed to the edge of the world.

The women were always pregnant, and the one-room cabins were so tiny that there were many of us always streeling about the road outside. Once out on these roads we gathered in a gang of children. The moon was swelling as if to burst. The only ones who weren't outside were in the houses with the whooping cough. We could hear them, even through the stone of the walls, with their strange barks and red faces. Suddenly, from nowhere we heard a group of horses come cantering up the hill. They galloped past our houses. About five horses. The road ended not far along so we waited. Strangely, they never came back. We waited every night for them. We looked for them in the fields in the morning. They were all we talked about for awhile.

'They must have jumped off Ireland and into the sea.'

'The hag got them.'

The last horse was white. I remember them as riderless but other children older than me said they had fairy riders on them. One night they came back from the forgotten edges and we children followed them in a frenzy and called out to the rider of the white horse.

'Oh rider of the white horse, what cures whooping cough?'

The old people were the ones we looked up to. They taught us everything. My grandmother taught me to smoor a fire. To cover it in ashes so it looked dead. You could go out about your business and come back and give it a poke and it would alight.

Sometimes the old people would say that a time would come when the stories would disappear from the country as sure as the forests, the harps and the wolves did. That we would be as tame and domesticated as a gelded bull. Fit for nothing but slaughter. There would come a time they said when no one would be able to speak their own tongue.

Mary

Mary's Plan to Save Seán from Seamus and the Cruelty Men (1945)

I had arranged for my sisters to be put into service so I knew how to do it easy enough. I could work and get Seán to school. I was to go to a family in Kilbride, Meath. The Lyons. Just outside Trim where I could see Maeve any time I wanted, which made me happy. The couple, Brian and Patricia, were in their late twenties and expecting their third child. Patricia was a schoolteacher and Brian was a solicitor. They lived in the schoolhouse at a crossroads at the edge of our colony. When I arrived I didn't even have a change of clothes. I walked those miles without shoes. My hair was grey and very short; my crocodile hands almost tore a hole through Mrs Lyons' rose-petal skin when she put her hand out to shake mine. We got an electric shock off each other.

'Loose electrons,' I said.

'I beg your pardon?' Her husband Brian looked as if a plank had hit him.

My English was rusty and formal. I had only been with my family and other Irish-speaking families in our tiny community. But I laboured on in the English I knew.

'That's what we're after getting a shock from, Mr Lyons, sir. That would be them electrons that spin around your atoms coming loose and when they find my atoms they give off an electrical charge.'

There was such a stunned silence that I added, as if in amendment, 'That's what the fellah says anyhow. My brother Seán told me that. He was good in school. The Christian Brothers are training him in Dublin. He'll be a priest.'

They were too mannerly to even look at each other, though it became a story they all told after. How I must have looked now brings a smile to my face. Grey cropped hair under a headscarf, a patched skirt and bare feet walking out of the Irish Colony into their world. Sure, I looked a bit poor and odd but I was as sane as a wet blanket wrapped around a burning child. I was sending myself away and I knew why.

Her husband Brian smiled. 'You must be walking a long time, Mary. I could have gone and got you. We didn't realize.'

They gave me tea and bread and butter. The next day Patricia and I took the pony and trap into Trim town and bought me my first pair of shoes and a change of clothes. I was reluctant to do this as I told her I needed to send all my money to my brother who had started school with the Christian Brothers on a part scholarship. I was proud to tell an educated woman this. She told me that the clothes and shoes were to be a starting gift and she would not take them out of my wages.

I had a little room by the kitchen. Enough to fit a bed into. The first time I had my own room, because wee Seán used to stay in mine. I rose every morning at 5 am. That was a lie-in for me. There was no farm outside to keep but I still filled the time. I made the fire in the stove and prepared the breakfast. Patricia got up and went to 6.30 Mass every day. She was a devout woman and often we would say a decade of the rosary together in the evenings. She would pray for her people in Mayo, and America, and I would pray for mine. When the children woke up I got them dressed and fed. I let the children take a turn at the churn when I made butter. They would turn and turn with fierce concentration, until the small globs of butter appeared on the cream. They would help me shape them with the wooden butter pats. I loved to see the shining yellow butter in the crystal dish ready to be spread onto my hot brown bread. It didn't last long I can tell you.

I even had Friday nights off and Sunday afternoons.

I had turkeys, chickens and a few pigs outside. They were mine, I suppose, as the Lyonses let me deal with the animals and I wouldn't have lived without animals about and liked to eat meat that I had reared and nourished myself. Daddy always said if someone showed me something once I could do it. The fellah up the road was a beekeeper proper and he gave me old hives and taught me to get the honey. I loved my bees. He told me that you have to talk to bees. That they would have to know who was born and who died in the family, otherwise they'd leave or worse, stop making honey. He seemed to have a lot of success with bees so I paid heed, and those bees knew more about all of us than the priest Fr Lavin in his confessional.

I cooked lunch and dinner and kept the house scrubbed clean. I washed and wrung out their clothes, and took care of James, the new baby, as soon as he was born. I polished the silver and the brass by the fire. I lit fires and chopped wood. I baked bread and tarts and made sloe wine. I still went up the lanes and got the berries for my jams with the children trailing after me and the baby on my hip. My feet were light as always, so even when I walked I could not hear myself. Sometimes I wondered was I there at all. In the evenings I could see, from the corners of my eyes, the spirits fly by me. I asked them to keep Seán safe and learning, and Padraig be taken care of in the asylum and not in harm's way, and Bridget in Dublin to have good fortune, and Maeve to find a good man and get a family of her own, and Seamus to find peace with Sheila, and Sheila to find some happiness with her new baby on the way.

Bitterly, Seamus and Sheila would not speak to me. They felt I had betrayed them by walking out and leaving all the work on their backs. But they had never paid me for any work and I needed money now. I had to keep Seán in that school. I prayed to the Virgin Mary, for I knew that though Meath was full of fairies and spirits, they were not inclined to heed us or help us. Wasn't it us that had taken the land from them right at the very beginnings before anyone wrote anything down? That's why we needed the Virgin. I never prayed to the man on the cross. Who could? He looked like he was otherwise occupied. He looked like he needed more help than any of us. The Virgin was a great comfort. One day I would kneel before Seán and he would bless me. The day of his ordination.

Patricia would smile when I said this over and over again, 'What if he doesn't get the calling?'

'If you met him you would know,' I told her.

Patricia was a gentle, dignified woman, tall and willow-like. I was small and steadily growing more stout with all the food around and the absence of hard labour on the farm that used to keep me thin as a whip. The school she taught in was just across the road. At the crossroads in Kilbride there was only a school, and our house opposite. The towns had electricity brought to them but we had none. I loved the Tilley lamps in the evening. I thought about Seán's atoms and electrons, and he wrote to me that loose electrons are what create electricity. Now we had discovered the essence of what we were made of we could harness it for good and evil. These were his concerns. He wrote no news of any teachers or priests or other boys. He did tell me when he was thirteen he went to a place called Booterstown and got the collar. He was very proud of that. It was as if normal reality did not exist for him nor he for it. I could read the letters and Patricia worked with me in the evenings to improve my writing and spelling. She too read Seán's letters and admired his thinking and his writing. She began to include him in her prayers. I wrote a letter each week to Seán. Some nights I would only manage a few lines, but I kept the pages and sent them off faithfully every

Friday. I would get a letter back the next Wednesday. We never missed this. I told him I was happy working for this wonderful family and he just wrote about atoms and theories, and bits of history he was learning. I wrote asking him to tell me the name of his friends but he never mentioned a living soul.

He asked me for more stories about Columcille whom he never tired of hearing about. At one point Columcille was excommunicated and banished from Ireland. He and his companions went to Iona, a tiny island off of Scotland, and there they started the great book of Kells. He only came back once to Ireland for the Synod of Drumceatt, in the year 574 AD. The bards and druids were about to be expelled as pagan troublemakers and he spoke on behalf of twelve hundred of them. In a way he was chief of the druids. He said if they were exiled from Ireland by the official new religion, then Ireland would lose all their knowledge and stories and it would never be replaced.

This particular letter was seized and an almighty fuss came out of it. I was told that all correspondence is read and opened by the Brothers. They didn't like my suggestion that St Columcille was a druid. I was mortified. Patricia had to intercede on my behalf and explain that it was just old folklore that I was repeating. That I was a native of Kerry, not Meath and I had come with all sorts of stories from the peasants down in Kerry who could neither read nor write. I was just a housekeeper writing to my brother. They allowed me to resume my correspondence if I kept it decent. I was worried that I had got poor Seán into a whole welter of trouble with my old nonsense. Patricia and Mr Lyons told me not to worry about it.

'The priests have their own interests to protect,' Patricia said, 'but be careful because you'll put your brother in danger.'

Mr Lyons even joked that they had a pagan in their midst.

Mr Lyons said, 'Don't think any more of it. I was always more of a Columcille man than a St Patrick man myself.'

I promised them I would never tell their children the stories from home and they just laughed and said more's the pity. Patricia taught me to play draughts to while away the dark evenings by the fire.

Patricia was pregnant with her fourth baby. I massaged her feet and legs when they swelled up. There was a healer down the lane and I would go and get herbs from her for Patricia to drink when she was very sick with the vomiting. The healer was showing me all the plants that worked as medicine, and I began to make up wee bottles myself. Patricia would tease me about this but she drank the herbs, at least I think she did, she could have been pouring them down the sink for all I know. Though I lived with her she had a privacy to her, a wall of calm serenity around. Her's was an educated way of living. I had never encountered anyone before who had no fear of the other world. Who had never seen a fairy. Who had never heard the banshee. Who walked through the ruins in the evening alone with the dog and did not fear that the pooka would carry her off.

'If he takes you off on a wild ride he'll leave you back in the same spot but you'll never be the same again. He can take you to the moon. Some have said that's where they went.'

'I thought you were done with your stories,' Patricia smiled as she read her paper and I fussed about her. Pouring her tea. Setting the table. Checking the potatoes in the stove pot. I looked at her, shocked.

'These aren't stories,' I told her.

She shrugged and suppressed a smile.

'And what if you saw the black pig?' I had my hands on my hips. 'What would you do then?'

'The same black pig that heralds the end of the world?' She was about to laugh but held it back. I bristled.

'The very one? If you saw it running by, what would ye do?'

'I'd wonder how they knew it meant the end of the world because if they ever saw it before then the world would have ended.' Then she relented and sighed. 'I suppose I'd say a decade of the rosary, Mary. Sure what could I do?'

This was the world of the educated people. Gentle people. Patricia and Mr Lyons never fought in front of me. They lived decently and quietly and dedicated themselves to their children. After dinner in the long summer evenings, Patricia and Mr Lyons went for walks together up the lane. They chatted and laughed with each other. I remember my father and mother; they had seemed desperate about each other. He had always craved her and she had teased and goaded him. That's what I remember anyway.

Here was another way of loving; a comfortable way.

The fourth baby was a girl, and they called her Teresa. I suppose I always had a grá for the youngest. I took her on as my wee pet. Baby, we all called her, as she was the baby. The name stuck, no one ever called her Teresa.

These were my second set of children to raise, Joseph, Eileen, James and Baby. There was not a quiet moment in the house, I can tell you. They had the run of the place. I loved them all as if they were my own, and in a way they were. I fed them and dressed them and it was me they came into at night if they were afraid. When Patricia and Mr Lyons went visiting and playing poker, the children gathered around the kitchen fire on long dark winter nights and begged me for stories. I told them a few and I told them facts about the fairies. It was their right to know, no matter what their mother and father believed. Beside us walk the spirits of the other world, though they do us no good, they will leave us alone if we acknowledge them and give them their place. In the gaslight and firelight the fairies seemed real but when the electricity came and they got the wireless in, it was then the fairies went out. We talked little of them after that; everyone preferred to listen to the radio.

I raised these bright children in the hope that they would not be like us. We were poor and the scatterment of the dog's family was in us. None of us in the same place as each other except for Maeve and me.

I saw Maeve every other day at the shop, which was a great joy. She was happy and plenty of men were courting her. We went to the pictures together every Friday night, and there was always some fellah trying to get with her. They all thought I was her mother and I was only twenty-one and she sixteen.

Maeve

A Very Pious Young Girl

They say a very pious young girl will make a right old devil. And Catherine, the daughter of this shop owner Mrs Boyle, was a plain old sap of a thing who spent her time on her knees on the landing praying to the statue of the Virgin. She was only a few years older than me but she didn't like me because, though she was the daughter of shop owners, I was tall and pretty, and she was a pasty, pudding-faced, uncooked dough ball. To top it all she had no ankles; her legs went straight into her brown sensible shoes with no interruption.

I was sent here when I was eleven to work in her family's shop. Her mother and father gave me bed and board and a few shillings a week. I never had a room, just a mattress on boxes in the storeroom. It was only when I was fifteen that they bought a screen to put up around my mattress. There were four rooms upstairs, they had a spare room but I suppose they used it for visitors. Despite that, I couldn't complain about Mr and Mrs Boyle. They were nothing but fair to me. I heard shocking stories from other servants and skivvies, but I had none to tell. If some of the delivery boys got too fresh with me Mr Boyle would loom protectively but not proprietorially. I became, by fifteen, one of the prettiest girls in Trim town. Mr Boyle, always a merchant, told me that that was currency.

'You've a great head for figures, Maeve. You could go study bookkeeping. You could be teaching the class in no time. You should look in the mirror and think about what you could get from your face. Don't be a fool. Choose a man who will support you or run a business. Stay away from these fly-by-night corner boys that sniff around trying to help you with your packing and lifting.'

'I will, Mr Boyle,' I laughed, flattered and pleased that he thought I had a future and wouldn't be forever working for them in this grocery shop in poxy Trim town.

I had a few savings and I waited for Friday where I could go to the flicks and dream my escape.

I was never a good reader but I was good with numbers. I could add it all up for the customers without using the till. Mr Boyle taught me to tie the parcels with twine, make a loop and break the twine with a sharp tug without losing a finger. Food came in bulk so I spent most of my time weighing and packing the flour, sugar, salt, tea, barley, dried fruit. The weights and measures man would come in and do inspections, and I gradually learnt to weigh and measure without any measurements. I was never off. Mr Boyle had an easy way with the customers and was well liked. He originally came from Northern Ireland and so never cheated anyone out of so much as a grain of sugar.

Most of the time their daughter Catherine was gone to secondary school. She was a border with them Loreto nuns in Navan. Mercifully, she only came home at holidays. In the summers we stayed apart from each other. She treated me as if I was contagious, for she never had a fellah and I had plenty on Friday to walk me up the town to the flicks.

I got my period when I was a few years in their service. I had known this was to happen as I had to wash Mrs Boyle's clothes and she told me mine would be starting one day and Catherine's. I just dreaded that because I would have to soak and wash three sets of these bloody, reeking cloths. The first year I got terrible cramps but they eased off and there was something about the blood that I began to like. The colour. There was not a lot of colour in the town and this colour was vivid and exciting. The brightness of the blood at the start of the week and the dark red it became. If I didn't have to do all the washing I would have looked forward to my periods.

When Catherine was nineteen and finished school she was put to working with me in the shop. Her lips curled when she saw me. She still knelt on the landing and said her rosaries. I pitied God, to have to be listening to her flat voice with no sins to spice up any supplications.

'Would you not say them in your room?' I told her as I came down the stairs with all the sheets to launder, nearly tripping over her fat ankles.

Her mammy and daddy were actually worried she would become a nun. She was the only child they managed to squeeze into the world. They wanted her in the shop, so they soon found her a man who had a business delivering bread in his truck. He had several trucks, and lorded it over many drivers. His name was Kevin, he kept looking at me. Couldn't take his eyes off of me. It used to amuse me. When he'd come around to do a bit of enforced courting, I would wear something really tight. A blouse a little too small. He would watch me breathlessly as I went this way and that in the shop. I'd make sure to have to put stuff up on the top shelves beside him so I could stretch up on a ladder and let him see what he was missing. I knew the buttons were straining around my breasts. I just did it for divilment. I liked to be looked at in that way. He was stuck with that sack of old potatoes, Catherine, and he knew it, but it was she who would own the shop. And even if I did, I wouldn't look twice at him. He knew that too.

Catherine said her prayers and I swished by him with my arms bare and my hair loose. Poor Kevin, he was a bit of a gom himself. He didn't know if he was coming or going.

Mary

You Got Two Ends of the Rope

I prayed every night and this was my prayer:

Seamus, may you be happy, may your household find peace, forgive me for leaving and taking Seán, may your wife no longer be as sore as a briar. I worked that farm for many years and left without shoes on my feet and my hair grey. You got two ends of the rope and leave to pull, so be happy now.

Bridget, wherever you are, send a letter to us and let us know how life has treated you. It's been so long without a word.

Maeve you go meet a good man and have your own family away from the shop, may I see you grey and combing your children's hair.

Padraig, after all is done I know to wish you well is hen's milk in a pig's horn, and a cat's feather for mixing it. For I have some fear of those places, cities of the mad they are, and no way out of them, but may God give to you according to your heart because you never hurt a soul or caused damage to a person or animal. When I have reared this lot of children for Patricia and Brian, maybe one day I can take care of you again. Sometimes I look at the oak tree outside and know you would love to shin up it. I still stop my bicycle on the road and stand in the bird song and cattle moaning and try to hear you again. I have a little collection of wooden whistles and small birds that I found out in the woods after you were gone, I have the birds here on my dresser between my comb and hairbrush.

Seán, my little man, my light, my heart, my best boy, a stór. Your gifts and good heart will raise us all up. Bless you, and one day you will bless us. I dream you will be a priest and I your housekeeper and Padraig in a tree in our yard and Maeve visiting with her children. One day, on the day of your ordination, I will kneel before you and you will lay your sweet hand on my head and give me grace. And that grace will wash me down and I will be absolved of all I failed to do for you all. It was not for want of love.

Out of all of them that I promised to take care of, Seán was the one I managed to do the best for. The promises I made to my mother were beyond me to keep. I didn't do a good job. I know that. But we were orphans pretty soon into it. I had to put aside my failure and guilt and live on to be of service to another set of kids who had their lives mapped out in better ways. All I know is, I never took a moment for myself out of it and I tried to steer our little currach to the shore, but the sea was rough and the shore was rocky and they swam away from me as I called out to them. But they were all alive at least. I didn't know that of Bridget for certain but I hoped that none of us were yet dust.

That's my night prayer. More to my mother and father than to God, but also to the Virgin that I loved. I felt her kindness all around me. I felt her in everything, the centre of every atom, of the pots, of the sloe berries, of the flakes of paint on the window sill, of the potatoes I pulled from the garden, of the rosary beads, of everything she hummed life into. We will not break her centre apart. We would surely destroy the world. She found me such a good family to go to live my days. My work was appreciated here, and my jam was eaten and my sloe wine drank. The children piled on my knee quicker than they did on their reserved, gentle mother's. They threw their arms around me and asked that I lie with them and hold them as they fell asleep. I chased them about the yard with my broom and brought them on long walks through the fields. They clung to my housecoat as the dogs barked at us and it made me feel strong to protect them.

Them it was in my bounds to protect.

'Tell us a story, Mary,' James would say of an evening.

'I'll tell you a story about Johnny Magory,' I teased. 'He was a jinnit and that's all that's in it.' After they protested, Eileen would pull me down into the chair, with the baby in my arms. I'd tell them the first one that jumped in to my head.

'Back in Kerry we believed there was a friendship between even the dead dust of the bones of kin. I remember on a windy day, the dust on the road whirled round, Seán the storyteller used to tell me that this was due to some particles of the dust of long separated kind rushing together in love. When a sudden gust of wind suddenly started on a calm day, whipped passed us and leaving the calm day behind it we watched it with awe. We were told we should not stand before, or in the way of, the blast. Rather we should take shelter even behind the walls, even if the nettles stung us as we got into the ditch. When it passed, Seán the storyteller taught us to throw after it a handful of sand, grass, leaves or something that could not be easily counted. He told us to say, *slán le gach duine a chluineas sin*, 'May all who hear that blast be safe.'

'Once my grandmother said they were out at Halloweve night when out of nowhere a dark cloud from the west moved towards her in a whirlwind. She remembered that she had been told to cast the dust that was under her foot against it, and at that instant, if they had any human beings with them, they were obliged to release them. So the old woman bent down and lifted a handful of gravel that was by her door. She threw it into the whirlwind and shouted out, "In the name of the Father, Son, and Holy Ghost." My grandmother told me a woman, weak and faint and feeble, fell on the earth with a heavy groan.'

Of course they had a hundred questions. After putting them all to bed, I prayed at night to the Blessed Virgin to bring me home. Home to Bolus Head. I would walk up the hill. The very hill that the man with the bicycle came up on. The man pushing his bike up that hill. His face red and out of breath. How we all ran around him in a swarm of curiosity. How much we didn't know where he would lead us. Each night after my prayers were done, I closed my eyes and imagined walking all the way home to Kerry, onto the rocky edge of the world. Retracing my steps; to Bolus Head, I would walk. I saw the islands before me. And I would wait for a whirlwind to whip up and come from the west, down past the houses. I would stand where the field leads to the standing stones. And so the hag would send me the whirlwind. I imagined myself breathless as the whirlwind came to me and I would bend and pick up a handful of stones and throw it into the dust. That I might free my mother and father from whatever spirits carried them off, that stopped them from ever coming back to me.

Maeve

Poxy Trim Town
(1946)

I was thinking of moving on somewhere else. I was sixteen and could be married, but I always let them go. The ones who came courting. I couldn't help feeling there would be a better one coming into the shop the next week and I was usually right. Blue-eyed boys in long pants. Eager to bring me to the flicks on Friday night. My only night. Blessed be Friday. Holier than any Sunday. As my oldest sister Mary used to say, 'Live horse, and you will get grass.'

The latest one, there he was. I was behind the counter dressed in white and red and with a bit of lipstick on to drive poor Kevin mad. The shop was quiet; Catherine's dad, Mr Boyle, was behind the desk in the office, reading a paper. I did all their accounts and paid the bills and I was good at that. I'd had many suitors. He was different. His name was Rory. He asked me out when he saw me the first time. He said he'd seen me on the street with my sister Mary. He knew the family she worked for. Rory had class, his family were country people and he had been in boarding school. He was only seventeen and had finished school.

He wasn't a groper like so many others. Not that the gropes were all terrible. Some of the kinder ones, I'd let them stroke me in the lanes on the way home. I'd move closer to them as we walked as a signal to put their arms about me. Only if I liked them, and felt like it, mind you.

Rory's arm linked in mine. He would rub his elbow off the side of my breast. Forward and backward. Real gentle, as if he was doing it by accident and then stronger so I couldn't mistake it. This, two Fridays in a row. Until I was biting my tongue and feeling myself moist and my breathing was shallow. I turned around to him in the dark lane and we leaned against the wall. It was I who was pushing him against the wall. And it was I who opened my silk blouse and put his hands up to my breasts. I reached around and undid my bra so he could touch the bare skin. His breath was taken in sharply and he let out a little moan. It was wonderful.

We kissed and kissed and he pulled on my nipples and my head swirled. He pressed me into his legs and I could feel him stiff and erect. Hours we passed in that alley and that was as far as we took it. I thought of nothing else all week. When I went around town on my errands and deliveries I pressed against the saddle and pictured him. Friday came again and he didn't have to ask. He would be standing there outside the shop.

'Is that the Greeley boy?' Mr Boyle asked. 'He's keen on you.'

'Indeedn't he's not,' I laughed.

'You could do worse. His family have acres all over the county and he's the eldest of thirteen. He'll inherit that farm to be sure.'

This darkened me somehow. I had seen enough of my sister and brother working on a small farm to know I didn't want to be a farmer's wife. Worse still, I had been raised around people that squabbled over land and feuds that lasted generations, and that's when things were going well.

'Are you a farmer?' I asked him. His hands didn't seem to have done a day's work in his life. I could feel no calluses when he slipped them up my skirt. That was where we had got to on our Friday nights. I had stopped wearing my underwear to the flicks and I told him this. It would keep him on the edge of the seat throughout the film. Keep him glancing at me in dark desperation as I touched my stockings with the tips of my fingers.

'I want to go to America,' I'd tell him and see the hurt look on him as I planned my life without a notion of him in it. That look was my power.

When we went into the lane I would guide his hands and hold them when I wanted him to continue. He followed my lead like a dance. He urged me to just skip the flicks but where could we go? It was also the only time I could spend with my older sister, Mary, who had Friday night off. She was the only family I had in my life and though she'd come into the shop during the week it was always too busy to talk much. I sat between Rory and Mary. He said he never remembered the film. And I thought it only heightened our petting after it because we had to wait so long to get to it.

Behind the lane I'd keep a hold of his hand when it was up my skirt, then I took his hand out and put his finger in my mouth and then in his. He would press his stiff thing against me and it would shoot off behind the material of his trousers, but he was so young it would be hard again by the time he pulled back. What I loved about Rory most was the little moans and sighs, like a small song to my body.

All week I waited for Rory. I'd wait to see him stand in the door, lank and tall and freckled. His head cocked and wearing a hat that only served to make him look more like a boy, his hands would be in his pockets. We could never pass up the town without the corner boys giving us a running commentary:

There she goes with that Greeley boy,
She'd want to get on it before she's an old maid like the sister,
His people won't have a skivvy,
He's a landed man, going to have a farm,
He's been up at the school and what's she been at?

Been out with every fellah in the town.
She'll throw him away like all the others.

On the way home I'd put my hands in his pockets and grab him there through the material. One night he had cut a hole in his pockets and he wasn't wearing underwear either. He put my hand in his pocket in the flicks. We were watching a Flash Gordon film. Mary was on the other side. I touched the soft paper skin on his shaft and we nearly leapt up and ran at that instant. I could gobble him up.

That night we walked Mary a bit of the way out of town until she got on her bicycle and said she'd go the rest of the way by herself. She smiled at me. I never knew how Mary could live without all of this but she didn't seem to mind. Rory said Mary was away with the fairies. She talked about them so much. I think she lived in another world surrounded by the unseen. I had been raised with talk of them too, but I never paid it heed and never in my life saw anything that would suggest they were around me. I was a numbers person and Mary was a storyteller. I pointed it out to Rory, she might be in touch with those from another place but she was a pragmatic and efficient person in her life. She had farmed, and fed us single-handed from when she was ten, and she had cooked and kept our house on top of that. She had sacrificed everything and baldy spotty Seamus had got the farm only on account he was a boy. Mary had no bitterness over that. I thought it wasn't fair. Just because you're a man doesn't mean you are entitled to it all. But Mary said that was the way of things and it kept everything simple. Dividing up land into small parcels led to starvation and bad farming. She said she loved the Lyonses. She doted on their youngest, Baby; she called her her luck-child. All the children she raised as diligently and patiently as if they were her own, but Baby she loved like she loved our Seán. Not many could do that, though many were forced to do it. I couldn't see myself in that situation. Not liking the idea of constant service I wasn't even sure I wanted children of my own. A bit of rest after all these years work was what I was looking for. A bit of the good life. Sure I had seen the life in films and maybe I could get to America and live like that.

Mary said she liked Rory too. But she warned me that his mother had already spoken to Patricia and Brian about her eldest son doing a line with a landless, penniless shop girl. Patricia and Brian were not concerned. They were gentle, non-interfering people. They did say that the Greeleys were big landowners and had a lot of power locally and with the priests. Other servant girls had told me that the Greeleys had a reputation with their workers and servants. That they rented out people, children too, and there was talk of beatings and other cruelty. I put it down to local jealousy. Rory was a gentle creature only interested in the one thing. That would be me. Or really my body. But that didn't bother me because I was enjoying every bit of it myself and hadn't asked him too many questions either. I wasn't looking to marry him like everyone assumed. I just wanted a bit of fun and to go to America one day. All these things were on my mind as I was walking along the lane between Rory and Mary. I was a calculator and could add up both sides of the balance sheet in any situation.

We said goodbye to Mary and turned to go back to the town. Rory nodded to me with a half smile. 'She's probably turned into a hare and bounded all the way home.'

I punched him in the arm. Mary talked openly about all those old things as if everyone around was party to them. Though I had no way into the fairy world myself, I did believe Mary was one of those. As he said it, I turned in the night and I thought I might see her transform. He was laughing, softly shaking his head.

He kissed my hand. I thought that was such a funny thing to do. Like he'd seen it in the films. I remember an old woman who came into the shop often; she had had twenty-three children. She had said something once that I never forgot. She had said that the men of Ireland were very rough with the women. But Rory Greeley was never rough with me.

We walked the narrow road, alone in the world. A harvest moon giant and red burned in the next field. There were foxes slipping away from us as I climbed a gate into a field and lay on the grass waiting for him. For a few minutes I thought he wouldn't come. He made me wait. I heard the swing and clank of the iron gate as he leapt over. I kept my eyes shut tightly.

I felt him stand over me. Could feel his moon shadow cross me like a chill. I shivered.

'What do you want from me girl?' he said.

Without speaking or deciding anything and without taking our eyes off one another both of us stripped bare. I'd never seen another human body naked and I doubt he had either. If anyone had come into the field they would have caught a rare sight in Ireland that summer night. At first we sat up facing each other. As if we didn't know where to start now all the obstacles of clothes were gone. I pulled towards him still sitting and facing him, our legs intertwining. He lay me down suddenly and it hurt like a knife thudding into me but I still couldn't stop. His legs were covered in blood and he touched it with his fingers and tasted it, which made us both laugh. We lay for a while in the field and we were not cold.

For a minute he sat up and opened my legs and looked inside me. I lay there knowing a boy like this would be looking at nothing but the mystery of the world. I liked that feeling of having it between my legs. He didn't say a word; he just kept looking, holding my knees. It made me catch my breath and pull him to me and we did it again and this time it was wetter and softer and I saw speckles of light dance behind my eyes and behind his head. I pulled him into me harder and harder, and I cried out when he moaned. I wanted to do it again. I lay back and let him shove his fingers up, with his head right down there watching it all. The light began to push its way over the hill, we got our clothes back on and by the time he helped me over the gate the birds were chanting and pouring their strange sounds into the air. But I didn't want this day. I didn't want to be cleansed, I wanted to feel that dirty night in me all my born days. As I swung over the gate I pulled up my skirt to remind him I had no knickers on, and his face contorted again and he kissed me beside the gate roughly.

'You're something else, Maeve O Conaill.'

'I know I am.'

We heard the sound of a cart coming up the road and we ran. It turned into a race. As we got near to the town and its big ruin of a castle we slowed down.

'Are you all right?'

I nodded.

'What can we do now?' he asked. He was pensive. He didn't hold my hand or link my arm.

'Will I see you Friday?' I asked.

We were compressed by the riot of bird song. Made tiny.

'Was it not lovely?' I reached out and squeezed his arm.

He smiled at that, 'I thought you didn't want to be a farmer's wife.'

'Who said I want to be anyone's wife?'

Maybe that was harsh and I regretted it, so I quickly took his hand. The morning hedges were lush and spilling over onto the road. We walked either side of the green grassy central line. Seeing the town I felt all of its pressure. We were like Adam and Eve leaving the garden. But I didn't want to trap him. I knew the whole town was talking and that his people would have heard of me. I felt him watch me go up the lane and into the back door, and through to my little corner in the shop storeroom. It was where I had slept every night since I was eleven. Five years on that mattress on wooden boxes. Not a real bed. And there was no door. Maybe it was just lack of sleep or the feeling that I'd pulled the plug and let all the water drain out of the bath but I thought I barely knew Rory Greeley. He was only a child out of school and kept by his family. We never talked much or told anything to each other. He came on Fridays, and we walked cringing past the corner boys and their chorus of disapproval that kept the whole town in its place. We would talk about what the film would be that night. Then on the way home we only wanted one thing from each other and that didn't involve words. Did I love him?

Sure I didn't know him. And he never said he loved me, he just kept telling me I was beautiful. But sure I knew that. And the competition wasn't much in poxy Trim either.

There was a hand mirror by my basin and I put it on the ground and squatted over it. I wanted to see what he saw when he looked at me. That was the part I would come back to the most. The most exciting part of it all. The long looking. I had looked at myself many times before but this time I looked with his eyes. Then I lay down on the bed. I would have to get up and start taking deliveries soon. I placed my hands between my legs. I decided I would not wash today. I would keep the smell there as a reminder.

Surely the world could make more room for me.

Upstairs Mr Boyle and Mrs Boyle, Catherine and Kevin, were just waking up. Each of them had chosen a bedroom to themselves.

Mary

The World Goes Around as if There Were Wings on It (1947)

Every Christmas puts another year on your shoulders.

Seán and Maeve went back to Seamus and Sheila for Christmas Day but on Stephen's Day they got up early and came over to us in Kilbride. The Wren boys would be about in the country doing their mischief. It was a great day, Stephen's Day. The bulk of the cooking would be over but we had plenty of food from the Christmas dinner. While I got the meal ready, Mr Lyons was good enough to pick them up in the trap. Seamus never came out to greet him, I was told, but that was Seamus. I was busy making everything perfect for Seán who was going to stay with us for the holidays. I had threaded holly together and hung it around the house. I had little oil lights and I placed hollowed-out birds' eggs over them as decoration. Maeve had to be back to work the next day.

I had stuffed two turkeys and boiled a lovely ham in my own cider that I had made from the apples in our orchard. They were my own potatoes too. Floury and soft and a little sweet. There was

Yorkshire pudding and cabbage and for afters there was my own plum pudding and Christmas cake. Oh I loved to pour the brandy over the pudding and set it alight, and carry it to the table with the holly burning and crackling on top. Seán was quiet, he barely said a word all meal. He didn't even eat much of the feast I'd put before him. As he scraped his leftovers into the slop bucket, I said what I always said to the children when they didn't clean their plates.

'One day you'll follow the crows to Tara for that.'

Like clockwork there was a shadow passing by the kitchen window. 'Suds and sins,' he called out.

Even on Christmas Day poor old Suds and Sins came shuffling out of the darkness, and I put half of the slops in his bucket and he went away without a word. Seán offered to carry his bucket to the gate as it was slippy on the ice, but I'll warrant he did it to get away from my scolding. Though I didn't mean to scold. For I loved him so much my heart could burst.

That night we said goodbye to Maeve. She sat up in the trap and waved at us. Her blonde hair covered by my shawl, for it would be a cold ride home. I had awful trouble making her wear it as she was worried about looking like an auld one.

'See you Friday,' she waved.

Mr Lyons was a bit drunk but the horse knew the way into town and would know how to get back. He had a cigarette in his mouth and his hat crooked on his head. Maeve's laughter could be heard down the dark cold road. Seán smiled to hear it. It was the only smile I saw on him.

'Are you not happy up at the school, Seán?'

'I just miss you, Mary. I miss everyone.'

'It's normal to get homesick. You'll get used to it.' He came up to me and hugged me. Seán was the only one who ever did that. He put his head on my shoulder. He was as tall as me now. 'Are they being good to you? The Brothers?'

'Some of them are alright, I suppose. Tell me a story,' he pleaded. 'I miss your stories.'

'I thought they were getting you in trouble.'

He shook his head. 'Tell me one now. There are no Brothers around to hear you.'

That St Stephen's night I told my favourite story, 'The Bull Bhalbhae'. Seán said he would walk up the fields with me tomorrow and we would look for a hole into the underworld.

'You're getting too big to share a bed with me,' I said.

But he wanted me to hold him that night. So I lay him down with his back to me and held him. He was a man of twelve but he had softness in him that was written on his face. I hoped it would never harden over but I never yet saw an adult man with that softness.

He stayed the week and helped me with all my work. Seán wasn't one for hard labour, he moved slowly about everything as if in a dream. And he didn't have a great amount of physical strength.

The children loved him and Patricia and Mr Lyons said he must spend all the holidays with us if he was allowed out again. For there were no voices raised here in this house and no one wanted for anything. The Lyonses listened to their children, shared newspapers stories with them, sat around the wireless with them on their laps, at ease with each other. The food was plentiful and the fire was lit from morning to night. The turf shed was always full.

Over the week Seán relaxed, and smiles came rushing back like a dam opening on the river. He raced around the yard with the little ones. Though he was already twelve years, for a moment I thought he was still a child.

It was the coldest day I can remember. A frost took hold that never lifted from the grass and the road. Mr Lyons put Seán in the trap to take him back to the train to get him to school. I pulled the cap down on my brother's head. His ears were red and numb. His hair was as blond as Maeve's.

Mr Lyons stamped his feet and said. 'That's it, Mary. We'll get a car by the end of the year. We'll be nice and warm then.'

Seán's eyes brightened. 'A car? Can I have a drive of it?'

'Indeed you can.'

'There you have it, that's something to look forward to.' I held him tightly to me and he gave me a long hug.

'I'm glad to see you so happy, Mary,' Seán said.

'You'll be happy too, Seán,' I said. 'One day you'll have a house of your own like Fr Lavin. Maybe you'll have his house and I'll mind both houses.'

He nodded solemnly. Mr Lyons managed to raise his eyebrows even in the frozen air, and so I got out of the trap and watched the horse paw the road warily. The wheels skidded on the ice and they went very slowly out of my sight.

Inside the house, I cried a bit for Seán and prayed to the Virgin that she keep him from harm. I picked up Baby from her basket though she was asleep and content and didn't need to be disturbed. I sat with Baby for a while by the stove. That was my place in the world. My chair by the stove in the kitchen in the Lyonses' house, a strong pot of tea on the range. Raising these lovely children who would never be sent away, who would be schooled on past eleven years, who would choose what they wanted to do, who would not have beds in other people's houses, who could stay with me forever. One leg tucked under me that would go numb but that was how I sat, like a fat old stork with Baby on my knee, she would curl into me, her fingers clamped around my hand, and I sang to her all my songs and more that would come to me out of nowhere, and others that I would have once sang to wee Seán when he was a gossin just like her. 'You are my luck-child,' I'd whisper to her.

Seamus

I Had Burnt my Coal and Got No Heat

Mary could make things grow, I'll hand her that. The ground listened to her and gave all it had. Even better, she could take what grew and make it into something. Breads, jams, meats, butter, cheese, when I think of how she fed us all. I don't know where she learnt all that. Little visits to neighbours' farms and she would come back with a new idea. She should have stayed with me and worked on her own family land. Plenty of sisters did just that for a brother. Sure she couldn't have married, but she wouldn't get a man while she was in service to that Lyons family either. It wasn't for her to be starting her own family. She wasn't the marrying type.

I saw her in town one day on a bike and she had grown stout and placid, and with her grey hair you'd have never guessed she was not yet thirty. The farm would have kept her leaner. No, Mary was not one for men or for gossip and she was a hard worker. I never raised a hand to her in all the years; I let her make all the decisions about the family and the cows and pigs and chickens.

She had a knack for them animals too. She had all sorts of potions to feed them when she thought they were poorly. Once, when we were visiting a neighbour's farm for a wake, a goose took a liking to her and followed her around the whole time we were there.

She never spoke ill of anyone, she tolerated that old fool Patsey who stopped coming around once Sheila was in the house. Though he still came out and met me in the field just to stick his nose into my business, pretending to ask how I was doing and did I need anything. I could see right through him. He looked at me with his funny eyes. If I had a shovel in my hand I always had a mind to bash his head in and bury him in the potato field and nourish my crops. At least he would be useful for something.

There was something funny about Patsey. I'd always felt it. Something not all decent. There was a want in him.

He'd bought a thresher. A huge machine that stood in his yard and he took it round to the other farms. He must have been stinking rich. He was always in the yard fiddling with it. He loved that feckin machine. I knew come harvest time I'd have to go and get it from him and that brought a dark fog into my head.

There was no quietness on a farm. Blasted armies of birds squawked, always dogs barking and cows and pigs squealing, and now kids wailing in the house when I went in and Sheila complaining. I was eighteen when I married her and I didn't know better. Then I saw I could have married a whole other type of woman. One who would have worked a farm alongside of me. I missed the woman I never married and never met. But I couldn't go back now. I burnt my coal and didn't warm my hands.

Every day I'd come in I wished that I'd find her dead in the bed. Then I could go find another woman who would want to be on a farm.

If Mary had stayed by my side we would have got by better but she didn't favour me. She spoiled that wee sap Seán. He was weak and girlish and she filled his head with stories of fairies and spirits and told him he was cleverer than the rest of us, and sent him off to get an education. I didn't know what that would be worth to him, it's not like he'd have training in a trade that could actually be put to use, because he'd still be poor, but then he'd be poor and useless. Mary wanted him to become an auld priest. Just to please her.

Maeve and Seán came for Christmas Day. Sheila wasn't much of a cook but I yelled at her to get something in front of us for pity's sake. Maeve prancing about, swishing her long hair and sparkling eyes and wearing lipstick, she wasn't up to much either. Neither of them could cook, and Seán walked the fields with me and was only interested in the fairy mound, he'd spent half his life on that mound on guard for the Cruelty Men. I stayed away from that. It was a burden to have it interrupting my fields. There was nothing in me that would make me touch it. I'd enough shite luck as it was. But Seán climbed on top of it and I told him to at least turn his jacket inside out but he didn't heed me. He thought he was one of them, I suppose.

I thought he'd stay the week and do some jobs for me but the two of them got up early the next morning. When that hoity-toity Mr Lyons turned up in his trap without warning, sure I was fit to be tied. Why a man like that didn't have a car at this stage was sad. Well Seán and Maeve were out of here as fast as shite from a goose. Sheila had a fit because there was still clearing up to do after the day that was in it. She cursed them both. They hadn't even told us they were going, and there was Mary sending her boss to take them from us before they'd given us any work for all the food they ate and the fire we had on for them. Sheila was going to go up the town and Maeve could have stayed with the baby.

Sheila deserved a bit of a break because she was having an awful time feeding the wee fellow. Her nipples were so bloody that the baby was shitting blood from drinking so much of it. She had told Maeve that, and Maeve had still gone early in the morning with a wave to us and a fake thanks. Mary would have known what to do about the feeding and all that, she'd have had a cream or potion to soothe it but instead Mary had taken my own brother and sister off to herself and her fancy house. I felt a terrible rage in me that day. I had sworn not to speak to Mary when I found out she was abandoning our land. All we had worked for, all we had left to ourselves from when we were dragged here by some half-baked government scheme.

Whenever I had to pay a doctor I cursed Mary for taking that money out of my hands.

Whenever I had to call a vet in to look at a poor sick animal I hated her for leaving. Giving all she had to a family who were not her blood, while me and me sons and me wife needed her right here.

A man of twenty-two acres of good farmland in County Meath could have got himself a better wife though. That one I couldn't blame Mary for. At the time she had sided with Patsey on that one.

Mary

Whatever Baby Likes

I waited in my sleep each night and each night she came to me. I heard her move from her bed. Feeling her way through the dark hall.

My door was open for her and she pushed it lightly. Wordlessly, she climbed into my bed. I folded the covers away to make room, and then wrapped her in the blanket tucking her in. She rolled towards my body and we lay pressed together. I felt her warmth. We said nothing.

Both of us fell into dreams and the soothing sleep beyond.

It was as if I waited for that every night to go off into my deeper dreams. In the morning she smiled and always said, 'How did I get here? I fell asleep in my own bed and I wake up here, how did that happen, Mary?'

'You're always welcome here, a stór.'

Her voice was loud, she'd never learn to whisper. She chatted to me like water rolling over the stones in a babbling stream. Her hand was flung about my neck.

She gave out to me. 'Did you brush your teeth? Your breath smells like the rhinoceros house at Dublin Zoo.'

'So does yours. And why didn't you ever take me to Dublin Zoo?'

No one had ever looked so closely at me. 'Why is your tongue cracked, why do you have little holes in your skin on your nose, what is that hair that grows out of your chin?' I could have been insulted but she was not mean, she was just interested in me, and my flaws were her anchor. Her skin was smooth, and her eyes white and her lips dry. I rubbed my nose on her temple until she laughed, 'It makes me sleepy when you do that.' She scrunched her nose. 'Why do you have a flappy tummy?' She squeezed my big tummy. It was growing bigger, I'd grant her that. All my weight was settling there. I told her it's because I loved my potatoes and butter too much. I told her singing softly,

The potatoes are the love of my heart;
They require neither kiln nor mill,
They only require digging in the garden and leaving on the fire.

She wanted to know stories; I told her a few I could think of. I made sure they had happy endings. The story of the Bull Bhalbhae was our favourite. I told her Maeve's favourite, 'The Children of Lir', but she cried all through it, and I swore that was enough of that. I dreaded the moment she would find out about her own death. That it comes to us all. I shielded her from it, but I discovered over the new years of her life that she accepted it. That she knew without me telling her. I had been telling my stories to the other children, a few here and there. But with Baby she harvested them out of me one by one. She would be the one to pass them on.

'Baby,' I said, 'we have to get up now, I have to go light the fires and get the breakfast and feed the hens.'

She popped up and came with me. I carried her into the kitchen and wrapped her in the chair until the fire was lit. Her feet were black. Taking a cloth I washed them gently before I dressed her in front of the fire. I plaited her curly black hair, and her eyes were so light blue I could see her thoughts in them. She drank milky tea as I made porridge, pouring honey into the lumpy centre for her.

'Ah Baby, what would I do without you?' I would say to her.

'I'm here,' she'd chirp back. 'You don't have to do without me.'

And that was the truth.

We were lucky we live opposite the school in Kilbride. The eldest, Joseph, was off to the Christian Brothers in Trim that year. He'd have to go on his bike a few miles. He said he couldn't wait. He wanted to be a big man. But I also saw the fear in the poor gossin's eyes, behind his bravado.

'You'll be all right,' I told him when were are alone. I had his head over the barrel outside and I was washing his hair in rainwater like I always did. I was sure not to put strain on his head so I cupped it in my hand. I'd done it like this since he was five. 'They say the Brothers are a fierce lot.' He closed his eyes and let the cold water run over his head. I had a towel around his neck so it wouldn't run down his back.

'I know there's talk of beatings up there, but your mother and father are respectable people. Your mother is the local schoolteacher so that gives you a bit of grace. Sure they only really go for the kids from the poor families. Don't you be worrying Joseph, ye hear me?'

He looked relieved to think of it like that. Patricia wouldn't allow any beatings in her wee school. She never raised her hands to the kids and forbade me from day one to do the same to her own.

'Why do they have to do it, Mary?'

'It's just the way they are. They're afraid you'll all run wild. Big boys like you.'

Joseph and James were lovely, natural boys. They robbed apples and sometimes took threepenny bits from their mother's purse, or worse, the church collection plate. Mostly, they played Gaelic up and down the fields or ran about with their hurley sticks waging war on Red Indians. Mr Lyons took them up to Dublin to Croke Park for All Ireland matches. They would come back full of stories from the Cusack Stand. Of how the Bishop walked onto the pitch at the beginning of the games and the players, all fine young men from their counties, would kneel before him and kiss his ring while the Artane Boys Band played.

In the evenings, their father, Mr Lyons, liked to take a small whiskey as he listened to the wireless. When I brought it to him he raised the crystal glass to me and said,

'Drink your fill: there is a plague in Kells.'

Mr Lyons was a gentleman.

Baby took her mother's hand every morning and they walked over to the school. She always ran back for one more hug from me. I waited for this. Her turn. Her pulling away from her mother. I bent down so her arms could go about my neck. I drew her to me and savoured the hug. Her spindly arms were soft but ferocious in their affection. I took a long a deep breath and let her go. She'd be back to me for lunchtime. I'd make her something special. Whatever Baby liked.

Maeve

I've Watched You from the Landing

Kevin delivered his bread and leered at me. The house was never empty, Mr and Mrs Boyle were always in the shop and Catherine worked alongside of us. She was growing fatter but not pregnant yet. God help her. I almost felt sorry for her. I could have told her to share a room with her husband Kevin, and something might have come of it.

This tick-tock of the town never wavered, never varied, never skipped a tock, nor missed a tick.

One night Kevin came creeping down to the storeroom and I sat bolt upright. He came around my partition and I could see he was drunk. He climbed into my bed and I pushed him away. He put his hand over my mouth.

'If you make a noise I'll have you thrown out on the street you dirty bitch, I know what you think when you look at me. I've watched you from the landing window when you take boys into the alley.'

He had his hands around my throat. I knew there was nothing to do and some things you have to put up with, so I let him crawl on top of me. I even stopped him putting his thing inside me when I was dry. I concentrated and held onto it and rubbed it quickly back and front on me till I was wet and then he stuck it in good and hard. I whispered to him to take it out quickly if he felt about to let go but he was not listening. He let go inside me and I thumped him on the back in silent rage. He collapsed on top of me.

'I can't get pregnant.' I pushed him off.

'You dirty whore,' he snarled and he was stiff again.

I'd never get rid of him now, so I just put up with it. I made him say it again. I liked the way he said dirty whore. I asked him to say more dirty things and he did. Rory was always silent. I liked the way it made me feel to hear dirty words. But when he went back upstairs, I cried and cursed Catherine for not having him in her room.

During the day he looked at me like he was looking at an animal and I felt a small pressure pain in my groin when he did. I knew he'd come again that night. I didn't want him to come but since he was going to anyway I tried to make it so I could get what I wanted out of it. Catherine went to her daily Mass and her flat feet slapped around the shop. As she stood on the ladder to get at the bags of flour, I noted that her bovine bottom was getting even bigger.

Before, with Rory and with the corner boys, I was the one who decided. I was the one doing things for me. I reached into their trousers and found what I wanted. I was powerful and they all trotted after me with their tongues hanging out. Indeed Rory couldn't stay away from me no matter what his mammy was telling him. He would have done anything for me. But I didn't ask anything of him.

Kevin counted the money at night. He took a cut himself though he did no shop work. Mr Boyle let himself be bullied. Mr Boyle was terrified that Kevin would leave his daughter. We all knew she locked her room at night. I didn't even have a door.

Did I have to do this for the family too? Was it not enough to be a skivvy?

Seamus

The Weaker Sex

The gate creaked and I was just taking me boots off, so I cursed that creaking gate. Cursed it even more when I looked up and saw the priest, Fr Gilligan with the usual face on him like the back of a bus. He was coming up the front yard to knock at the door. Sheila had taken to the bed and the boys were tearing up the place. There was no fire lit.

'Father, what can I do for you?' I kept him at the door. I couldn't have him in but he kept looking over my shoulder and I had no choice but to let him walk into the awful mess. There was stuff thrown all around the place like a mad woman's shite.

'It's filthy, Father, I know, but she won't get out of bed to clean it.'

He looked for somewhere to sit that wasn't strewn with nappies and clothes and I took a bunch of dirty washing off the chair and dumped it on the floor. Then I booted the babies out of the house into the yard where they could do less damage.

'Seamus. How is Sheila?'

'She's a pain in me arse, excuse me language, Father, but you're lucky you have to steer clear from women, because first me mother left us and took me father with her probably to America, then Mary left me and now I'm with Sheila. I don't know if there is such a thing as a good one.'

The priest winced, but I could see he hadn't come to my house to talk to me about my woes with the weaker sex.

'If it's Padraig you want to see me about, I don't have money for his keep.'

'No. No. Padraig is fine. He's where he should be. You can put him from your mind entirely.' He cleared his throat and looked at the teapot on the stove. I had been out on the farm all day digging and I didn't feel like serving a priest when I came home, when I had a woman lying in the next room who was meant to be up and doing it. I went to the door of the room and yelled, 'Sheila, get up and get the priest some tea, will ya, for God's sake woman.'

She arrived at the door half dressed, pulled an auld cardigan around her and shuffled out to the stove. She was pregnant again. Her face was greenish and her eyes were as dead as a dead sheep's eyes.

'The fire's not lit, Seamus,' she said accusingly.

'And whose fault is that?'

'How can I make him the tea when the fire's not lit?'

'And I don't suppose there's dinner either.'

Fr Gilligan stood up quickly. 'There's no need for tea, Seamus. But thank you. I had a visitor, a Mrs Greeley. She's a fine woman. They own a lot of land beyond Trim.'

I stared at him, if it wasn't about Padraig, what was he still doing here?

I had a sudden flash of me getting the teapot and poking his eyes out with the spout. That's after I thrashed Sheila within an inch of her life for making a holy show of me. Got those stockings that lured me in the first place, and which she never wore now, but kept in her suitcase, which was always packed under the bed, got those stockings and put them around her scrawny neck and pulled tight till her dead sheep's eyes fired up with a bit of a spark of protest and then I'd extinguish them forever.

There was a bird in the house and it flew out of the rafters and between me and the priest, and I didn't murder either of them but sat down on the other chair and all the newspapers on it.

They were Sheila's newspapers. She read one every day. I'll say that for her and I didn't mind her buying them because I was proud to have a wife who would read about the world beyond these fields.

'Mrs Greeley was worried about her son, Rory.'

'What's this to do with us?' Sheila asked as she knelt on the sooty floor and fumbled to get a fire going in the stove. Mary could light a fire by looking at it.

'Rory has been seeing Maeve, your sister. Mrs Greeley feels it's not going to go anywhere.'

'Are ye worried about Maeve, Father, or Rory, or Mrs Greeley?'

'Is he the oldest son?' Sheila perked up. She lit a match and it burnt out in her hand. There was so much ash stuffed in the fire grate no air could keep a flame there.

'He is.'

'Do you want me to tell Maeve to stay away from this fellah because she's a servant in a shop and he's got land?'

The priest walked to the door. 'I'm caught between both parties here. The Greeleys are friends with the Bishop. Their next two boys are going into the seminary.'

I was going to take him by his collar and put him out of my house when he turned and said, 'I don't like to say this in front of your wife but there's word Maeve is with child.'

We were never a normal family. Everything went wrong with us. We had no luck. And a big fairy fort stuck into our fields and spirits that took the cattle in the night that weren't sick, and the potatoes I was pulling up were small and tough and chalky tasting. Now Maeve was bringing us to shame. Now we wouldn't be able to go to Mass on Sunday without all the tongues wagging.

'I'll kill her,' I said. I pushed past the priest and got on my bike and I pedalled all the way to Trim without letting a breath out of me, seeing nawthing but pure rage.

Maeve

It Was Just a Bit of Diversion

If people's characters were written on their forehead they would rather meet a blind man than one who could read.

I had grown to like Rory. He had gone away to study agriculture, for that was the new word for farming. He had come back though and each time sought me out in the shop. He asked me to stay true to him but I didn't. For I guessed he would not have me in the end. I had not many friends but Mary. Every Friday night she came to the shop and walked me to the pictures. We didn't mind what was on. It was just a bit of a diversion. If I didn't have a man asking me out she would walk me home again. Mary was easy; though she was older than me she never gave me advice. She just accepted anything I did or told her. She just told me to be careful. Nothing else.

She was embarrassed by such things and would go beetroot when I would point out men in the theatre and tell her how long or short their things were. And I had felt enough of them pressing up against me in this town. What was I meant to do? I was bored in the shop. Could have done the accounts in my sleep. The same people coming in, at the same times of day. Everyone had a pattern, as if the whole town was moving like the insides of a clock and everyone knew their place and function. Tick-tock. And who was I? A skivvy from a poor farm that didn't learn English till I was eleven. We left the Irish behind quick enough. So much for the government hoping people would listen to us and want to be like us. Fat chance of that.

At night I'd take my hand and stroke myself to sleep. I closed my eyes and it wasn't Rory I saw, or any of those gombeen men who I led into the lane to amuse myself. Rory was the only one I'd go all the way for. He had a bit of decency about him. He wasn't a corner boy like most of the others. Them corner boys were frozen in motion, they had nowhere else to go, and stood where they could see everyone go up one street and down another, the eyes of the town. They made a smart comment at everyone who went by. If the wind was blowing hard one way they curled around the corner to the sheltered side. They'd never marry because no one would have them. They were poor sons of big families with neither land nor trade. Some would disappear to England. Corner boys never got to America. I imagined New York and Boston with empty corners.

I'd lie on my mattress at night and imagine two of them together. At the one time. I'd stare them straight in the eye the next day after having had them in my dreams.

Rory was there again. Home from agricultural college. He was getting handsomer and quieter at the same time. I didn't like the quietness. I wanted him to tell me stories of all the things he was learning and what he knew. He said he loved me when we would be out in the fields. But when he spent himself and rolled over he'd never say it again. He knew he wouldn't be allowed to marry me.

There were no girls at agricultural college, so his mammy must have been trawling the country for suitable matches because she knew he always came straight to me. I couldn't make my mind up if I wanted more from him than what I got in the field. Sure he was nice, but a bit dull.

I was bored of the street; bored of Rory; bored of Kevin forcing me; bored of poxy Trim; bored of the castle that lay in the town. The big ruin took my breath away the first time I laid eyes on it. I was only eleven then and Mary couldn't come with me because wee Seán had a fever. I had walked myself all those miles and miles of road and hedges in the lashing rain.

Padraig

Whisper It from Tree to Tree

There are woods outside the walls. The trees could take a message, whisper it from tree to tree all the way down the road, over the oceans of stony fields and yellow furze to the home trees. Home trees would uproot, come walking. Home trees would march in plain anger – say that this stolen child had not harmed even so much as a beetle yet sick green walls won't open up and let go. They would bend over the wall and brush branches off grass, curling roots grasping air, somersault into the grounds. Run, scramble, crawl into their branches – be carried home.

PART III

A MARRIAGE, AND A BIRTH AND A DEATH

O Silver Branches that no sorrow has shaken,
Hear one thing more!
The Earth wails all night
Because it has dreamed of beauty.

Bridget, after returning from her first visit to the Earth speaks to the other gods: Angus, Dagda, Midyir.

Bride

The Earth Wails All Night Because It Has Dreamed of Beauty (1847)

Night fell early here, and it took so much with it. I was born in 1825, on Bolus Head, Cill Rialaig, Ballinskelligs, in the Barony of Iveragh in County Kerry. When I was born, the island of Ireland had twice the population of the United States of America.

Bolus Head had many families living along it. Ours was a threshold world. Backed by dark blue mountains we jutted out into the sea, barely attached to the land, and there was nothing after us. The night was full of stars, and black wind, and spirits, and people changing shape; but come the day we forgot all of these gnawing mysteries and concentrated on feeding ourselves.

My father, Batt, said we should all learn English for fair days. When he went to sell some cattle he said he sometimes needed it. He warned us against learning the reading and writing though. He said people who did that sometimes forgot how to read the land. In winter days, such as those, the sun barely made it over the mountain, and was so weak you could stare it in the eye. It scraped along the horizon and sunk, leaving a yellow light that the birds glimmered in, as if they were dust. Our mountain was our world. When we died our bones went inside it.

Our house was an important one, as it was the one where people gathered fireside nightly. Batt told the stories. He held them in his head. He had thousands of stories, and if he missed a sentence my mother interjected and corrected him. This stopped his flow but he didn't get irritated with her. He paused and nodded, and, as if placing the lost phrase back into the trail of words, he exhaled and continued. The hag, he said, lived behind the mountain in the caves. She had lived there for millennia. The hag had no age. St Patrick tried to kill her but St Bridget stopped him. Don't go near the cliffs, Batt told us. Her hand will reach out and carry you off. Otherwise, he had no argument with the hag. He sometimes waved his stick in greeting to her and she stared back at him. You only saw her if you were alone, he explained. Two people together could not see the hag.

One day we were gathered outside the cottages and two funnels of dust rose on the path. They joined together and came speeding towards us. In excitement, my father stood from his stool.

'You see those whirls of dust?' said Batt. 'What are they but two souls separated in life that have found each other again.'

We ran at the small, child-size tornadoes. Breathlessly, he pulled us back.

'Out of their way now. Let them have their joy.'

My mother came out and went to throw some gravel into the small whirling.

'If there's a soul trapped in there we should get it out.'

He stopped her too, and held her arm as the wind whipped them into a field and out of sight.

'Ach sure I know, but when you think how long they've been apart.'

They stood, my mother and father, surrounded by us all, outside our little cabin. We were happy there on Bolus Head. We knew who we were. We weren't afraid.

But it would come. The fear. Perhaps, it was there all along. Maybe even before the first settlers came to this island. Those who my father, Batt, said were called the De Danann and were driven underground with the arrival of the settlers from Iberia. For no one who came as invaders had any luck here, not the Iberians, not the Vikings, not the Normans, not the Brits. And those who came to help got even worse shrift. The Spanish Armada broken off the side of the island, or the French lost and unmet.

'Why didn't any invader have luck here?' I asked. For I followed my father around like a shadow.

Batt said, 'On account of the shining ones who live in a world beneath us. They were the first in this land and they were well versed in druidary and magic. You could walk through the land and not know they were in it.'

I looked at the ground beneath my feet and Batt banged the wet grass with his stick.

'They are there all right and most people can see them when they are very young, up to the age of seven, or very old, in the time before death.'

There were a few like my father who had the gift and he could see them all his life. They knew him well and accepted him. He could identify who it was to pass the gift onto in the next generation though it wasn't up to him to choose, and it wasn't necessarily of his blood. It was the story that was the key – those who could keep the stories.

'If you are identified and walk away from it or squander your own gift the night will come down around you.'

He saw me shudder and he shrugged. 'But you could always leave the land. Once you get away from Ireland, there aren't people underground.'

'Where would I go?' I asked, sure that I had the gift but not sure I wanted it.

'Find a land that hasn't driven its first inhabitants to extinction, I suppose.'

But he looked at me with his hard blue eyes and I felt a heat in my bones and my head melt into the wild sky behind because I understood that I was able to hold the stories.

'There are men of learning coming round from the towns to take down the stories into writing. But that won't save them, a stór. They're only alive by the telling. Do you understand that?'

I said I did, though I wasn't sure.

'The stories are our shape, Bride,' he said. 'If we lose them we're lost altogether.'

Evenings we'd get in by the fire and listen to Batt's stories. There was some gossip. Some distant noise about far-off British governments in Dublin, but that was the other side of the world to us. They didn't speak our language; they didn't know us. We never left our parish. Even the priest rarely came up to us.

When my sister Grace died of whooping cough my aunt said that they didn't bury her quick enough. She was already changing shape. That you could hear her big paws batter the light wood of the coffin as they put her into the mountain. My aunt said many of our family could turn into hares. Our great-grandfather could turn into a wolf. He had a wolf's tail on him.

The priests told us if we didn't baptize the babies into the Holy Roman Catholic Church then they would not be allowed into Heaven. When anyone had a baby, they were quick to baptize it for fear of this awful fate. There was a limbo graveyard up the mountain. It was always cold there. We were afraid of the spirits there. The hag watched over that. None of those unbaptized babies would ever get anywhere off that mountain. Those burials were left up to the men. I have an early memory of my uncle putting a baby in a sack and leaving the cabin to walk up Bolus Head on his own.

Batt learnt the stories from his mother. His grandfather Connaire O Mac Tire had been asked by the master to come to the hedge schools and tell the children the stories so they would know them alongside the Latin and Greek they were taught, and from other people in the parish. Sometimes he left the cabin on the edge of the cliffs to walk to the next parish to get a story he did not have. He could remember a story after one telling, word for word. But he did have to work to keep them in his head. He would come home at night, over the rivers, and low stone walls, and up the road to the stone cabin, repeating the new story.

My mother said the fairies themselves, on dark nights, with the fish, the seals, and the dolphins dreaming far down in the sea below, would be the first to hear him tell a tale. And that's how he liked it. The stories were sacred to him. They were medicine from the land.

Batt was a mild soul who never raised his voice, for there was no part of himself that he was not comfortable with. He never got too drunk. He took care of his few cattle, and we had a bit of land planted with potatoes just for us to eat, but no more could we get out of it. On rare days if the food was short, he went out with his brothers fishing, though he dreaded the sea. Two of his brothers drowned, and his own father. He was afraid if he drowned all the stories would drown with him. Every time Batt saw me he would start testing me. He asked me who Bride was, because that's my namesake.

'The saint,' said I, 'her day is the start of spring; we make the crosses out of hay and hang them in each house.'

'True,' he said, 'you wouldn't find a house without one. One time there was a barn in Kilorgan and the farmer forgot to hang the cross.'

'What happened?'

'Sure it burnt to the ground with all the cattle in it. You could smell the burnt meat for days after. No one around here ever dwelt in a building again without Bridget's Cross.'

I was walking the road beside him; the sea was spread out like Bride's cloak, light swarming on its surface.

'She was there at the beginning of the world, Bride, she brought it all in,' he said. 'Some called her Bright, some Bride, some Bridget. It's what we call a woman on her wedding day.'

It made me love my name, and all the different things people could call me: Bridget, Bride, Bright.

'She brought life to the earth,' Batt said. 'She was the first to hear its song and know what it was longing for. She visited the earth and felt its pain. She came back to the gods, Angus, Dagda, Midyir, and told them she had heard the song.

"*O Silver Branches that no sorrow has shaken*," Bridget said to the other gods, "*hear one thing more. The Earth wails all night because it has dreamed of beauty*." They couldn't get the song out of their heads and they followed her down here.'

We stood and looked at the islands out in front of us. He would talk slowly and allow me to repeat things. He was making sure I could carry the stories. That there were no leaks in me.

When I was twelve I was sent away to work in a wealthy Protestant house near Dingle. It was the next peninsula, but it might as well have been America. I never came back to Bolus Head except the once.

My father's smile was always saying, everything is sad but don't get too serious, a stór, my love, macooshla. All the old people said the same thing to us – in the end life will break your heart. He seemed happy and peaceful always. He had eight children, sure I was only a daughter somewhere in the middle, but I felt he had selected me. I would not be the heir to his small rocky patch of a farm, but I was to be the keeper of his stories. He didn't invent anything or make anything up. He used to get fierce cross with me when I'd embellish and add extra bits onto a tale. For you never knew what was happening inside the people's heads in them and I was sometimes tempted to add bits to show their feelings. He said it wasn't our place to go changing them.

His eyes used to glaze at first when he told the stories and then they would settle into a trance. The only other sound, apart from his lovely voice, was the wind that pierced and shook the stone houses. But we felt safe inside the story. When he came to the end he would say the same thing. The same thing they all said, the storytellers, and he taught me to say it too.

That is my story. If there is a lie in it let it be so. It was not I who composed it. I got no reward but butter boots and paper stockings. The White-Legged Hound came, and ate the boots from my feet, and tore my paper stockings!

I was twelve when I left. It's hard to understand when you leave a place how much you feel alone without it. Batt's stories I'll never forget. For I thought he was as ancient as the hag behind the mountain, though he was not yet forty. I missed my family and friends terribly the first years, but my father, Batt, I missed the most. I didn't feel I was up to the stories. I felt there were things he hadn't told me that would now be lost to me forever.

When the crop failed everyone tried to hang on for another year till the next crop. There was some food from the sea but most didn't have boats or skills. It took energy to get out there in a boat you didn't have. The next crop failed, and the next, year after year. We were hearing terrible stories from all over the country. Herds of people were walking away from their fields and trying to get to workhouses to stay alive. I worried about my family. By the time I got back to Bolus Head I had some provisions on me. Something for my family because working in a farm there was at least flour and grain. In fact, there was plenty of other kinds of food in the country if you weren't relying on the potato.

The end of the world had come to the end of the world. As I made my way back home, I found the hardest thing to look at was the houses rapidly fallen in on themselves. As soon as a family left the house the authorities would tear the roof off it so they'd not be able to go back.

The headland was all but abandoned. People had just walked out of their houses and off down the road and died. There were unburied bodies in ditches. My father's cattle had been eaten and only my mother was left in the house with my brother and his family. They told me my father, Batt, had starved to death rather than leave his family landless.

Only birds lived in our houses now. The fires exposed their black throats as the gables fell.

I walked up the mountain to the standing stones just to get away from my starving family in the cabin. They had looked at me as if I could save them. The limbo graves on the hill whistled with ghosts. No one to haunt. I sat on the side of the mountain and let the baby ghosts into me for a while so they could feel some relief. I took in multiple infant souls into my breathing body and hung onto the grass with my fists. The hag came to me then. Her eyes were cobwebbed and cloudy with cataract, her skin was so deeply furrowed it looked as if time had ploughed her through. She had hair as a harvest growing from her chin. I thought she was the banshee. If she were, she should have been busier with all those dead and dying I saw on the road to here.

'I'm Batt's daughter,' I said aloud to her.

The hag lifted me to my feet and I, leaning on her, put my back to the standing stones. I heard a scald crow screech above me but when I looked it was off in the distance. And the stream that flowed through the boggy mountain was in my ears but in truth far off in another field. The sea was bright in some parts and black in others. The sky was about to stamp me out. My outstretched hand reached out and flattened on the standing stones. I could feel their cataclysmic loneliness now that the mountain was emptying out.

By those standing stones I clung for hours until Sadhbh, my brother's eight-year-old daughter, came looking for me. Her eyes were bleary and ringed with dark circles.

'How did you find me?'

'They said this is where you'd be.'

Sadhbh kept looking over her shoulder.

'I'm going to America,' she said to me.

'How are you going to get the fare, a stór?'

'I heard you are going. Take me. I'll work for you.'

'Musha, I've only the fare for myself.

'You have to take me, Auntie Bridget, or I'll starve on this mountain.'

We sat against the stones. Too tired to talk anymore. The children around here had stopped playing months ago. We watched two birds, one a hawk, and one a scald crow swoop together.

'They're not the same species at all. It's a wonder that they are playing together.'

'Are they playing?' my niece said. She squinted up.

As if the birds could have known what trouble we were in.

It began to rain so we got up to climb down the hill to the road below. There were no stories around the fire that night because everyone was in a shocking state from the hunger. My brother's wife made bread with what I'd brought, but some were so far gone they had a hard time eating anything. The children's swollen bellies stuck out from their skeletal frames and they were half blind from the smoke. The air itself gnawed at the children's cheeks until they were hollowed out.

Was this the worst time?

It was the worst time.

I lay by the fire that night on an old cow-skin rug. As I slept, the hag's hand reached down the chimney and she stuck her bony crooked fingers down my gullet and dragged out all of those ghost limbo infants from me and took them back up the mountain. When I woke up I was feeling lighter. Without saying goodbye I started the long walk home. I couldn't help them anymore. I would have to leave and send money back to them. I hoped the food I left would keep some going until other help came or they walked off this mountain into the workhouses. I turned to look back just once and saw Sadhbh standing on the hill looking after me with hatred.

Despair was my only companion on a walk over one hundred miles. I won't tell you what I saw on the way because it won't do you any good to know. Except it was the worst time. I was witnessing a world dying. A world that we would never get back on this earth. Our language, our stories, our spirit would be starved out of these mountains. To keep the rhythm of the walk day and night I told my father's stories to myself. My feet were raw and I was walking on hard skin that wore away and shredded my soles to a pulp. No one I met looked at me or greeted me. Everything had changed here. The worst thing was the fear. It was more powerful than the stench of death. The crops were pulled out black with it. A fear had settled down among us and that would be hard to unstick. The land would be seeped in fear. It would evaporate off the wet roads and rain down on us in an endless circle.

I collected one new story from a family I met that took me in one night in Kilorgan. The man had it. He had got it from his mother. She had got it from a family she was with. They gave me a blanket and I slept in front of their fire.

I told him the story of the Bull, and he said, 'The person who brings a story to you will take away two from you.'

As it turns out I only got the one story from him. As was my father's habit, I told the story to myself out loud several times that day until it lodged in my head.

The hawk sought out the grey scald crow to spend a year learning tricks from her. They lived together while she was teaching him, and he had learned a great many tricks from her. They were very happy and content together until the time was up, and the hawk said he would be going if she had no more to teach him. She asked him to stay another year, as she had one more trick that would be better for him than all the others.

He stayed another year with her, and when the year was over he had learned no more from her than he had learned before. He said to her he had seen nothing but the tricks he had learned already.

'O, there is one! I forgot about it,' said the grey scald crow. 'When you and another bird are together, dart away, turn bottom up, fly in under and upward. Come on,' she said, 'and I will show it to you!'

They both flew off. She went out before him and he followed her. She returned to him on her back, swooped upwards and killed him.

That was the wage he got for the year – his death.

Maeve

My Eyes Were Painted On (1949)

Mr Boyle was not a stupid man. He was an ordinary man. He was bald, and brushed his few hairs over the top of his head in a way that made him balder. I used to think of him as a father in a way because he was always nice to me and took his time to explain things. But I never ate at their table nor walked to Mass with them. I had to walk to the church on my own. There was an early Mass for the workers in the town so I could get back and open the shop for the few hours on Sunday so the town could get their milk and bread and papers. Mr Boyle was never a father to me, even though he was a good man.

I fantasized that he came to me too at night. Or that I would creep up to his room. I was getting tired of Kevin. He repulsed me, but I was stuck with him. I thought about killing him. As I cut the brown wrapping paper with the big scissors I held it up and made a snipping action to him. He broke into a smile. He liked it. He knew I wanted to cut his thing off.

As revenge I thought of going to Mr Boyle's room and getting into his bed, though he wouldn't have been up to much. That I know. I wasn't sure how I'd get out of this situation. I had to go up in the mornings and empty the chamber pots. I did all four rooms. Mrs Boyle had yellow-green piss and lots of it. I carried that to Mr Boyle's room. His piss was pale and I poured her piss on top of his and left her pot there. That's the closest Mr and Mrs Boyle get to each other, I thought. Catherine's room was full of holy statues and pictures of Padre Pio. They should have let her become a nun, she'd have made a right old mother superior. Despite all the praying she still had a pale yellow piss like the rest and I poured it into the others, making a solid yellow stinking concoction. Kevin always left a shit for me. He was meant to do that downstairs but he liked to make me carry his shit. I had to carry the full chamber pot down the narrow stairs. Catherine was usually praying to the Virgin's statue on the landing, for deliverance. All that praying had kept her a virgin, a married one at that. I thought of pouring it on top of her head. I thought of even letting a little drop onto her big flannel grey nightie, but I felt sorry for her those days since I was forced to please her horrible husband.

But one morning this job made me gag. By the time I got the first chamber pot I was vomiting into it. Now the mixture was so repellent I was rushing down the stairs, stopping to gag. Catherine squealed, 'Jesus, Mary and Sweet St Joseph! What on earth is wrong with you?'

'I don't know.'

I did know.

It couldn't be.

I had a dream where my eyes were painted on.

Oh Virgin Mary forgive me, for I have sinned. Oh God, I'd do anything, I'll run from here and never go near another man. Never have those shameful thoughts. I'll never stroke myself to sleep again. Please don't let me be. Please.

When I told Kevin, he folded his arms.

'But sure, it could be anybody's,' he said.

'No,' I said.

'I see you down that alley. It's you always takes their hands and puts them on you. It's you who goes rooting in their pants. We've all had a look at ye.'

'I don't do it all with them,' I said. 'It can't be them.'

'We all know you go to the fields with that Rory fellah,' Kevin said.

It could have been Rory's. Though Rory was more careful than that ape Kevin. He'd been to agricultural college. He knew to pull out. He didn't want to ruin his life. But my life was ruined.

I'd have to marry Rory.

What if the baby came out as ugly and stupid as Kevin?

I could get money off Rory and go to America.

There was a lurch in the tick-tock of Trim town, or was this meant to be? Was I part of the workings of the town or was I the grain of sand in their clock? What did they do with girls like me?

'A woman may live after her kindred but not after her shame.' That's what they told us. I could kill myself. So what if they buried me with the limbo babies outside the graveyard? I was never once spoken to by a priest anyway.

Seamus

A Letter from Brooklyn

When I got there Maeve laughed in my face and said she was going to America and she couldn't give a damn about Rory. He could marry his mammy, she said. She asked me for the money to go to America then. I told her I'd get it for her. I'd sell a field but she should never come back here as long as she lived, she could go to Hell, and her wee bastard. She was delighted with that and she went off in great excitement to Mary to tell her she was going to America.

The funny thing was a letter had arrived from New York, a while back. It was from our sister Bridget who we hadn't heard from since she went into service in Dublin. She was over in America working for a family in Brooklyn. I didn't know what to do with the letter. She had enclosed some money in it and was asking for all of us. She said she had had some tough times but was fine now. I didn't want to hear her story. I barely remembered her, even if I put my mind to it, she was a child when she left and I couldn't imagine her now. She said something in the letter about getting one of us over there so she could have family about her. It was as if God had answered our prayers for once.

But why should bloody Maeve benefit from her disgusting sins and the shame she was bringing on me. For once Sheila agreed with me. Sheila said she'd write back and there would be more money where that came from but she told me not to tell Mary or Maeve. Sheila said she'd like to go to America. We could sell the land and go get better work in Brooklyn. For one day I tried to think of it. I imagined arriving in America with a bit of money for a business, open a shop or something. I wasn't wedded to this bloody land. I only came to it as a child, no one wanted us here when we came.

But then I saw that smug bastard Patsey tinkering with, and polishing, his thresher, even though it was a long way from harvest time. And I knew he'd be the first to snatch up this land in his podgy red paws. So I told Sheila, no, we won't go to America. And she raged, and cursed me and threw all the dirty clothes at me. A full nappy of shite came flying through the kitchen and I ducked. It was the best laugh I got for a long time. I told her to clean it up and we struggled for a bit. Until I got her by the scrawny neck, with my hands clean around it, and I squeezed. I dragged her to the bed, and gave her a right good hammering, and the little boy was watching me, screaming for his mammy. Though she'd never done much for him. I kicked him out of the room and I went back to her. I wanted to finish it off but she curled up on the bed and was silent. We both stopped and looked at each other. The baby outside was crying behind the door.

'If I'm not going to America, then that whore, Maeve isn't going either.'

'Well what are we going to do with her? She's going to make a holy show of us with her bastard baby.'

I sat by the small choked fire and ate my dinner that night, and I had too much to think about, and the boys were bawling and howling, and Sheila was back in her bed writing a letter to Bridget. I was dammed if I'd sell even so much as a blade of grass to Patsey for my sister's whoring. Then the priest called again.

Padraig

The Land of Boiled Cabbage

The walls smell of cabbage. Smells cabbage on skin – stops eating.

The sun creeps into the rooms, boiled. Boiled sun's watery light does not warm cold floors. They stick an injection in. Fights back till they strap down. Blue circles spinning, all colours fill up, angry colours with sharp edges – insides are wrenched by slicing green red yellow squares, blue dots form in blackness.

A voice says, 'Drink this down, and you will be better in no time, love.'

Love? Love? Love?

Whisht!

Big mug of shiny white sticky fluid slides down throat. Retches at each gulp – a man puts his hand over mouth so the retches are swallowed back down.

Whisht, would ye, whisht. What happened? Far inside a shell but always saw everything. Had seen Patsey behind sunlit evening windows of his cottage in a dress – high-heeled shoes. Had seen the crows lining branches of trees. Had seen new mother croon talk to the pigs before she sent them to the butcher. Blood lilting. Singing into slaughter. Seen little boy beckon to follow on the fairy mound hunkered watching the hares hop circle dance. Had seen sisters, Bridget with Maeve link arm in arm walking to school with no turf for school fire. Their bare feet legs blue in winter from the cold slap of a mud road – they are laughing. Knows what love is. Has seen it.

Man behind, rough, pulling, drink gone in dribbles on skin, roaring through rivers inside slippery landing in core, spreading curling into sick, rising vomit bubble lips. No one wipes it off, shaking head be free, arms tied, legs tied. Lilting to slaughter without song.

Can't sit up. Whale caught. Can't spout shoot through web sky into dark tight free star streaks. Sick chin running neck sticky. Captured by Fomorians – held hostage by Balor.

Mary

She'd Go to America and Start Again

Oh I cried the night that Seamus turned up to the door. He declined to come in, so I went out to the yard to him. The rain was sheeting sideways but he glared at the house and shook his head as we stood under the eaves of the shed.

'Oh Seamus, it's good to see you. I'm glad you came. I hate a feud in the family.'

'It was you started it, Mary, by disobeying me.'

'I've heard you've three wee sons.'

'Aye, but they're not good for work yet, and I still have to feed them, and yer wan's pregnant again.'

'Seamus, can we put it all behind us? What has you here?'

'It's good news, so it is. I suppose you could say that.'

I closed my eyes. I could take anything now.

'I suppose you know about Maeve.'

'God I do. What are you going to do to her, Seamus?'

'You mean what did that hussy do to herself?'

'She's a great girl. She made a mistake, that's all.'

'A mistake that has the whole land talking about us. I see the looks in the people's faces up there at the church on Sunday. They always thought we were dirt and this is more dirt for them.'

'There's plenty of people that judge others but I'd rather not. All them that's judging us has done the deed themselves.'

'They've done it with the blessing of the church. Not her. Like an animal in the fields.'

'There's plenty a sinner who made a mistake after seeing stockings hanging on a washing line. What about Maeve?'

'She's off to the convent in Castlepollard to have the baby and then Bridget is taking her in in Brooklyn. The family she's with don't want a scandal and she's had to leave. Her name is muck around these parts. She won't find service anywhere.'

'And the baby?'

'The baby will go to a family the nuns have in mind.'

There was so much in my head that I almost missed the most vital part of the story. 'Bridget? You've heard from Bridget?'

'She wrote a letter, she'd take Maeve over to America. She's a job there as a maid and can get Maeve one. After the baby is born.'

'Oh God I'll miss Maeve. For three years we've never missed our Friday nights together. What will I do without her? Can I have Bridget's address? And I want to go see Padraig too. He's sixteen now. Maybe they cured him? Patricia says they've all sorts of new treatments now.'

'Aye, the priest told me they put him on an insulin treatment, and electric treatment. He's been looked after.'

'Have you gone to see him? I really want to go!'

Seamus looked at me slyly and darkly. 'I'll not have you meddling. Next I know you'd have got him out and he'd be back with me.'

'We can't just abandon the poor wee gossin. I made a promise to Mammy.'

'And she just abandoned us, didn't she? I signed him in and I'll sign him out. You stay away. You'll not be able to take care of him in this house.' He gestured to the big pebble-dashed back of the house.

'Can you at least tell me which institution you've put him in?'

Seamus shifted; he pulled his shoulders up to his ears and his cap down over his eyes, and walked back into the rain. 'You're lucky I'm telling you this. That I've the decency to inform you. I don't want you talking to Maeve again. You should have been keeping an eye on things here. You've not done well by any of us.'

That cut me to the quick. Seamus always knew what would hurt the most and never hesitated to use it. He began to walk away. I couldn't bear losing him again.

'Wait, I'll get you some jam and tarts I've made. And some sloe wine.'

I went into the parlour to get them but when I came out he snatched them without so much as a bye or leave, jumped on his scaggely pony, and hightailed off up the lane.

When Patricia came home from school with the elder ones, she found me still crying by the stove. I had it in my mind that I should tell her, as she'd hear it around town soon enough but I was too shamed by it. I told her Seamus visited and then told her the shocking news. Patricia took my hand and looked very sad.

'Poor Mary,' she said.

'Poor Maeve,' I said, wiping the tears from my face.

Patricia looked shocked, but not disgusted. 'It's good she'll go to America and put it all behind her, and the baby will find a good home with a family who long for a child. Now you know your sister Bridget is safe and well.'

'And Seamus came to me even.'

'Leave Seamus alone for the moment. He's made a first move to come back and tell you what was happening. Eventually, he will come round. It is good of Seamus to keep you informed.'

I brightened up. Patricia was a woman of education and kindness. She knew things that I didn't, and reacted in a different way. I went about my evening's work and Mr Lyons came home. I knew Patricia would tell Mr Lyons everything. But I tried to hold my head high and not be ashamed.

That evening he made a special trip into the kitchen.

'Mary do you need some time off?' he said.

My heart stopped cold, was he getting rid of me?

'I don't.' I kept at the sink and didn't want to look at him. My cheeks and neck were inflamed with mortification.

'If you need anything,' Mr Lyons said, 'just ask us. What would we do without you? You're part of the family.'

Mr Lyons got a car, and spent an inordinate amount of time polishing it and looking at its engine. Cars were rare out on these country roads. When you'd hear one coming the kids would run to the gate and watch it go by. Staring at it as it disappeared around the corner. At night, if a car passed, I would watch the lights ride across the ceiling and down my wall, and I'd wonder who could be driving by at this time of night and I'd bless myself.

That night I lay on my bed and I would have liked a car to come by and light up the walls for a moment. I cried again for Maeve and her baby and hoped she would write to me. I knew she was in the convent to have her baby and I was sure the nuns wouldn't treat her well in there. But it wouldn't be for long and soon maybe she would come by, before she left, and say goodbye. She'd go to America and start again, she was pretty and good with figures and Bridget would take care of her. They would write to me and maybe we would see each other again.

Then I heard, as I usually did, Baby making her way down the stairs on her little bottom. She pattered across the cold kitchen tiles and over to my room. Wordlessly, she crawled into my bed and I put the covers over her. We cuddled up together and she was soon asleep, her faint bad breath warming my eyes, and her tiny arm thrown fiercely around my neck. I felt such a roar of love that it kept me from crying.

Padraig

Put One About You

Pray to Mananaun Mac Lir that he will send an invisible cloak. A cloak coloured like the sea where the shadow is deepest. Remember sea?

Caught in the shadow – the man on the bicycle. His shadow passed over. A sticky shadow that one was. A bit of it stuck – a small piece of broken shadow always.

No one went ever to Bolus but in hope of getting something there. What did he get?

Put one about you, Mananaun Mac Lir would say. Wearing the invisible cloak. Now let a small light go before us. A small light would go before us on the road, for there are no stars in Balor's sky. Cross the wall – reach the dark strand, there would be a boat of pure crystal waiting before the boiled sun rose.

It is the *Ocean Sweeper*. Mananaun has sent his own boat; good fortune to us while there is one wave to run after another in the sea. No sooner stepped into the boat then back. Not in the small woods by the little cottage. Taken back in all longing to lonely Bolus Head, back to where the land is a magic finger pressing down into the shining sea. Where islands blink and shimmersham; back to where the cloud-dancing sky is an unfolding story about to be told. Back to where Mammy and Daddy are outside the wee cabin. Mammy would be waiting. For the *Ocean Sweeper* goes as fast as a thought goes – to the heart place.

Here in the Land of Boiled Cabbage – doesn't make a sound. Doesn't look at them. Shuffles near the sun spit grate, the licking flames, the puny coal. Waits for hag to chimney stretch and finger grasp, ankle pull up dark tunnel spout over sky to home. No hag, no hag. Corner curls in smelly armchair, head bird buried in arm crook – waits for new mother to come.

Maeve

We Have the Songs You Taught Us, That Is All

The Boyles, whom I had lived with since I was eleven, never came out to say goodbye when baldy-headed Fr Gilligan, with his stop-a-clock face came to drive me to the mother and baby home in Castlepollard. None of them would even look at me the last months, and I was glad to get out of there. Though if I'd known where I was going I wouldn't have been so quick. I'd have run to the dockyards and swam to Liverpool. I heard from another servant girl that it was better to go to England, if you had the means, and stay in a place there. She said in England you could leave as soon as you had the child and find work. But I let myself be swept along in a tide of shame, and was feeling so sick and heavy I had thought I'd do my punishment and then get on with things. The new beginning I dreamt of.

Mary's favourite story was that of the Bull, but Bridget and I always loved 'The Children of Lir'. So, as Fr Gilligan drove me, I was relieved he didn't speak to me and I told myself the story that Mary used to tell me.

In those days sorrow was not known in Ireland: the mountains were crowned with light, and the lakes and rivers had strange starlike flowers that shook a rain of jewelled dust on the white horses of the De Danaans when they came down to drink. Lir was a fairy king but his new wife was jealous of his love for his four children. So the wicked stepmother turned them into swans and cursed them to spend three hundred years on the lake, when that time was ended they had to swim three hundred years on the narrow Sea of Moyle between Ireland and Scotland, and when that time was ended they would have to spend three hundred years on the Western Sea that has no bounds but the sky.

I thought to myself that if it weren't for Mary's love and relentless work, we'd have been orphans and sent away to the industrial schools. But if it weren't for her stories we'd have pined away those evenings, as lonely as anything ever known. The stories were the shape of our souls. I wished to God Mary could be there with me. I might have even let her tell her old bull story after she told me my favourite one.

This was my first time in a car and I was trying to enjoy myself. Now and then I'd look at the neck of the priest. He had a hairline that went down in a V under his collar, and I thought of reaching out and stroking it. I giggled, for he glanced at me in the mirror and frowned. He didn't say anything but I'm sure he thought I was in no position to be smiling. I smiled more. Then I couldn't hold it in. I was pinching myself and clenching my eyes to stop the laughing but it just came anyway. More out of nervousness than anything. His face grew red and when we arrived he got out of the car, all huffy, and marched into the big building without looking at me. I tried to push the door open but I couldn't figure it out. He came back with a nun and she opened the car door.

'What were you waiting for?' she said brusquely. 'This is not a hotel, young lady.'

I didn't know what to say, so I said nothing. She looked at my bump under my coat and I felt the shame of it rise up. Fr Gilligan never so much as even glanced at me. Another nun came out to him all smiles and chatter and offered him his tea. By God, but them priests loved their tea.

I was shown a bed in a big dormitory and they took my suitcase and that was the last I saw of it and anything in it. I was given a uniform of starched rough sack and told I would be working in the kitchen and could start after I went into the office and answered questions, and saw a doctor.

I was a good reader and the nun didn't expect that, because she left my file out in front of her, 'Marked tendencies towards sexual immorality.' That I read. A doctor was brought in and he did a quick listen to my belly and poked me about a bit while the nun looked on with too much interest. I imagined kissing her on that hairy shrivelled mouth. I always imagined kissing and stroking anyone I met. I imagined holding them in my arms. My heart was wide open.

'We'll have to give you another name.'

'Why?' I was shocked.

'You'll be called Teresa from now on. It's a good Christian name. I've heard things about you, Teresa. You are a first offender so you'll be sent to the kitchen. Do you have the hundred pound adoption fee?'

I shook my head. I had not imagined they'd charge me for my own baby.

'Don't the new parents pay the fee?' I asked.

She glanced up, surprised at my insolence. 'Teresa, speak when you are spoken too. They have a fee to pay too. Our costs are high, picking up the pieces after you lot. You'll have to work your debt off.'

Raking it in, I thought. But I didn't say it. These nuns are raking it in off our marked tendencies towards sexual immorality.

Fr Gilligan arrived, full of scones and cream buns and milky tea, to talk to her. I was led away by another girl in a white cap. He never looked at me in the eye but I felt him stare after me so I turned quickly to see him and he went red again, his lip curled in disgust.

There were about two hundred of us. We weren't allowed to

talk to each other. I worked in the kitchens. We were forced to pray out loud while we worked. Though the nuns patrolled at night we could whisper to each other in the beds, they were that close to one another. The girls from good homes were kept separate from us but I don't think they were treated any better. Not all were pregnant. The girl beside me said her name was Aggie but they renamed her Maire. She had had her baby a year ago.

'You're a first offender but you must have said something to the priest because they have you in with us second offenders.'

'You've had two babies like this? Are you mad?' I whispered. 'When I get out I'm never touching a fellah until I'm married to him.'

'They keep the first offenders in for about two years. They get all the work out of them. But the ones from the good families can go after the baby is born. Some of the girls here are kept five years. They work in the laundry. Then they're sent on to other laundries.'

I groaned and rolled over in my bed. 'I should have gone to England. I just didn't have the fare. I let the priest take care of all this.'

I never saw another doctor. My waters finally broke in the kitchen and the other girls screamed. The matron came running and dragged me into the rooms at the end of the corridor where you could hear the others screaming in labour. I had grown up on a farm and had watched cows and pigs and sheep but nothing prepared me for the nuns. They tied my hands and legs to the bed. I couldn't move. I screamed out and cursed them and bled and shit. In the end I had two babies instead of one. They untied me and I rolled to my side.

A boy and a girl. I called them Fionnuala and Conn after the children in the story of 'The Children of Lir'. The nun sniffed. I could call them any heathen names that I liked because those who got them would change their names anyway.

I was moved to a different room, as they took another girl in, a look of terror on her face. I saw them get the same rope to tie her. The rope was bloody. I hadn't noticed that when they brought me in. It struck me that it mightn't have been just my blood, but the blood of us all.

The matron spoke to me as I sipped a cup of milky tea. 'You don't have the adoption fee. Usually children of first offenders are separated quickly from their mothers. For a period of a year they are carefully vetted for abnormalities, and if showing no signs of such, we adopt them out. Children of second offenders are subject to Poor Law regulation and are either transferred to industrial schools or fostered.'

I felt my heart tighten and my stomach lurch. 'Sister, I'm a first offender. Sister, I'll never be here again. I can tell you that now.'

'You should have thought of that before you laughed at a priest. And you with a big stomach on you. Twins makes you a second offender anyway. You will be transferred to the laundry tomorrow,' the matron pronounced, and got up to go.

Another nun was bringing in my babies for me to feed. I was too tired to say anything more and I didn't want all her hate and bile inside this moment. The moment I held Fionnuala and Conn I felt my heart open inside out, until I knew it would have to break.

I whispered Lir's words to his beloved children when he found them turned into swans, '*The woman who ensnared you is far from any home this night. She is herself ensnared, and fierce winds drive her into all the restless places of the earth.*' And I swear I thought of the matron when I was whispering this to them. '*She has lost her beauty and become terrible: she is a Demon of the Air, and must wander desolate to the end of time – but for you there is the firelight of home. Come back with me.*

But they could not come back.'

I worked in the laundry for two more years after that. I saw my twins as often as I could to feed them and I never prayed. If them nuns prayed to the same God, he wasn't the one for me. My twins had red curly hair like Rory and I was relieved they were the spit of him and not that yoke Kevin. They gave me a book about St Teresa, the Little Flower, so I prayed to her only, since it was my new name. I dreamed an American couple would take them. The other girls (we were all called girls no matter how old we were) told me that the nuns sold the babies. But then the rumour went around that the courts weren't sending so many children to the industrial schools anymore and the religious orders running the schools were putting pressure on the nuns to give them children to put their numbers up. Those schools paid by the child so the church wanted the numbers up to keep the schools going, even though the schools were meant to be for the children and not the children for the schools. But that's when I could think straight.

They held hands in the nursery. Fionnuala was rounder, with a mop of curly red hair like her father, and Conn had red curly hair and thin legs. But their minds were as entwined as branches on the same tree. They played with each other's toes, sitting in front of each other. Hands and toes. They had no toys but none of the children had. In the laundry I had scraps of cloth and made them both rag dolls. I called the dolls Aodh and Fiachra after the other children of Lir.

That matron said they would be observed for deviancy before adoption, because of my wicked nature. If only they knew. It wasn't just one man. I didn't want just one man.

They let me feed my children and I had so much milk I fed other babies who weren't thriving on the bottles. I was called often from my laundry duties to feed the babies. Them nuns were cheap to the core so I saved them a fortune in milk. But they let me know that they despised me for it. That all my endless milk was a sign of my wantonness. One of them said, 'Look at you there, like an old sow.' Jealous, she was. It got me near my babies so I spent as much time as I could in the nursery and the nuns hated the babies, so they were happy enough to have me taking care of them.

I heard a rumour from one of the women who worked at the laundry that a batch of kids were to be taken to the industrial schools. I got up in the night and went to the nursery. I found them asleep and I took both of them in my arms.

I walked down the road carrying both of them. They were twenty months old and big, so they were all I could carry.

Where was I going? I was walking to the lake. I had nowhere to go. I thought I could walk all those miles to Mary in Meath. But

I didn't even know what part of the country I was in because I had not been out of the grounds of the mother and baby home for two and a half years. The lake I could see from the attic of the house. It was cold and the children woke up and were holding onto my neck. A few years before I would have had more strength, but the starvation diet I had been on all the time left me weak and with little energy. I had boils on the back of my neck. Their little hands cut into the boils and I kept stopping.

I was going to the lake to jump in. My children would be saved from what I knew would be their fate at the schools. For they would never see each other, or me, again. They would be raised as slaves. I was hungry and poor, but I was never stupid.

The way the twins moved meant they had to be together. They were balanced to each other like bird wings. They moved in synchronicity. A perfect boy–girl mirroring. I was allowed to love them until they were almost two years old. I had dreamt, hoped, prayed for life for them in America. But I really wanted to take both of them somewhere with me. I didn't know where somewhere was. I didn't have the means to get there. I didn't even have a coat.

They had each other.

They were my wings, those tiny children. When I walked between them in stolen moments I was the bird body and they were my flight.

If they were taken I would be just that. A wingless bird body. A bird can only hop a few steps before becoming exhausted.

My friend in the laundry said, 'Believe you'll be out of here soon. And your children will have good homes. What kind of life can you give them?'

But I was selfish. Being pretty had always made me selfish. I never had to try as hard as my sisters or friends. I had my long blonde hair and sparkling green eyes. My soft, pale skin and rosy cheeks. I was a wolf among those nuns. They smelled my rage, the way I looked at them, I wanted to tear them apart. Being pretty made them hate me because that was a sign of sin. It led to the other things, the touching and the longings. But I hadn't counted on this huge love I'd feel for the twins. I loved my brothers and sisters and I once loved my mammy and daddy before they left me. I hadn't yet met a man I loved for himself, I just wanted them for the feelings they would give me, feelings where my mind would swirl and my breath would cut short and the visions I would get when it came to a peak. But the twins. My babies. I had grown so vast in the inside with this love that if they were to leave there would be a hole that would never fill.

I had asked that they be adopted together. I could see that their tiny souls and minds were entwined like spirals on old tombs.

They were never allowed call me mammy but they knew what I was. I had my breasts out for them to drink. They knew who I was.

I sat down by the lake and we all shivered at its shore. They held onto me and I gave them such last bits of love as I could. I gave them a feeding and they trembled until their legs were blue. I stood, to walk into the water. I walked in with a child on each hip the cold water to my waist as they clung and cried and pleaded. I don't know what made me, and I was sorry for it often, but I couldn't take it that they were holding onto me for protection and I was murdering them. I was able to give them more love than any of the other poor wee ones in the nursery but now I realized all that love only hurt them more. Love burrowed inside them, expanded their hearts; the bigger the love the bigger this emptiness when it left. But here in the cold lake in spring I came right to the centre of love. A centre that had no fear in it. This was the love I had been waiting for. A love where you could give and give and give and not want anything. My terror was gone and in that second I carried them from the water.

But as I came back out of the lake the guards were pulling up in a car and shouting.

Two guards ran to me to grab the children. They put blankets around us all, and drove us back to the mother and baby home.

'Don't take me back there please, please, please. Take me to my family. My sister is with the Lyonses in Kilbride. My sister Mary will take care of me. The children are going to be sent off to the industrial schools. They're going to be separated in those awful places. I want to see Mary. The nuns will kill me for this. They'll take it out on these wee ones.'

Fionnuala and Conn were screaming. The guards were looking at each other.

'I haven't done anything wrong. Take me to my family. Don't take me back to them nuns! These are my babies. They're mine. I'll decide what happens.'

'Look here, it's Teresa, right?' one very young guard spluttered.

'My name is not Teresa, it's Maeve. Maeve O Conaill. Remember that. The nuns gave me the other name and I don't want it. I'm Maeve. These are my children. Their names are Fionnula and Conn. Remember that. They'll change their names too. But this is who we are right now.'

The young guard was staring at me, at my beauty. He was moved.

'Go to Kilbride in Meath. My sister Mary works for the Lyonses in the school house. Please tell her I'm here and need to speak to her. At least do that.'

He looked pleadingly at the older guard who shook his head.

Four nuns were waiting at the door, in a line. The matron trying to look on me with pity, but she couldn't even muster that, and her hatred written into every line on her horrible old face. So much so that I felt the guards hesitated, but they handed us all over. The young guard carried both Fionnula and Conn and I thought he couldn't take his eyes off of me. If only he could have helped me.

When my children were taken the next day I begged to know if they were adopted but the matron was only too pleased to tell me that my reputation for sexual lewdness had got around and they couldn't afford to adopt those children out because they might end up back here again as often happened with families who weren't satisfied with the children they got.

When she confirmed that my beautiful swans were separated, and sent to the industrial schools, I lost myself. I ran away again, this time to drown myself for real. The same guards picked me up on the road before I could get to the edge of the water. I asked them again to go to Mary. The young guard seemed to understand. I thought of running again the next night. I had nowhere to run to in truth. But I thought I could get to Mary. The Lyonses would get them back for me and I'd take them with me to England like I should of in the first place. Christ but that was my big regret.

The Children of Lir answered their father's invitation to come back and live as swams with him. 'May good fortune be on the threshold of your door from this time and for ever, but we cannot cross it, for we have the hearts of wild swans and we must fly in the dusk and feel the water moving under our bodies; we must hear the lonesome cries of the night. We have the voices only of the children you knew; we have the songs you taught us – that is all.'

The guards found me again, lying by the lake in the night dreaming of swans. The young guard was especially kind to me but I felt they knew where I was from and that was always the shame. That was what them nuns did. More than changing our names. More than the back-breaking work. The bad and scant food. It was the shame they put into you that I would never get out of me. And none of us could find our way back from the belief that we were to blame for all that was done to us.

That was my first beating that night. The matron stripped me, and with a belt flogged my back. She said I would be sent on to Mullingar, to the big house where my brother was. Because I was as mad as him.

To comfort myself I remembered that when the swans got separated on the rough waters of the sea on their second three hundred years they had a place, The Rock of Seals, where they all would come back to.

Fionnuala would come to it broken-feathered and draggled with the saltness of the sea and call, 'O Conn that I sheltered under my feathers, come to me! O Fiacra, come to me! O Aodh, Aodh, Aodh, come to me! O three that I loved, O three that I loved: the waves are over your heads and I am desolate.'

We loved when Mary would tell that part. We would all be around the fire leaning in to her with our hearts broken and then something would come into her eyes, as if she saw the swans coming back through the walls of the house. And all the brothers would come flying back, one by one, torn and cold and she would take them under her feathers. And we by the fire would feel the love they had for each other even though they were cursed to be swans. And I always felt that this was the love Mary felt for us. That she was our Fionnuala.

Could she not hear me now? Maybe she was our Lir? It was like when the swans asked for their father, Lir, they were told that he had wrapped his robes of beauty about him and was feasting with those from whom age cannot take youth and light-heartedness. He retreated further into the fairy world to forget his pain. And Fionnuala was happy for him because she loved him – *he cannot hear us calling through the night – the wild swans, the wanderers, the lost children.*

Could she not hear me now?

I sat up that night in the dormitory with all the frightened women and I told them the story of the Bull. I told it for Mary's sake. But that story didn't do much for me. A woman who was let wander the countryside sleeping with a bull was a bit far from my experience. More of them gathered around me. Some left their beds and sat close but I didn't care about keeping my voice down. Most didn't move for fear of being caught. But every last girl in that dormitory was listening. Then I told them the story of the Children of Lir, and they all began to snuffle and weep.

The memory of all beautiful things came to the swans, and they were sorrowful, and Fionnuala said, 'O beautiful comrades, I never thought that beauty could bring sorrow: now the sight of it breaks my heart,' and she said to her brothers, 'Let us go before our hearts are melted utterly.' And they flew off to spend three hundred years on the stormy sea of the Moyle and they were there till three hundred years were ended. 'It is time for us to go,' said Fionnuala; 'we must seek the Western Sea.'

The nun on night duty didn't stop me. She too listened to the story. The matron arrived. Even the matron didn't stop me. They stood in the door and listened. The stories had their way with people, if nuns were people. And though everyone saw them two nuns stand there listening, not one girl moved. Everyone knew we were protected as long as I could keep the story going.

So they came to the Western Sea. The swans were on that sea and flying over it for three hundred years and all that time they had no comfort, and never once did they hear the footfall of hound or horse or see their faery kinsfolk. A sorrow on them, for the sea was wilder and colder and more terrible than the Moyle.

The girls began crying in hysteria. There was weeping and moaning on all the beds. Like a contagion. They were using it as an excuse to unleash all the lonely sorrow stuffed in them. My voice rose to make sure the story would be heard. The matron didn't even put on the lights. When I got to the end of the story she said, over the din of tears,

'Teresa, are you quite finished?'

'I'm all finished,' I said. I wasn't crying though. I had cried enough down at the lake with my babies.

I waited for her to drag me out and beat me again but she didn't. Instead she contacted Seamus and he willingly went along with their plan and signed me away. Fr Gilligan, who must have taken pleasure in chauffeuring poor unfortunate fallen women about the country, was the one who took me. He drove me in silence all the way into the very centre of the country. I could feel it. I who had been born by the edge of the world could feel the great coast and wild Western Sea retreating as the land swallowed me up. This journey reminded me of the journey we took as tiny children in the horse and trap.

My father sitting in the front with the reins. We crossed the entire country under the open sky. I had sat with Seán on my knee for most of it. I had tickled under his arms and felt him laugh into me. We had been shocked when the mountains sailed away from us like blue ships and the country had flattened out. We looked around us in wonder, and all agreed that Ireland was the most beautiful country in the world.

We had crossed through woods and towns and green open spaces until we found Rathcairn in County Meath. We had found it in summer and the hedges were flowing into the road and our land seemed endless. The little house, with its baked earth floor, was filled quickly with us.

I had only known my mountain, and then our fields in Meath, and then I only knew the street that ran from my shop to the cinema. I only knew the lanes that led to the field that got me into all this trouble. I hadn't seen much of the world. I had certainly not seen something as giant as the big house in Mullingar. I had known so little of the world, and now I knew I would have to be mighty clever to get myself away from here.

Mary

The Veils Were Thinner at This Time of Year (1951)

The veils were thinner at this time, when the earth was tilting away from the light, preparing to sleep and shed its colour. I found it hard always, this late October time.

I knew we needed this time of year. We needed this darkness. So I took it into me and tried to feel every bit of it.

It was a time my family came to my mind. My mother and father mostly. They were phantoms opening doors in my sleep. But I never caught sight of them.

I braced myself through the shortening days. This was the time of year when the horizon made its incision and the trees shook their disguise.

It was All Souls Night. I had the dead to remember. My mother and father. So I went to the Mass with the Lyonses and closed my eyes and prayed to the Blessed Virgin Mary that she had scooped them up instead of the old hag. The priest Fr Lavin was chatting to

Patricia and Mr Lyons and they beckoned me over after Mass. We walked to the priest's house by the church and I hesitated at the door. I'd never been invited into a priest's house before. Fr Lavin saw my hesitation and smiled kindly at me. He took me by the arm and said,

'Is it an escort you want over the threshold?'

The Lyonses laughed but I felt fierce awkward inside the house of a priest. The children were all at their uncle's place, so I came in. It would be too quiet to go home by myself. I couldn't bear an empty house at that time of year.

The priest poured the women glasses of sherry and Mr Lyons and himself took whiskey. His housekeeper, Miss Quinn, was a very tall, slim, young woman, with a pretty face, and shoulder-length, thick curly hair. She didn't seem to mind me standing there with them all in the living room. She never looked at me as if I shouldn't be there. In fact Fr Lavin addressed her as Beth and asked her would she join us for a sherry. She poured one for herself but didn't sit down. I wasn't sitting either. She looked closely at me, and I wished she would ask me to the kitchen with her, but she didn't look like she was going to the kitchen.

'Can I take your coats?' She smiled at us.

The Lyonses gave her their coats. They were talking gaily with the priest about politics and the local hurley team, which was doing so well, and Joseph was the star player.

The priest was pouring the second whiskey, and I was still standing up, when Miss Quinn pulled a chair by the fire for me. Sure didn't I have to take it out of politeness? My mother and father would have been proud to see me sitting with all these respectable people by the fire.

Suddenly, without asking, Miss Quinn sat on the couch beside the priest and joined us. I glanced at Patricia and I saw that she too raised her eyebrows in shock. Mr Lyons cleared his throat and adopted that amused look he had when he was confused by a situation. Fr Lavin didn't blink, he kept talking about hurling.

'Brian, do you remember when we were both on the team for Westmeath?'

I found it strange that a priest would ever talk about a time when he wasn't a priest. Mr Lyons beamed and said,

'Ach indeed I do, Jimmy. Remember what Gallagher used to tell us?'

This was the night of nights; I looked at Patricia for support. Mr Lyons was calling the priest by his first name. They had been great friends in their schooldays but I didn't think this was an excuse. No one else seemed to notice. Miss Quinn topped up all the ladies' sherries before I could put my hand over my glass to stop her. She had rings on her fingers and lipstick on. I even saw Mr Lyons' eyes linger on her for a moment. The fire flushed her cheeks red and her eyes were bright.

'He was the coach,' Fr Lavin told Miss Quinn. 'An awful man, really. But boy did he put us through our paces.'

'Remember what he'd always say as we'd take to the field.'

Patricia smiled indulgently, she knew this story.

Fr Lavin and Mr Lyons spoke together and clinked glasses.

'If you can't get the ball – get the man!'

We laughed.

We all drank a bit too much that night and I asked Miss Quinn, who kept asking me to call her Elizabeth, could I help her in the kitchen and we'd rustle up something.

I got to the kitchen and there wasn't much in it by the way of food.

'Miss Quinn, I have some tarts and ham and pudding and all sorts of things down at the house. Maybe I should go and get them and bring them back.'

She laughed happily as she threw open the cupboards with her long arms. 'The cupboards are bare.'

I found some brown bread and a biteen of cheese on the counter. The kitchen fire had almost gone out but I stoked it up quickly, and disappeared into the garden. I found a few herbs and pulled them up. She came to the door.

'What are you doing, Miss O Conaill? Can I call you Mary?'

'Yes, of course. Just thought I'd find something growing in the garden.'

'Hunting and foraging? Are ye?' She giggled.

I glanced around and saw a few cigarette butts on the ground.

With a shrug I came in, and toasted the bread and melted the cheese over it, and sprinkled some rosemary I'd found that she didn't even know was growing. I thought of Seamus and his wife who knew nothing about how to get a meal going or take care of a house. But Miss Quinn stood at the door and smoked, pulling her cardigan around her, and chatted happily to me. She was great company, and so at ease with herself that I could see why the priest would want her around even if he'd starve.

'I eat too much anyway,' I confessed. 'It's my only comfort.'

'No other vices?' She raised her eyebrows and offered me a cigarette. 'Maeve O Conaill who used to serve in Boyles' shop was your sister?'

'She was,' I said. 'Is.'

'I always liked her. Ye don't look alike.'

We could hear the men in the other room singing songs. Patricia wandered to the kitchen and Miss Quinn handed her a tray of bread and cheese to bring in. Patricia took it in surprise but I quickly saved her the embarrassment and took it off her. The men were very glad of it.

Miss Quinn sat on the edge of Mr Lyons' armchair. It didn't seem to matter a whit to Fr Lavin but Patricia stood up to go and Mr Lyons told her to sit down and take it easy. 'We haven't even heard one of Mary's stories yet. The night is young.'

'She tells the children the most amazing stories. She has thousands of them if not more,' Patricia said proudly. 'Don't you, Mary? Tell us a story. It'll stop these two from singing.'

Miss Quinn was sitting on the floor by the fire now. Fr Lavin saw what I thought of this and patted the couch for her to sit on. She threw herself on the couch and lit a cigarette. They were all smoking except me. I never had the grá for them. Miss Quinn whispered something to the priest and he looked at me.

'Mary, Beth tells me you're Maeve's sister.'

Patricia put her arm on my arm protectively.

'Your brother Seamus came to me and told me that she had gone off to America to join your sister Bridget. He told me to tell you. I was going to come over.'

The air of the world was sucked out and I sat in a little vacuum with the voices going on around me. Patricia never took her hand off my arm and I loved her for it. For if she had let go I would have shot up out of my chair through the roof, and through the seven veils of the sky, and I would have never come back. I couldn't tell them that I hadn't heard where Bridget was in America. That I hadn't heard from her since I got her a job in Dublin as a maid for a doctor's family.

'Tell us a story, Mary,' Patricia urged. And how could I refuse this woman? Who had been like a light in my life. Who had taught me to read and write properly, who had allowed her Baby to come every night into my bed. Who had given me Baby, my luck-child.

'A happy one, mind you,' Mr Lyons warned. 'Most of them end in woe.'

If I told a sad one I might have cried myself so I told them the story of the Luck-Child. The happiest tale of all tales.

On the way out of the house it was 2 am. We were all very merry. Many songs had been sung and stories been told.

Fr Lavin stood at the door and said, 'I'm sorry to bring family matters up like that, Mary. Forgive me. I had a biteen too much to drink. I'll come see you. I can take you to your brother.'

'No. He won't see me. We're not talking, so we're not,' I said.

'Did you know about Maeve?'

'Indeed I didn't. I hope she'll write to me. I'm glad she's gone, she had such trouble. The Boyles were a good family but she was always a wild one. America will suit her though, to be sure. She had her heart set on escaping there.'

Miss Quinn came and joined us so I went to walk away. I didn't want my business all over town.

'Lucky her,' she said. 'I'd love to see America.'

'Oh I say you will.' Mr Lyons had his arm around Patricia who was wavering in the dark night.

The priest laughed and we all bid each other farewell.

In the cold car I breathed onto my hands. Patricia said to me,

'It's better for Maeve. I'm sure, for all of you. The child will have a good home and she can start again. God love her. We'll pray for her.'

Mr Lyons said nothing; he cleared his throat and concentrated on getting the car back to the house as full of whiskey as he was.

The Lyonses were good people. They had never said a word against Maeve, though the entire town knew she had to be sent to the mother and baby home a few years back. I was sad that I'd never see her again, she being so far away. But I was happy she and Bridget were together. I would take moments to imagine them in a big sparkling city with tall buildings like New York. They would have each other just as they did when they were wee ones, they could comb each other's hair. That was the last we spoke of it. In a way I was more shocked that I had just sat in a priest's living room.

Everything was changing.

As we rode in Mr Lyons' car I gasped when a fox crossed the road and Mr Lyons slowed down so we could all look at it in the headlights. The fox's eyes shone in the night like a mad orange money. What new currency was this?

Maeve

He Had Taken Out My Soul and Opened It

Fr Gilligan came once more for me. We did not exchange a word and I never looked at him as I got into the back of his car. Another journey across Ireland through drab little towns and endless twisting roads. I tried to imagine what New York would be like. There was a man with him who sat in the front of the car and kept a close eye on me. I thought of the Cruelty Men. As children Mary trained us to stand up on the fairy fort in the field and scour the horizon for them. When Fr Gilligan got out of the car at one stage to go into a hotel for tea the man sat with me in the car.

'Are you the Cruelty Man?' I asked. He gave a little snort.

'I'm just helping out,' he said. Then he got out of the car to stretch his legs and I lay down on the back seat. The nuns never gave me my suitcase back so I had nothing in this world, and the thought of that exhausted me. After a while I heard the priest come shouting and the man say, 'She's sleeping. She's here. She's here.'

The hospital in Mullingar was enormous and terrifying as we pulled up. But I felt no fear. My brother was there and I would find him, and we would be together, and we would escape and go find Fionnuala and Conn.

Fr Gilligan, who had said nothing to me all the way, leaned into me as a nun came to the door to lead me to admissions.

'You're not laughing anymore, are ye?' And he smiled at the nun, who seemed to know him and light up at his presence. She told him to come in and she would get him a cup of tea and some scones and fresh cream. They were jokey together. He put his hand on my back and guided me towards her.

'Teresa,' she said. 'Let's get you sorted. I hear you are a great worker.'

'Oh by God. She is that.'

As I sat behind an open frosted-glass door I could hear Fr Gilligan talking to a matron, outlining my case. They knew I was there but they talked as if I wasn't. Nobody asked me anything, they'd have rather talked to a priest who I met twice. He spoke as if he had taken out my soul, sliced it open and found an empty purse.

'Matron and I discussed this one. She'll need some treatment before she's ready to take her place usefully here. She's also prone to running away and has caused an awful lot of trouble. The guards had to be called twice. She attempted to murder two little children. Drown them in a lake. We have her transferred here to avoid sending her to prison. She's lucky the nuns are good women with forgiveness in their hearts. I'd put her down as At Risk.'

'I see she has marked sexual tendencies.'

'You've a lot of work on your hands with this one. She almost ruined two very respectable families in Trim.'

Always the respectable families. The ones with the money. They were busy trying to separate themselves from the likes of us. When a few generations ago they were, like us, struck by famine and in workhouses and losing their land themselves. Ireland had independence from England, and we had been taught of all the evil England had done to us, but I didn't see much freedom here. So far in my twenty-one years I'd gone from the farm, to the shop, to the mother and baby home, and now to an asylum. And I had worked seven days a week in most of them places without stop, without much food either. I wanted to tell this to the priest and the nun but they looked at me as a murdering whore. Though I was sent to no court. Court had gone on behind my back.

The nun nurse pursed her lips. I was looking at the big heavy crucifix, up so high on the wall where none of us poor mad could grab it and smash their heads in. Jesus was out of reach, as usual.

'I was told she was a great worker in the laundry. We always need more hands here. But it's only fair to offer her treatment first. We'll probably start her on insulin and see where that takes us.'

They wrote down my name as Teresa Boyle. This was the only time I spoke up to them. I was trying to play it clever and get out of there. My plan was, when they thought I was well in the head I'd go get Fionnuala and Conn and take them to Mary who would get me the money to take them to England. The other girls said England was big enough and no one had any real religion there so you could live with your babies no questions.

'My name is Maeve O Conaill. Teresa was a name they gave me at the home. Boyle is the name of the people who I worked for in Trim.'

Fr Gilligan and the matron swung around in surprise. They hadn't expected I could read what they were writing. They hadn't expected I could talk. The nun looked at me with a certain amount of sympathy and Fr Gilligan shrugged.

But they went on doing what they were doing. I got really angry with them and went to grab the book.

'If I go down as Teresa, like I have been for the last few years, when will I get back to my own self?'

Two male nurses came in and pulled me out of the room, and the priest didn't even look in my direction. I went quickly limp, as I didn't want trouble. Because I had a plan. And I knew who could help me with it.

They gave me a uniform of rough clothes and I put it on. I lay in a big ward that night listening to the screaming and crying of the poor mad people. But most of all, I heard the silence in between all of us women, lying in beds, strangers to each other from all over Ireland.

After my three hundred years in the mother and baby home, I was transferred for another three hundred years to the big house in Mullingar. I hoped to find my lovely brother Padraig. Padraig had a look in his eye, as a child that could not be contained. Surely he would know how to get free.

Mary

The Luck-Child

The morning after I had sat drinking whiskey in the priest's house, I woke with a fierce head on me. And Baby told me my breath smelled like a dead cat, and so it did. As I lit the fires and got the breakfast all the Lyonses slept in because it was a weekend.

The night before, on All Souls Night, I dreamt of Bolus Head. The islands in the shining sea and me on the balcony of the world, up in the old village. As it is with some dreams that are trying to tell you something, it stuck in my head the whole day.

I once asked my father why the standing stones never fell, in all these thousands of years, and he used to tell me that they had roots that went to the centre of the world. We would stand together by them. He had a few cows that grazed around them though it wasn't our land. He would point out at the raw finger of land behind the two islands.

'That's the Beara Peninsula, Co. Cork,' he'd say. 'They have a rock there that is known to be a frozen hag. There are many that talks of the Hag of Beara. But I never knew her and it is not she who appears to folk on the road in these parts.'

'Did you ever see the hag from around here?'

'Indeed I did. An old woman whom I saw walking with icy feet across these heathers. In a way, she felt like one of the family. I wasn't afraid.'

Only once when I was a child did I see a priest walk up the road on Bolus Head. And I saw a grown man jump over the wall in fright. The priests had such powers.

Baby was five years old, and she had a head of curly brown hair. She had brown eyes, though the rest of them had blue eyes and so did her mammy and daddy. We didn't know where she came from. I had her spoiled.

Patricia didn't go to the early daily Mass in winter. She got up an hour later and sat at the table. I dressed Baby. I had all the children's clothes by the fire so they would be warm for them, draped them over the iron bar on the range. Baby was always dressed by the fire; I wouldn't want her getting cold. Sometimes I worried she was chesty and caught every cough going. Croup, whooping cough, bronchitis. I worried for Baby when she was sick. I made her rhubarb tart from my own rhubarb and I melted marshmallows over the top like icing. That was her favourite.

'You have her ruined,' Patricia scolded me. But we all loved Baby. And I knew when the children are seven they change and they don't really belong to us anymore. Up to seven they have their inside eyes open to the other worlds, then the age of reason comes upon them and they grow blind to the hidden things. I hated to see a child turning seven, if truth be told. But Baby would never change on me.

On this day I told Baby I'd take her to the bog. Mr Lyons and the boys had cut the turf in the summer and they let me take the trap up there with Baby to collect a bunch of it when the mountain of turf in the shed ran low. Mr Lyons always said he would do it, but he hated the cold ride in the trap and wouldn't dirty his car with the turf. Besides, Baby and I liked to go to the bog with the pony. I wrapped her up in blankets and we harnessed the pony up to the trap and off we trotted. And the best thing to do for the four miles or so was to tell her a story.

'Aidan, Osric and Teigue were cowherds of the High King of Ireland. They slept in wicker huts on the edge of the forest.'

Baby said quietly but with authority, 'And tell me what each of them was.'

'Don't you know that by now? You tell me.'

She laughed. 'Teigue was the eejit, a fool. Osric was young and fierce and Aidan was like you, the storyteller, and really old and kind.'

Teigue found an infant child at the foot of a tree. She smiled at him. He was immediately enchanted by her and told his fellow cowherds that she was a gift from the hidden people. His friends couldn't let the child perish so they carried her off. She was wrapped in a mantel that was thickly embroidered with gold flowers.

'This is the child of some queen,' Aidan said. 'One day great folk will come seeking her.'

'I will not let the great folk take her away,' said Teigue. 'She is my Luck-Child. She is Osric's Luck-Child too, and we are going to make a house for her, and she will bring us good luck every day of our lives.'

'She is my Luck-Child too,' said Aidan. 'We three will make a secret house in the forest and there we will keep her from prying eyes.'

The Luck-Child loved to hear Aidan's stories. She loved them even when she had grown tall and wise and beautiful and was no longer a child.

'Mary. Am I your luck-child?' Baby would always ask at this point.
'That is what you are, a stór. You are my luck-child, without a doubt.

One day when she was grown she took out her flute and played the music which she heard when the wind swept down from the hills and into her forest. Suddenly a great white hound came through the wood and when it saw them it stood and barked. The hound had a gold collar set with three crystals.

'O my Luck-Child' said Teigue, 'a king will come after this hound. Go quickly where he can get no sight of you.'

She had the will to go but the hound would not let her move and through the trees came the High King of Ireland and his foster brother. The King stared at her in astonishment.

'Who is she?' he said to his cowherd.

Teigue said, 'She is my Luck-Child, Oh King.'

They looked him up and down and snorted. The King's foster brother said,

'She is no child of thine!'

Teigue sighed and moved closer to the Luck-Child, he put his arm around her shoulder and he was trembling.

'She is a child of the hidden people and she had brought me luck every day since I found her.'

The King stepped closer to her.

'This is extraordinary. Tell me how you found her.'

'I found her under a pine tree, a nine-month child wrapped in a mantle all sown over with golden flowers. She is my Luck-Bringer since that day.'

'She is mine today,' said the King. 'O Luck-Child, will you come and live in my palace and bring me good fortune? I will make you High Queen of Ireland.'

'On the day ye built the little hut in the forest for the lost baby ye built truth into the word of my druids and now I will build honour into your fortune. The day you took care of a child who would have perished is the day that brought luck into your life and mine. Ye shall rank with chiefs and the sons of chiefs. Ye shall drink mead in feast halls of your own and while I live ye shall have my goodwill and protection.'

'I love you,' said the Luck-Child to the King and they all returned to the castle.

The people of the land were struck with wonder when they saw the Luck-Child and her three foster fathers. They said that since the days of Queen Étáin who came out of fairyland, no one so beautiful and bright was seen in Ireland. The King called her Étáin and there was feasting and gladness on the day they married and Teigue said the sun got up an hour earlier in the morning and stayed an hour later in the sky that night for all the joy contained in the world was spilling out.

'That,' said Baby, as we had the bog in our sights, 'is the bestest of all the stories.'

'And why do you think that?' The horse, knowing where it was going, broke into a trot.

'It's sooooo happy,' Baby said. 'What's *your* bestest story?'

'My favourite story is 'The Bull Bhalbhae'.'

'That has the scary bits in it.'

'The hag is a biteen fierce alright. My sisters Maeve and Bridget loved 'The Children of Lir'.'

'But that's the saddest of them all.'

Baby leaned herself forward and put her head on my knee. She was wrapped up like a worm.

'This is a head hug. Will I be your storyteller when you die?'

'Yourself and my brother Seán. You'll be the ones to remember them and pass them on down to whoever will listen. Maeve had a great head for the stories but she's in America now and she'll have no use for them.'

'We'll pass them to our children?'

'No, life isn't that simple. It's storylines not bloodlines that it goes by. I only got some of them from my father, and some from a storyteller in the village, and others from all over the place. Ye mightn't have children and worse ye mightn't have children that will listen. It's a rare gift, listening. You'll pass them down to whoever has a big enough space in their head for them.'

We walked across the bog; the November light barely lifted the lid off the world. The day was raw and biting but we warmed up as we put the turf from the Lyonses' stacks onto the barrow and rolled it over the rough ground to the trap.

Baby wasn't satisfied with the fairy stories. She wanted my own history as well, and she knew it inside out more than she knew the history of her own blood.

'Seán in the village had half his stories told to me, and he asked me to tell them back to him. There was a university man who came every summer on his bicycle and he'd stay down in the village of Balie Na Skeligs and come up to us on our balcony that looked over the world, to write them down. So there's a book of them somewhere.'

'A book of them?' She was impressed.

'It's not the book that will keep them going, a stór. It's the telling.'

Baby loved to put the turf on the barrow. She reminded me of me at her age, except she was brighter and prettier and her voice was like the flute itself.

'Was it always your father that saw the hag? Did you ever see her, Mary?'

'Oh many's a people saw her. But your mother has told me to stop telling you stories about the hag because you'll have nightmares.'

'What did she look like?'

'My father saw her by the well once up the mountain and she was taking water in a bucket, he froze and she looked right past him. He said her hair was long and grey down to her knees. She took the water off in the direction of the limbo graveyard. The burial place for wee babies who didn't get baptized.'

'Why didn't they get baptized?'

'They must have died too soon. But you have to be baptized to go to Heaven.'

'Maybe they were thirsty, Mary,' Baby said. 'Maybe she's the only one who can hear them.'

'Baby, you are wise beyond your years,' I told her, and we wheeled the last barrow over to the trap and loaded it on. Baby danced around me.

'Can the hag love anything?' Baby asked.

'*Is fuar cumann cailleach*, they say.'

'What does that mean?'

'The affection of a hag is a cold thing.'

'Remember the time we saw the hares out here?'

'It's not the season for them now.'

'Last time we were out we saw a group of hares gather in a circle and up they went on their hind legs. They faced each other and bowed.' Baby made a bow.

'I saw this display many times before, and often with Seán as a child.'

Baby lifted the turf with both hands and smelled it. 'Maybe they're your family, Mary.'

Baby walked only on tiptoe, she never really walked. She danced and skipped. She sprang about the pony. And the pony leaned down to chew her hair and she squealed happily. I picked her up and together we sat. Side by side. She was bundled up and that's when I started calling her Bundle. My own little Bundle.

I always let her hold the reins in the summer but today she was swaddled and leant against me. I breathed in the lovely sweet smell of the turf. The bog here was deeper than at home and you had to go down further, but it still had that lovely smell.

'I thought the hares would come even in winter because they're your family, Mary and it was All Souls' Day.'

'No. When my father left us to go find my mother he never came back. Not even in a dream.'

She chattered away, her voice clear like water flowing over sparkling mica stones. The quiet was a sunken enclosed November quiet. We were the last two people in the world. The horse's clip-clopping rang through the air as the only sharpness.

'Are you listening, Mary?' she said every now and then.

'I'm listening, my own little Bundle.'

The night before I had fallen asleep with too much drink on me and dreamt of Bolus Head and the hag. But never my father, or never my mother, or never the new baby she must have had if it survived. Though I longed for them to come to me in my dreams to explain what happened, they never did.

Seamus

Then Something Queer Happened
(1952)

I'd cut the wheat and put it into stacks. I had no storage on the farm, so I had to thresh twice a year and that meant one thing. I'd have to take that walk over to Patsey, and tolerate him coming over to me, all smiles and back slaps and auld plamaus. No one round here ever touched anyone, but Patsey was always at it. He'd stand right beside me in a big open field as if we were at the stands in Croke Park. He'd be talking to me and nudging me with his elbow to make a point or to get a reaction. Asking after me wife and me sons.

He'd always try to convince me to get someone else to feed the mill on the thresher. He loved that machine. Granted it was an impressive beast, about twenty feet wide. Not many would come help me with the threshing because I never went to help anyone else. But Patsey would get a few lads and I'd always tell him there were too many, for he made me pay for their work. I wanted to feed the mill meself. I didn't see that it required so much skill. Patsey relented finally, and drove the machine and let me at it. Off we went across the field.

The blades swung and chopped, and we were going and going. Patsey said we should take a break, but I waved him away. I wanted to finish the job and get them all off me farm. I told the wife to have something laid out for our food but she never heeded me. I could see the lads itching to get away as quick as possible, and we were all getting hungry.

Didn't I put my arm in too far, and the wheat was sucked by the blade. Before I knew it my sleeve was caught and a bright slash of red sprayed before me and I pulled back. I could hear a shout from far away. Patsey turned off the machine. By the time he stood beside me I was standing without me arm. There was Patsey yelling and screeching like a woman. The lads tried to lay me on the ground but I backed away from them. Me eldest son was beside me and holding onto me jacket. I felt like the air had been sucked out of the world. Then the pain whooshed into me as if the air had brought it back. I doubled over but I didn't fall.

The bastard Patsey had me in his car with a blanket around me that was filling with blood. We were on our way to Navan hospital. I remember the look of me wife at the door and she narrowed her eyes, not with concern but with hate, when she saw what had happened. Patsey was forcing me to drink whiskey. As he drove he held it to me lips and I gulped it down. He swerved all over the road.

'Jaysus boy. I told you we needed my man to feed the mill. Jaysus. You're a stubborn creature, Seamus, you always were.'

'Would you fuck off, Patsey. Watch the road, or we'll have an accident.' I told him. And he laughed out loud like a maniac, taking a swig of whiskey himself.

A month after I was out of the hospital, I found meself standing on me field where it happened. Me arm was now in the earth, scattered and shredded. Me fingers were down in the soil in bits. How was I going to lift a shovel? How was I going to feed the animals? The wife was triumphant, this was our chance to sell and move to town. She had never been a farmer's wife. I couldn't say that this land was my father's land and my father's father's. This land had been taken off someone and given to my father by the government. He had barely spent a year on it. I'd no photo of the man and no recollection of his face. I don't remember much of him, except his bad and worsening mood when me mother didn't show up. The wife had already gone to Patsey and told him to make an offer. When I found that out I took her by the hair and banged her face off the wall, the boys screaming around me.

Me arm and elbow and wrist and fingers were here now, under the soil. I'd never sell it to that fucker Patsey who had probably planned for me to lose me arm. Sure he'd bought that thresher and tended it like a new baby, and all with the intention of ripping me to shreds and getting the fields here. And he still had the gall to slime his way over here to offer me any assistance he could.

'You've done enough,' I'd snarled at the fucker.

Then something queer happened. Standing here on this sloping field, with the grey thud of a sky above me, I felt me arm come back to me. Just like that. I could move the fingers and swing the elbow. Me arm was reaching to pull something out of the earth. I'd always done that without thinking. If I was standing next to a bush I would always find meself pulling at the leaves. It was a habit. And here it was again. The feeling was so strong I looked down in shock but the arm was not there. Me sleeve was hanging loose. And so it was from that day on, I could feel that arm as if it had never gone. I reached for things. To open the gate, to grab a bucket, to push a cow through the gate with it. But the arm was gone. It even waved over at me sons if I wanted their attention. But it wasn't there.

I told no one about me arm still being there. Until I woke in the night and me fists were clenched and the fingernails were digging into the palm of me hand. I groaned and rolled around the bed. The wife stirred up.

'Seamus, what are ye at?'

'Me arm. It's killing me. Me nails are ...'

'Which arm?'

'The feckin arm that's gone.'

'Jaysus, Seamus, you'll end up in the big house in Mullingar with the rest of your feckin family.'

I swung out the side of the bed trying to grab the arm that was gone but of course I couldn't. The nails were digging, digging. The pain was awful, more that it had even been when it was tore right out of me shoulder.

'You'd love that wouldn't ye? Ya useless clart. Then ye could sell this place from under me.'

'Tell your feckin sister to come back and work for us.'

I was down on the floor trying to concentrate and uncurl me fist with all me might. I closed me eyes to imagine the arm was fully back but it wouldn't unclench. The sweat was breaking out on me brow.

'It's her who has you cursed,' Sheila hissed. 'I heard tell she was a bit of an old witch. With her hair grey at fifteen.'

One of the boys was at the door.

'Daddy? Are ye alright?'

'Now you're waking them all up, Seamus.'

'Daddy? Daddy?'

'Would ye fuck off,' I howled. 'The lot of ye.'

Mary

It's a Blessing to Be in the Lord's Hand as Long as He Doesn't Close His Fist

Patsey stood at the door. He took off his hat and at once I knew something had happened.

'Here's to the light heart and the heavy hand.'

'A blessing is often an upside-down curse,' I told him, smiling.

'Arra, sure you're right there Mary. To be sure.'

'Come in, come in.'

Patsey fingered his hat and shook his head.

'It's good to see you, Mary, just came by for a cup of tea in the hand.'

As he stood in the kitchen, he looked down at the floor.

'Is it Seán?'

I had two hives out the field and the honey was in a square, wooden box. He dipped into it with a knife and spread it on the scones.

'Mary you're a wonder. Honey and homemade scones. You have a light touch when it comes to the baking. I should have swept you off your feet and married you. But you wouldn't have wanted an old fellah like meself.'

I was a bit taken aback at Patsey talking marriage. Old farmers like him, you just expected to stay bachelors. 'Is Seán ok? You haven't come to talk about my scones.'

'I might come again just for them, they're that good.' Patsey scratched his head and his eyes darted to the corner of the room. 'I'll just say it to you. It's Seamus. He lost the arm in my thresher.'

I gasped and sat down in the chair by the fire.

'He's out of the hospital a month now but he's having a hard time of it.'

'That's shocking awful. How did it happen?'

'I told him we needed a few lads to help with the threshing and I told him not to feed the mill, but to let my lads do it, as they know what they're doing. But you know your brother as well as I do, would he listen? He was putting the shafts of wheat into the drum and I was driving. I heard the lads shout and turned the machine off, and there was Seamus standing very still with one arm gone. He didn't even scream. He just looked at me as he usually does.'

'As he usually does?' I had to start making tea. Do something.

'Ye know. With a face on him like a boiled shite.'

We both laughed at this but stopped guiltily.

'The thing is, Mary, he can't do around the farm what he could. And that wasn't very much. I never thought farming was really in Seamus's blood. I always thought he looked miserable at it. Not like you. You could farm a bog, Mary. You could harvest a prison yard.'

'His wife ... his sons ...' I knew what was coming but I didn't want him to say it.

'Sure they're only wee ones. Raised like weeds. They're running wild, half the time they don't even have pants on them. They never have shoes. They don't look well fed. She's ...'

'I know. Patsey. I know. She thought she was getting away from something didn't she?'

'Aye.'

'But she wasn't. She was getting right into it.'

'And who's to know if it was worse than what she was getting away from.' Patsey stuffed another scone into his mouth and chewed vigorously. 'Sheila's a tongue of ivy – and a heart of holly. She's not much good to him on the farm, or for the wee ones once she's produced them. As Daniel O'Connell once said, she has all the characteristics of a poker except its occasional warmth.'

'I can't go back there, Patsey. They wouldn't pay me. And she wouldn't have me back. You have her number alright, she has a tongue that would clip a hedge.'

'She'd have you in a minute, are ye mad? She's dying for you to come back.'

'And work as their slave? I need my wages. I'm paying for wee Seán to stay in school.'

'He's about fifteen now.'

'He is that.'

'Most of us never went schooling beyond twelve.'

'He's different. I'm making sure one of us gets to go. I promised Mammy and Daddy I would take care of them all and Seán is the only one I've managed to take care of. At least Bridget and Maeve are in America.'

'Maeve in America?' Patsey started to say something. He looked at me in silence as if to look right into my head and then he began to speak but hesitated.

'What do you know, Patsey?'

'Nothing, Mary. I just care for your family. I kind of looked out for ye all. Ye were left all alone so young. Them Cruelty Men would come for ye. I made my mind up to keep ye all away from the industrial schools that would have surely scooped ye up. I couldn't help Padraig, but when they got one of you they backed off a bit and I hoped that would happen. But if you don't come back Seán will have to leave school and come help Seamus, for he won't make it with one arm.'

'I know you did, Patsey, you were a good neigbour. Why did the eejit put his arm into the thresher? God, he was born a donkey and he'll die a donkey. Would you not buy the farm from them and let them do something else besides farming?'

'Seamus has a bee in his bonnet about me getting the farm. I don't want the grief. Mary, I have my own lads I hire to feed the thresher but you know Seamus. He wouldn't let them onto his farm. Mostly everyone will help and we'll do the threshing in a rota, but Seamus likes to keep to himself. He wouldn't work any other man's farm and so the men don't come to his. Many's a fine man has lost his arm in the thresher. Any man can lose his hat in a side-*gaoithe*.'

'If a man is his own ruin let him not blame fate, Patsey,' I said. 'God forgive me.'

I took a wee dram of whiskey from behind the bread bin and we both had a glass. We sat in silence for a while.

'Sure you've found yourself a nice home here, Mary.'

'I did. The Lyonses is decent people.'

'So I've heard. And they're lucky to have you.'

'I'd better be getting the lunch ready, Patsey. You're an awful time-waster.'

'I didn't come here to waste your time.' Patsey got up and I walked him out.

'You've got yourself a car.' I laughed.

'I do alright. The thresher has ...' Patsey caught himself before he'd boast about the monster that ripped my brother's arm off.

'Patsey, why don't you just offer to buy the land? They don't need to be farmers. They could go into town and buy a shop with the money or something. They could buy a wee bar.'

'Could you see Seamus behind the bar with a face on him like the letter Z? Jaysus it would curdle the pints.'

I smiled at the thought of it. He was right, of course.

'Seriously, Mary. That would be a solution but he'd never sell it to me. He's had some notion that I've been after it all along when all I did was try to help. If I wanted it those years back I'd have had it when ye were left orphaned. The priest would have been only too happy to send the Cruelty Men in and gather ye up. Listen, Mary.

You think about it. Either you or Seán is going to have to come back.'

'Thank you, Patsey. Thank you for bringing me the news.'

'No bother, Mary, no bother. You stay now in the Lord's hand.'

'It's a blessing to be in the Lord's hand,' I replied. 'As long as he doesn't close his fist.'

Patsey gave a gentle wave and I watched his stout frame get behind the wheel of a lovely new car. I couldn't begrudge him that.

I went back inside and made breads and tarts. The boys had brought me a pheasant from their hunt so I plucked and prepared it for dinner. My fingers found the gunshot all through the flesh and I rolled the metal in my hand and bit my lip. I saved the tail feathers for Baby. We liked to stick them in the potatoes I pulled out of the ground that had unusual shapes. We had a collection on the window of all sorts of creations.

I always walked over to the school to pick up Baby. We would cross back together and she would chat to me about her day. There were only two classes in the school and it was divided by a wooden partition. Patricia would come over and take food back for many of the children who wouldn't have lunch with them. As a result the numbers in the school kept increasing because word got around it was a good place to send your children. Many from the Gaeltacht areas Rathcairn and Lambey – the Colony, as the locals here referred to it – came because they felt their children would be better off doing their schooling through English. For there was still a shame attached to the speaking of the Irish.

Evening came and I couldn't get Patsey's visit out of my mind. Poor Seamus losing his arm like that. Shocking altogether.

I told Patricia about his arm but not about Patsey's plea that Seán or I go back and help him on the farm. Fr Lavin was over that night. He always came on a Tuesday for a poker game. We had Padraig O'Donnell the bank manager and his wife Maura, Fr Lavin, and the local solicitor, James Duggan. I would bring in trays of food and drink and stay in the kitchen to see if they wanted anything.

I would sit and watch the fire, and listen to the wireless and sip my tea. Fr Lavin would never leave without peeping into the kitchen and saying, 'God bless the washers up!' As if there was a team of us. I'd laugh. It was nice of him to think of me, but I was raised so afraid of the priests that I never knew what to say back.

This time he came right in and sat opposite the fire.

I felt myself blushing red.

'Mary, a man came today to talk to me.' He looked at my face. 'Don't look so alarmed, now. He was a neighbour of yours.'

'Patsey, Father. He came to see me too.'

'I'm awful sorry to hear about your brother's accident.'

'Aye, shocking, Father. Shocking.'

'Patsey says he's having trouble with his arm. The missing one is still giving him a lot of pain.'

'In all fairness, Father, if it's missing how is it paining him?'

'Oh there is such a thing as a phantom limb. After Lord Nelson attacked Santa Cruz de Tenerife and lost his right arm he had terrible pains in his missing arm. In fact he said it was proof of the existence of the soul.'

'I'm not sure I get you. Father.'

Fr Lavin, who had drunk a lot of whiskey throughout the game, seemed to be just warming up. Patricia stuck her head around the door but he waved her away and she discreetly closed the door again. I knew then they had discussed me over their poker game and the thought of all those fine people contemplating my lot made me very frightened indeed.

'If you think about it, Mary, like he did. By the way, the attack was unsuccessful ...'

'The arm attack? But it was a thresher, Father.'

'No no, the attack on Santa Cruz. You see he deduced that if his arm still existed after its removal then the entire person must exist even when the body is long gone. The spirit of the arm was there you see.'

I looked into the fire. What could I say?

'I don't know, Mary. Maybe he wishes it was still there and that's all that it is.'

'But he wouldn't wish it to hurt him would he?' Why were we talking about this? Fr Lavin wasn't an ordinary priest really. 'You seem to know a lot about it, Father.'

'Phantom limb, it's called, since the American Civil War. It was a phenomenon that always fascinated me. I have a lot of useless knowledge, Mary.' Fr Lavin looked downcast and he too stared into the fire. I was waiting for him to ask me would I be leaving.

'We don't want to lose you, Mary. What would Patricia do? You're the anchor to the household.'

My face went redder and redder.

'And the children.'

'Baby,' I said, suddenly afraid.

'Baby is your pet, she is that alright.'

'I'll not go and work on my brother's farm as a slave. He'd never pay me, Father.'

'I've heard that. Patsey seemed to say he was a difficult character alright.'

'His wife is worse. There's two of them in it. They're so mean they'd give you one measle at a time. I'd take their children in hand, for I love children, but I won't live with her and Seamus.'

'When is Seán finished school?'

'Seán will not go work for Seamus either. He's no skills for farm work, Father. It's too hard on him. He's a delicate wee lad. I swore to my mother I'd look out for him. God rest her soul.'

'I've heard from the Brothers at the college that he is a fine young man. They told me he wins all the medals in Latin and mathematics.'

'Truth be told, Father, Seán's not happy up at the school. They can be hard places and he's a soft lad. He'd probably go to the farm in a minute just to get away.'

'Mary, you're right. I'll look into it. I'll see what we can do.'

'Thank you, Father, thank you. If I leave here I won't have the money to keep him in school.'

'No, that's not the solution. You're family here now, Mary. We can't lose you.'

Fr Lavin went back and there was much laughter and talk from the front room.

When everyone had left I cleared up the living room and did the washing up. It was long past midnight. I looked around my kitchen. It was my place in the world. Outside the window were my garden and my rows of vegetables and potatoes. Beyond that, my bees. There was a fairy tree at the end of the garden and I left offerings by it many's a time to guard my little world. It was the first time I thought of it all like this. Baby wasn't in her bed. That bed lay empty, and was filled with crates with my jams in it. By now she went straight to my bed by the kitchen and she would stir in her sleep when I climbed in and her little arm would drape over my neck and she would stay close to me all night. If I moved she would move. This was my place. I was part of the Lyonses now. They were mine and I was theirs.

I turned the wireless off and closed my eyes by the fire, and drifted off into sleep dreaming of an arm spread into the land that was reaching up to pull me down into the underworld. It woke me with a start and I went into my little room and got into the bed beside Baby. I smelled her soft hair that I had washed only that day with the rainwater. For the first time in my life I realized that I had found my place in this world and I might even be protected.

Padraig

Balor's Eye

Balor's eye is giant murder and kept closed, only to be opened on the battlefield. Weapon eye. It takes four big strong men to open it, the eyelid has a rope woven into it – the grunting sweating men grab the pulleys and hoist it open. Heave ho! Death is not in the eye but in those seen.

Hiding from their gaze in the trees, trees weep shedding, breathing budding, sing blossoming – all hiding from the Cruelty Man – his snatching death eye, but now there is nowhere safe to hollow hide. Under the gaze.

A long strong arm held down. It was a working arm, hairy and muscled – a farm arm. This arm has detached – and burrowed underground, worm nuzzled all the way through bog-rock – slithered through roots to ooze pop up on gravelly flat where cars park, this arm has bristle hair, stretching – contracting down sick green corridors to room, edging up table to hold down.

The doctor never makes sounds from his mouth. They pulled the curtains around the bed, put wires on head. When the doctor turned to the machine – Balor's eye on the back of his doctor head. It knew this eye. The priest had this cruel eye. The Cruelty Man had no brain no head only this eye. The very one who took me here. The eye could kill anyone it looked upon.

New mother told that when Balor was a wee child poisonous fumes rose into his eye – made it foul.

Balor stands with his back to the battle – the four nurses wrench the lid open. Twist head, can't look, can't be seen. The nurses listen – the doctor is saying things. Rubbish things, nonsense things. The doctor is mad. After all these years here can tell the mad ones. Where the light is bent in them – their speeches are like hammering on tin.

They stuff mouth. The brother's arm has crawled over half the country to pin to the table. He gave up his own arm to keep stolen child away.

The blight eye zaps in. The eye does not kill at once. Fizz in body moves everything around. Soul has to go inside a hollow bone. Don't come out of there. Shut up soul.

New mother said that Balor's eye if ripped out of his dead head would bore a great hole in the ground – water would fill up crater until a lake.

Many shocks zap, zap, arm held lighting up inside glowing – flips into air like a fish in a bag – CRACK. Lands, but core trunk, part that holds it up, centre where everything sticks out from. CRACK. Eye nailed. Worm arm dissolves.

Everyone stands back. Balor's nurses tiny mouths open in crooked tooth chorus. The eye closes.

Maeve

This Is Not a Hospital

We were promised a band, but mostly it was just a wind-up gramophone playing scratchy records at the dance in the big house. When the dances were in full swing, the clatter of feet shuffling in poor rhythm drowned out the music. I went anyway for the bit of diversion. I went to everything they offered, which wasn't much. They had started to hold dances every couple of months. It was viewed as rehabilitation, but since they kept taking more people in and not letting any of us out I wasn't sure what we were being rehabilitated for. We women were let into the big draughty hall first. Some had make-up, but most of us just brushed our hair but still had nothing nice to wear.

This was not a hospital. It was a city of the mad in the land of the mad. We had shoe shops, carpentry shops, a farm, a laundry, a bakery. I worked in the laundry. The women's and men's worlds were kept separate. I asked for my brother for many years but they would not let me over to see him. They knew who he was. The Grass Man they called him. They told me if I looked out the back of the hospital there was a place where he went behind the trees and wove clothes out of grass. He made whistles and birds. That was him alright. They put him into the carpentry shop and he learnt to make chairs and cabinets, but they say he never talked. He would have been eighteen years old. I could not get to the men's rooms at the back of the hospital.

The only time the men and women were allowed together was at these dances, but Padraig had never been to one. I danced with a man from the carpentry shop and I asked him about my brother. He told me he was a fine carpenter but after the last round of shock treatments a year ago he didn't come through and now spent all his time out behind the trees.

'Maybe he'd make a grass ladder,' I said. 'Then he can sling it over the wall and escape.'

The man laughed with me. 'Maybe. Maybe.'

The man I danced with didn't seem mad either but he did seem settled into this place. I didn't want to become settled.

I asked them when I was going to be released.

'When you are cured,' the doctor said simply.

'If I'm not mad what can I be cured of?' I asked him.

'You wouldn't be in here if you weren't mad. Only your brother can sign you out.'

I wrote to my brother Seamus every week. I wrote to Mary but she never replied and I knew Mary would help so I worried that she was not getting the letters. She would not leave me here.

Padraig

Crack. They Break the Back

Finds a place by the wall behind trees – makes whistles, birds. Pulls up grass – makes a grass shirt. Made a grass hat for head – made grass trousers. Hung them in trees.

Drank their sugar drinks. Vomited – had to drink more. Stays away from all. Knows where to go to hide from the eye.

Became a man here. Digs holes behind the trees – sticks it in them, sends crazy grey yellow into earth. The nurses kept telling not to keep touching. To take hands out of pants. But it likes it. Two bare winters where shivered in grass shirt – grass hat – wove a grass long coat. Don't want to be inside even in the rain.

The eye finds even behind trees. Even wearing grass. More shocks. To stop going behind the trees – stop fucking the ground. They're afraid the Midlands will get pregnant. But land wouldn't be a bastard for would marry the hag. Knows what the first kiss of her craggy cheeks and thin lips would do for her. Kissing the hag makes her beautiful. That's the secret.

CRACK the electricity breaks the atoms in head. Huge rearrangement like a shake of a b-b-b-bag of b-b-balls. The frogs inside head turn blue – yellow – tongues dart from eyes – some burst into flames.

Hides from eye farther away. Soul takes shape of an eel – slimy soul slithers to hide in spine. Only exists in the hollows of own bones but the mad doctor has Balor's Eye – must know this because doctor wants to get to that place. Bone hiding soul is spied. Gottya.

CRACK. They break the back.

Maeve

Meeting the Grass Man

I was delivering the laundry to the hospital part where the very sick were. I saw a man in a cast on one of the beds. He was tall and his feet stuck out of the sheets pointing away from each other. I saw his face. It was he. My brother.

I walked to the bed and he looked right at me and smiled.

'Padraig,' I whispered. 'Is it you?'

A nurse came right up beside me.

'Teresa what do you want? Have you got the fresh sheets?'

'Nurse, this is my brother.'

'This one? The Grass Man?'

Another nurse was beside her. She might have relented just for a moment but when there were two of them I had no chance.

'What happened to him?' I asked.

'He broke his back during shock treatment,' she said warily, glancing at the other one.

'He didn't break it, THEY did,' I felt an anger rising in me. A fury. A helplessness. I reached for his hand.

'Let me sit with him.'

'Who is this woman?' the other nurse demanded.

'Teresa Boyle from the laundry.'

'Well this man is Padraig O Conaill. He's no relation.'

'My name is Maeve O Conaill. Teresa Boyle was a name they gave me in Castlepollard mother and baby home.'

Another nurse came up and the three of them led me away. I knew not to fight.

'Padraig, I'll come back to ye. Padraig. I have to speak to him. Padraig, it's Maeve.' They were holding my arms and I shook them off. I went back down the corridor to the laundry.

I could hear them mutter to each other, 'Brazen hussy. Two children she had. She could be in the laundries for that.'

I didn't know what they meant. I was in the laundry.

I had to keep my head. That was all I had in here. I had been a model patient. Though, that could be the very trap I had been ensnared in; a completely sane patient in a mental hospital. I had never shouted, never told my stories, never complained. I was waiting to get out to go home. I asked the doctor how my children were doing, and when could I go and see them. He said they were well taken care of in an industrial school run by wonderful priests. I was desperate to get out to see them. I told no one of my plan. I would go visit them and then take them to England. Not to be fed this slop food, not to be working all day in the hot laundries until the veins popped out on my legs.

No one ever came to see me. I never received a letter. I knew the procedure to be released, and I knew, year by year, it was going to be closed to me. There were four thousand patients living in this big house and only eight were released every month. More were streaming in than ever left. The place was growing bigger and bigger. The new psychiatrist was young and just out of university. He chatted more than the others and I was able to get more information out of him than I had ever had before.

'One percent of the country is incarcerated behind walls of various institutions,' he casually told me.

'You seem proud of that fact,' I said, cautiously.

'I am, Teresa. It's the highest rate in Europe, if not the world. It shows that the independent government is taking care of its people.'

'I'm ready to take care of myself, doctor, I feel I still have something to give on the outside.'

'But Teresa, to get out you have to have your family agree. In this case, it was your brother who agreed to your time of rest here. And in fairness, you were caught trying to drown your children in a lake ...'

'I was distraught! I knew they weren't going to be sent to families. I wanted them to be adopted, at least. They were beautiful children, doctor. If you saw Fionnuala and Conn, they'd break your heart with beauty. Them nuns were telling me they were dirty creatures tarnished with my sin. I walked out of that lake, Father, I mean, doctor. I walked out. I never went through with it. I knew it was a mistake. I was in a terrible state. I'm better now. Rested. One mistake, doctor, that's all.'

'Be that as it may. The procedures are as follows: your brother would have to write to us and request your release. Then we would call you for inspection. If the letter arrives too late for this month you'll be deferred until next month. We have to decide if you are ready to be called up. Then we let your brother know. He has to claim you in writing. The board will then decide if you should stay or leave.'

The release procedure had never been laid out before me like that. I took time to take it in.

'But doctor, my brother never answers my letters. No one does. I write to my sister but she wasn't the one who signed me in and anyway I don't think she's getting my letters.'

'Your brother has requested, from the beginning, that all your letters be forwarded to him and he will distribute them.' The doctor regarded me with something akin to tenderness. 'You've been here a few years now and your behaviour has been exemplary. I see in the notes here that you take your medication and you've undergone insulin treatment.'

I remembered the phrase we used as children all the time. 'That shook you!' It really meant that showed you. But, right then, every tiny part of my insides was shaking. My intestines rattled inside me. I had to empty my bowels.

'Did that work? The insulin treatment?'

'My sister. Doctor. You have to let me get a letter to Mary. She's the only one with a head on her shoulders.'

'Tell me about the insulin treatment, Teresa.'

'I was very sick on it doctor. I don't want it again.' I shifted in my seat. The sudden dawning on me that I was just like the rest of them in here. The poor, the mad, the half mad, the painfully sane whose families had wiped their hands of them. I would rather be like Padraig. At least he had his grass weavings and his place behind the trees. What did I have?

'I need to go, doctor, sorry.' I was always apologizing to him and the nurses. The doctor stood to let me out. I was in a position of trust in that I could walk the corridors without an escort. I ran down the corridor and into a toilet. I sat on the seat and emptied my bowels. My frame trembled, and colour drained from my hands and legs. There had been weeks where every morning they injected me with insulin until I went unconscious. Then, as I woke, tiny stars flashed before my eyes and they made me drink a big mug of thick white sticky substance that one patient said came from pigs. I would retch but force myself to gulp back down whatever I vomited up because a nurse would stand there and make sure that happened. I did whatever I was told because the doctors and the priest had told me that I was lucky I was not in jail for bringing my children to the lake.

I had been a model patient. Doing messages. Helping the nurses. Working so hard in the hot laundries, dreaming of my two beautiful children as I walked among all the waving forest of suits and clothes that swung on the laundry lines. I comforted myself with the idea that they had not been adopted. I had signed nothing. When I was released I would take them over to England where we could live without all the prying eyes of the moral brigade. That was my plan. But my talk with the doctor made me realize why Mary wasn't helping me. I was left in Seamus's hands. I had offered him my services for free on the farm as pretence so he would let me out but now I knew I had no control over anything. Only he did. And the doctors and the board. And the priest who drove me here. And the nuns at the home who beat us and tied us to the beds to punish us in labour because we were wretched.

I had strength until this moment. Now I lay on the floor of the toilet and I whimpered like a desolate child. I tried to clear my head. To plot my escape.

But all I saw, in my addled head, was Padraig, with a broken back lying in the hospital infirmary.

Seamus

Where Comes a Woman, There Follows Trouble

What was it that St Kevin said, and him living the life of contemplation over there in Glendalough? Where comes a cow, there follows a woman; where comes a woman, there follows trouble.

And when a milkmaid came tempting him, didn't he drown her in the lake? No wonder they made him one of Ireland's favourite saints. The man had some sense in him. But, by God I didn't, and I lived to rue it every day. It was always a relief to me when I went into the room after the midwife was finished with Sheila and they'd show me another boy. I'd look first at the thing between his legs and I'd breathe a sigh every time. Women are treacherous beasts when they come in human form.

All these bloody women and their letters. Letters from the nuthouse from Maeve. Crawling to me like the repentant whore, swearing she'd come and help me on the farm now that I'd lost me arm. That she'd live out her days as me faithful servant. Now if you knew Maeve like I knew her then you'd know she'd be lying. She'd no more come and be a servant than she was fit to do her job in the shop in Trim without shaming the lot of us with her whoring. Producing bastards and trying to drown them. She was as mad as Padraig. And then letters from Bridget in America that came every year and then stopped. Just a card from her at Christmas asking us to let her know what became of us all. Sheila, the wife, wanted to keep in with her because she sent money the odd time for the boys. Sheila started to write to her about my arm but I wouldn't give Bridget the satisfaction of knowing something like that. I'd live in fear of her coming over and putting the cat among the pigeons. I didn't want her going to see Mary who thought Maeve was with her in New York. No matter because I'm the one who signed her in. Fr Gilligan assured me that I was the only one who could sign her out. She was better off where she was now. I couldn't have her around me sons. She made her bed now she could lie in it. Plenty of other women might feel like it, but they waited till they were married. And word back was it wasn't even in a bed that she did it, but she was out in the fields like an animal. They always said that it was the yellow praiseach of the fields that brings the Meath women to harm. She'll not come near us.

And Sheila, what could I tell ye? A dumb wife and a blind husband might make their marriage work but what chance had we? I sometimes found myself standing out in the rain in the field with me foot on the shovel and letting the big slimy drops fall into my collar and crawl down my back rather than go take shelter in the house and feel the lash of her tongue.

It was bad enough with a neighbour like Patsey who would live in your ear, but worst of all was the visits from that busybody priest in Kilbride, Fr Lavin. This was not his parish at all. I was never a priest man myself. We were always told to be neither intimate nor distant with the priests. I went to the church on Sundays and minded me own business, but our family was never one to be running after them.

Fr Gilligan took Padraig and Maeve both off my hands. I could respect him. He had a bony face and a bald head and a stern manner.

When he was doing confession sometimes that Fr Lavin came up to help him on busy days. There was always a big queue for Fr Lavin because he was known to be soft, and he'd have a chat. That suited me just grand, I headed straight to Fr Gilligan's booth to get it over and done with. Though he gave an awful lot of penance (whole rosaries sometimes if you caught him in a mood) and Fr Lavin only asked you to say a Hail Mary. What chance does a man like me have to sin anyway? You knew where you are with a priest like Fr Gilligan. His heart was as hard as any stones on these walls. There's no sides to the man. You did what you were told and he'd leave you alone. You stepped out of line and you'd be taken care of.

Fr Lavin on the other hand, was a priest like I'd never seen before. He smiled and waved at everyone and his face beaming like an idiot. He was in the habit of arriving in his fancy car. They said his family had plenty of money. Half the time he had his housekeeper and her friends with him, and they all looked like they're off on picnics and other nonsense. A priest on a picnic! He was asking to look at the fairy fort but I wouldn't show it to him. What would a priest care about fairies? I had enough of them with Mary and Seán always blathering about them and telling stories by the fire. Fr Lavin had soft hands, he'd never done a decent day's work in his life. I hated to take his soft pink hand in mine. I clenched tight now that I had to shake with my left hand.

I made the mistake of letting him know how me missing arm was bothering me. Paining me. I felt like an eejit telling him, but his face lit up and he seemed to know a lot about it and told me, no I wasn't mad at all. I never thought I was mad. I just told him that was all. But it was good to hear that it wasn't a curse. Sheila had me convinced Mary had put a spell on me. Sheila thought Mary was a witch on account of her grey hair and all her talk about the world underneath us. She said Mary could turn into a hare. That was a fact known around these parts. I told Sheila she should spend more time cleaning and cooking for us than listening to women's rubbish and chatter at the wee shop down the road or when they went to get the water from the pump. Didn't they go there and stand for hours filling each other up with notions, and frightening each other, and discussing, when they were only meant to be getting the flour or filling the cans with water?

Fr Lavin wanted to nose around about the family on account of Mary. It seemed simple to me. I wanted Mary to come back and work as only she could. She had kept us going on this farm. Even when she was only eleven, she somehow worked it by herself, and though we were starving half the time it was a miracle she got food on the table to us the other half. We only survived because of Mary. But Mary was stubborn and Fr Lavin said she was happy with the Lyonses and Seán was doing well in school and maybe would come back when he finished his education. Which was a lie too. Why would he come back and work for me for nothing?

Everyone was trying to trick me. I lashed out at the arm even though it wasn't there. The nails dug into me palms and I rolled around the bed. When it wasn't paining, it was itching like bejaysus. The itch was almost worse. Be gobs, I'd be out in the field doubled over trying to control an itch that wasn't there. Something that didn't exist but that was worse than anything that did. There were times I was so desperate that I sat on the fairy fort and begged them to stop their playing. The doctors took me back into the hospital and said it might be the nerve endings in me stump and they operated again to take the end of the stump off. So that worked for a month or two. And I was relieved it was all over when it started again. The feeling of me nails in me palms. The terrible itch. And the doctors took the rest of the stump off but they were just chasing the phantom into me head, for always after each operation the pain and the itch would return. I would reach for a shovel with the missing arm. I would try to turn out the light. Sheila nagged and nagged to get the electricity hooked up because it was coming out our way, but I put me foot down and said it was all a waste of money and we wouldn't be paying the government for light. The feckin woman wanted to put a toilet inside the house too.

'It's far from that ye were raised,' I told her. She hated me I know it, but she was me wife and she did as she was told.

Then Fr Gilligan came to me. Cycling on his black bicycle and not in a fancy car, I might add. He told me Padraig had broken his back in the loony bin. But what could I do?

'Do you want me to visit him?' he asked. 'Do you want me to bring you to visit?'

'Arra, I've enough going on. I'll go see him someday but not now.'

'Fr Lavin is taking Mary to see him,' Fr Gilligan said.

'He's not like a priest at all, that fellah. No disrespect now.'

Fr Gilligan gave a rare snigger. 'Oh these young priests. They're full of notions. There's even talk of the Mass not being said in Latin. And that the priest would turn and face the congregation.'

I was gobsmacked. 'Surely that won't happen father. That will never change.'

'I hope not, Seamus. For all our souls. Sure that would be the beginning of the end. I hope not.'

'We might as well be black Protestants if that happens.'

Mary

We Learnt Their Tongue and Not They Ours (1953)

Fr Lavin heard from Fr Gilligan that Padraig had broken his back in the big house. Now usually it was custom not to talk about those who had to go to asylums. Many's the person that just disappeared from our conversation. But I never would have a brother or sister forgotten, so I had always been straight about where my brother was with anyone I met. Fr Lavin offered to take me to visit him. Sure wasn't I that stunned and overjoyed, didn't I say yes?

It was an icy morning. I walked gingerly on the slippery roads. The frozen muddy puddles reflected the white sky. I wore a headscarf and had my coat buckled and buttoned and my silver mints in my bag for Padraig. To my surprise, Elizabeth Quinn, the priest's housekeeper opened the door with her coat and hat on. Though she was tall she always wore high heels. I stood inside the hall and she put on a bit of lipstick in the mirror, wordlessly she offered me some but I shook my head. Sheila, Seamus's wife, was the first woman

I ever saw close up with make-up. I thought it made women look like dolls. Patricia wore a little powder and I copied her, and that was all I'd have in my bag by way of make-up.

'Are you off somewhere, Elizabeth?'

'Oh yes. I thought I'd come along for the ride.' She smiled. 'If himself is not here there's nothing to do.'

I shuddered at her casual way of referring to the priest and looked around the hall. I could see plenty to do but I said nothing because I was delighted I wouldn't have to drive the long way into the middle of the country with only Fr Lavin. Though he was a chatty man he was still a priest and I could never think of what to say to him.

Fr Lavin breezed into the hall, in that friendly smiling way of his, and put his hands to his forehead in mock shock.

'What have I done? How will the Lyonses make it through today?'

'Father, I've left a pot of stew and a pot of soup on the range. I made them bread for the day and wrapped it in tea towels on the range too. All their clothes are ironed and laid out, Father.' I had wondered the exact same.

He shook his head and grabbed the car keys from a pile of papers and envelopes on the dusty hall table.

'Even so, they'll never forgive me. Come on and we'll have you home before it all falls apart.'

On the way down they made me tell stories to pass the time. Elizabeth sang some songs and Fr Lavin joined in with her. We had a merry time, but what was weighing on me was that I would soon see Padraig. He was just a boy when he was taken away. Would he even recognize me?

We were led through the hospital and Fr Lavin took my arm. Since we arrived with a priest we were treated like nobility and I was glad of it. It was a queer lovely world the priests lived in. The hospital was a bustling place, with patients walking through the grounds and nurses hurrying down corridors. It was clean but very cold. Or was it I that was cold? Elizabeth was complaining it was too warm.

There was a hospital for the bodily sick and in the men's wards there were six beds, all full. Padraig was by the window and he was in a big body cast. His eyes were closed and the nurse indicated that he was on heavy sedation to keep him quiet. All the patients were the same, and very quiet as a result. We felt the need to whisper. I took a sharp intake of breath when I saw him, recoiled a bit. Fr Lavin and Elizabeth held onto me and propelled me forward to him. I stroked his forehead. I would not have recognized this man.

Yet I would have known him anywhere. He was so like the men from back home. Those tall dark men, with deep blue eyes, and gentle natures that didn't match their fierce looks. My Padraig was very beautiful, with a thick head of dark hair, and a fine, sculpted face and firm jaw. He hated to be touched before but now he opened his eyes and looked right at me. But he did not smile. Instead big tears flowed down his face and down mine and we just looked at each other. For the first time since he was twenty months old Padraig allowed me to hold him. Musha, he could not wriggle away from me, for his back was broken and he was frozen in plaster of Paris.

Elizabeth looked at Fr Lavin. 'I didn't expect him to be so young and handsome. How old is he?'

Fr Lavin shrugged.

'Has it been five years? He's a year older than Seán,' I said. 'He must be twenty.'

I began to speak in Irish to him and his big eyes softened. For he would have never heard a word of English until he had been brought here. English must be the language of devils and doctors for him.

I whispered stuff in his ear. The old stuff he loved about the beginnings of the Earth, and Balor of the Evil Eye fighting with the De Danaan and great battle stuff and lovely poetry. I told him that I had another family to raise and once I had that done I would come back for him. I would not let him die here. I would have a field with a biteen of woods at the bottom and he could stay there. I would build him a shelter under the trees and he'd never have to come inside again. I would tell him stories out there under the trees and I would give him a knife to start his carving again.

> *Balor was to be killed by his grandson so he locked his one child, a daughter, Ethlinn, in a tower made of crystal to keep her from becoming pregnant. However, Cian, with the help of the druidess Birog, managed to enter the tower dressed as a woman. They spent the night in each other's embrace before Birog took Cian back to his land. Ethlinn gave birth to triplets by him, but Balor threw them into the ocean. The druidess followed them to the sea and managed to save one whom she called Lugh, and gave him to Mananuan Mac Lir, the god of the sea, who became his foster father.*

Padraig was listening, I could tell, and he always loved those particular stories. Those ones about the very beginning. He would creep in the door of the house, and sit a little apart from us all, but just where the warmth of the fire could reach him. We knew not to crowd him and we would all shift a little to make room and give him his space. We were all only children in that wee house. Children of a defeated people who had been summoned back to reconquer stolen lands in a newly independent country, but little job we made of it, instead we became their servants. We learnt their tongue and not they ours. Children, hiding from the Cruelty Men, trying to avoid being scattered to the wind like a dog's litter.

'That's enough now, Mary,' Fr Lavin finally said, gently, as the nurse gave him a nod. 'We don't want to tire him.'

I whispered quickly to Padraig, 'My Seán is be the only one of us who will not be a servant. That was why I could walk away from the farm and give my life to strangers. For Seán. They had chosen him as the brightest in the class. They had come around and asked who wanted to be a priest and Seán had put his hand up when he was only nine. He had got the scholarship on account of that. I paid the rest for him. Whenever things are bad think about Seán. Oh and Maeve is off with Bridget in America.'

As soon as I told him that his head began to swivel and his eyes grew large. He began shaking his whole body. The nurses leapt forward and ushered us out.

I stood in the corridor of the hospital after I left the ward and I thought, either I go mad myself now or I pick up and walk away and resume my life and caring for the Lyonses who need me. Elizabeth saw a look in my eye, but Fr Lavin took her firmly by the arm and led her away.

'Give her a minute,' he said.

One nurse came up to me and asked, 'Do you have a sister by the name of Teresa?'

'I don't. Why?'

'Oh just that another patient thought Padraig was her brother, but then people here have all sorts of notions in a place like this, sure otherwise why would they be here?'

I stood for a few moments. In the distant rooms I could hear screaming, and then quietness. A dread came crawling over me. I had always felt this dread in me. The pressure to survive. But now, as I had seen what they done to my Padraig, I could have ignored the dread, and gone mad myself. But I made my choice to not go mad, to go on being me, and walked on towards the kind priest and his untamed housekeeper.

They let me ask some questions when we were signing out, and they answered them on account of me having a priest with me. It was Seamus who had signed him in so it must be Seamus who would have to request in writing to get him out. But I had nowhere to bring him to and Seamus wouldn't have him home with Sheila and his brood of boys, so I suppose he must have been in good hands. I had asked were the treatments working. They said they were, but they had stopped the ECT since he had broken his back. They would resume it once he was healed. Fr Lavin said this would be best as the doctors were highly trained and qualified to deal with patients like Padraig. I knew in my heart that he would never be released. What would my mother have thought of me for letting all this happen?

Padraig was harmless on the farm, I told them. He wasn't right in the head but he never hurt anyone. They agreed that he had never hurt anyone while in the asylum and I was glad to hear this.

As we crunched down the icy gravel drive to Fr Lavin's car I thought I heard my name being called. I turned and looked back but saw nothing except that terrible, big, stark house in winter, and kept walking.

We stopped in a hotel along the way. As I drank my brandy, they got me another one at the bar, and I drank that one too. It was more than I was used to, so I felt queer wobbly in my legs and had to go to the toilet and be sick. I washed my mouth out and ate one of the silver mints that I had brought for Padraig and forgotten to give to him. Elizabeth and Fr Lavin had a third drink and I had a water. Elizabeth asked me how old I was.

'I'm around twenty-seven or eight. I forget. I don't know when my birthday is.'

'We're the same age!' She didn't even try to hide her shock. Fr Lavin smiled at us both.

'Maybe we should make up a birthday for you. Or we could go and find your birth cert.'

'I burnt it, Father,' I said wearily. My Baby would be missing me and asking for me. Who would she sleep with?

'Why, you strange old thing?' Elizabeth giggled.

'She's as old as you are, remember?' Fr Lavin said, speaking quietly into his glass.

'Only in years. Mary is one of the ancients, don't you know that?' Elizabeth said. 'She has one of the old minds.'

'What are the old minds?' Fr Lavin was amused.

'Everything is sacred to her.' Elizabeth shrugged.

'I had to burn my birth certificate. When we came from Kerry my mother stayed behind to have her child. She never came to us, so my father went back home after a year to get her. He never came back. I was around twelve. If they knew that, the neighbours would have sent the Cruelty Men around to get us all. That's what Patsey said.'

'But maybe it would have been better. They'd have looked after you,' Fr Lavin said.

'Patsey said that we'd be put into them industrial schools for orphans. There would have been plenty who would have taken our land. There weren't many from Kerry where we were resettled. Most were from Connemara and we weren't close to any other family.'

'They're not just for orphans, them places.' Elizabeth was agitated.

'I see the wee boys and girls from the schools marched down the road in rank and file,' I said. 'Like a little ragged army. Poor things.'

'At least they are being looked after,' Fr Lavin said. 'Years ago they'd have been on the streets.'

'We wanted to stay together. Patsey said we should hold onto our land and he was right. Seamus would have lost the farm.'

'So you burnt your birth cert in case they found out you were only twelve?' Elizabeth said.

'I did.'

'Patsey was right, I suppose.' Elizabeth drained her drink. She looked over her shoulder at the bar as a signal to get more, but I stood up to show them I wanted to get home.

'Sometimes I see their feet and they're all bleeding,' I said. 'And they look starved and tiny and you can see bruises all over their legs.'

'If it wasn't for the church,' Fr Lavin explained, 'those orphans would be dead or in gangs, like in Charles Dickens' time. The church is doing the best for them with the money they have.'

Elizabeth shrugged. 'They could sell some Vatican gold and feed them and put shoes on their feet and stop beating them. I spent time in one of them places. Remember?' Her eyes flashed a challenge at the priest. She turned to me. 'I know I'm not supposed to mention it. Keep it all hidden. Wipe my head clean of it. My dad died and there were thirteen of us. My mother got herself a boyfriend but someone reported it to the priest.'

'Whisht now, Betsy. Mary has her own troubles.'

Elizabeth sat up to her full height. She was almost six foot and taller than the man she worked for. Fr Lavin instinctively looked around, not wanting a scene.

'I've just seen her brother with his back broken in a place like that. I think I can let her know a bit about myself.' She leaned in close to me and I could smell the drink on her. 'Mary, I was ashamed. They drummed it into us that we were the spawn of Satan. We were taken because someone ratted to the priest that my mother had a boyfriend. The priest and the guards sat outside the house one night and saw him go in. When the man came out in the morning they went in, and we were scattered all over the country into orphanages. My mother never could get us back. She left for England and I've never heard from her. Don't even know what happened to my brothers or sisters. I was put into service when I got out at sixteen and it was to a brother of the head nun I was sent. They never paid me. Had me sleep in the shed. Then I went to a family in Dublin who were horrible too. Finally, I came to Fr Lavin for help and he took me in as his housekeeper.' She smiled at the priest. 'Why do you look at me like that? Mary is the soul of discretion. She'd never tell a secret. Have you ever heard her gossip or talk about another person?'

Fr Lavin rolled his eyes at me as if to say he was used to such talk from his housekeeper. I had never imagined to be sitting in the lounge of a hotel with a priest and his housekeeper and they drinking three drinks apiece and talking so loosely, so I said nothing.

'I'm just saying, Mary,' Elizabeth leaned towards me again, and poked my thigh with her finger, 'you were dead right to keep your brothers and sisters out of them schools. I wish someone had done it for me.'

'Now, now,' Fr Lavin said. 'The Sisters of Mercy gave up their lives to look after you when your own couldn't.'

'Mercy? Mercy? My mother could have taken care of us. She wasn't allowed.' Elizabeth looked as if she was going to cry. Her head hung down. She was the only woman I ever knew who wore her hair loose and free like a girl. I held onto my lovely friend's arm on the way out of the hotel. I was small beside her, and she tall and thin and leaning on top of me.

It was a quiet car ride all the way home. Each of us thinking of other things no doubt.

I had a little whistle in my pocket that Padraig had carved when he was a wee gossin. I doubt they let him near knives at the hospital but the doctors told me he wove stuff out of grass and liked to be outside for the most part, no matter the weather. I wasn't surprised. I had meant to give him the wee bird whistle but had forgotten that along with the silver mints. Now I kept my hand in my pocket and clutched it, as the maze of icy Midlands roads, with their high hedges cutting out the sky, twisted and turned pulling us three confused souls on into the holy empty centre of the night.

Maeve

I Had Two Beautiful Children

I had two beautiful children. The two red curly heads on them like their father. They came from me just as they were put into me, under the stars on the soft grass. At that moment I might have loved their father. At that moment I hope he loved me.

I was taller than most of the nurses but I was thinner than them too. I was always cold there, that is why I didn't mind the work in the laundry – it kept me warm at least. I hadn't the patience or the skill for sewing or other work. I huddled in my bed, and sometimes I was so cold that my dreams were all hunts for blankets that wouldn't cover and fires that wouldn't light. Funny, I only spoke English but my dreams were still in Irish.

I was killed trying to remain myself. To find beauty in this strangled world. The grey shadow of a bare branch twisting up a wall. I had trained myself to smile at everyone from the moment I entered the big house. I smiled and I didn't talk much. I did secret investigations to find out what the nurses' and doctors' interests were. When I found myself alone with them I brought up the subject of what they cared about. Then they brightened up and did all the talking, I nodded. They told me I was intelligent and a good conversationalist, without me ever having to reveal anything of myself. Nothing is as interesting to someone as themselves. Nurses and doctors began to seek me out to chat about their hobbies. One doctor loved hunting and I only had to ask him an innocent question about pheasant season and he thought I was a genius for having listened to him. Another nurse fancied herself a great dancer and loved music. I asked her to show me some steps for the dance, and there she was coming to me on every shift and twisting and twirling in front of me with great authority, but no rhythm.

The food was so terrible, mostly just stale bread and cabbage, and occasionally boiled meat and cold, runny shepherd's pie. Boiled cabbage, boiled beef, some days boiled mutton, boiled whiting fish on Friday. The water they boil the carcasses in became the soup. They served us stewed tea with the meal. I worked for ten hours a day in the laundry. It was not just the hospital laundry we had to do, which was huge in itself, but we took in laundry from the outside. We did hotels, uniforms, gowns and suits. The work was strenuous and the machinery heavy. I felt faint with hunger much of the time and my hip bones stuck through my skin. Blue and red rivers of veins popped out on my legs. Who would have me? I who was once the beauty of Trim. Or maybe I just thought I was. God, how I loved the attention of all the men coming into the shop to eye me up. No matter how ugly and smelly and rough they were, I loved how they looked at me.

Sometimes in the bed in the morning I put the soles of my feet together and let my legs hang to the sides. Just to open up again. I did it under the covers for if I was seen it would be reported.

I never hurt my children. I only brought them to the lake. I was so sad those days. I was still sad, but I could cope. They came in my dreams, sometimes as children, and sometimes as swans. They spoke to me in Irish. Every day, working in the steam and the noise, I rehearsed the moment when I would see them again. I would get out of here soon enough, for I had committed no crime. I was not mad.

I would go to the nuns and inquire as to where they were sent. I would go to the orphanage and take them both away. Of course they wouldn't know who I was at first but I'd take them to a hotel and buy them afternoon tea. The kind of cakes and buns they wouldn't have seen in an orphanage. I'd bring them to Mary and show her her beautiful niece and nephew. She'd know what to do then. She'd help me get the money to go to England with them. No one in England would care that I hadn't a husband and no one would know I'd spent time in an asylum. I'd work as a maid for some nice family or in a big hotel, and my children would be sent to a good school and looked after.

Small patterns the ice made on the inside of the window, I scraped it with my nail when I awoke. The frozen pattern looked like tiny leaves. Leaves and feathers were so alike. It was a shape that the world tried to fall into. Trees grew into it, birds flew with it, water froze to it. The way our ribs fanned out from our spines, sure we were all only auld feathers and leaves.

On the other side of the hospital my brother lay with a broken back. I knew someone might come to visit him so I kept going to the nurses to tell them that if he had a visitor to let me over to see them. It might be Mary. She would come. When she would see that I was here she would know that it was a mistake and she would get the Lyonses, who were respectable people, to help. A solicitor and a teacher, no less, decent good people. They would get me out of here.

The nurse in the hospital had a thing for St Teresa the Little Flower. She wore her medal around her neck. Every time I came I asked her about the saint. She gave me a book on her. I read it cover to cover and quoted parts of it to her. She thought I was as devoted to this wretched saint as she was. She promised to let me know if Padraig had a visitor.

I brought the laundry to the hospital and I was warned to stay away from Padraig or any male patient. I tried to move up close to him and I knew from his eyes he knew who I was. The nurse was not as amenable as usual.

'Teresa.'

'Sister Patrick.'

'Teresa, there was someone in visiting Mr O Conaill.'

I stopped in my tracks. My heart twisted in my ribs like a fish pulled from water.

'A priest and two women. I asked them about you but they never heard of you.'

'Did you say my name is Maeve O Conaill?'

'No, Teresa O'Boyle.' The other sisters began to snicker. 'I said it was Teresa O'Boyle, so I did.'

'Did the woman have short grey hair and was she kind of stout?' I was trembling, my ribs and spine turned to feathers and leaves.

'Yes. Two very different women. One was very glamorous with high heels and the latest fashions.'

'That might have been the woman she works for. Mary was here. She's my sister.'

'I'm afraid she said she never heard of you.'

The other nurses began to titter.

'My name is Maeve O Conaill. I told you to say that.'

'Now run along, Teresa. Are you sure you want to claim this fellah for your brother? Being related to the Grass Man will not look good on your record if you ever want a release.'

The others burst out into raucous laughter at this.

'Sure would you look at the black head of hair on him and you a blonde!' One nurse said.

'He's my brother. I'm sure the doctors could tell you. We were signed in here by my brother Seamus O Conaill. My name is O Conaill. He's always been like that, Padraig. Since he was about one, we said he was swapped by the fairies.'

They all fell about in stitches of laughter. I knew I shouldn't have said that. I knew that outside our world people took a dim view of spirits and such. I approached Padraig in the bed and went to hold his hand.

'He's a handsome one all right. Maybe you fancy him?' One of the nurses squealed and they all laughed until the tears were rolling down their face. Sister Patrick came over and took me away from the bed. Padraig was looking right at me and I at him.

'*Slán*,' I said. '*Slán, mo mhuirnín.*'

It was around that time I began to get terrible headaches. My head would fill with ice and swell and push my skull out as if it was about to crack open. Darkness would frame my vision and grow into the centre. I was being buried alive. I told the doctor. They continued with my usual treatment, salts in the morning, sedatives during the day and liquid paraffin at night.

I slept in a ward. One night I was lying in my bed I heard them lock both doors into the wards. There were four beds in the middle dormitory laid out with no one in them. The nurse came and whispered that I was to move into one of those. I was terrified for I knew what that meant. She went and got the other patients and we all shuffled towards the middle dormitory. They put screens around the bed. The beds were tidily made and I lay down. A nurse bustled in with a basin and swabs, saline and other medical stuff. Seven nurses stood around me and finally the doctor swept in with a black box held by the handle. They had a gramophone and turned on music quite loud. It was John McCormack singing 'Danny Boy'.

'Teresa,' the doctor said gently. 'You are to be the first tonight.'

I went to sit up but the nurses all gathered round and held me. There was no point in fighting. I began to think of my children. And how I would see them so soon. I felt them put saline on my temples, and strap the contraption around my head and buckle the front. The doctor put some machine on himself. As if our brains were connected. I began to scream and he fiddled with all the buttons. I was knocked out with the shock.

I woke up with the screens removed and all the other three patients in the beds lying unconscious. The doctor was nowhere in sight.

There was a bowl of porridge in front of me and I went to pick up the spoon but it dropped to the floor. I wasn't hungry. A nurse tried to feed me.

'So how are things out there on the Colony?' Did she just say that? Or was I thinking that.

My mouth opened but words were lost inside my head. I could think but not in words, so I couldn't speak. The woman was staring at me. I felt a love for her that came from nowhere.

Suddenly, I realized that all my fraternizing with the staff and doctors had not got me anywhere. I had distanced myself from every other wretch in here. I had convinced myself that they were all mad and I was the only one wrongly incarcerated and forgotten. My plan had been clear, I would prove my sanity and they would have to force my brother to request a release and let me go. But a patient had told me once that the state paid for me to be here. I worked hard in the laundry for free. So why would they let me go? I had ignored her, thinking her cruel and spiteful. I lay back on the bed as sorrowful as the last wave that would ever hit the shore.

The ECT had shifted my thinking. My brain had got a good rattle and now I dragged myself over to my neighbour's bed and I put out my hand to her. She was a little afraid but she was groggy. She took my hand and we sat side by side not looking at each other. It was the first time I'd ever touched a fellow patient in my two years there.

The nurse stopped in her tracks when she saw us, at first she looked bewildered and then she smiled knowingly, 'Don't ye two make a fine couple.'

I was to have six weeks of therapy. They came for me every night except Sunday. I found it very hard to work in the laundry during the treatment so they put me in the sewing rooms, where I sat by the window mending strangers' clothes. Really they let me sit with some cloth and needle in my hand, as I couldn't focus on any task. My headaches did not go away, but I never talked to the nurses or doctors again. My long blonde hair started to go grey and I stopped brushing it and let it tangle around my head and hang loose like the hag. The nurses were delighted. They were always jealous of me and they preferred me looking like the wreck of the

Hesperus. I spent time kneeling by the window and praying and they thought the electricity in my head helped me get closer to God. But it's not their god I could pray to. I closed my eyes and prayed to the hag.

Hag

I Send Her Leaves and Feathers

I send her leaves and feathers. I put them on the window in ice, they look like swan feathers. These gifts are to remind her that the perfection of the world is in its tiny details. Sure they are cold gifts but that's all I can give. *Is fuar cumann cailleach*.

My arms reach out from my cave at Bolus Head. I spent a while watching the monks watching the sea from Skellig Island. I snickered as they abandoned the island and came ashore with their toes frozen after only a few centuries. Couldn't hack it, could ye?

She is young and broken and I let her crawl into my hands and I cup her in my craggy palm, and her heart beats back to me in code. She is cold and growing colder. She can't get warm this little one. She grieves for her children, but they are alive. She wants them but they have forgotten her. They have forgotten they were ever loved.

Mary

Face the Sun but Turn Your Back on the Storm

Seán was in my kitchen. He had grown to be a slender tall man. His hair was bright blond like Maeve's was. Though he was training to be a Christian Brother, they were sending him to the university in Dublin to study mathematics. He wanted to be a mathematics teacher. He didn't go into the living room with the family but preferred to stay by my side. Really I would have loved him to be a priest like Fr Lavin and have his own house and motorcar. I thought I might be his housekeeper one day when the Lyons children were grown. As a Brother he wouldn't have his own housekeeper. He'd live in a house with all the other Brothers, which seemed a bit like a nun or a monk. But I knew better than to say anything to him. He told me he preferred numbers to people and had made up his mind. I was so proud a brother of mine was going to university in the city. Mammy and Daddy would know that I took good care. I got one thing right.

Tonight was Tuesday, there was a poker game on in the living room and we were expecting the usual crowd. It was nice to have such fine people in the other room eating my scones and rhubarb tarts. Mr O'Donnell, the bank manager and his wife Maura. Fr Lavin and the local solicitor, James Duggan. If you had told me, as we grew up so wild on the edges of the world, that I'd have been around such people from Trim town I'd have never believed it. They were all polite gentle people and sometimes when the whiskey was flowing they broke into song. I opened the door a biteen, and heard Mr Duggan sing a lovely version of 'She Moved Through the Fair'. He had a big voice like an opera singer and I'd never heard it sung with such vigour.

Who came whistling into my kitchen but Fr Lavin's housekeeper Elizabeth Quinn? Elizabeth had a funny habit of whistling when she walked. Now I understood why she didn't behave like other women I had met. She was brought up in an orphanage. Seán got off the chair by the stove and she sprawled into it. Her long arms stretched halfway across my kitchen. I made her tea and she looked at me and smiled.

'Are you happy, Mary?'

Seán looked at her sharply and moved towards me. I didn't know how to answer a question like that. I'd never heard anyone in my life ask another soul if they were happy or not.

'I keep thinking of your poor brother Padraig and his broken back. It was nice to hear the Irish again. I wish I could speak it. What was the story you told him? I never met anyone who told stories before. Someone should write down all your stories before we lose them all.' She looked at Seán as if to draw him in. I hadn't introduced him to her.

'Elizabeth is Fr Lavin's housekeeper. This is my brother Seán.' They shook hands. 'He's to be a priest.'

Elizabeth curled up her nose. 'What do you want to do that for? How old are you?'

'I'm nineteen,' Seán said quietly.

'You look about fourteen,' Elizabeth giggled. 'Not enough of Mary's food went into you.'

'Oh I fed him plenty. And he's very tall. If he's too thin it's because of the Brothers not feeding him. He's in university studying mathematics now.' God love him he was almost by my side now. I could see how this woman, with her face painted and her hair flowing down her back, was scaring him. He was taller than her though, and most men around these parts weren't.

I gave her a cup of tea and a mince pie and cream. She wolfed it down. Seán looked awkward, as if he was about to cry.

'Did you visit Padraig?' he asked me quietly.

'I did.'

'I didn't know his back was broken.'

'You have enough to contend with. No need for you to go near the place. He's getting all the modern medicines. New stuff from America. The doctors were giving him the new treatments. The electricity. Sure everybody loves the electricity now. Though I won't have it in my kitchen.'

Elizabeth looked at a space between us. 'What was wrong with Padraig? Was he ever violent?'

'No,' Seán and I said together. It wasn't right to be discussing family business like this. I wasn't even going to worry Seán with the story about our visit.

'He was just innocent in the mind, that's all. He was fine until about his second Christmas.' I walked into the scullery to start a bit of washing up and I heard Elizabeth try to talk to Seán, but the poor boy wasn't able to talk to a woman. He had known no life outside boarding school with the Christian Brothers and our farm, and the university would have no women in it either. Mr Duggan was singing 'Danny Boy' in his lovely loud voice and Elizabeth threw her eyes up to Heaven.

'God, that auld eejit murders those songs, doesn't he?' she said. Seán smiled.

'Oh I don't know, I think he has a grand strong voice,' I said. My black cat came to the window and I put out a saucer of cream for her.

Elizabeth got up. 'I've never heard you say a bad word about anybody, Mary. I suppose that's to your credit. But it makes for long evenings.' She looked at Seán. 'You don't seem like a priest. Would you not think of going to America or somewhere? Even for a few years. When did you want to be a priest?'

'She's the priest's housekeeper,' I reminded him quickly.

'It can be lonely life,' she sighed.

'For you or for him?' Seán asked.

'Not when you have God,' I said firmly. The idea of Seán in a place as big as America was such a notion.

Maura and Patricia came into my kitchen and I gave them tea and fried up some bread and rashers on a pan. They sat at the table and Seán was motionless on a chair. Baby heard all the commotion and came down to see what the craic was. She sat on his knee and he clung onto her as a shield. I almost whisked Seán out of there, but the night was too cold and there was no one but Eileen sleeping in the upstairs house. Elizabeth whistled a little tune.

'Do you remember they used to say?' Maura smiled. '"There are three things that Christ never intended: a woman whistling, a hound howling and a hen crowing."'

Elizabeth stopped whistling, she didn't look offended. 'All those things came in threes. I bet Mary knows them all, don't you, Mary? I was telling her brother here to write them down for her before they're all lost.'

'Sure I'm not going anywhere. He's more to be doing than that. It's only a lot of awld rawmeash I know.' I said, pouring the tea through the strainer.

Maura leaned into Seán. 'I heard you're training to be a priest. It's a great honor for your parents. They were Irish speakers weren't they? Given land by the commission?'

Seán nodded and looked at me for protection. Baby was holding up his hand and measuring hers against it.

'The silent are often guilty.' Elizabeth had mischief in her voice. She took her tea black, without any milk. I could see that Maura, the bank manager's wife, didn't know where to place her. Was she a housekeeper like myself or was she something else? I could swear there was a bit of the gypsy in her, but if she was raised by the good nuns in the orphanage they should have been more adept at smoothing out the creases.

'A silent mouth never did any harm.' Patricia smiled at Seán. There was a time before he went off to the Brothers that Seán would follow me around the farm talking all day, his chattering as sweet and constant as the birds. But he had grown morose over time. On the rare occasions that he was let out I would have liked to take him in my arms like I did when he was a wee child, but now he was a man, and a Brother in training.

'I'm not to be a priest,' Seán blurted. We all looked in shock.

'The Brothers are a congregation rather than an order.'

'What's the difference?' Baby asked.

'We take simple vows, not solemn ones. The orders are for the well-to-do children.'

We sat in stilted silence. I felt a biteen ashamed of him.

'Elizabeth is Fr Lavin's housekeeper,' Patricia said to Maura.

'Ah! Fr Lavin is a great man,' Maura said respectfully.

'Oh isn't he just,' Elizabeth snapped. 'Sure I'd no idea about sin until I came to him.'

Patricia glanced at me; she would never talk behind a person's back but I could see that Elizabeth made her extremely uncomfortable. Elizabeth had become my friend, as she dropped into my kitchen almost daily, if only to take food home to her priest who might have starved if it wasn't for me. I felt it an honour to feed a priest. Priests were the chosen representatives of God on this Earth. I never imagined that it would be something I'd get the privilege to do. Fr Lavin never failed to compliment the food I sent off with Elizabeth. She herself seemed to have a good appetite too. The Lyonses never complained that I was feeding another household, as Patricia fed half the children in the school with my scones and sandwiches. They were decent to the core.

'I'm not cut out for it,' Elizabeth sighed. 'He's gone all the time visiting the sick and dying. Even when he's there, there's a constant stream of people all knocking wanting something, or he's over here playing cards or off to the races with Mr Lyons. I hate cleaning and I can't cook. I was raised in an orphanage. All the food was slop when they weren't starving you. But I was never alone. I used to long to be alone. Now I am all the time. If it wasn't for Mary here no one would talk to me in the whole town.'

We were all silent. I had never heard anyone admit they were raised in an orphanage. Elizabeth was half wild. She was so tall. She stood and stretched, and started loping into the next room where the men were. 'Let's have a whiskey. I drink enough of tea all day long.'

There was a soft wheezing outside and at the sound of footsteps everyone looked up expectantly.

'Missis, do you have any Suds and Sins?' rasped a voice.

I went outside and gave him a bunch of rasher rinds I'd tied together with string and shooed the poor innocent away.

Elizabeth came back with the whiskey from the living room. Patricia and Maura looked to me.

'Fr Lavin is such a pet,' Maura said.

'Sit down now,' I scolded Elizabeth. 'You're like a hen on a hot griddle.' I got glasses for us all. 'I'll get you a wee sup in a minute. Do you know what they say the three worst pets are?'

'No.' Elizabeth flopped into the chair. She didn't cross her legs like other women do but planted them firmly on the ground and took one ankle up to her leg like a man.

'A pet priest, a pet beggar and a pet pig,' I said.

Everyone laughed, but Seán went bright red. Elizabeth lit a cigarette by opening the stove door and putting her hand into the fire. I threw some turf on it while it was open. She inhaled deeply and said to Seán, who sat in the corner a little apart from us all,

'Don't you just want to run like the hammers of hell and get out of this country?'

He shook his head. 'I'll stay near Mary,' he said softly and Patricia smiled affectionately at him. 'I wish my sons were so devoted. They need some manners, those lads. They're as mad as March hares.'

Seán's face relaxed. He'd have never sat among the company of men like this. He seemed so fragile and sheltered, it was hard to believe he was nineteen. Though he was tall, he was still slight for his age, his fair hair cut short. He had fine bones like Maeve and the two looked so alike.

'Maybe Elizabeth is right, Seán,' I said suddenly. 'Maybe you should try America and go to your sisters out there. Sure aren't you the image of them?'

'Where are your sisters, Mary?' Maura asked with interest.

'America, Bridget went over there and Maeve joined her.'

'What city?'

'I don't know. There's probably a few cities over there. Trim is the biggest town I've ever been in. I'd ask my brother but ...'

'Yes, Seán.' Elizabeth's eyes flashed. 'Why don't you find out for Mary where her sisters are?'

'Seamus's not talking to me either,' Seán said. 'I wanted to go home and help him out but Mary said ...'

'I'll get Fr Lavin to go ask Fr Gilligan where they are so you can write.' Elizabeth helped herself to another glass of whiskey. 'Even your brother would have to tell his priest.'

'Mary,' Patricia said sharply. 'Sure tell us a story.'

'Oh yes,' Maura said. 'I've heard you're a great one for the stories.'

'Arra, I'll tell you one if you've one for me,' I said. 'I need a few new ones. These old ones are turning to rust in my head from want of telling them. Now the kids are getting older they just hare off when I start.'

'No I don't,' Baby protested.

I opened my arms and she came running. I took my place by the fire, with Baby on my knee, and closed my eyes to see which story would come to me first. A small one I thought. Because the men would be back soon.

'Did ye ever hear tell of the fairy cows that do be coming from the sea sometimes?'

'I've never seen the sea,' Baby said.

'We grew up by the brink of the sea. The wild Atlantic, but I haven't seen it since and begod I miss it,' I said.

'Go on.' Patricia topped up all the whiskeys.

Padraig

Crom Cruach in the Form of a Priest

'I hear your back is broken, you poor craytur,' he said.

Slaughter head. Crom Cruach. Bloody crooked one. To you, on the plain of prostration, one third of the children of Ireland sacrificed. So more milk from the cows, more wheat for the bread, more fat pigs to muscle strip for breakfast, blood congealed throat slide?

No, more than that.

Dangerous the night he came to bedside, not Balor, the doctors were Balor. Crom Cruach, the priest. Could not crawl away – again – again he came. A man in black like a neat jackdaw came hopping – again – again. Crom Cruach gave the last rites, in a white collar. Pulled the curtain around the bed with a metal screech.

Father Crom Cruach, worshippers perish in the act of worship. One third of the children for what? Bloody head.

New Mother said St Patrick fought not only the hag but Crom Cruach as well. But he was only a mortal – a stolen child – a slave among pigs – foreign born – a measly peasly. The hag outlived on in her cave. Crom Cruach would sneak back in, oozed from under the ground – he was everywhere.

The priest touches. Touch of a priest – consecrated – sacrificed.

Tomb cast. Frozen. Under the eye. Spread out for the touch. Call to them. Whistle. Hag call. My bog brothers come take home. Underground seeps the dirty water of the land. Freeze in leather. Empty out. Slaughter head. *Nach mé atá tuirseach!* Crom Cruach screech pulled the curtain open then crept away, black shadow softly slimy shame padding through snoring ward. Whistle the needle through worlds' deeper worlds until reaching home. Soon. Soon. Not yet as dead as bog brothers, not yet as dry. Can't move but can still cry.

Mary

The Rubbish of Ireland

Eileen announced at dinner that she would become a nurse and Patricia was silent, and then, as I was serving them the roast, she said. 'Why don't you become a doctor?'

The boys laughed and Mr Lyons looked at his wife in exasperation.

'A doctor?' Eileen was surprised.

'She's a girl,' Joseph scoffed, and took three of the best slices of meat. I took one of them off his plate and gave it to his father.

'There are women who go to university,' Patricia said. Almost sounding unsure herself. 'We could arrange it. You have the brains. It doesn't seem fair.'

'The three most difficult to teach,' I said. 'A mule, a pig and a woman.'

The men all agreed with me on this point.

Patricia slammed her fork down. 'I teach girls everyday, Mary. They are every bit as bright as the boys and exhibit far more in the way of concentration, I'll have you know.'

'Sure,' I said. 'Eileen will be a gentlewoman like yourself. She won't need to work.'

'I work,' Patricia said. 'Teaching is work. I love my work. I want both my daughters to work.'

'Why do they even send girls to school?' James asked. 'They don't do anything with it, it's not worth a cuckoo's spit.'

'James!' Mr Lyons said.

'Surely you see your mother working, James.' Patricia was red in the face. We were all quiet as it was unlike her to get flustered over anything.

'I couldn't anyway,' Eileen said. 'They don't do honours maths at the convent after third year.'

'Girls aren't good at maths,' Joseph stated. 'Everyone knows that.'

'Well how can they do it if they don't offer it?' Patricia was about to cry. 'You are well able for it.'

'Sure my Seán could teach her maths,' I said off the top of my head. I was so proud of Seán I thought he could do anything for anybody.

So that was how Seán began to come to the house one weekend a month and Eileen came home from boarding school. He taught her honours maths much to Baby's chagrin, for she had thought Seán was hers to drag out over the fields and go find the colonies of fairies. Seán could find the trace of a fairy unlike anyone else.

To comfort Baby, Seán would take her on his knee and show Eileen and herself number tricks. Seán blossomed, his shyness disappeared and he laughed and grew in confidence.

Elizabeth Quinn, the priest's housekeeper, who spent most of her time in my kitchen, teased me that Eileen had taken a shine to him. But then Elizabeth went off inexplicably for a few months and I saw neither sight nor sound of her. When she arrived back she was not herself at all. She always had a wild look in her eye, but now the look was dark and fierce and she wouldn't let on where she had gone. Just that she had been to see a sister of hers who had also been raised in the orphanage. I gave her nettle soup and always made sure to cook extra so she could feed the priest. The school and the church and our house were all very close so it was only a hen's race to her door.

Once I found poor Elizabeth lying in her bedroom in a rumpled heap. There were cigarette butts and ash all over the covers. I went into the kitchen and made her an egg flip by warming up some milk and stirring a raw egg in, then adding sherry. There's not many thing an egg flip can't cure.

'Musha, maybe you need a rest,' I told her as I put the drink up to her lips. 'You're not yourself, at all, at all. Go back to your sister. You're in no fit state to be a housekeeper. Fr Lavin is too decent a skin to move you on.'

'Was I ever a housekeeper?' she would say in a small voice from the bed. Her voice seemed to get smaller and sweeter the sadder she got.

'The night and day are as long as they ever were,' I said to her, as I cleaned her room. I pulled her up in the bed and began to brush her hair as I brushed Baby's every day. But Elizabeth's hair was like a bird's nest. 'So what's got into you?'

'Ah Mary. You've had a hard life too,' she whispered. 'Why are you never down? You're always in the same mood. You're always busy. You do the work of ten people and now you come and do this work too.'

'We all need a reason to go on. That's what you're lacking. I have my Seán to look out for. He needs a lot of keeping up in Dublin, the poor divil. The Brothers are paying for his education but there are always extras. He's a good lad. Doesn't even drink.'

'He's fine now. Soon to be a priest.'

'Oh I'd have liked him to be a priest. But it's a Brother he's to be. I suppose it's the next best thing.'

'He and Eileen seem to have found each other. Maybe he should just be a secondary school teacher.'

'He has a calling. Eileen might have a wee crush, but Seán's not like that.'

'Have you ever been with a man?'

'Hold your whisht.' I blushed. Elizabeth hadn't been raised right, but she still should have learnt how to be around decent people. I finished brushing her hair and she seemed to want to get up. I led her out into the tangle of garden and she sat on the bench.

'It's wild here,' I said.

'Don't go turning it into a feckin farm now, Mary. I like it like this. The garden is just being itself.'

'It's a jungle.'

'Exactly.' She lit a cigarette and pointed to her head. 'If you think that is a mess you should see what it's like in here.'

'Elizabeth, you're a lovely-looking girl. Surely you could find a fellah to take care of you. But even then musha, he'd want you to keep his house. Maybe you're not cut out to keep house. If you'd just do a bit of tidying up, I could teach you cooking. My poor brother married a woman who couldn't kick snow off a rope.'

'Maybe she's like me.'

'I didn't mean that, a stór. Sure you're a lovely girl with a lovely manner.'

'Have you ever thought that maybe she was in one of them schools and was raised not knowing how to keep house? Sure we were just fed slop, cocoa in dirty tepid water, bread and porridge. So many of us had rickets and were small and scrawny and they didn't even teach us anything well. We had to spend every day for hours after school making rosary beads. If we didn't make sixty sets of rosary beads a day we were sent up at night to the corridor for a beating. We sat there in terror, beading class they called it. But it was a big racket for them.'

'Surely the Sisters of Mercy were just trying to teach you an occupation or something.'

'Stringing beads on wire? Did we ever see any money from it? You must be codding me. The nuns would take you into the room and make you strip off and they would be frothing at the mouths like wolves, and beat you naked on the beds. They'd have a look in their eyes I'll never forget. As if they were in ecstasy.'

'That's awful.' I stopped brushing her hair. 'I never heard the like of that.'

'It's just that it's happening to people like me, so no one cares.'

'The orphanages?'

'They're not feckin orphanages, Mary, because the children aren't poxy orphans. But if anyone tells they just say you are a mental case. I wasn't an orphan, they took me from my mother and she loved us but it wasn't the beatings that were the worst. It was what they didn't do.'

I felt awkward but she was gripping my hands and crying and shaking so I hugged her as if she was one of the children.

'Did you tell Fr Lavin all this?'

'But sure he just thinks that the church is doing their best and everything. He's feckin brainwashed, so he is.'

'He is a priest, a stór,' I said. 'He would support the charities.'

'But, Mary, they're not charities. The government is sending money to them for each child. That's why the Cruelty Men are scouring the country. They prey on the poor and get more and more children. And they keep the women having more and more babies in their ignorance. Babies that they can't take care of, and then they feed them into schools that are no more than concentration camps. Sure there are children as slaves all over the land. Do ye know that?'

I sat down. 'Elizabeth. Maybe it was just your orphanage. They can't all be like that. Sure aren't the church doing their best? Otherwise they'd be running around the streets like in the olden days. And prey to all sorts.'

'Right. Instead they're prey for the evil nuns and priests in the schools. And they are evil. Why do they do it? I keep asking myself every day. Why did they do it to me? But no one cares, Mary, even you don't believe me. My sisters and brother, I don't even know what happened to most of them. If I hadn't come to Fr Lavin I would have had nowhere to go. They'll be coming out now, at sixteen years, and I don't know how they can cope because by the time you get out of there you are nothing. You have nothing left. You have nothing inside. And you could take the beatings, the starvation, the forced labour, but you know what you can't take? I keep telling you, the thing that is missing. I'm serious, when I see you take Baby by the hand and tell her your stories and take her on your knee and sing her your songs. And the way you look at your Seán when he comes into the house as if he was the sun itself. No one ever looked at me like that. I went in there at four. What was my crime, Mary? I wasn't a bloody orphan. My mother wanted us. They stole her off us. They were waiting outside in a car to take us. The priest and the guards. You know what they used to say to us all the time? "Ye are the rubbish of Ireland." That's what they said. From when I was four I was never held or hugged or even smiled at again.'

Fr Lavin came round the back and stopped when he saw us. I checked Elizabeth instinctively to make sure I had brought her out decent. The poor craytur wouldn't have paid any heed if she had sat there in her birthday suit. As it was, her nightie had a button opened at the neck. Her shoulder bones were sticking out she had lost so much weight.

'I'll go get your gown,' I said.

'I don't have a dressing gown.' She shook her head.

I tut-tutted despite myself and Fr Lavin smiled weakly at me.

'I was wondering what all the ruckus was. Betsy can get very lively. Thank you for cleaning up in there, Mary. What would we do without you?'

'She's an able lassie is our Mary.' Elizabeth pulled hard on the cigarette. 'She and I should get a wee house together and she'd teach me her spells and we'd be the witches that live at the end of the lane.'

'That's all my eye,' I said. 'She's not herself at all, Father. Maybe we should call Dr Macintyre?'

'Dr Macintyre? He's the two ends of a hoor! I'll not go near him.'

'There's no call for that, Elizabeth.' Fr Lavin was looking visibly distressed and out of his depth. 'Go on now, Mary. I'm sure they'll be waiting for you at home. Did you tell Joseph and James I need them to serve Mass with me for a funeral this afternoon?'

'No bother, Father. Elizabeth has been a good friend to me.'

Elizabeth looked up, surprised.

'I have? What have I done for you? Ever?'

'I suppose you keep her company in the evenings, Betsy,' Fr Lavin said. 'There are other skills to being a woman besides cooking and cleaning. Remember the parable of Mary and Martha?'

'Don't preach,' Elizabeth snapped sourly. Fr Lavin looked at me helplessly. 'She's been feeling out of sorts lately.'

'Since she came back from her sister?'

'Her sister?' Fr Lavin looked puzzled. I figured it really was time to go. Seán would be arriving from Dublin soon and Eileen after him and I without even the fires lit. As I left I said, 'Come see me, Elizabeth. Sure I've missed you terribly. Whatever has made you sad will pass. We're all in God's hands. I'll say a rosary for you tonight, when my work is done.'

'It's too late to be praying for me. I was cast out long ago. I'm the rubbish of Ireland.' Elizabeth was lighting another cigarette off the last one. 'But thanks anyway. Actually do keep me in your prayers. I'd like that.' She waved her empty cup of egg flip towards me.

'Our lives aren't really our own at the end of the day,' I shrugged. 'You know what they say? Face the sun but turn your back on the storm.'

As I closed the gate behind me I glimpsed the two of them sitting silently on the bench, staring into the weeds and bushes and long grasses.

Eileen and Seán were already home. Uncharacteristically, she burst into tears in my kitchen.

'What's the matter?' I asked her, the pot still in my hand.

'The nuns hate my guts for this.'

'For what, Musha?'

'For doing honours maths. I have to sit the exams in the boys' school, and they have to escort me over there. Now one of the other girls in my year wants to do honours maths too. They blame my bad example. Mother James said, "You used to be a good girl." They pick on me all the time. They call me out for everything. I was taken away from the school play, and I had the lead part. Sister Michael bullies me every chance she gets. I can't bear it. Worse! At the boys' school I'm the only girl, so they point and throw bits of sucked-up paper at me. They flick it onto my back all class and when I come out I'm covered in balls of paper stuck to me. All in my hair,' she sobbed. 'And sometimes I have to walk on my own to the boys' schools if that ancient crone Sister Assumption can't come with me. And then it's awful. The boys really jeer at me and the maths teacher encourages it. Brother Thomas, he asks me all the hard questions and I swear he turns red as a beetroot when I can answer them. I know he hates me being there. He puts a face on him as soon as I walk in the door. And the girls make all sorts of jokes when I come back to the convent.'

Seán stood up. 'Then we'll stop.'

She looked bereft. 'It's my favourite subject.'

I saw myself losing Seán on the weekends.

'What would Patricia say?' I said. 'She wants you to do it. Says you are well able for it.'

'Of course she is more than well able for it,' Seán said. 'She's really good. I don't have to teach her. I only show her something once. She could do maths at university.'

'Hear that?' I said triumphantly. 'Don't mind those gobaloons. They're all as thick as a double ditch. It's only jealous they are.'

'But I know what it's like at boarding school if you're singled out,' Seán said to her, not to me. 'I was.'

'Why were you?' Eileen wasn't crying, suddenly she was fascinated.

I was furious at the self-pity of both of them. 'Ye both were lucky to get the chance of further schooling. Seán you were the only one of us who did. And you, miss. You've had the expectation of it all your life. Well the dogs have not eaten up the end of the year yet!' I said and marched off to find Patricia at her roses.

'What does that mean?' I heard Eileen ask Seán.

Patricia was kneeling and pulling weeds. I told her what was happening and she bent her head low and sighed. 'Maybe I was too hasty. What's the use in all this pushing if her life is a misery?'

That night Mr Lyons agreed. 'A young girl like her should be out doing other stuff with her pals. Spending the whole weekend studying maths is not normal.'

And that was that. The end of the idea of Eileen being a doctor. Everyone seemed relieved except myself, I thought it was a crying shame, but sure what could I do?

Padraig

Bloody Slaughter Urges

My brothers.
Sacrificed.
Still waiting.
St Patrick was a foreign slave.
He couldn't know
That the pigs he minded could see the wind,
But Crom Cruach crawled out again
Because it's in the land,
Under the ground.
All the time.
The urge.
Bloody slaughter urges.
Last orders please?
Power – hate – fear – merciless – there was no stopping them.

Mary

The King of Everything

They had set up a big marquee tent, and people from all around arrived on bicycles and pony and traps and motor cars, as well as on their own two feet. There was a charity dance in Dunderry and you can be sure James and Joseph found their way up there even though they were meant to stay at home. The two scuts were lying on their bellies lifting up the flap of the tent to get a look at all the shenanigans of the adults. Men on one side of the hall, and women on the other. Fr Lavin and two other priests organized it to raise money for The Sisters of Mercy Orphanage. They also kept an eye on the proceedings to make sure nothing got out of hand. Elizabeth had begged me to accompany her. Seán was home for the weekend, so I insisted he come along. He wasn't a priest yet. We took the trap and guided the horse with the odd click and whistle. He was too gentle to ever touch a horse with the whip. We were singing all the way to the dance. There was to be a big showband there. Elizabeth looked stunning in a satin turquoise dress and her hair piled on top of her head. It did my heart good to hear her happily whistling away as we arrived in Dunderry village. All the people were dressed to the nines.

Seán and I danced with each other. Otherwise no one asked me to dance and Seán would be mortified to ask anyone. Joseph and James ran about outside with other lads their age. They picked up cigarettes off the ground and smoked them among the cars. Even Suds and Sins had shown up, with his hair greased over his baldy spot, but he didn't dare walk through the door of the tent. There were a few around who were like that, men who hadn't ever fully come into themselves but always lived on the edges and the corners.

Elizabeth had no shortage of admirers. She was soon having tea and custard creams with a young man. Fr Lavin could not take his eyes off of her.

'I'm sure she won't let you down, Father,' I tried to reassure him. 'She knows she has her place as your housekeeper. Without that job sure she'd be lost altogether.'

'You do her job for her, Mary. Don't think I haven't noticed? Do you know who that is?' Fr Lavin said sourly. You'd swear she was his daughter the way he was hovering and guarding her.

'No, Father.'

'He's from outside of Trim. John Greeley.'

'Is he a brother of Rory's?' I gasped.

'He is. And there's Rory over there.' Fr Lavin pointed out a nice-looking young man dancing with a girl. Sure I remembered him well, with his curly red hair. 'She's the pharmacist's daughter in Trim. They're engaged.' I nearly fell out of me standing. 'I shouldn't have told you that Mary, I don't know what I was thinking.'

Someone came over to discuss something with him so I drifted off to watch the dancers.

Mostly, I stood and watched Rory Greeley and his lovely young girl. They were obviously in love. I was glad Maeve was in America. I hoped the child she bore was in a good home somewhere. I couldn't help thinking that the little one, whether boy or girl, was the first of the next generation and would not know, nor would it matter, that she or he was an O Conaill from Bolus Head. We had stopped speaking our language and now we were giving up our children to be raised by strangers. Then I thought there were always Seamus's children but somehow I wasn't feeling them to be the heirs to our story because Seamus was so set on cutting me off.

'What's the matter?' Seán said, as he handed me a biscuit. I shrugged; he knew nothing about any of that mess that Maeve had made for herself. Fr Lavin came back to me.

'Are you all right, Mary?' he said. 'Why don't ye all go home?'

Seán had had enough and readily agreed.

'The boys can walk away without a stain, Father,' I said, staring at Rory.

'That's the truth,' Fr Lavin said. 'But it's up to the women to keep the men good. That's the way nature made us.'

'What I see from nature is that the birds and the bees have no shame, only us, Father.'

'We're not animals, Mary.'

'What are we then? No, the animals don't act out of malice and they know who they are and what they have to do. I do want to leave but Elizabeth looks like she's just getting started.'

Fr Lavin laughed. 'I'll take care of her, don't you worry. Seán, you can take your sister home. He's a fine young man, your brother, Mary.'

'Oh indeed he is.' Fr Lavin knew how to cheer me up and take my mind of things. 'May I never take life too seriously, knowing I'll never get out of it alive.'

Fr Lavin was right to get me out of the dance at Dunderry for I had a good mind to go up to that whelp of a curly-headed boy Rory and ask him did he know where his first born was? Impossible to have done that and I wouldn't have. But I wanted to do something and I'm sure I saw him look over at me. There was many a night I walked from the cinema in Trim with them and then I parted on my bicycle and them into those cursed fields. I should have gone and pulled them apart under the moon. I could have saved Maeve, but not a word I said, for I adored her so much I was hoping she was not going all the way in the yellow grass. None of us had a mother or any guidance in those matters. We knew all about it alright from raring animals but then, as the priest said, we weren't beasts.

Seán went up and whispered to Elizabeth. She implored him to stay but then shrugged, gave me a little insincere wave, and took John Greeley onto the dance floor when the band started a new song. I don't know where she learned to dance like that; it wasn't in the orphanage that was for sure. But she was good. And you'd think at twenty-one years old she'd have more sense. But there was always something of the eternal child about her. It was odd that she was my friend, for I had never been a child.

Seán rounded up a very reluctant Joseph and James and we made our way home. We weren't singing and the boys were sulking.

'Feck it! Why are we leaving so early?'

'Hauld your whisht now. Aren't ye lucky to have been let here at all? Your sister was begging to come but there she is at home with the wireless.'

'She's a girl,' James said. 'That's different.'

'So it is,' I said. 'So it is.'

Seán clicked his tongue and the horse made a turn down the dark roads, the trees moaning softly as we interrupted their sleep.

'Give us something, Mary. Some blessing for the road. What was the one Daddy said on the way from Bolus Head?'

I was in no mood for blessings. I kept thinking about Rory Greeley.

'Go on, Mary. You're in a buck as bad as the boys,' Seán teased me.

'What was it my father said as a blessing?' I took a deep breath.

'Jaysus here we go.' I heard James mutter to Joseph and that just made me more determined that I'd do it for Seán. If it was left to those young pups all the wisdom of old Ireland would be buried with the last of us.

'I call on the seven daughters of the ocean, that one,' Seán said.

I call on the seven daughters of the ocean
Who knit the stitches of the sons of longevity?
May three deaths be taken from me,
Three lifetimes given to me,
Seven waves of good fortune bestowed on me!

'I'm famished with the cold.' James shivered and I put him under a blanket. I stopped as I tucked him in but he peeped out from the blanket and said,

'Is that it?'

'I thought you were sick of all my auld palaver?'

'Well ye might as well finish it,' Joseph said.

I took a deep breath. I don't know where they all were in my head but they came when I didn't think too hard. I just let them come themselves.

May the Spectres not harm me during my journey
Without hindrance, in Laserian's breastplate,
May my name not be promised in vain!
May old age be mine
And death not come to me until I reach it.

'I'm cold!' Joseph muttered, so I put a blanket around him too, tucking him in as much as I could. They were good boys, those fine Lyons sons.

'What did happen to your father?' James asked, muffled from under the blanket.

'He went back to Bolus Head to look for my mother that's all I know. I haven't had sight nor sound of him since. He didn't like this flat land. The mountains were in him and called him back to them. God rest his soul.'

'If he's dead,' Seán said quietly.

'Some say you can take a man from the mountains but you can't take the mountains from a man. And sometimes you can't even take a man from the mountains.'

'Why don't one of ye go back and see what happened?' James said.

'Arra, it's a long way to Bolus Head,' I said.

'Especially if the news is not good,' Seán said.

'Mammy cycles all the way to Mayo every year. If ye'd lay off the spuds you could do the same,' Joseph said and James kicked him from under the blanket. Joseph stared at his little brother in contempt.

'What are you looking at?' James said.

'Not much,' Joseph said.

'Look in the mirror and you'll see less,' James retorted.

'If ye go back ye could find out from someone,' James said. 'I'd have gone back if I were ye.'

'If-if-if. Only for if the sky would fall,' I said.

'Go on, finish the prayer,' Seán said.

Joseph and James looked at me and I closed my eyes to get the rest.

May my tomb not be prepared,
May I not die on my journey,
May my return be granted!
May the headless serpent not catch me,
Nor the green water-beetle
Nor the foolish cockroach!
May no robber harm me,
Nor troop of women,
Nor troop of warriors!
May the King of Everything
Cast more time my way.

'I like that line,' James said. 'The King of Everything.'

'I'M THE KING OF EVERYTHING!' Joseph yelled suddenly at the top of his voice and an owl flew out of a tree in fright so that we ducked in the trap as its wings brushed our heads.

'Look,' James was cheering up. 'The moon has gone behind the hill. It's got so dark now. There's not a stim of light.' He lit a lamp in the trap and his face glowed as he held it up.

Seán began to sing,

When I'm gone, oh! May some tongue,
The minstrel's wish fulfil,
And still remember him who sang
'The Moon Behind the Hill'.

He stopped.

'Go on what's the rest. Can you teach us some?' Joseph said.

'That's all I remember of it, do you know that one, Mary?'

I shook my head.

'How do ye remember them all?' James groaned. 'I have a hard time remembering the stuff for school let alone all the stuff ye have in your head.'

'People around us had huge memories because they had no pen and paper,' I said. 'Ye have your books on the shelves. Ye keep your knowledge outside your heads.'

'We could have come home with Fr Lavin,' Joseph suddenly remembered to be aggrieved.

'Hasn't he enough to be doing?' I asked them.

'He'll have his hands full with Elizabeth, I'll bet.' Seán smiled to himself.

'She looked mighty tonight.' Joseph actually licked his lips.

We all laughed.

'We saw women and men out in the fields,' James blurted out. 'They were on top of each other. Like dogs fighting.'

'Whisht now. There was none of that there. That dance was for decent people,' I said. 'Sure didn't Fr Lavin and the priests organize it and made sure there was no drinking.'

'Right,' Joseph snorted. 'You should have been out with all the cars. There were plenty of people sneaking out for a sup of whiskey. Women and men. Elizabeth was out there with her new man pouring it down her throat.'

I tut-tutted.

'And the young farmers before they went in were rubbing petrol on their collars.'

'Why would they be doing that?' I was baffled.

'To pretend they had a car when they asked the ladies to dance,' Joseph said.

'The ladies would smell it off them and they might have a chance,' James said.

All of our laughter rattled out into the vast night.

'That's some carry on.' The laugh had done me a world of good and I wiped my eyes.

'It's good then we left,' Seán said.

'I hope she behaves herself,' I sighed. 'Poor Fr Lavin has his work cut out for him with that girl. She'd better go home with him otherwise she could step on a stray sod.'

'What's that?' Little James was tired now. The dark night's cold had crept into us all. He cuddled up to me despite him getting to be a big lad.

'Oh have you never heard tell of the stray sod? Many a man's been caught out by that. Sometimes if a man be walking home through the fields and he steps on the stray sod he'll become suddenly lost and disorientated and he will be all spun around and won't know where to go to get home.'

Seán smiled at James who was curled up beside me under the rug.

'There's plenty a fellah tonight coming from that dance that might step on a stray sod,' Seán said.

'I think I've stepped on a few meself.' Joseph laughed.

'Mary, do you think that Elizabeth will make a holy show of the priest do ya?'

'Whisht now, James,' I scolded. 'None of your guff.'

'Mary, what if we see the black pig?' James's eyes grew wide in the lamp light.

'Merciful hour! The world is not going to end tonight,' I told him.

'Say us a prayer.' James pulled closer, spooked by his own mention of it.

'Go on, Seán. You're the one that's doing the training.'

'I still prefer your ones, Mary,' Seán smiled. 'The old ones.'

'Well say one then. I taught them all to you as I teach them to Baby. You two will have to carry on my stories when I'm dead or they'll die with me. But sure maybe that's for the best. The world is changing.'

Seán's head arched back as if looking for the words in the star written sky, '*May Bridget save us and may we live under her cloak and the Holy Spirit protect us from fear, from caves of white death guard us and keep us company*.'

Joseph put his head in his hands. 'I can't believe it's Saturday night and we left the dance just as it was getting started and now we're saying prayers on the way home. Sure I have to serve at half six Mass tomorrow with Fr Lavin.'

'That's true and all, ye poor craytur.' I laughed.

'I don't mind serving for Fr Lavin,' James said. 'Fr Murphy, when he's over, gives you a puck in the gob if you miss ringing the bell at the right part.'

'Fr Lavin said he doesn't mind if they do away with the Latin. He said it would be better for the congregation to understand what he's talking about.'

'They'll never understand what he's talking about,' Seán said softly.

We could see the house up ahead and there was light from the living-room window and smoke still coming out of the chimney. The light went off downstairs, and we knew it was gentle, soft-spoken Mr Lyons not wanting to let on he had been waiting up to make sure we all got back in one piece. Jess the Irish Setter ran out to greet us.

Padraig

Goes to the Centre of the Sun

Whistles heard.
    Brothers are there.
    Bog brothers,
    Tattered bodies
    In bits of themselves
    Undissolved,
    What remains?
    All are tired
    Of waiting
    Without living long enough,
    In the end
    Life will break your heart,
    And your back.
    Your head
    Will old your soul,
    Your soul
    Will slither into your spine

And see with the eyes of an eel,
Your throat
Will host the moon,
Eyes close,
Seeing everything but nothing.
Opened up to save,
In the end
No one came,
Not first mother,
Not new mother,
Not little brother.
Only the hag comes with her cold love,
The dread feeling
Has to go,
Escape the rasping searching eye.
Only one place left:
Has to become I.
I go,
I leave them all,
With the bog bodies I lie down
In my forever bog bed
But they drag even you up again
To poke, to stare,
So I don't want
To dream death with you
That's still unsafe
So I go
Into her
Hag's cold embrace.
Wet is the dark
I go to be unseen.
Inside the centre of the sun
Is a hole.

Mary

The Morning After the Sisters of Mercy Ball

There was a bird trapped in the chimney. It had been trapped there a few days. I could hear its sounds, the eerie panicked squawking, and the wings bashing around in the flutter of darkness. I sat waiting for it to come out but it never did. I cleaned the fire, finding a few tiny black feathers in the grate, and headed off to Fr Lavin's early half-six Mass. Joseph streeled along with me, rubbing his eyes and moaning.

'You're well fallen. At least we had the sense to get you home early from that dance,' I said.

Fr Lavin wasn't at Mass. A small group of us, mainly servants who had to get back to our Sunday duties, sat waiting. At a quarter to seven there were murmurings, and Joseph the altar boy was dozing off in his little frock. Someone coughed loudly and deliberately and he got up bewildered. He came off the altar and stood before me.

'Mary,' he said. 'What should I do?'

'I'll go and look in on him,' I sighed.

'This is not like Fr Lavin,' a woman said, shaking her head.

No one would be so rude as to say anything about a priest in the church so everyone shuffled out into the brightening spring morning. I sent a delighted Joseph skipping home. The dawn chorus was deafening, a world ruled by birds. I walked around the back of the church to the priest's house. I was thinking of the trapped bird and how to get it out before it flew into the room and destroyed the Lyonses' long cream curtains.

The priest's house hunched in stone silence and I rang the doorbell. No answer. I walked around the back and opened the gate as I was accustomed to doing so. The back door was open. The house was as black as the inside of a cow with its eyes shut and its tail down. I called out.

'Elizabeth?' No answer.

'Fr Lavin?' No answer.

I heard a shuffling from down the hall and the priest emerged like the bird from the chimney.

'Betsy? Betsy? Is that you?' He was dishevelled and ashen and when he saw me he cringed visibly.

'Father, I'm sorry. You're sick. I just thought I'd check in on you. We were at the Mass.'

He winced and put his hand to his head.

'It's alright, Father. They've gone home. Do you want me to contact anyone to say the other Masses if you're sick?'

'She's gone,' he squawked.

'Who?' Though I knew.

'She's taken all the money from the church collections that I had here. And the takings from the dance.'

I led him into the living room and opened the curtains, and he covered his face.

'Over a thousand pounds. From the dance alone. We never had such a sum before. How am I going to explain that loss to the Bishop? It was to go to the orphans at The Sisters of Mercy. I had the money here last night and was counting it. She helped me count it. It was the only thing she helped me do in a long time.'

'Should we call the guards?' I asked.

Fr Lavin shook his head furiously. 'NO. No no no no. She knows I won't. She knows I won't. I rue the day she ever came to me looking for help. I swear she was in such a state when she came. I took her on out of pity.'

I went quickly into the kitchen and made him an egg flip and poured a big dose of brandy into it. The poor man gulped it down.

'I don't understand,' Fr Lavin said.

'Well Father, she's a bad article. I'm going to go get Mr Lyons,' I said and took the glass from him and rinsed it.

I ran back up the road to the Lyonses. I had to go upstairs and knock on their bedroom door. When he heard the news, Mr Lyons rushed out of the house without a hat on his head.

It was me who she left a note to, that Elizabeth Quinn. I could hardly read her scrawl but the note was there under a rock on the windowsill. I had not seen it on the way out. But then I hadn't been looking for anything unusual.

Seán was coming back from an early walk through the fields as was his habit. He took the note off of me and I told him the situation but said to say nothing to the children.

'Mary,' he read the note out loud, 'I wouldn't have stayed in this awful country so long if it wasn't for you. Forgive me for not letting you know but I had to get out of here for once and for all. This was my only chance. There's no place for me here. They took everything a long time ago. Thank you for being my only friend. Poxy Trim ha ha I'm heeding your words and putting my back to the storm. Your friend, Elizabeth.'

'The nuns were too busy working them to teach her how to spell,' Seán said.

'She was clever enough to say nothing of the money she stole from the church,' I said angrily. 'I'll hand this over to the guards.'

'I thought Fr Lavin didn't want the guards.'

'He's too good a man. He took her in as a housekeeper on account of her having nowhere else to go, and she who couldn't drag a herring off the coals. Sure didn't Mr and Mrs Lyons have to provide food for the poor man, and him busy out doing God's work and nothing to come home to except her, with the speckles on her shins from sitting too long in front of the fire. He didn't have the heart to throw her out, and she came to him from the orphanage.'

'Which orphanage? Elizabeth was an orphan?'

'Goldenbridge in Dublin, she said. She was taken from a bad mother and the family scattered where the church could look after them. The money was to go to that very place. And the baldy-faced lies she told about them nuns. This is what she pays them good nuns back with.'

Seán suddenly bit his lower lip. 'You don't know what you're talking about, Mary. If she grew up in one of those places, she deserves a bit of compensation.'

'And you to be a priest!' I was livid. I tried to grab the note from him but he held it away from me.

'You never spent time in a place like that. I have.'

'You weren't in an orphanage. I made sure you were sent to a good Christian Brothers school where the sons of respectable families go to. How dare you.' I took it out of his hand.

'Mary, you're in no mood. And this note implicates you.'

'What?'

'It says, she heeded your advice.'

'No one would believe that.'

'In the end people believe what they want and we don't come from here really. We have no people about. What did we come from? The Christian Brothers are quick to remind me. You used to tell us yourself: A smoky cabin, a handful of spuds and a flea-filled bed.'

'That was only an auld saying. It was I who used to say that to you? God forgive me.'

'Respect Fr Lavin's wishes. No guards.'

'I'll see what Mr Lyons says. He'll know.'

'I know the church, Mary,' Seán said. 'They don't like gossip and scandals.'

Seán and I went in and I lit a fire in the grate that I'd set earlier. We both stood and listened to the rasping of the bird wretchedly slamming about the chimney as the smoke rose up.

'Poor auld thing,' Seán said. 'Is it a crow making her nest up there?'

'No. It's a jackdaw. Crows make their nests in the tops of the trees. Jackdaws are divils for the chimney.'

Seán took Elizabeth Quinn's note from me and put it into the young flames, but it lifted up. I tried to put my hand out to prevent it rising up the chimney but my little brother stopped me. I who had been a mother to him, and now he was a man stepping in to protect me.

'Careful,' he said in a whisper, as we watched it fly burning away on up to the wretched bird that had taken residence uninvited.

'Where will she go?' he said.

'She'll fly out the top where she came from,' I said.

'No, not the bird. Elizabeth.'

'I bet that one will go to America,' I said. 'That's where she talked about all the time, and cut up pictures of, and spent every last penny of hers going into the cinema in Trim to look at. Poxy Trim she always called it. After I told her that's what Maeve called it. Oh she used to make me laugh. Poxy Trim.'

'I bet she's down by the docks already securing passage over to Liverpool and on to New York,' Seán said wistfully. 'She's rich now.'

'Rich, pah! Put a beggar on horseback and she'll ride to Hell,' I said, and left the living room to make sure I had everything for Sunday dinner. We were to have roast lamb and my homemade mint jelly, and Yorkshire pudding, and potatoes and carrots from my garden. I would make rhubarb tarts for desert, ladled with home-made cream. I was thinking of all I had to do, and Baby was up in the kitchen shivering and looking at me with expectation for her sausages and rashers. I would go outside and get some nice eggs from the hens for her.

'Come here to me, me auld segotia,' I said to her. I took a moment to cuddle her on my chair by the fire. The embers were still warm from last night, so I stirred them a bit. Seán stood looking out of the window.

I sat up suddenly because I thought I heard her outside the window. For Elizabeth Quinn, the priest's housekeeper, had whistled everywhere she walked. So it was true what they said about women who whistled. Suddenly, it occurred to me that the whistling was in my mind. Just like Padraig's that I still heard every now and then as I worked outside. I heard them all the more if I was tired and the sun had gone down, and the old light left in the sky like a lonely guest who won't part company because they've nowhere to go. In this guilty light I would now stand and hear two whistlers.

'Tell me a story, Mary,' Baby whispered and put her hands up to pet my ears. 'Just the one. Please.' I took her little wrist and kissed it on the tiny wrinkle.

'Musha, sure I've work to be doing.'

Patricia came down in her dressing gown and went outside to the outhouse. When she returned she said what she always said. For this house was the teacher's house and her boss refused to put in an indoor toilet despite all her supplications. It was the only thing Patricia ever complained about. 'I must write another letter to Mr Sullivan asking for the indoor toilet to be put in. This is so tiresome. We're the only house of decent people now without one.' She saw me and softened. She took Baby from me.

She had never hugged the other children but everyone hugged Baby.

'I can help you today, Mary. You must be upset. Just tell me what you want done?'

'No. I wouldn't hear of it. This is your day off.'

'You never get a full day off, Mary,' Patricia said and looked at me closely. Did she think I'd run away with all their money like Elizabeth?

'Sure what would I be doing with a full day off? The hens and the pigs, and the potatoes growing out there, don't take days off,' I said. 'I'll need the boys to go get some water at the pump though.'

She bit her lip and nodded, pulling Baby close to her and kissing her head. 'Poor Fr Lavin. He took his chances with employing a girl from the orphanages. Goldenbridge. The nuns do their best but sometimes breeding will out. Goldenbridge, that has such a beautiful ring to it, doesn't it? How was the dance anyway?'

'I want a story at breakfast!' Baby demanded.

'I'll tell you a story,' I said. 'About Johnny Magory. He was a jinnit and that's all that's in it.'

'Another hug?' she chanced, and I couldn't refuse. Patricia smiled and left the kitchen and I took Baby on my knee if front of the fire.

'What's this?' I said grabbing her chin and opening her mouth and looking into it.

'What?' She was frightened.

'Be gobs my child I think there's an alp luachra in you.'

'A what?' Baby was wide-eyed.

'Have you been sleeping out by the fairy fort?'

She shook her head vigorously.

'There's only one way to get rid of an alp luachra.'

I walked my fingers up her tummy and chest and she began to smile, her eyes shining. 'Do we have to go to the well at the end of the world?' she said.

'Oh no. Even the well at the end of the world won't help if you've an alp luachra inside of you. I'll have to feed you salty beef and then bring you to the stream and the alp luachras will hop out parched with the thirst when they hear the water.'

'How do you know they're there? Can you see them? I think I can feel them jumping in my tummy.' She earnestly held her tummy and looked down, her mop of black curls falling over her face.

'*Fadó fadó in Éirinn*, there once was a king who had everything until he fell asleep on a fairy ring ...' I began. Seán came and sat by the kitchen table and I could see him putting his chin in his hands ready for the telling. And when I finished I said,

'That is my story. If there is a lie in it, let it be so. It was not I who composed it. I got no reward but butter boots and paper stockings. The white-legged hound came, and ate the boots from my feet, and tore my paper stockings!'

Seán stood up and said, 'We have to get ready for Mass. You didn't get to yours.'

I gave Baby a last squeeze and a kiss and got up to do my work.

PART IV

THE CURSE

Sheila O Conaill, may harm overtake you
A child crossways in you and never born;
Or if so may he not be like a Christian.
The snout of a pig rooting in the dung.
For fear he would be a hangman that would hang the people.

Old Irish curse

Hag

I Chose Him, You Killed Him

I had to take him away.
He wouldn't lie with his brothers
In the bog,
He knew you'd come digging.
I put him into the sun
But in fright he would not go
Because he knew it was the end,
Jumping out of my grip he ran along my arm and jumped into my mouth
So I shat him out into my hand and put him back up quickly
Into the sun.
He flared into the centre of nothing,
Incinerated.
I cried crows for him. We had been close. He had come as no more than a baby to me.
His chubby arms reached up. I picked him up, and nuzzled

him. But I don't know my own strength. I forget what you are, what I am. I make mistakes. I held him close and whispered a web into him that caught his thoughts like flies.

He had carved birds for me. He had whistled for me. He was my signaller. He was got. Him I could not help. Among so many others.

But he was beautiful. I could leave him with that. Don't blame the hag. I merely chose him to love. You killed him.

You'll all have to go from this land if you keep this up.

Sadhbh

Woe to Those Who Are Lost in the Time of a Storm (1900)

The lucky ones got away to America. America was like Heaven to us. A place above the water where you grew wings and flew but could never come back down below. Indeed they were always part of us. Those who left here. We imagined them leading grand lives in tall buildings as they disembarked off great ships.

We relied on the money they sent us from time to time. When letters dried up we could only assume they were dead. Sometimes the letters would start again after a long time of silence. Nobody felt too much then because there was so much suffering you would be overwhelmed. Woe to those who are lost in the time of a storm.

Everything was a secret. Who you were, how many there were of you, what part you came from. You never even told your children stories about your own life because it would weigh them down and turn their lives rotten by the telling. We moved as in a great exodus and cut off our ties to the past. We started to make our children speak a different language to us. English, even though our English was bad. My grandfather Batt always said that, though English was good for hustling and bartering, it was Irish you should use for lovemaking.

But Batt starved to death. Many couldn't talk too well to their own children but they wouldn't pass on the Irish because it was contaminated with bad luck too. A language is something that dies quickly and never comes back. Indeed we could go sorrowing for that too, but what would be the use?

I got letters with money from an Aunt Bride who went to America and married a black fellah. I don't remember much about her but I kind of remember once she came to visit us from Dingle with some food. The food kept us going for a few weeks and then most of the family took to the road in search of something else to keep us alive.

I had begged her to take me with her but she had walked away. If it wasn't for Bride we wouldn't have made it through. She married a *fear gorm* as we called them, a blue man; *fear dubh*, black man, meant the Devil himself. We thought that was fierce exciting. The time she had come she gave us food and then she went up the mountain. I remember her, for I was sent to find her. My father, her brother, said she would be up at the standing stones because that was where she spent her time as a child. He said those stones were family to her. I climbed the hill to the stones. I was weak and tired because at that time even though we were children we were too sick and hungry to run about. She wasn't there.

But there was an old woman. An ancient one. With cobwebbed eyes and a gaping toothless mouth. And she said nothing to me as I took a rest by the stones. The old woman had a pet hare. At least, it seemed to be her pet, as it sat beside her and didn't startle when I sat down. I was too frightened to say anything but she pointed to the sky. I sat with my back to the stones. They were warm even though the day was windy and cold. The wind stilled. She gave me bread, and I was afraid to eat it, but I was so hungry that I was afraid not to eat it. So I chewed on it. It was the most delicious buttery hot bread I had ever tasted. She pointed to the sky.

There were two birds flying there. A hawk and a scald crow. They were engaged in trickery of flight and then the scald crow killed the hawk and it fell with a thud to the earth. The woman gestured to me to fetch it. I ran and found it in the long grass. I looked back and they were gone. The hare and the old woman. I brought the hawk back to the cabin and we ate it that night. We even chewed its bones and fed the berry-black eyes to the youngest babies mashed up with its tiny brain.

It didn't do them much good in the length of things. We were eating kail, a wild grass that grew by the side of the road, which we called praiseach, but it began to poison us. The younger ones all died of hunger, or the priaseach, before the month was out, and only me and my older brother lived by going to the workhouse. Just walking off our land. That was Gregory's Law they passed in the English Parliament especially for us. The problem in Ireland they said was the people, the small cottiers with little land, and if they could reform that everything would be better. Which meant if they could be rid of us everything would be better. If you asked for help at the workhouse you forfeited your land to the British government. My grandfather Batt said that this was the land they had driven us to when Cromwell's armies came from England and massacred us. Survivors were pushed to the edge and now they would take the edge from us. That's why he wouldn't go.

'Cromwell rid us of harps, woods, wolves and land,' he said.

I don't know what he was dying for. There was nothing left.

I would have gone to America in a heartbeat but I never got the chance.

My grandfather Batt was raving at the end. Seeing things. Talking to the hag, he was. His long legs trembling when we folded him over and took him back inside the cabin, his face sunken and grey, his arms and legs like wet feathers. He was dying hungry with his eyes open. I had to put stones on his eyes to keep the lids down, we were all too weak to dig a grave. Someone came around to get the starved bodies from the houses and put them on carts in piles and they were buried, God knows where. When they took him from the house the stones fell from his eyes and they opened again. I could have sworn he was making sure we'd not leave the land.

Once Batt was dead and his body gone from the house, the wee childer died one by one. My mother made me brother and meself get up and leave our cabin. Leaning on each other for support, we walked the long miles to the workhouse. That was how we survived. She remained home and died of the hunger rather than go into the workhouse. Because of her we didn't lose this cabin.

Thinking of it all now, I did remember Aunt Bride, maybe she had been there in the cabin after Batt was dead and before we left for the workhouse. That night she told us a story about a bull. There was always money in the letters she sent us from America, so she must have done alright there. We would not have survived without it.

I have one of the letters here and I had to bring it to the priest to read it.

My dear Sadhbh.

I have never forgotten your small self, standing there on Bolus Head as I walked away and on into my life. I'm sorry that I did not write sooner but you and the family are much on my mind. I hope this few bob will do you, and I'll send some more as soon as I hear back from you that you got this much.

I know you want the stories but I have put them out of my head. America has its own stories and I settled into my life here in New York.

There was a man in Baile na Sceilge who could read and write and I gave him eggs and he'd write back to her. I hope she enjoyed my letters as much as I did hers. I told her what happened to us all.

After a year in the workhouse I came back to Bolus Head. The brother made his way to Dublin and maybe beyond that. I never heard tell of him again and he wouldn't have known how to write a letter.

Why did I come back? To the house where all my ghosts were. I didn't want to leave it to go to ruin. Truth be told I had nowhere else to go and no one else to serve. The house was mine though the land around it was lost because of that same Gregory's Law, which required that those who had gone looking for help during the famine were forced to surrender all but a quarter acre of their land.

It was a different place now. Emptied out of people and the ghost houses with their torn-off roofs full of skinny cattle. Ours was the only wee row of houses with anyone left on this mountain.

I told her that there were fierce rows over here now about the land. What else? Land land land. The Great Hunger had shifted everything. The landlords kept putting up the rent and few could pay it, and many of us were finding ourselves out on the soft side of the road. The Land Leagues were up and started, but the landlords were still evicting.

There was talk of Michael Davitt from Mayo who wanted all the poor to stick together and take what was our due. The land of Ireland for the people of Ireland. I liked the sound of that, so I did. And there were Ladies Land Leagues. There was Charles Stewart Parnell, who, being a landlord himself, favoured a softer approach and less rent, but didn't want the revolution Davitt wanted. Fair play to him though, he arrived once in the West on a white horse to stop an eviction. The crowds gathered all around him.

Things went more Parnell's way than Davitt's. And the men around here, when they got the little biteen of land they wanted and the title to it themselves, they became very settled into it. There was word of *an Gorta Beag*, another famine that broke out in Connaught, and we were fierce wary that it would all start again. But it didn't, people might have been hungry, but there was a not a big dying off.

All of them politics and great men didn't have much to do with me. I heard of the ructions and could see things change though. We lived here on the edges and were left with the scraps, but them who were getting the good land were becoming frequent church-goers as far as I could see. I told her enough of all that. She was reading it in the newspapers all the way over in New York. She probably knew as much as I did. She just wrote back wanting to hear of life on Bolus Head.

There was a young neighbour of mine, Seán. He was a great man for the stories. I had no head on me for them but I told them me Aunt Bride had a great one about a bull. I only remembered part of it because she told it to us when we were too hungry to have ears. He pestered me for the story but for the love of God I could not remember how it went.

In my letters I asked her for the story but she paid me no mind. She told me that, like fish, the stories don't last long out of their place. In them days there were old people who had nothing left to them but wander the roads and beg food from us and a night on the hay in exchange for a few stories and songs. Each time I let one into the house I asked for this story of the bull but none had it. I began to wonder did I hear it at all in my childhood hunger fevers.

Finally, I told a man at the fair that Seán was wanting that story and he was able to tell me that a man near had it. Maybe it was from me Aunt Bride. For she had walked out to us on the edge, and that was a good hundred miles or more, as far as I knew. She had always paid her keep by telling the stories along the way. That was the old ways she had. The man confirmed that it was a woman from this village who had passed by many years back during the Great Hunger and had told it to him.

'That's the very one,' I said.

It was days later when I mentioned this to Seán's wife, and she told Seán, and he went looking for that story. He left one night and his wife came to me fretting that he had not come back. There was a storm and he fell in a river on the way back. Didn't he come back up Bolus Head drenched and nearly dead from the cold? But he had the story. And it was a mighty one at that.

He told me the man was dying and the story would have gone with him. He called me around to the house and we sat by the fire and he told it to me and I nodded. That's the one. I said. I remembered it now. The princess demanded to marry the bull. And I was glad to hear it again though it brought pain to think of the very hard times we had here in the house when all the tiny ones died with wild grass in their mouths, and my grandfather Batt couldn't stop seeing even when he was dead.

Maeve

Most of Us Smelled of Paraffin (1953)

Still tall and mostly blonde despite my long twenty-three years on this earth, I had many offers at the dances in the big house. Maybe it was my vanity but I witnessed scuffles with the men over who could make it across the room and ask me to dance first. I had my eye on a nice young man who worked in the cobbler's shop. As I did my errands with the nurses he would stare at me. Not that I thought of that anymore. I never touched myself and my fantasies had faded away. They had me cured for sure. There was a doctor who looked at me with that look. As soon as I saw that look I knew I could get something from him. I always knew that. So I made sure to endear myself to the doctor so that he would be on my side, for I still harboured hope that I would get out of here and get my children back to me and go to England or America. Any day now. Any day now. But there were no doctors here to dance with us. The big rough male and female nurses who leaned with their white coats against the walls watched us wretches with a sneer.

Most of us smelled of paraffin, as that was what they used for dandruff. So I never got too close to anyone. Along with Jeyes Fluid and boiled cabbage, that paraffin smell was inescapable.

The cobbler skulked in the background, I danced with other men and looked over to him. When he finally got the nerve up, another man was in front of him. I quickly walked around the first man and took the cobbler's hand. I was never one for messing about when I saw something I liked.

'What's your name?' he asked, when we were attempting a stiff waltz that none of us knew how to dance well.

'Maeve. But they call me Teresa.'

'What should I call you?'

'What does that matter?'

'Why are you here?'

'Why are you?'

He put his hands in my dress pocket. I thought he was making a pass so I pushed him away. He looked around in fear at the nurses who lined the wall. None of them were even looking at us.

The music ended and he went back to the men's wall. I put my hand in my pocket and felt coins and went crimson. What did he think I was? Who told him about me? Should I call the nurse? But that would get the poor man in trouble and he was so young that I felt for his stupidity. When the music started the men walked again across the floor to the women. Boldly he came up to me. I could hear a nurse snigger behind me and I tensed. Had she seen the sordid transaction? I had never taken money from a man. Perhaps I should of. I could have married Rory if I wanted to. He was in love with me. He was probably heartbroken when I went away. He probably thought of me every day and would for the rest of his life. But I didn't love him. I just wanted to be free. And now here I was, a captive in a free society. There had been no trial and no sentencing and I did not know how many years I had been condemned to serve so I couldn't even start counting.

I took his hand and gave him back the money, he blushed.

'I need you to find out about my brother. They call him the Grass Man. His back was broken. I didn't see him in the hospital yesterday. What happened to him? I'd like to get to see him.'

The music stopped and the dance was over. He leaned in and quickly whispered, 'I heard tell that the Grass Man died in the hospital. His back was broke and his head fell back and he choked while the priest was giving him communion.' The cobbler squeezed my arm as if to say sorry. He was herded out with the rest of the men, like water running down the bath drain, and we women standing watching them swirl around the door and disappear.

'Look at yer wan,' the nurses nudged each other. 'Weeping in the middle of the hall watching the men leave her.'

Seamus

For Fear He Would Be a Hangman That Would Hang the People

When Padraig died, I had a letter from a doctor in Mullingar suggesting it was time Maeve get out. She wouldn't be worth a trawneen on the farm and no one would stay with Sheila in the house.

Padraig's body had been brought home and laid out in the house and only Patsey came to wake him with us. Patsey made a holy show of himself crying over the coffin and petting the dead lad's face. They had taken the cast off his back to lay him out and he looked like a fine young man.

'It's nothing to do with you, Patsey,' Sheila said. 'I told Seamus that I wasn't coming into a house with a lunatic and that was that.'

'Don't go telling Mary now,' I warned him and he began to sob more.

'Ye were a good-looking family for the most part. But Seán and Maeve and Padraig got the real looks,' Patsey blubbered. 'How old was he?'

'It says he was born in 1933 on the cert. So he'd be twenty now.'

The room was dark except for the Tilley lamp and I wasn't going to be giving Patsey any more of the one bottle of whiskey I had, so he said, 'Maybe it is none of my business but Mary has a right to bury her brother. She was a mother to ye all.'

'Not to me,' I said, and closed the door on him.

'Why is he always sniffing around?' Sheila said.

'Ach, he's not the worst.'

'You're the one always giving out about him. Now you say that just to disagree with me.'

The children kept putting stuff into the coffin with him, bits of potatoes and leaves they collected from outside. Kevin, the eldest fellah tried to climb in with him, and Sheila had to knock him out of it with the broom. Even though it was the cheapest coffin it wasn't cheap, we set him on the kitchen table, ate our dinner around him that night and I was glad to see the back of him in the morning. Little Michael was only about two and a soft lad; he kept kissing him and shaking him to wake up. I can't say any of us cried. One less lunatic to think about. I suppose I'd have to get Sheila to put it in a letter to Bridget.

It was an odious wet day when we buried Padraig. Of course feckin Patsey couldn't resist telling Mary. She came with that smarmy bastard Fr Lavin. Fr Gilligan said the Mass. There was hardly anyone in the church. It was probably the smallest funeral Rathcairn had ever seen. Padraig had never been to school because he was too wild to have indoors. He had spent his life running about on the farm and in the woods and no one but the family and Patsey had met him. His life wasn't part of anything.

Mary sat right behind me and cried and cried, making a holy show of herself. The kids thought it all great gas and kept squirming around to gawk at an aunt they'd never seen. She had given them all mints outside and they stuck their grubby hands out for more.

Padraig was to be buried out in the graveyard but the rain filled the grave so they wouldn't put him down into it. They told us to go home and they would bail out the water and put him in when it was not flooded. Sheila went on, and Fr Gilligan and Fr Lavin went to the priest's house.

But Mary stood in the rain by the grave and Patsey climbed inside the grave with the gravediggers, bailing out water with buckets. As much as they'd bail out, the sky gave them double. They were up to their knees in water.

'It's useless, Mary,' Patsey said, shaking his head as the gravediggers got out and pulled Patsey up after them. 'You come up to me now and get dry and we'll come back.'

'Are you going over to Seamus'?' She pulled her headscarf tighter around her head as the rain ran down the inside of my coat. I turned to walk away but I heard the fecker Patsey say, 'There's not enough in that house to baptize a fairy. Come over to me and I'll cook ye some spuds and dry you off in front of a fire and you can make us an egg flip. I could do with one of them yokes now. Or a hot whiskey. Ye were great with them egg flips.'

'I'll not leave him in the rain here without even a burial.'

Patsey was wet and his teeth chattering and he gave me a lift back to the house. Even the gravediggers scurried off to take shelter. So Mary was left all alone in the graveyard sitting on the coffin itself, beside the flooded open grave, and the rain bucketing from the heavens.

Hours later, the rain did take a break. Patsey went back and they got him buried. Mary stayed there until she saw the job done.

Mary came in that night, with Patsey and Fr Lavin. They were after Bridget and Maeve's address in America but I threw them all out. Sheila went wild. She was holding her big pregnant belly and ran up the road after them as they made their way up the hill to Patsey's house.

'May the Devil catch you and take you where you can't be found! And your precious sister Maeve isn't in America anyway. That trollop went as mad as the rest as ye and ended up in the big house.'

Mary came running back to her and Sheila blocked the door.

'Is this true? Seamus, is this true?' She shouted into the house, as the kids clamoured at the door, delighted.

I knew then that I had to get Maeve out of the big house. I didn't want any more interference from anybody. I went to the door meself and gave Mary an awful reading as she stood in front of me.

'Yer not welcome here. Don't ever darken me door again. Stay away from this family ye auld witch. Does your priest know that yer a witch? Does he know you be doing spells and making all sorts of potions and healing the sick with your piseogs? Go take a running jump at yourself, ye hoor's melt. Before I'll give ye a puck in the gob.' The children were yelling blue murder around me and I smacked her in the face, so I did. She went reeling into the gatepost. Patsey and Fr Lavin must have heard the commotion and came running down the hill.

'Do ye know she's a witch?' Sheila screamed at them as they appeared at the gate. Sheila grabbed a shovel that was leaning by the gate and was waving it over her head. Her belly was bursting out of her dress. 'Her hair was witch grey as a child. She turns into a hare at night. She should be locked away too with the rest of them. There's none of ye worth the steam of my piss. Oh I rue the day I got involved in this wretched family.' Sheila swung round and belted Mary with the metal of the shovel, it came down on her shoulder and she fell like a tree. Sheila stood over her, she raised the shovel up again and brought it down on her back as Mary tried to get up. She poleaxed her with the sharp end of the shovel and then dug in into her neck as if trying to chop her head off.

Patsey and Fr Lavin were frozen, and too scared. The shovel came down on Mary's head this time and I thought she might kill her so I came up behind and caught the shovel as she held it to strike again. Sheila howled at me and tried to get it off of me, but even though I had only the one arm, I was stronger than her. Fr Lavin finally came to his senses and jumped in front of her; even Sheila wouldn't dare hit a priest. Patsey looked as if he was about to shite himself. The two of them dragged Mary away up the lane, leaving a bloody patch by the gate. The fat old thing was too heavy to drag for far so they went either end of her. Her battered head was lolling to the side and her dress was slipped up her legs. Patsey, the old goat, got the end of her where he could see her knickers.

I'd never seen Patsey angry in all my born days but he was yelling back as he carried her, his curse words clear over the air. I'll never forget that curse, because, by God, it came true.

Sheila O Conaill, may harm overtake you,
A child crossways in you and never born;
Or if so may he not be like a Christian.
The snout of a pig rooting in the dung.
For fear he would be a hangman that would hang the people!

'Don't ever darken our door again. Any of ye.' I yelled after them. 'Good riddance to bad rubbish!'

And then the night was still and the kids had all run out of the house and up the fields. I let them away. They'd come back, when they needed feeding or the rain started up again.

Mary

And Death Not Come to Me Until I Reach It

What was I like? My eyes swollen shut, my teeth knocked out and my jaw in a wire, my shoulder bones broken. In Navan hospital the hag visited me. Wee Padraig was safe in her cold arms. I felt relieved to grieve him, for I was as broken as he had been when I last saw him. It was the only way to get through it. I could not speak or see but I could sense everything. Patricia and Mr Lyons came in as often as they could but were wise to never bring the children. The hag tucked me underground. From beneath the earth I felt them all hover above me with love and concern. Fr Lavin and Patsey sat beside me with guilt, but I wanted to tell them that this was exactly where I should be and the pain was just what I needed. Often I thought of Elizabeth Quinn and all my anger was gone. I knew she was right to do what she did, and that she had told the truth about them places, even though it was hard to fathom why those who were meant to be the representatives of the Holy Family on the Earth would be so full of hate for the poor. When Seán came in I felt his glow, he was one of the shining ones here on this Earth. He told me the story of the Bull Bhalbhae, held my hand, and the healing began. His visits did not drain me and we journeyed underground together for he could always walk between worlds.

May the Spectres not harm me during my journey.

The hag sat at her cave in Bolus Head looking out to the Skellig Islands and fed us her sustaining broth. Seán stood with his back to me, silhouetted tall and thin at the mouth of the cave. I saw the bull tell the princess to go home when the hag reached her long arm down the chimney and snatched their third child from her breast.

'I will not return home. I will follow you until I die,' she tells him, and so she follows the bull. The bull walks on ahead. Sometimes he stops and waits for her. As soon as she catches up he tells her to go home to her father. Her answer is always the same.

'I will not return home. I will follow you until I die.'

I would have to find Maeve. She needed me. I knew she was in the big house in Mulingar and had found Padraig in the infirmary. Also, I knew she had tried to contact me but her name had been changed to Teresa. In that cave, the tattered grey bog bodies told stories of their sacrifices. The hag gathered my ancestors, mind you it was by storylines not blood lines, Batt, Bride, Sadhbh, and Cormac Mac Airt himself hunted to the West by Cromwell's men, son of a wolf. Cormac Mac Airt leaned back against the wet, riveted dark walls in the hag's cave and said:

'A thief took my eyes from my head.
They said if I ate wolf meat it would protect me from seeing ghosts.
But a wolf has eaten the moon,
A wolf devoured the sun,
Now it has turned wide-jawed
To the ice-cold frozen
Tide-wild earth,
A wolf has eaten the world.'

I couldn't make head nor tail of that even though it stuck with me.

I could not stay forever with the hag, Seán was standing guard as he had always done and gave me the signal using one of Padraig's whistles. The Cruelty Men had followed me down through the underworld. Their shadowless shapes stalking me. We had thought we were staying one step ahead. But they had taken their sacrifices anyway. If the Cruelty Men had the power to journey under the ground and mix among us, I would have to resurface and protect the ones I could.

May old age be mine,
And death not come to me until I reach it.

But there were those above who were still in the Cruelty Men's sights. Once I heard the whistle, the hag led me above the earth. The swelling went down, light slivered through my watery eyes, the wire was removed and I could open my dry mouth gradually. I took small steps with Seán or Patricia holding onto me. I would be ready again to see Baby, my luck-child. I was loved and protected. We banished children of Cromwell had been restored.

Once Patsey came in with a shot pheasant draped over his knee. It sickened my heart to see the broken beautiful bird but I let him leave it for me. I knew he was fierce guilty that he hadn't done more to stop Sheila and her shovel.

'Sheila has had her baby,' he said, 'They had called him Ignatius as he was born on the feast of St Ignatius. Sheila was convinced you cursed him so she won't go near the poor wee craytur.'

'I never cursed a soul,' I murmured softly. For I could not speak loudly or clearly still. They had fitted me with a set of new teeth and I wasn't used to them yet.

'It was I who cursed him,' Patsey petted the dead bird. 'But Sheila has it all mixed up in her mind. I'm sorry I did. But sure what power do I have?' He looked at me for reassurance. But all I could see was the shining blue and red feathers of that once-lovely bird.

Seamus

The Wiremen
(1954)

Them feckin Wiremen were coming up the hill. My hill. Patsey had taken in lodgers of course, the sleeveen. An electrician and another fellah. There were no flies on Patsey. He never missed a chance to make a shilling, a cute hoor alright, he'd put me in the ha'penny place. They were after sticking feckin poles in my feckin field and yer wan Sheila was in a latheration with excitement. She wanted the electric light. I had me Tilley lamps and me oil lamps and couldn't see the use in it. But that clart Sheila wanted to modernize, she said. And she was pregnant with the sixth of our litter. Even Fr Gilligan was out to me insisting that I didn't run any man off my land, and take the wires into the house, and let them Wiremen traipse all over the drills of me fields, digging holes in the paths along the roads, and erecting them huge wires.

Let me tell you, I was livid one day. It was the idea of the invisible power that would run into me house that I didn't trust one iota. It would be an indoor toilet she wanted next. Always in some sulk, she was, and streeling around the house with a face on her. While the wee ones were growing up muck savages.

I was making the slurry to spread on the fields. I had the yoke fixed onto the back of the tractor and it got jammed. It kept jamming. I needed the job done, as I had rented it out from Patsey himself and didn't want to have to pay a farthing more, and the cute hoor would ask for it if the job went on another day. Didn't I have to climb up onto the back of the tractor and I put me foot down to stamp it and unjam it and me right leg got caught in the machine. The next thing I know, I'm falling off the tractor and laying on the ground roaring and the boys are running about me screaming. Their snotty faces raw with terror and blood spurting everywhere. I looked up and blood spattered on the lid of the sky.

'Go get Patsey,' I gasped at them. The eldest ran like the hammers of Hell over to Patsey's house.

'*A Mhuire, is trua!*' Patsey yelled when he looked at me. He took me in his arms and took off his shirt and tied up the leg that was all in a mush. He put me on his back, and shouting at the children to go tell their mother, he carried me to his car. I bled all over the back of the seat but to his credit he never mentioned that until later. The Wireman came in the front with him and kept turning to look at me.

'Hold it together, boy; we'll get you seen to.'

They couldn't save the foot.

The doctor looked at me arm stump and said, 'Well, Seamus, to paraphrase Oscar Wilde, to lose one limb is a misfortune. To lose two is beginning to look like carelessness.' He could be as smart-arse as he liked, but I stared at the ceiling and knew the farm was eating me alive. The land would take everything.

The wireless was on beside the bed. I lay on me back and stared at the ceiling while Meath won the All Ireland. I remembered when we won in 1949 against Cavan and meself and the boys lit sods of turf, speared them with sticks and marched with everyone down the roads in a grand procession. I didn't mind being with people that night. The one time in me life I mixed in with the village and felt them not to be looking down their noses at me and me family or whispering about us. We stayed up all night singing and dancing and I was a whole man then, not like the shredded amadán I'd ended up like for this big win five years on. The whole hospital was in a state of celebration and activity. Little did they even think of me and my plight. Grown men weeping in their beds with joy. But I didn't feel any of this.

Would it matter to me boys that they've won the All Ireland and the Sam Maguire Cup was to be brought back again when they had spent the morning scrubbing their father's blood out of the yard and off their faces? What did the feckin Sam Maguire matter to them now that their father had lost a leg?

It was weeks I lay there, and they finally gave me a wooden leg to wear home. No one but Patsey and Fr Gilligan came to see me. I knew Sheila would be in a rage with me on account of the leg. Sheila believed in curses, it was about all she believed in. That woman was sure of the Devil but not of God. She had been pregnant again, and the child was breech, which she took to mean crossways. When Ignatius was born she checked him for a pig's snout. I told her that it was an old familiar curse he said and there was nothing in it. Patsey was never one to talk ill of anyone, I'll give him that. His curses were as useless as his blessings. But that only made her more convinced, she thought Mary was a witch and had a hand in it, until I began to look at the baby Iggy in a funny way and Sheila wouldn't give him the breast. I had to tell one of the other lads to stick a bottle in the baby's mouth a few times a day or he would have starved.

I knew Mary would go looking for Maeve in the big house and I was afraid with all her connections now she would arrange to get her out. I didn't want her coming back and shaming us or being a burden. I talked to Fr Gilligan and the doctors and I signed more papers and got her moved to the laundries in Dublin. Fr Gilligan said that the Sisters of Mercy needed able strong women and Maeve was noted to be a good worker. She'll be in good hands there he said. Out of harm's way, he said, the nuns will mind her, he said.

'What about that priest, that Fr Lavin fellah?'

I had a feeling Fr Gilligan disliked him as much as I did.

'He's an awful blabbermouth. I don't want him telling Mary.'

'I'll read him the riot act. He won't say a word. Priests are used to keeping secrets. It's our job.'

And as soon as he said it I knew it to be true.

'That'll be the last we'll hear of her,' I told Sheila who seemed as eager as myself not to have Maeve coming back anywhere near us. Sheila and I would sit by the fire and sometimes would laugh remembering the time she battered Mary.

'That shook her,' Sheila said. 'Coming back all hoity-toity because she's a skivvy to solicitors and teachers and has an in with the priest and all those pusthagauns.'

'That priest is soft in the head,' I'd say.

'You won't be getting any trouble from them again. They're a bad lot. And that fellah Padraig, the one we buried, he was stone mad. Sure he hadn't even made his communion or anything.'

'You're right an all.'

We'd be almost civil for a moment but then she'd start in on me for something.

'When's them potatoes ready to be pulled? All we've eaten is turnip for a week. A crippled beetle could look over the potato skins on this table.'

'You could shift your arse and help me. Fr Gilligan said he'd send me more boys from the home but they're always trouble.'

'That's because you beat them and starve them. This is the only place that they go running back to the Brothers for mercy.'

'You could send your sons to school and then clean this house sometime. Would it ever strike you to do that? If ye do that I'll get you that cat you've been asking for.'

'What's the use of keeping a cat when all the mice have died of malnutrition?'

'What's that meant to mean?' I'd start yelling.

So there was Patsey, a year after all those shenanigans, at the side of me hospital bed. I was cursed with Patsey.

'With you gone Sheila never has the kids in school, Seamus. Ye would want to watch or they'll take them off to them industrial schools.'

'Fr Gilligan wouldn't do that. He's had two of mine already. And I'd have sent Mary to the nuns if I could to be rid of her. She works like an ox, they'd have loved her.'

'Mary wasn't the worst of them, Seamus. She had to spend months in Navan hospital after the doing Sheila gave her. Fr Lavin wanted to go to the guards but Fr Gilligan talked him out of it and Mary said she wouldn't leave her nephews without a mother. I told her it was you who pulled the shovel away in the end before she got kilt.'

'Don't come here to talk to me about that wan. Mary's not welcome in my house.'

Patsey let out a deep sigh. As if he was the one with all the troubles. 'Your wee fellahs are up in the fields. They're wandering around like strays. I give them spuds to eat, they're starved, Seamus.'

'You stay away from my fields, Patsey.'

'Arra, I don't want your fields, Seamus. I'm a bachelor. Sure I've nobody to leave my farm to and it's too big for me at this stage. I'd rather go around and do the threshing at this stage in the day. There's more company in it and I like a bit of company. It was Fr Gilligan who told me that I should help you out with the fields and I'm trying me best.'

Patsey heaved his trousers up under his chest.

'By God but you're getting big Patsey.'

'Sure food is my only pleasure.' He smiled shyly. Then he frowned. 'I have a few sheep now. But they're bastards. More trouble than they're worth. I'll not do that again. I let them out in your field. They're up at the fairy fort. Did you ever see why sheep are so happy? Be gobs, they're eating the fairy cheese, them mushrooms.'

'What are your sheep doing in MY field?'

'I put them in there to eat all them mushrooms and keep yer chislers off them. I saw your boys pick tins and tins of them. Their eyes are spinning in their heads.'

'Just go out with a stick and bash the bejaysus out of them.'

'The sheep have taken care of that. They love them mushrooms. The sheep's mind is a different kettle of fish altogether. It's what keeps them looking so contented. How's the leg?'

'Gone. Patsey. Or hadn't you heard?'

'Well the arm never went, did it? You ended up with a ghost hanging out of you.'

'I did that. I still feel the leg too. When the surgeon told me he'd had to remove it on up to the knee sure I didn't believe him because I still felt it there. They never go. I can even wiggle me toes and they not there.'

'That's a strange goings on.'

'It is indeed.'

'Bit like family, Seamus,' Patsey said slyly.

'What does that mean?'

'Ye can cut your family off but ye can't. That's what I meant.' Patsey stood up. He had the rumpled look of a bachelor farmer and the smell. A priesty smell.

I got out with a wooden leg and the feckin electricity was in the house. In all the feckin houses, like. Some people were even putting in toilets inside, which I thought was a filthy thing to want in your house. There were poles in me fields and the crows were delighted now to have a place to sit and gather and eye me seeds. There were more cars coming down the roads now and one of me lads, Michael, the fourth one, got hit and flew into the ditch. I had to go in the car with the fellah who hit him and he died before we got to the hospital. That kept the others off the roads at least. Michael was buried in a small white coffin on top of Padraig. There would have been a stillborn girl in there, but since we never had her baptized she had to be buried outside the holy ground, in a place for the limbo babies. I'd asked Fr Gilligan to make an exception but he was a man of the letter.

The women on the farms around us tried to come over to help but after a few weeks everyone goes back into their own lives and

I was glad. They love a tragedy, do the women. They love to sit by the fire weeping and thinking of all the dead at once. That's what's obscene and terrible about the grief of a woman. It's not just the sorrow at hand they do be grieving for, but the sorrow of the world and all the sorrow that's ever been. It reminds me too much of the sorrow to come. The grief of a woman is an ugly spectacle.

A queer thing happened when I got on top of Sheila after me leg was gone. It was something I couldn't go to the priest about. Not even in confession. He'd stick me in the big house in Mullingar, and they'd break me back and choke me like me little brother. When I'd shoot it into her it didn't just come spurting out of my boidín like normal. I'd feel it in my foot. I would get a double whammy. The foot that was missing. That's where I felt it every time, and it was much better than before. It was as if me missing foot was an extra boidín. And I couldn't even tell that to Sheila or anyone. I'd stand out in the fields and wonder what spell Mary had put on me at all, at all.

There were evenings when I'd be coming in through the fields, and I could wave over at Patsey. We were on waving terms again. Though he never came round to the house he would walk over to speak to me in the field. Could I tell him? Tell him that when I climbed on top of my woman and shot it into her it was in the foot I felt it as well. The missing foot. No, I could tell no one. And then I'd see a hare bound over the edge of the horizon and I'd know it was her. Keeping an eye on things. She was probably wondering how her spells worked out. To be sure, I wouldn't let on to her that finally this was a spell that was to me liking.

Maeve

Going Underground

I felt a change coming. I was excited. Once I was out for the funeral there was no way Mary would let them take me back. My journey to Hell would be over. All these years lost, but what of them. At least I would make the best of what was ahead. The day after I heard Padraig had died another nurse came into my cell in the morning and told me to not get dressed but to follow her.

'Where are we going? Should I get dressed for the funeral?'

'Well, child of grace, you complained yesterday about headaches, did you not?'

'I did. Are we going to the doctor?'

'We've registered your complaint. You complained last week that you couldn't sleep with the noise of the other patients. It was only a year ago you complained about the food.'

'Yes.' My heart sank as she led me further away through the hospital and down a long corridor. I stopped in my tracks. The stout nurse pulled me on.

'We thought a rest in the hold would do you good.'

'A rest? In no-hope hold? You're messing with me? I'm fine. Honest I am, nurse. I can sleep fine. The headaches are gone. I'm used to the food.'

'If you don't cooperate and come with me and do everything I say you will stay in the hold indefinitely. Do you understand?'

'Yes, nurse.' I walked on in a trance, quaking with dread as I stepped closer to a big door with several wooden bolts. As she knocked on the door it opened and a nurse let another patient out. The patient and I glanced shamefully at each other.

'This one is coming for a rest.'

The nurses smiled at each other at that word.

'So this is the one that all the men fight over at the dances?'

'Can't think why. She's a skinnymalinxmaloney.'

The other nurse appraised me and agreed. 'More hair than tit. Like a mountain heifer.' They roared at their own wit.

'I've heard she was a floozy in her last life. She's lucky she's here, not the laundries.'

'What have I done?' I said as the nurse shoved me in the back over the threshold. The door was closed and I could hear the bolts one by one shutting me away. 'This place is for the people who are really away with the fairies.' The nurse inspected me closely to ascertain whether I should be here or if this was just punishment for my expectations. We entered a ward.

There were five beds very close together, facing each other, and patients lay in some of them with the covers pulled over their heads. There were rooms to the side that the nurse said were nicknamed igloos.

'They're for the free-thinkers,' she quipped. 'They're padded and we can strap you up in a jacket so you'll not harm yourself. But I reckon you won't need that. You're not at the end of the line yet.'

But how did I get here if I wasn't at the end of the line? This felt like the end of the line to me. The end of the world. What had happened? There were women pacing up and down, and women rocking on beds back and forth, and women picking their noses.

I felt I was among a bunch of apes at the zoo except I'd never been to the zoo. I'd never been anywhere. From leaving Bolus Head in a horse and trap, to a farm in Rathcairn, to a shop in Trim, to a mother and baby home, to the big house in Mullingar. My life was slipping away month by month, year by year, and I couldn't seem to get a hold of it or see any end to it.

The walls were whitewashed and it felt like we were all down in a hidden cave. I said the prayer my sister Mary had taught us: '*May Bridget save us, and may we live under her cloak, and the Holy Spirit protect us from fear, from caves of white death, guard us and keep us company*.'

I had never known what they meant by caves of white death, but now I did.

A group of three nurses approached me. They looked right through me as if they couldn't see me. I wasn't a person to them at all. But I was relieved when I saw it wasn't the shocks again. Was this going to be like the sickly insulin treatment they had me on when I first was committed? They came at me, sticking a tongue depressor in my mouth, and began to pour paraldehyde down my throat. I jolted and gagged but they were firm. My mind shook. My grey brain rattled off the yellow bone of my skull. The nurse said I had a fit for twenty minutes, which was a normal part of the treatment, and when I was finished they took the tongue depressor out. 'Lie there, love, and let it do its job,' she said. What was its job? And after that I don't remember anything for a few days, or was it weeks, and I saw into the future as I crawled through the past.

I was going underground. Under my life. Under the country. Under the barley. Under the potatoes. Under the churches. Under the lunatic asylums. Under the cow shit. Under the wild primroses on the hedges. Under the schools. Under Bridget's cloak. Under the bed where I gave birth to my twins. Under the courts that stole my children. Under the chieftains and druids who sliced our son's nipples and stuck them face down in the Iron Age bog. Under Patrick's staff that pinned me to the bed where the doctors held me down and attached electrodes to my head. Under my womb madness.

Under the connivance of monks that took our stories and twisted them into their own. Under the Vikings who plundered our treasures. Under the betrayers, the snitches, the deal-makers that welcomed our enemies to the shore. Under the Normans pouring tar at us from their freezing green-zone castles. Under the flight of the Earls who left us to ourselves, what a joke, as if we stood on the edge of the cliffs with hankies waving them off, poor miserable peasants that we were. *Come back, oh nobility, and fuck us again.*

Under Cromwell who scoured the land of us and banished us to windy wet mountains where even the sheep lost their footing. Under the Brits who beat our language out of us. Under the landlords who put us out on the soft side of the road. Under the world where the fairies are. Where the limbo babies' tiny skeletons still cage their earth-stuck souls; because Heaven won't open to them. Under the tangled roots of imported trees. Under the huge machines that stripped the bogs empty.

Under the music that squeaked out of the boxes, the air that rushed from flutes, the bang of the drum. Under the low-lying, eve thickening clouds. Under the blight. Under the boats that shipped corn to England. Under the decks of the coffin ships. Under the people of 1916, the children of the starved who had crawled out of the West. Under Pádraig Pearse's gammy eye and bad poetry. Under the stone yard in Kilmainham Gaol, where they tied the wounded James Connelly to a chair and shot him. Under the Black and Tans. Under the constant grey sky. Under failed negotiations of poor leadership.

Under each other now. Under the Blue Shirts. The uncivil war. Under Béal na Bláth. Under Archbishop MacQuaid rasping in de Valera's ear as they made plans for us. Under the poets who ordered us to open the door without giving us the key. Under the picture of the Sacred Heart, offering us his inedible organ pressed with thorns. Under the singers who made us shiver but would not warm us. Under the endless decades of the rosary. Under the museums that hid the

Síle na Gigs from us. Under the pricks of self-loathing men who stuck it into us, and condemned us as dirty with their juice.

Under the Virgin Mary who will one day show no mercy to the child in Granard. She is the one and only, the holy and immaculate Virgin that renders all us mothers whores.

Under the cassocks of the bishops and cardinals and the popes with their useless cocks ticking like metronomes, marking out time until the chickens come home to roost. Under Ben Bulben. Under the endless verses of rebel songs. Under the drink. The poitín that could turn you raw blind, the Guinness that blackens your shite, the *uisce beatha* that bursts your liver. Under the fierce watch of the bad nuns who ate their sandwiches and drank their lemonade as the starved children in their care collected turf for their parlours.

Under the solicitors, the guards, the school principals, the doctors, the bank managers, the decent people of Ireland who you need to sign for your passport.

Under the thud and hum of the laundries. Under the heaps of banned books from exiled scribblers. Under the shoeless bloody feet of slave children in the obscene care of the church and state – uncounted lives melted like snow off a ditch. Under the fairy forts in Meath, the hag stones in Beara, the disappeared Georgian buildings. Under the INLA, the RUC, the IRA, the UDA, the UFF, the SAS, the UVF, the MI5, under the bombs, the assassinations, the murders, the kneecapping, the man who was shot dead outside his house last night.

Under the toll roads that they built to slice through a Neolithic world they refused to understand.

Under the tribunals, the confessions, the recessions, the depressions. The brown bags of money under tables. Under the heroin, the flats, the dirty canals, the coke come-downs, the cathedral shopping centres, the developers, the bankers, the crap, ugly buildings standing empty, *the Great Ongar*, the unlandscaped blank green spaces in the sprawling housing estates built on floodplains, the unsignposted roundabouts. Which way now? Which way now?

Under your shrivelled breast, oh hag, that I sucked and sucked, but it was too late to come to you for nourishment, so dried out were you with our neglect. And when you cried out in pain, it was only black crows that squeezed out of your tear ducts and flew at me as I lay in your embrace, and all of these hag crows plucked chunks out of me, until, dismembered, I was taken off inside the black noise of the flock in small separate pieces, and squawkingly digested, and shat out onto the forest floor, and eaten by insects, and inside these creepy crawlies, under the canopy of trees, when the insects died and dried up, the soil of this land took me for what it could suck out of me which, of course, wasn't much by then. Was it, Oh Ireland?

PART V

THE CLEARING

I am Eve, great Adam's wife,
I that wrought my children's loss,
I that wronged Jesus of life,
By right 'tis I had borne the cross.

I that brought the winter in
And the windy glistening sky,
I that brought terror and sin
Hell and pain and sorrow.

Tenth-century Irish poem

Hag

You Dreamt of Losing and You Lost

The sun spun me around this galaxy twenty twisting times and I have felt your dreaming straining and stretching before you even took form. I was a spider and can still do spider things. I can take your dream threads and weave traps with them. You dreamt you would find this land, and out of the fog the craggy cliffs of Bolus Head appeared. You dreamt of slaves but they came with new gods that ate your own. You dreamt of powerful strangers and they cut you open. You dreamt of castles and you became servants in them. You dreamt of silence, and your harps were piled high and burned. You stopped dreaming of wolves and I took them away. You dreamt of the West until you were pushed out to there. You dreamt fear and pulled the fear out of the land, the crops rotted and black with your dread.

The sun spun me around this galaxy twenty twisting times and I felt your dreaming straining and stretching before you took form. No stillness is possible. Time is not a stairs to climb. There is nowhere we are going. Yet we are moving all the time. Time spirals.

You come back and back and back, swirling around in dim recognition, but never exactly where you were, always one degree darker, one degree brighter, one degree farther, one degree closer. Every birth is an expansion. This serpentine tale is told in storylines not blood lines. Their story is not a straight line. Now there are three children who can carry the stories through the whorl; these stories that are the history of your dreams.

You dreamt of freedom from one master but you didn't dream yourselves clear. You dreamt of riches and they came, but as soon as it was given you dreamt of poverty and it came back. You dreamt of gleaming buildings by glittering rivers and they were built, but you didn't dream yourselves in them, so they stood empty and the rivers turned foul. If you are dizzy it is because you have woken up.

Inside your national museum the bog bodies lie exposed. Waiting for their sacrifices to be worth something.

435

Curly Hair Is a Sin (1956)

My curly hair, they told me, was a sin, so it was. In the Bible a curly-haired woman was a harlot, so she was. I pulled and pulled at my curls and Sister Michael shouted at me, '435 have you been curling your hair, you brazen hussy?'

But I hadn't. She beat me with the hairbrush, slammed the hard part on my cheeks and stuck the bristles into the back of my neck. I was put in the coal room because of my curly hair, so I was. It was red and sinful they said, and in the dark I clutched it and dragged it smooth but it always bounced back about my head like the spring of the divil himself.

At night we slept in long rows of beds, the number on our bed was our number. I tried to keep awake because I knew what would happen if I slept. I felt the warm wet around my bottom and at first I liked it because I was so cold, but then my stomach sank and I tried to lie on the wet spot to soak it up and rub it off with my body. But Sister came and pulled us all out, she knew who we were, night after night. We stood out of our beds shivering and crying, and, in the dark, with her thorny hands around my arm, she sat us in the icy cold water. Sometimes the water was hard at the top and she broke it with a stick and kept me in there till I was blue numb, so I was. She made me stand with the piss sheet around my head, the wet part in my face. I couldn't breathe, so I couldn't. She made us walk outside, around and around wrapped in our own sheet after the cold bath until the sheet dried. Once two of the Sisters scooped me up and threw me in the dryers with the sheets. They told me they would turn it on and they shut the door. There were laundry women there and they gawked at us. I saw out the thick glass and I put my hand at the window and the world seemed far from me.

There were only women in the world; I didn't know there was any other thing but us. The priest came in and said the Mass but I didn't know he was a man. I didn't know that anyone was soft or kind, or anyone could say nice things or you could be touched without being hurt.

Baby

Day of My Beloved, the Thursday (1958)

I was excited to be growing up and going somewhere where they wouldn't all call me Baby. Still I would crawl onto Mary's knee for a cuddle and I would ask her about when I was born. She said I was born twelve years ago on a Thursday, no less, just like Colum Cille and just like her little brother Seán, who had joined the Christian Brothers.

'Tell me about Thursday, Mary.'

'Musha sure you've heard it so many times you could tell me.'

'Ah go on, Mary.'

'Thursday of Columba benign,' she would put her arms tight around me and say, 'day of my beloved.'

'And are you really related to Colm Cille?' I'd ask.

'It was said that we were, musha. Colum Cille's father was a grandson of the Conall who gave rise to the Donegal Cenel Conaill dynasty, and we ruled the north-west of Ireland and beyond.'

'So how did you end up in Bolus Head in the south-west of Ireland?'

'That I don't know, but sure Cromwell scattered us all over like a dog's litter.'

'And now you're back!'

'Indeed I am. Now go on and practise your piano and let me get the tea. You're an awful time-waster.'

I knew she loved to have me in the kitchen chatting to her. My life had a lovely slow rhythm to it. Mary would get out of bed and I'd roll into her warm spot. She would get things ready in the kitchen, clean and light the fires, fill the fuel buckets with turf, and off she'd go to an early Mass. She cooked a hot breakfast for us all and when I'd be walking across the road to the school with Mammy, Fr Lavin would be coming in for his breakfast. She fussed over Fr Lavin and if he said the moon would fall out of the sky and bounce along the road between the house and the school Mary would have believed him.

It was like having Jesus himself there in her kitchen.

I had a great time in school as Mammy was the teacher, and I got to run any messages. My brothers were in boarding school so some of the lads from school would get water for Mammy from the village pump and pour it into the water tank for us. We kept the water in a big ceramic urn and there was a tap on the bottom. Mary would boil it for cooking and cleaning. From morning to night, Mary would be on the go and never once did I hear her sigh or complain. On top of all the housework she had a little farm in the garden. Rows of turnips and potatoes and rhubarb. She kept a few geese, chickens, a pig and a goat.

Mammy and I would come home to Mary for lunch and sometimes Fr Lavin would have it with us. He and Mammy talked books mostly, they both liked to read. Fr Lavin brought Mammy lots of Agatha Christie books.

After school I did my homework in the kitchen and played outside with my hoop and stick or skipping rope, but mostly I liked to shadow Mary, and she would leave the caring of the animals for us to do together. We would go to the bees at the bottom of the field and tell them any news we could think of. And when I'd feed the pigs she would always say, 'Pigs can see the wind.' I never questioned that.

But now I was twelve and I had to go to boarding school to the nuns where my sister Eileen had been. Eileen had left to study nursing in Dublin, and everyone decided I should be a teacher like my mother, as I had a great memory for the stories Mary told, and was good at school, though not as good as Eileen.

Fr Lavin used to come often with a little boy from Cavan by the name of Jimmy. Jimmy was only six years old but tall for his age and Fr Lavin let Mary spoil him and we'd take him out and show him the animals and he was happy-out to be with us. Sometimes Fr Lavin would collect myself and Mary on a Saturday, and we'd drive to Cootehill where he lived with his parents who were old and had no other children. They had a house on the main street of Cootehill and had pictures of the Sacred Heart and Mary and Padre Pio with his bleeding hands.

One day we picked up Jimmy and off we went to see the head of Blessed Oliver Plunkett, it was only the size of an onion and kept in the big church in Drogheda. So I suppose heads shrink when they're pickled like that. Jimmy loved to hear about how he was hanged and then taken down just barely alive, then pulled along the road by horses and then slowly sliced in quarters and yet he didn't betray his faith or Ireland. Boys were into all that stuff. We'd kneel and pray in front of the relic and then sometimes, if there was more time, we'd go to Newgrange.

Fr Lavin and Mary were divils for the old ruins. An old lady had the key at Newgrange and we'd climb over the stones. She led us down the passageway with our heads bent and she held up the lamp and we could see carvings by ancient people.

'These were from the people who lived here first. They were Stone Age people but, by God, they knew their astronomy and mathematics,' Fr Lavin would tell us. 'Then the Celts came and there was a great battle and they were pushed underground.'

'The ancient people of this land were the sídhe. That's the Irish for fairies,' Mary whispered to us in the dark, cramped stone passage. 'They live on to plague us still as we take their land. Though there are those about us who have great relations with them and they can cure all sorts of ills.'

The old woman led us down the passage to the centre of the stones and she would extinguish her lamp. In the stony, deep dark cold we felt we were in the centre of the earth.

My favourite time was when Mary's brother Seán was home from the school he worked in. Though he was an adult, he always was easiest with me and never interacted with my mother and father. Mary would cook a goose and bring it with us on the picnic and Seán and Mary and Fr Lavin would bring Jimmy and me to see the castle in Trim and the Tower of Leprosy where the crusaders had come home with the disease. All ruins now. We'd go to the Yellow Steeple where there once had been a statue of Mary that was sacred and people came from far and wide to get cures from her. There was a great pilgrimage in Trim in the Middle Ages. Fr Lavin would point along the shining Boyne.

'What happened to her, the Idol of Trim?' I asked one time, 'Where is she now?'

'That was donkey's years ago. She was burnt during the Reformation.'

And the grown-ups sighed as if they still missed her.

We'd put our feet into the Boyne and Seán would teach us to skim stones. Jimmy and I would climb over every corner of the castle and scale right up to the top. I thought I was the most blessed of all children to be gallivanting around town and country with Mary and two priests.

'Why does Fr Lavin take you out like this every month?' I asked Jimmy as we sat with our legs in the sacred Boyne, where once Fionn had found the salmon of knowledge.

Jimmy shrugged. 'Dunno.'

I came over to the picnic where the adults where telling stories and eating sandwiches and drinking tea from flasks.

'Why do we take Jimmy with us?' I asked Mary.

Mary frowned at me and said, 'Musha would you watch your tongue. Don't be disgracing us.'

Fr Lavin smiled. 'Sure I thought you and he were the best of pals. Isn't that so Baby?'

Jimmy seemed very still, listening carefully, his head cocked to the side.

'His mammy and daddy are quite old and need a rest,' Mary said sternly and that was enough about that. I was scolded for my impertinence when I got home. Indeed those days you didn't ask adults much because they never told you anything.

We learned not to pester them. I had seen the animals jump on each other in the yard but I didn't realize that humans might have to do it too. Everything was a mystery.

Ignatius

A Walking Hoor
(1962)

They called her Bridget because we have an auntie Bridget in America who sent us money sometimes. She was the first girl after six boys. My mam would have her train as a skivvy from the beginning.

'At last someone to help me,' Mammy said.

More like, at last someone to wait on me hand and foot and do all the stuff I'm meant to do. And Da put the water from pipes in the byre for his animals but he wouldn't put it in the house for the women to use. Bridget was seven, and every day had to fill the buckets up with water from the pump in the barn and bring it back to the house for Mammy. And I saw her white face and her grey eyes and she had a tiredness about her and never a smile. I'd sometimes go up to her and kick over her bucket, she hated me.

Me and my brothers expected her to wash our stuff and get us food, and clean up after us, and we were happy she was born to serve us. Daddy and Mammy told her to stand up and give us the chair when any of us came in, and Bridget was growing up into a right miserable streel of a creature who looked like she'd been bet with a shovel. And she dressed like a boy, because with five brothers over her and one dead, there were no girl's clothes for her.

Bridget wailed when I kicked her bucket over and Daddy had seen it and I was in for it now. He came with his one peg leg and his one arm and a stick in it and he crashed it down on my head and yelled at Bridget to shut up the noise and go get more water, but he kept pounding the stick down across me back and me face and me ears and, then, when I was on the ground, he stuck the stick into my neck until I thought, it's going to go through me and he telt me.

'You know what ye are? Ye'r a walking hoor.'

I squirmed but he pinned me with his foot.

'What are ye?'

'A walking hoor,' I gasped.

Bridget stopt wailing and looked as happy as Bridget could ever look, which meant the look of absolute misery left her pale face for a moment and blankness took over. The blankness of satisfaction that another creature was more miserable than she was. Mammy came to the door. Maybe she'd stop him from killing me outright. Maybe not. She'd be glad to be rid of me too.

'Seamus. We need feckin water in the house. I've been telling you for years.'

Da kept his foot on my chest and snarled.

'If ye can't go to the well and pump the water then what good are ye anyway? Why would ye need water in the house? First it was the feckin electric lights that ye have to get out of bed to turn off, next it's water. What will it be after that? Yer useless enough as it is.'

'Go get more water. What are ye just standing there looking at?' Mammy yelled at Bridget. She never called any of us by our names. I thought she just mixed up the boys' names, but it was then I realized she never used Bridget's name either. This made me think, and as I was lying on the ground under me da's foot, I got new strength and I pushed back at the stick and grabbed it. I toppled me da over with his peg leg. Then I knew I was in for it as Kevin, who was sixteen and the eldest, came out from the barn and tried to grab me and give me a kicking too. I wiggled away and ran and ran and ran.

The fields were flat. There were no real hills to hide me but I sometimes went down to the woods at the end, or sometimes I spied on Patsey and went stealing from him.

This time, I ran over to Patsey's house and he was there, so I stopped.

'Ignatius!' He let out a big sigh. 'What are ye up to now? Look at the state of ye.'

'Da gave me a beating.'

'Ya probably deserved it. Did ye? Come in, boy, and I'll clean you up.'

Patsey lived on his own, and as me Da said he had a priesty smell about him. His house was very tidy and he had daisies in a glass on his table. And the table had a red and white check tablecloth on it. I sat down and took the petals off the daisies. A grown man picking daisies for himself seemed a bit odd, but Patsey was the only one who called me by me name and he didn't beat me like all the others, even when I stole from him. He'd caught me many's a time stealing eggs and other things but he usually gave them to me and didn't tell on me so I kept doing it since he was soft in the head like that.

Though me ma says Patsey cursed me when I was in her.

He had a box with plasters and Dettol and he washed me face, and me ear was swollen and I had a pain in me side.

'Why are ye clutching yer side?'

'Daddy had his foot on it.'

Patsey sighed as he lifted my shirt and put his big red hand on my chest, and said 'I'll take ye down to the doctor. Your rib might be broken. But don't tell your mammy and daddy I did, right?'

'I don't want to go to the doctor,' I said. 'I'll be kilt.'

Patsey shook his head and said. 'A rib will fix itself. Ye'd better get off then before Seamus finds out yer over here.'

He went into his bedroom and I walked over to his big display of blue china.

'Why do ye have blue china?' I called out. 'Yer such a Granny Knickers with it all out on display.' I took a little cup and put it in my pocket. He called me into the bedroom.

'Give me back the cup,' he sighed. 'And I'll give you a penny.'

So we made an exchange. I'd never been in his bedroom before. There was a picture of President Kennedy and a picture of the Pope and a statue of the Virgin Mary on the mantelpiece. The walls were bare. His bed was high and narrow and there were rosary beads and prayer books on a table beside it. He grunted a smile at me.

'Not much for you to steal here, Ignatius.' He really was the only one to ever call me that. The schoolmaster called me O Conaill. 'What are we going to do with you at all?' He was sitting on the bed and patted the side of it for me to sit down. But I would only sit down if he gave me more money.

'You've a great head on you, Ignatius. I do think you're the cleverest of all your brothers. You have a spark in you. A glint in your eye. I can see that. But you've grown wild as a weed and you'll end up doing some damage.'

'Me da says I'm a walking hoor.'

Patsey laughed. 'He's right, Ignatius. That you are.' He gave me another penny and placed the china cup on the dressing table. 'Go on off now, Ignatius. Stay out of your daddy's way till he's calmed down a bit. And leave your poor sister alone. She's a wretched time with all those men around her. Poor wee craytur.'

'Can I sleep here tonight?' I asked.

'Ye can in your arse! Sure there's no room. We can't be having that at all, at all.' Patsey was grinning.

'We can share the bed,' I said.

Patsey burst out laughing. 'I've been dreaming of having someone share my bed for a long time now but it's not you I've been dreaming of.'

And he kept laughing till it annoyed me and I went out and took a plate from his china and then he came out after me yelling for me to give it back so I turned around and skimmed it through the air and saw his big arms reach up to catch it and his hairy belly flop from his trousers over his belt as the plate sailed over his head and into the wall of his cottage and into smithereens. And he didn't look back at me as I ran off with the two pennies in me pocket and him on the ground with the crack of his arse sticking out as he picked up the pieces of the plate. Knowing that buck eejit, he'd be up all night gluing it together.

Baby

Vast Emptiness, Nothing Holy
(1958)

Mary was cleaning the church now too to get extra money. She was able to send her brother Seán to France for six months with a visit to Rome, but she wasn't impressed when he came back from 'out foreign' as she put it. France changed him, she felt. For me Seán was like a key to a door to the world. I used to wait at the gate and listen to him walking, jangling keys and loose change in his pocket, all the way from the bus in Trim. I'd see his blond head and his long stride. And he'd brighten when he saw me. Though I never could hug him now he was a priest and I was older, but I could run beside him and walk, trying to mirror his steps, and I knew Mary would be fussing to have everything just right for his arrival.

Mammy and Daddy ate in the dining room and Mary served them. When Eileen, James or Joseph came home they ate with them. But I would never leave the kitchen and Mary. Though Seán was a priest now, and an educated man, he chose to stay in the kitchen with us.

We three walked up the lane to pick blackberries and Seán tried to explain things to Mary that Mary didn't want explained.

'We went to Aix-en-Provence and saw Mary Magdalena's tomb.'

We filled our tins and reached into the hedges for more. The sky was Saturday blue, with jaunting white clouds.

'How did she get to France?' I asked. 'Is France near Palestine?'

'No, indeed it's not,' Seán said. 'When they excavated the tomb they dug her up and she had a piece of flesh still not rotted on her forehead where Jesus touched her to push her away from him when she tempted him. And her tongue was a branch still growing.'

Mary blessed herself with one hand to hear of a miracle. Miracles were nothing to Mary really.

Seán laughed. 'Turns out there was a rival tomb elsewhere in France. You see, if they could get the pilgrims in, in the Middle Ages, the whole economy of the town could change. She must have left about five corpses scattered around. The truth is she probably died in Palestine. The church accepts what the most powerful prince says and what suits them in the rush for relics.'

'Relics are powerful things,' Mary said, putting her hand right into the bush to get the sweet berries. 'Fr Lavin gave me the gift of a splinter of the cross and a thread from the shroud of Turin. I carry them about in my handbag. Sure they have great power in them.'

'That cross must have been a hundred foot tall with all the relics they give out. Look, Mary, the Romans had their main gods and then their household gods. We've substituted their polytheism with all our saints. Your St Jude, for impossible cases. Your St Antony, for lost items.'

'Blessed be!' Mary was pretending to be cross now. 'There's nothing wrong with saints. I didn't send you out foreign to become a Protestant.'

'I went to Rome and walked through the Vatican. I saw the Sistine Chapel. Michelangelo's paintings. And I had an audience with the Pope himself. Our head Brother and four of us younger Brothers were chosen.'

Mary stood. 'If Mammy and Daddy knew that would happen.' She stood and tears filled her eyes. I held onto her arm to steady her and she squeezed me close to her and wiped her eyes.

'I was out walking in Paris and I met a man in a café. He gestured towards me and I sat and had a coffee.'

'What's coffee?' I asked.

'It's a drink like tea but very strong and bitter. I didn't like it, but they drink it on the continent.'

'Seán has never had a drop of alcohol in his life.' Mary proudly told me. But Seán was so different from all the other grown-ups that nothing surprised me. I watched him stride ahead with long, loping steps, reaching out to pick the farthest blackberries. He was soft-spoken, tall and rake thin, his hair was light sandy blond and his eyes were deep blue with a grey rim. To me he was holy and had come from another planet. To me he was one of the shining ones from the lost race underground.

I caught up with him. 'Do you still talk to the fairies?' I asked hopefully.

From the days when I was little he took me out to the fields to talk to the fairies, I associated himself and Mary with the other world. They could both put their hands in and get the honey from the bees without getting stung.

'Now I talk to men in Parisian cafés.' He laughed.

'What did the man say?'

'He spoke very good English. He was Russian but had travelled to the Far East and had seen my robes and my collar and wanted to ask me some questions. He had converted to Buddhism.'

'What's buttism?'

'It's another religion.'

'What did he want to ask you?' I pestered.

'He asked me, "What is the absolute truth?"'

'What sort of question is that altogether?' Mary interrupted. 'I thought you were being minded by the older Brothers, not wandering about a city like that on your own.' She paused. 'What did you tell him?'

'I'm not a child, Mary. I might be a Christian Brother but I'm a free man. I told him it was in the teachings of Jesus Christ that the world could be redeemed. His sacrifice brings our savage species back to sacredness.'

'Good. That shook him. Giving up his Catholic religion and becoming a pagan.'

'He was Russian Orthodox, not Catholic, to begin with, Mary. Then he asked me who my leader was. I said it was the Pope in Rome. I told him I'd been to the Vatican, and he said he had heard of all the treasure amassed there. We talked awhile and I asked him about his truth. And he told me a story. For he was searching for truth.'

'What's the story?' I asked and sat at the side of the ditch to eat blackberries, and ready myself, for the O Conaills were great ones for the stories.

Seán looked at Mary for permission and I knew she would never resist a story no matter its source.

'When one of the great Buddhist holy men arrived from India to China, he was summoned by Emperor Wu.

'The Emperor questioned the monk. "What is the holy truth?"

'The great holy man thought for a while and finally said, "Vast emptiness, nothing holy."

'Emperor Wu was not satisfied and asked, somewhat frustrated, "Then who are you standing here before me?"

'The holy man smiled and said, "I don't know." And off he went.'

Seán laughed to see our stupefied faces.

'Well much good that did him,' Mary said, gathering our tins of blackberries. 'Summonsing an eejit like that and asking him difficult questions. More money than sense, that emperor. As for the holy man, there were two of them in it. At least with the Pope ye know where you are.'

'He gave me a lot to think about and we met a few more times and played chess and talked. We shook hands and he wished me luck with my journey and I with his.'

'Keep in mind, you were once devoted to St Colm Cille, Seán,' Mary said wistfully. 'He's kin of ours. St Colm Cille went out from Ireland with twelve men to convert the pagans of Scotland. He brought the word to them so they could be saved when England and Scotland were lying in ignorance and darkness. Of course they quickly reverted back to it when that scoundrel Henry wanted all those wives.'

'It is ironic,' Seán said as we headed back home, our tins full of blackberries, 'that he went to all that trouble to get a male heir and there was Elizabeth his daughter and she made the best ruler England ever saw.'

'She wasn't much good to us. None of them were. We're well rid of them,' Mary said.

'We're free now,' I echoed.

'Are we free?' Seán said. 'I've been studying Brehon Law, the old laws of Ireland that served us well until the 1600s and the consolidation of English rule. There were many in 1916 who, when they created an Ireland free from empire, wanted to go back to the old Brehon Laws. But we didn't. We took British law and Roman Catholicism.'

'What I meant, Seán, is that you should be out converting that poor man when it sounds like he was converting you. I'm going to get Fr Lavin to talk to you.'

You see that was the kind of talks we used to have when Seán came home. No one else in my life talked like that. That is why I stayed in the kitchen.

Seán and I were eating so many blackberries we were stained on the mouth and fingers with red juice. Mary gave us bowls of water to wash ourselves.

'The last thing he said to me, Mary, was, "If you meet the Buddha, kill the Buddha."'

'He sounds like a right demon altogether. Aren't all them Russians communists?'

'Is that because he has the wrong religion?' I asked. 'Maybe he knew you were right in the end and the Pope was the Holy Father of us all on Earth.'

'I don't know what that means, Baby,' Seán said.

'Stop filling her head with nonsense, Seán.' Mary scolded. She was banging pots around and sticking the poker into the stove and rooting it around making an awful racket. Fr Lavin knocked at the kitchen window. He came most evenings now for his supper, it was a Saturday so he had little Jimmy with him. Jimmy ran in and Mary gave him a hug and a tin of blackberries. Fr Lavin nodded at Seán and shook hands.

'Welcome back from your travels. Sure come in and regale us with your adventures.'

'He met the Holy Father!' Mary said triumphantly. Fr Lavin gasped and put his hands to his heart.

'A man who has an audience with the Pope should come sit with us in the dining room. We need all the news.'

Seán smiled. 'I'll stay in the kitchen. I have to be going back early in the morning and I'll talk to Mary.'

'Go in, go in.' Mary ushered Fr Lavin out of the kitchen and Mammy and Daddy got up to greet him.

So we ate, Mammy and Daddy and Fr Lavin in the dining room and Jimmy, Seán, and myself in the kitchen. Mary never sat down but ran back and forth serving us all.

'I sometimes go with Mary when she's cleaning the church,' I told Seán. 'I say some prayers to the Virgin.'

'Mary won't need to be cleaning the church anymore. I've done my travels. I'll soon be teaching and I'll be able to take Mary to Rome, and the Holy Land, and Lourdes.'

'You'll have your pick of schools,' Fr Lavin said, entering the kitchen to ask for second helpings. 'A maths degree and meeting the Pope. I hear you are quite the star of the Christian Brothers.'

'Sit down, sit down, Father; I'll be in in a minute.' Mary said from the scullery.

'I want to go to one of the industrial schools. They want me to go to Blackrock College or somewhere like that.'

'Why would you go to one of those places?'

'I feel they need changing and sorting out. I feel my mission would be most fulfilled there, and not among the children of the wealthy and powerful.'

'He's got all sorts of queer notions since they sent him out foreign,' Mary said, returning with a plate of more spuds.

'Mmm,' Fr Lavin said. 'I always felt he was a bit of a Jesuit in Christian Brothers' clothing but now I'm afraid he's a missionary.'

I picked up a spud and proclaimed, 'If you meet the spud, kill the spud.' And I bit a chunk out of the potato.

There was a shadow by the window.

'It's Suds and Sins!' I yelled to Mary. Suds and Sins was a queer fellow who used to live in a one-room house down the lane, with half of his roof fallen in. When it rained he sat in the other half of the house. The odd time, Mary had him in for a cup of tea. But he had a habit of flinging the dregs of his cup over his shoulder at the wall behind, so used was he to doing this in the ruin he lived in. He had a few pigs that lived with him in the house, and he would come looking to all the neighbours for spuds and skins to feed them. The poor man was a bit innocent of the mind and had a speech defect so it came out as 'suds and sins'.

Mary went out to whoosh him off. 'We're running late tonight, musha, come back in a few hours.' She bustled back in, shaking her head. 'Honestly you'd think I had no pigs of my own to feed.'

435

We Prayed to the Blessed Virgin (1957)

The Sisters made us take the first baths when the water was steaming. Sister Joseph pushed me into the basin, and I didn't have clothes on and the boiling water burned me all over until my body was red and I was screaming and scrambling at the edges to come out howling, so I was. When I lay on the ground after she beat me with the belt that tied up her black robes the other girls looked away, so they did.

Then we had to pour the boiling basins into the baths to take care of the babies. Some of the babies would go away to families and some would stay or go to other schools. If one was to be given to a family then we had to spend a few days fattening it up and making sure it was kept clean and its bottom wasn't red.

Sister Joseph told us to put a small girl in the bath. She was three years old, and I told her the water was too hot. 398 put the wee girl in so we wouldn't get beaten and the wee three-year-old girl was screaming. 398 held her down like she was meant to and I took the little one out but the little one was falling into my arms and was dead. An inspector came and talked to us. Sister Joseph said we would be severely punished and it was a terrible mistake. The inspector said we were eight and ten years old, so nothing could be done about our murder. I prayed to the Blessed Virgin Mary every night to forgive us for the killing and when the nun put me in icy water to punish me for wetting the bed, I hoped I'd die and God would consider it even.

I thought of the little girl and I remembered her snotty round face, and her hair brown and thin, and I was jealous. Because she got away from the Sisters and I was still here, so I was.

Ignatius

Bad Egg, Bad Bird
(1962)

I wasn't going back to the house to sleep with me smelly brothers because they'd skin me alive for knocking me da over in the yard. I was cold as a witch's tit but I spent the next two days down in the woods with nothing but berries to eat and I didn't go to school, but that was normal for me because I didn't like the schoolmaster, he was always belting me with his leather belt and cursing our whole family.

Bridget actually liked going to school, but I think she went for a rest as it was the only time she wasn't working cos she was a bit of a dimwit just like me and not able to do the reading or writing no matter how much the master hit her knuckles with the ruler. She just sat and stared into space with her mouth open and her teeth yellow and crooked, like the last little flicker of light, sometimes there, sometimes not. She never talked much or played in the schoolyard, but just sat in the shelter and wanted to be left alone. It was bad enough coming from all them brothers who caused trouble, and having the others laugh at us because we had no shoes and were ragged and gormless, but then our sister was a plain little dunce with a face on her like a pig licking piss off a nettle. And our da was a disgrace losing an arm and then a leg in separate farm accidents. The feckin eejit. And our mother never did much for us either except whinge and blame us for all her ills.

So when me uncle Seán arrived with Fr Gilligan and was talking in the kitchen and me da called me in I finally went back indoors. He wouldn't lay into me in front of them.

'Look at the state of the little savage. He's a walking hoor, he is. Ask any of them. He's the worst of them all and they're all pretty bad,' my da said and Fr Gilligan nodded in agreement and beckoned to me.

He looked behind my ears and checked my fingernails.

'Maybe give him a bath before he goes,' Fr Gilligan said with his nose all scrunched up. My mother was sitting by the fire and she snorted.

'Don't ye know, we don't have the water in the house yet, Father? He has it for his cattle though.' She spit into the fire and it hissed green on the turf.

'Seamus, why is his ear swollen like that and his face all bruised?' my uncle Seán said.

'I won't tell a lie, I beat him because he was torturing his poor sister and her getting the water for her mammy.'

They glanced at Bridget who was standing on a stool peeling a stack of potatoes for the dinner.

'I wouldn't put a child in the place I work,' Seán said, 'it's like a Siberian gulag. There's 250 beds in each dormitory and we have four dormitories.'

'She won't have him anymore.' Seamus pointed to Mammy who shrugged.

'Sure he hasn't been inside in days. He'll just turn out like Padraig,' Sheila said. 'Your sister Mary put a curse on him when I was carrying him.'

'I thought it was Patsey did that,' Da said. 'We don't want another Padraig alright though, she's right.'

'Padraig was away with the fairies,' Seán said. 'He had no harm in him.'

'Aye, it might have been Patsey that said the words but it was Mary egging him on and she's a witch mind you,' Ma grumbled.

'Padraig was innocent in the mind. But this one isn't.' Da glared at me. 'He's a little bastard, excuse my language, Father but you only have to ask the master. He can't read or write and he doesn't care. He's always tormenting his sister and the other wee ones in school and he won't do a drop of work here for us so he's no use to me. He's a bad lot. Maybe your school will put some manners on him.'

My big brothers were all in the kitchen now listening and grinning. Loving that I was getting it in the throat like this. They had their arms folded and some of them were spotty and all of them had their elbows hanging out of their gansies. Steadily, I looked around at my family. An ugly lot.

'Only for a temporary stay mind you, Seamus.' Seán looked at me and I looked hard at him. I narrowed my eyes so he wouldn't think I'm soft and try to give me a hiding for good measure. 'I'll keep an eye on you. Since you're my family they'll go easy. I'll tell you something, I was ready to go to another school, but if Ignatius comes for a few months it might straighten him out and he'll be happy to get back here. I can try to get him reading.'

Fr Gilligan nodded vigorously. 'It's the only way. An ideal solution. You being there and all. I thought maybe another industrial school would be smaller and less of a change. There's a good one locally that I have boys placed in all the time, but since you are up there in Dublin you can make sure the boy learns a trade and gets sorted out. Because he's a bad egg so far. There's an evil in his heart from an early age and maybe he needs to be taught a lesson.'

'I'm not doing it to teach him a lesson,' Seán said. 'I'm doing it to get him out of here.'

'What do you mean by that?' Seamus roared. My brothers sniggered slyly.

'He's black and blue.'

'Sure he's been sleeping in the woods for two days now.'

Kevin my eldest brother said, '*Drochubh, drochéan.*'

'What does that mean?' Mammy said. 'I've told ye, no Irish in this house.'

Uncle Seán closed his eyes. He looked like he hated being here as much as I did. 'It means 'bad egg, bad bird', Sheila. This is a Gaeltacht area. We got the land to speak the Irish. Come on Ignatius, let's get out of here.'

'Right so. What does he need to bring with him?' Fr Gilligan had drank his tea and set the cup back on the table, a sure sign he was off. There were never any biscuits or cake in our house for the priests to scoff down their greedy gullets.

'I don't have nothing,' I said. And I didn't. 'Even if I did there's nothing I'd take from here.'

As pleased as punch I walked out of there without looking at me mother or any of me brothers. Me da hobbled up to the door and took me by the scruff of my neck.

'You be civil up there and we'll have you back on the farm. Do ya hear?'

'I don't want to come back,' I said.

'Good riddance to bad rubbish,' me mother snarled from her chair by the fire. It had a print in it from her bony arse; she had wore it down over the years.

And the last thing I saw was Bridget who ran up to me with tears brimming in her grey ordinary eyes and she threw her arms around me. I looked down and I could see all the eggs in her hair from the lice behind her ears. I was so shocked that I let her squeeze the life out of me until I unpeeled her arms and pushed her away.

Baby

Firbolgs and Fomorians Running Amok (1958)

I brought Mary's bread and butter, and honey, in a basket up to Fr Lavin and stood beside him as he looked under the cloth at the food. Seán walked up the road behind me.

'He doesn't look like an Irish man at all,' Fr Lavin said. 'He's like a Viking. The O Conaills mustn't have been pure Irish after all.'

'What is pure Irish?' I asked as he took the basket and broke off a bit of hot bread.

'Well,' he said through a mouth full of crust. 'The people who lived here first were the shídh and they had a big battle with the Firbolgs, then the Fomorians.'

'Were they invaders?'

'They were states of mind, my child. There's still plenty of Firbolgs and Fomorians running amok in this country with all sorts of notions, I can tell you. Extraordinary isn't it that Seán and Maeve were Vikings and the rest of them are small and dark like the Celts. Two things in the one family.'

'Have you ever seen a fairy, Father?'

'No, Baby, I have not.'

'Mammy and Daddy say it's all piseogs and rawmeash.'

'Your mammy and daddy are educated people.'

'But Mary says ...'

'Mary is a good woman.' Fr Lavin put his hand firmly on my shoulder. 'Sure if all we believed in was what we saw, we'd be letting our blindness take over. And I'd be out of business to be sure.'

Seán was smiling. Though he was now a Christian Brother I still saw him as kind of my brother. In fact my brothers were just into the football and hurling and their friends. They had never talked to me like Seán did.

'This child is asking me deep questions, Seán.' Fr Lavin patted my head.

'I need to talk to Fr Lavin, pet,' Seán said. 'Run along. I'll be over soon and we'll go for a walk up the lane.'

'Now that you're educated do you still believe in fairies?' I asked Seán, and Fr Lavin burst out laughing.

'Come in, come in. Let's have some of Mary's bread. She's a great woman altogether.'

'I want you to hear my confession.' Seán looked serious.

'Is it the man in Paris?' I asked. Both of them looked at me in astonishment and I realized that once again I had said something that would stop the adults in their tracks entirely. Fr Lavin, being the consummate professional he always was, made light of it.

'Come in, come in. Sure we're starved of intellectual conversation until you come home to us here. Come in, come in.'

I skipped off. I felt a bit old for skipping but I did it deliberately. As excited as I was to be growing up, I was anxious at leaving my home and Mary and going away to school. I wanted to stay in this part of my life for longer. I was hoping the men were watching me skip and think I was a lovely innocent child. I wanted to be a picture of a little girl to lighten their hearts. After skipping down the road I looked behind but they had gone inside the priest's house and I was alone on the road.

It was like my house had two worlds inside it. There was the electrical world of my parents. They had the living room where they played poker and had their social evenings. They drank whiskey out of Waterford crystal. The picture of de Valera and the men of 1916 were on the wall. A metal Jesus writhed on a wooden cross inscribed with Latin.

Then there was the kitchen with its gaslight. On the wall hung Bridget's Cross made of rushes. While my parents listened to the wireless every evening in the living room, Mary stared into the fire. The living room world of my house belonged to St Patrick and Romanized Europe, and the kitchen to the older, wilder way of St Colm Cille, Bridget, hags, fairies, and ancient Ireland. What she was looking for and what she found in the flames was a mystery to me.

That evening I made Mary tell me a story and Seán was leaning at the threshold listening. We had not heard him come in. He was smiling at his older sister. I saw a look pass between them of pure love that made me a tiny bit jealous.

The next morning Seán was leaving. He was to start teaching maths and Irish in St Joseph's Industrial School in Dublin.

'Fr Lavin said you could get a post in any school. You're very well liked he said,' Mary fretted.

'I chose this school,' Seán said. 'I've been clear all along. I don't want to go teach the sons of the rich. By the way, Mary, I got up this morning and filled up your water from the pump. Look, don't worry about me. The rich will be fine without me. Why am I in service to God? Would Jesus be out in Blackrock College, St Michael's, Gonzaga? I want to change someone's life.'

I loved when he talked like this. Like a hero in a storybook. Mary bit her lip and shrugged.

'Musha, sure there was always a want in you, but you're a man now. Don't forget us.' She held him close and we walked to the door and to the gate and watched him walk away. The disappearing Viking on an Irish country road.

'I don't want to go to the nuns in the school, Mary,' I said. 'Everything will change.'

'Child of grace. That's the only thing we can be sure of in this world.'

'What?'

'Change. Everything changes all the time.'

'But I don't want it to change.' For I was so happy with her in her witch's kitchen.

'Neither do I, *mo mhuirnin Bán*, neither do I.' And she turned from the fire and we looked at each other for a long time. I don't think in all my life I have ever held another human's gaze for that length of time.

On the day at the end of summer that I got ready for school, Mary and I went to the bees to tell them I was leaving. We were walking down the lane with our arms linked and we met an old neighbour on the road. The old lady was sick and it was shocking to see her with her grey hair hanging down around her shoulders, for adults never went out without their heads covered in either a scarf or a hat. We nodded to her but she looked right through us. She began to walk across her field and she stopped and turned and we saw her on the ridge staring off at the trees. The old lady with her long grey hair seemed to have nothing left in her. She was a marked contrast to the crows' maniacal industry.

'That's old Mrs MacTiernan,' Mary whispered.

Mary and I stood and watched Mrs MacTiernan for a while. And then Mary shivered and we walked back to the house, slowly, reluctantly, making each step last. She recited one of her poems.

I have news for you: the stag bells, winter snows, summer has gone,
Wind high and cold, the sun low; short its course, the sea running high.
Deep red the bracken, its shape is lost; the wild goose has raised its
accustomed cry.
Cold has seized the birds' wings; season of ice, this is my news.

I said the words after her in my mind so I would never lose them. As we walked up to our gate I looked at the house of my childhood. Just as countries have their stories and fables, so too have houses. This was the house where, according to our family folklore, Mary had walked barefoot for five miles along the roads, out of an Irish-speaking world, with her short grey hair under a headscarf. My parents, the schoolteacher and the solicitor, had met her at this very gate and when she shook my mother's hand they got an electric shock from one another. And Mary who at that time couldn't speak English all that well, her reading and writing about the standard of a five-year-old, who had never been much farther than her farm and the church since leaving her home in the south-west, had told my parents that that shock was caused by the electrons leaving the atom. We all would tell that story all our lives for it said something about our assumptions. Really it said something about Mary.

What would I do without her? How would I sleep, in a dormitory, without her? How would I eat that horrible food? It said a lot about those religious people. How they fed you.

'Should we go take her inside?' I asked. 'We can't just leave Mrs MacTiernan in the field.'

'No.' Mary shut the gate and sighed, looking at me with love and pity. 'She is just taking a last look, that's all.'

Ignatius

He'll Be With Us for a While (1962)

This was my first time in a car and I got to sit up front. Uncle Seán stopped off in Clonee and we went to a shop and he bought me an ice cream with a chocolate stick in it, and said it was a 99. I never had ice cream or chocolate before and bejaysus it was the best thing ever.

'That's just the cat's bollix!' I said to Uncle Seán as we sat in the car. He laughed and rubbed my hair. As his hand came near me I winced.

'You've nothing to worry about, Ignatius. I've never hit a child in my whole life and I never will.'

'But you're a master, a Brother.'

'We're not all violent bullies, Ignatius. Some of us are trying to change the way things are done.'

I stared out the window as the green of the fields disappeared until there was nothing but houses and buildings.

'Where do they grow their food here, Uncle Seán?'

'They buy their food from farmers like you.'

'But where do they keep their cattle?'

Soon we sat in the office of the head Brother. Uncle Seán told me to be quiet during the interview. I sat on a chair behind my uncle. He was so tall and thin and his hair was as yellow as the hay we fed the animals. His fingers were long and fine. His hands were soft from only having to hold a pencil and never a spade. I had never seen the likes of him in all me life. The head Brother was a small man beside him, small, with a big belly and his eyes pierced right through me as if he could see everything inside of me. He wrinkled his nose as if it smelled bad.

'So this is he.'

'Ignatius O Conaill, Brother Peter,' Uncle Seán said. 'He'll be with us for a while. Till the end of the year.'

'We have to get him down on the books all the same.'

They made a file for me then and there. I was now a part of St Joseph's Industrial School, Dublin.

Baby

A Respectable Institution
(1962)

I didn't hate all of them. Sister Assumption was a blue-collar nun, which meant she had entered the convent at age twelve with no dowry. She was assigned to work in the kitchens for life. The blue-collar nuns had a separate common room from the white-collar nuns. The white-collar nuns had entered with dowries, and so were educated and became the educators. I hated Sister Assumption's first cousin, Mother Peter, who had entered with a dowry. Sister Assumption's brother was a priest and when he came to visit he would sit with Mother Peter in the parlour and Sister Assumption would come in, and bring them tea and sandwiches, but was not allowed to stay and sit with her own brother.

I sometimes wondered if there was anything else I could do besides teaching or nursing. The mother superior told me how my exam results were superlative and that I could go into teaching. My older sister Eileen was one of her favourites. She had finished her training as a nurse and had landed a job in a hospital in Dublin.

All the nuns loved Eileen. Except for the one mistake she made when she thought she could do honours maths and had to go to the boys' school because they didn't teach honours maths in the girls' school. Eventually, they forgave her her ambition and were only too happy to guide her in a more feminine way. She was Joan of Arc in the school play. She was head girl. It was only through the grace of Eileen, and the fact that the nuns were inveterate snobs, that they tolerated me at all. I was good in school, but my attitude and handwriting needed working on, so they kept saying. I wasn't ladylike enough for them, not like Eileen.

We were put at a table in the dining room with all the rich farmers' and bankers' daughters and our food was better than the others'. The scholarship girls were at their own tables. They were smart but poor and the nuns seemed to bear them a grudge. Finally, there were those who were not allowed sit at all. The nuns had the 'home' girls who were orphans, and they did all the skivvy work. They had to even take our used sanitary napkins and burn them on a pile. I watched them do this once. The air full of sweet burnt blood and acrid cloth. I tried to talk to them once and other girls spied me and reported me to the head nun. I was in severe trouble and I didn't know why. No one could tell me why.

'Just don't talk to them,' the nun said.

'Is that what Jesus would have done?' I said. 'Didn't he talk to the Samaritan woman at the well?'

No one dared beat us because we were paying students. Sister Assumption warned me that I was in a lot of trouble just for trying to talk to those girls and that I might get them in trouble too.

My parents were called to the school and I was reprimanded for insubordination. I walked down those long polished corridors into my mother's fury. They were strangers to me since I'd been away months now. Sister Michael was scathing.

'Don't think you're doing those poor unfortunate creatures any favours by your attention. You're only getting them into trouble too, you know. This is a respectable institution.'

There was so much I wanted to say. I looked pleadingly at my parents. I thought they might understand, but we were not allowed to be alone together. The nuns were everywhere. And they had their spies among the girls. I hadn't seen Mammy and Daddy since September and now here they were, and I couldn't even touch them.

'We assure you she won't do anything like that again,' Daddy said.

'She's a good girl,' Mammy said. 'She's a good heart. She sometimes doesn't know what's appropriate.'

'Can you explain yourself, miss?' Sister Michael said. She said it with such authority that my words got stuck in my throat. I saw my parents looking pleadingly at me. I wondered did they miss me too. I wanted to ask how Mary was. I wanted them to take me home and send me to day school in Trim. I'd cycle in and home. I'd see Mary every day.

'I ... I just wanted to ask them where they were from and what were their names. They're in school with us but no one knows their names.'

My parents cringed. I'd said the wrong thing again. And then my mother said it and I began to understand.

'It's our fault, Mother Michael.' Mammy wrang her hands. 'We had, have, I should say, a wonderful housekeeper Mary, but maybe we let Baby around her too much? She slept with her until she came here. My fault. Maybe I should have had her around us more ...'

'Baby?' Mother Michael shrieked. 'Who's Baby?'

I blushed to the soles of my feet; my blush went down beyond my feet. Down into the floor of the office, penetrating the wood, down the foundations of the grey old school, down into the earth, down where the fairies were until they were blood red with my blush.

'Teresa, I mean. Baby is her nickname at home. Of course now that she's sixteen ...'

Mother Michael's piggy eyes bored a hole right through my chest until the icy wind whistled into my heart.

'This explains a lot. She's not Eileen I'll warrant you that ...'

'No she's not,' my mother agreed a bit too quickly.

My father remained mute throughout the whole meeting. Though he was a solicitor and would stand up in court and battle with a judge, he too quaked in front of this formidable nun. I suddenly wanted to be a nun just to have power over even the men. No other women I'd ever seen had any of this power. Maybe that was why all the nuns took men's names. Why did they take all men's names? I suddenly had the urge to ask.

But my parents were respectable middle-class people of Ireland and Mother Michael took a deep breath. Her shoulders sank a little below her ears and she seemed to purse her lips in restraint.

'She's a bright girl. Her Inter Cert results were excellent. In the top three of her year. I'm sure she'll do teaching. How is Eileen doing?'

All three adults brightened up at the mention of my sister.

I twisted the sleeve of my sweater around my finger until it had formed a knot.

When my parents got up to go. I lingered, waiting to see them by themselves for even a minute, but Mother Michael waved me off and Daddy looked at me pleadingly as I turned to go. Mammy clutched her brown handbag on her knee, she had tears in her eyes as I closed the big oak door.

That night in the dormitory, I lay and stared at the ceiling. There was a world outside and I would just have to wait it out. Next year I would do my Leaving Cert and be gone. Gone from this institution, this world of nuns and their rules, gone from the long polished wood corridors with the statues of demure Mary and her eyes cast down. My mother had an aunt in America and Mary had Bridget and Maeve, her sisters, over there. I would go to New York. I would live in a tall skyscraper where I could see the Statue of Liberty and the Golden Gate Bridge and Elvis Presley. My world would be full of people with ideas. I would escape the mean, rat eyes of the nuns.

That following week I sneaked into the kitchen garden to see Sister Assumption. Officially, we weren't allowed to speak to the blue-collar nuns; they were the servants. The teaching nuns had white cuffs that set them apart. But the blue-collar nuns were nicer to us.

'Teresa, pet. How did it go?'

'Ach, I got a scolding that's all.'

'Are ye in for it with your mammy and daddy? For making them come all the way?'

'They'll have calmed down by Christmas. That's a whole two months away.'

'Teresa?'

'What?'

'Do ye know what happened to the girls you tried to talk to?'

'No.'

'Mother Michael stripped them naked and beat them with a cane.'

'They're mad but I never heard them give a beating.'

'Not to you girls. Ye have families. But they beat the girls who don't. They tied them to the bed and beat them.'

'I don't believe you. How do you know this?'

'They were sent to the infirmary after with their injuries and I went there and gave them bread and jam and listened to them.'

Sister Assumption saw how sorry I looked and she touched me, patting me on the arm. She had a country, relaxed, open way about her that reminded me of Mary; maybe that's why I always sought her out. I was stunned to be touched, even a hint of affection was a revolutionary gesture in that world.

'I'm just telling you so's you'll know it's better to keep to your own kind. For everyone's sake, like a good girl.'

Ignatius

The Saint of Workers (1962)

'St Joseph is the saint of workers, Ignatius,' Brother Peter told me. I said nothing. 'You'll learn a trade here. Learn how to take part in society, be useful, and be close to God.'

I was about to leave when Brother Peter looked closely at Uncle Seán.

'I thought you were thinking of leaving us. I suppose this means you'll be staying.'

'I was applying for the missions, Brother Peter. I came here for the boys but I don't think I've been of any use.'

'You're their favourite teacher, that's for sure. But you're a bit soft on them. You have to learn that sparing the rod spoils the child. You are part of a great institution.'

'I didn't want to be part of an institution, I wanted to be part of a church. I don't feel I'm serving God here. I don't even feel I fit into the institution. The other Brothers certainly don't trust me.'

'They think you're watching them, Brother O Conaill. They think you're judging them. Are you?'

'There has to be a different way of doing things.'

Jaysus, I thought. The taste of the chocolate was gone from my mouth though my tongue rooted around for it.

'These are children of a bad element, Brother O Conaill. They have no breeding. If we don't sort them out now and put the fear of God in them, then they'll be lost and in and out of the prisons as soon as they get out of here at sixteen.'

'What about the Love of God?'

'Let me tell you something, Brother O Conaill. In 1831 there were only forty-five Christian Brothers in the world. Then, by 1900 there were a thousand. Now, in 1962, there are four thousand Christian Brothers in Ireland. We know what we are doing. We know where this country has to go.'

'But I would like to see us expanding our notion of compassion.'

Brother Peter laughed, and leaned back in his chair. 'Now you're sounding like a Quaker! Ireland might not have necessarily been such a Catholic country. Around the beginning of the 1800s the church was disorganized and in the west of the country, where your people originally came from, no one was adhering to rules and rituals. It was around the 1830s that the church began to consolidate its power.'

'Really?' Uncle Seán actually looked interested. 'What changed?'

'There were a lot of other churches, Protestant churches evangelizing and trying to take the souls of the Irish people. Our strategy was to take over the social services, hospitals, education. It worked!' He pounded his fist on the table. 'By the early twentieth century we dominated everything and had managed to get the treasury to fund us.'

'Even though the government then was British and Protestant?'

'Yes because we were disciplined and organized. That's what I'm trying to tell you. We know what we are doing. You have to have some measure of trust.'

'Of course now with Independence, the Catholic Irish state has written into its constitution that Ireland is a Catholic country.'

'Yes indeed, Brother O Conaill. Our discipline paid off. We have become a centralized Roman organization and all that folk belief and other nonsense, that went on for thousands of years with ignorant peasants and their piseogs, has been stamped out.' He leaned back in his seat, I could tell he was a man who liked an audience. 'Look at the Sisters of Mercy. They were clever in that their order answers directly to the Bishop himself, so they have all the schools and orphanages. If you see the convents in any small town, they dominate the town architecturally and otherwise. I visited one a few weeks ago that had a laundry, a secondary school, a mother and baby home, and an industrial school all on the same complex.' The Brother glanced over at me and back to Uncle Seán. He turned his hands up as if to receive something. 'Don't you see? We control all women, men, boys and girls, of every class. The people of Ireland are here, in the palm of our hands.'

'That's a lot of power,' Uncle Seán said quietly.

'Your power, Brother O Conaill. Power for good. Without so much as an election, we guide this country.'

This sounded great to me. I immediately decided then and there to join the Christian Brothers as soon as I could. I'd be on the pig's back, for sure. But Uncle Seán's lips disappeared as if he was eating what he was about to say.

'Boys are coming to me, Brother; they talk of badness being done to them.'

Brother Peter suddenly stood and walked to the window, though I could see from his gaze he wasn't looking out. He was still as a church statue.

'I'm not saying all our Brothers are good men. We have to weed out some of the bad apples. You let me handle that.'

'It's endemic.'

'Brother O Conaill.' Brother Peter swung around and faced him. 'What is the main part of your mission as a Brother?'

'Love?'

Brother Peter spluttered and went red at the mention of the word. He narrowed his eyes at Uncle Seán. 'Obedience. Love will stem from obedience. These boys need guidance and a firm hand otherwise, with their numbers, it would be them running amok, chaos.'

'Is this really a church or is it just an institution?'

'Enough,' he snarled. 'I know you're clever. I know you are bright. But you are arrogant. We own you, Brother O Conaill. We own you body and soul. You are a sensitive chap, a gifted teacher of maths and Irish. We have many industrial schools. Artane, Letterfrack, Salthill, Glin and Tralee. You can be transferred to anyone of those. I don't know if you are cut out for it. There's a weakness in you, dare I say it, a femininity.'

I didn't know what that meant but it made my uncle flinch.

Brother Peter saw he'd got to him, and he smirked. 'You are a man of talents; you could get out of the industrial schools and teach the sons of the respectable people of Ireland. All the same, maybe for a man of such a contemplative disposition you would be more suited to Letterfrack, it is in a beautiful setting in the West surrounded by the Connemara countryside. Didn't your people come originally from there?'

'No, Brother Peter, we came from Kerry. I was just a baby. Though, I can't really call myself a Meath man, as most of the other families around us were Connemara. I'd like to leave Ireland, Brother. I found that trip I took to the Vatican and holy sites in France to be very enlightening.'

'Not too enlightening I hope.' Brother Peter smiled slyly, he cleared his throat and stood up and began to pace behind the desk. I'd never been in the presence of anyone who talked so much. Though it wasn't a conversation. 'That's possible if you play your cards right. We have ninety-five houses here in Ireland. Thirty houses in England, five in Gibraltar, seventy-five in Australia, twelve in Canada, eighteen in the United States of America, eighteen in India, and ten in South Africa. Take your pick. Where do you want to go?' He opened his hands wide. I was itching to get out of here and ask Uncle Seán where to sign up. I had never even been to a town before, and now I was hearing names of places that sounded so wonderful. Africa. Gibraltar. Australia. Where were these worlds?

'I'd like to go to India, Brother. But my nephew has been taken into the school for a few months so I'll stay while he's here, to watch out for him. He's a troubled boy and his parents felt that he needed my guidance and a more disciplined environment.'

'Well there you go; obviously you have faith in this fine school if your own family is now in attendance. That's great news. An endorsement.'

'To tell you the truth, if I hadn't taken him our local priest would have sent him somewhere else, so I intervened. We could make a difference in these children's lives. I saw it as a mission once. But many of the Brothers are out of control. There's no stopping them.'

'Look, Brother O Conaill, I'm aware of your concerns. There has been an internal dialogue about discipline techniques for many years. In the 1930s the Superior General himself advocated the banning of corporal punishment. Of course this proved to be unfeasible.'

'Unfeasible?'

The big man came and stood in front of me. He looked me up and down and didn't seem to like what he saw. He swung back around to Uncle Seán. 'Brother O Connail, you have been singled out as a young man of great promise. You have a brilliant future in this order. Granted, so much so that you don't belong here. Mission or not, you just don't belong. I know that most of the Brothers here can't get posted anywhere else. Just don't make waves. We have our ways of doing things. These children are from the worst elements of society. They are tarnished before they are born. They all hail from the lower elements, unmarried women, criminal fathers, the poor, they are the detritus of our new independent society. If they weren't here they would be where? Through original sin, these children are born savage animals, with our rigorous discipline, and, yes, that means force and fear, we mould them into useful citizens. What could your objection be?'

Uncle Seán hesitated and spoke softly. 'It seems they are being punished for the perceived sins of their parents, if being poor is indeed a sin. We are also, I believe, receiving a stipend for each child from the state, yet the food is inadequate. We are starving the children while using their labour for free. We are, in fact, profiting. I'm a maths teacher, I can work that out. I do the books for the school. But the so-called badness is what I'm most concerned about.'

The Brother's face went red with rage again; he contained himself, leaned over his desk, on his fists. His voice was soft and restrained. 'Obedience, Brother O Conaill, obedience. You are young, there is much you don't understand. Your scallywag nephew is welcome here of course, and we hope it benefits him. He will have special protection here as your kin. Once he is in the system though we have the right to decide when he leaves and how long he needs.'

'And after that I can go to India?'

'Yes, no doubt that can be arranged. But I'd advise you to stay in this country and with your formidable intellect you will go far in this organization, but you need to learn obedience, Brother. That is your fatal flaw. Your vanity and arrogance have been duly noted. There's something of the fanatic in you. Do not question everything. Your compassion is misguiding you. Making you insolent. Untrustworthy. Trust is crucial. Can we trust you? We have the interests of the organization to protect.'

'It is the interests of the children that I came here for.'

'The interests of our organization are the interests of the children, the two cannot be separated.'

I looked between the two men and I realized that they hated each other. Why had I only noticed that now? Usually at home, everyone would be yelling at each other if they were angry. But this was a different kind of anger. That was the end of the conversation, I had learnt a lot and I now knew what I wanted to be when I grew up, so I followed my tall uncle out and down the corridor where he showed me into a giant dorm with rows and rows of iron beds, and gave me the number 100332.

'Never get on Brother Peter's bad side, Ignatius. I think I just have. You'll be cleverer than me. This will be your number. You'll be known by it from now on by everyone except me.'

'I want to be a Brother too, Uncle Seán, like you.'

He laughed, sudden and high-pitched. 'Why would you want to do that?'

'That buck eejit Kevin will get the farm. I have to be something and I like how strong he made it sound to be a Brother.'

Uncle Seán smiled and patted me on the back. I had never had anyone touch me like he did.

I followed him as his shoes squeaked through the quiet dormitory, I was barefoot. I had never owned shoes in me life.

'This is Dormitory 3. Let's find your number, what's it again? 100332?'

'I don't know, Uncle Seán. The master never learnt me to read very good. He said I was as thick as two planks.'

'You can't read and you're nine? By nine I was learning about atoms in that school, from the same master.'

'He just beats me.'

'He used to give me the odd clatter but he was a good teacher. But then I had Mary at home taking care of me. You really didn't have anybody. I'll teach you how to read, Ignatius. You'll get it in no time at all. Any fool can learn to read.'

He stopped abruptly. There was my bed in the line of beds all top to tail all the way down like a snake of white beds. The place was very clean and sparse. There was a huge crucifix with a metal Jesus twisted in pain on it, hanging on the wall. That was the only decoration. There was a number on the bed. 100332. My number. My bed. My life.

'Uncle Seán. Will you still call me Ignatius?'

'I will, but no one else will,' he said.

'1000332 adds up to 9 at least,' I said, wiping the snot off the end of my nose with my hand. Uncle Seán's head shot back as if he had been threatened. Then he laughed out loud and the laugh had an echo in the giant room. He gave me a funny little bow and turned and squeaked off, abandoning me. I sat on the side of the bed and rubbed me snot from me hand onto the iron bedpost.

The other boys came in to sleep. They looked at me and looked away. I crawled into bed and wished I had asked Uncle Seán for a blanket. No one had blankets, just sheets, though it was very cold. My teeth chattered. I used to sleep outside with the cows sometimes or the pigs and they kept me nice and warm. It was the first time I thought about home. I used rather sleep outside to keep away from me brother and Da's temper and me ma's tongue.

There was a Brother walking up and down between the beds. He stopped at mine but I did not look up. I was too terrified. He had a stick of ash plant in his hand and I saw that. He walked on. I heard him at one side of the big dormitory bring his stick down on a boy in the bed and I heard screaming. I sat up in terror.

'Lie down, ya thick,' the boy next to me hissed. 'Or they'll larrop ya too.'

Two more Brothers ran into the room and I was relieved that they would stop him. But they all took the boy and gave him a kicking on the floor. The boy was screaming and I noticed that all the boys around me were whimpering and shivering in their beds. I didn't miss me family a bit but I missed those warm hairy peaceful pigs that allowed me to lie against their pink hairy wall of hot skin and had no badness in them.

Baby

Finally, I Was Home in Kilbride
(Christmas 1962)

My father had broached the subject as he drove me home from the convent for Christmas. I told him what I thought,

'Daddy, those girls are orphans and they make such a big hoohaw that they're allowed to go to the secondary school but they're taken out of classes to clean and cook. I hate the nuns. Except for Sister Assumption, she's lovely but she's a blue collar with no power.'

My father laughed at this, he patted my knee as we drove.

'You've only a couple of years left at the convent and then you're done with the nuns.'

'Do you know they make those girls scrub the corridors every day? You can see them on their hands and knees and the nuns walking behind them with a cane to whip them if they try to talk to each other or slow down.'

'At least those girls are getting an education. Most children leave school at eleven.'

'They have been picked out just to be skivvies. And none of them go on to Leaving Cert. They all leave after Inter Cert to be maids. That's what the nuns are training them for. That's what their lives are for. To be handed over to clean up after other people. I only tried to talk to them. I did nothing wrong.'

'Oh, Baby,' he sighed, but he wasn't angry. 'It's just the way things are. The boys have the Christian Brothers, the girls have the nuns. We all went through it and survived. Just mind yourself and it'll be all over in no time at all. Once you finish school you'll be away on a hack. Eileen is out of there and working and living in digs in Dublin and going to dances. You will be too.'

'The nuns run all the hospitals, don't they?'

'Yes. But there is an escape in the evenings for her. And you don't have to be a nurse. In fact I don't think you'd be cut out for it at all.'

'What am I cut out for?'

'You could be a teacher like your mother.'

'Janey Mack! The schools are all run by priests and nuns. I'll never escape. Ever.'

'Baby, it's just the way things are. You're only sixteen. You have your life ahead of you. You'll teach and get married and have your own family. Your mother is very happy. She loves all those children who she's taught over the years. She's very satisfied.'

'I'm not my mother.'

'No.' My father sighed and pushed the rim of his hat higher on his head. 'That you're not.'

Finally, I was home in Kilbride. And home was Mary's kitchen. I still slept with her in the bed though I was a young woman now. She loved to brush my hair before we slept. She lit the fire early in the morning and did all her chores and prepared the food for the day. Just as in the old days, she brought me eggs and toast and bacon and sausages on a tray before she woke the others, and she smiled at me as I ate.

'You're still my Baby,' she said. I nodded with my mouth full.

'When is Seán coming?' A bit of egg dribbled down my chin and Mary automatically leaned in and dabbed it off with her dishtowel.

'He's coming tonight and he's bringing my nine-year-old nephew, Ignatius, who I've been warned is a handful.'

'I've never met any of those nephews,' I said, and Mary went quiet and sad. I remembered a time she spent in hospital after a Brother's funeral. I had missed her something rotten and as usual no adult would tell me anything. When she came home from hospital all she said was, 'I fell over a straw and a hen pecked me.'

I also remembered a time she had gone looking for her sister Maeve. I'd overheard my parents get Fr Lavin to make inquiries in the big house in Mullingar, where her brother who died had been, but no one of her name had been there. I didn't know what that place was other than it was big. Mary said her two sisters Bridget and Maeve were somewhere in America. They never wrote to her and she was sad to say they had forgotten her. Perhaps, she said, she had raised them badly, or maybe they were hurt she had not been able to do the best for them. She always took the blame herself, though I was disgusted at them for not writing her. Eating my buttery toast, I told her about the nuns, and the school, and how I hated it and dreaded the day Christmas was over and I'd have to go back.

'I'd have given my eye tooth to get the kind of education you are getting. So don't be bitter. A light heart lives long.'

Later that morning, Mary let me hollow out the birds' eggs and place them over the little lights. I loved their glow. I loved that she collected them all year for this day. Christmas Eve was my favourite day of the year. Seán and a young boy with wild grey eyes came. The boy, Ignatius, stayed close to Seán at every moment, and his eyes darted about suspiciously at us all.

Fr Lavin came over with Jimmy. They were the only children in the house so we made a fuss of them.

'Why would Jimmy not stay with his parents for Christmas?' I asked Mary, but as usual she gave me a look.

'I was wondering if there is an age I have to be before people begin to tell me things,' I said, and Eileen laughed. She was very pretty now and had beautiful clothes and my 24-year-old brother Joseph was studying law to join my father in his practice, while my other brother James was working in the Bank of Ireland and was twenty-one. They all hugged me as they entered, and the house became full, and my father went to plug in the lights. It was the first time we had electric lights strung on our tree. Us women stood around with glasses of sherry and the men nursed whiskey, and we went 'oooooooh, ahhhhhhh' as the lights came on. Even Mary, who kept electricity out of her kitchen, nodded in approval.

My mother proudly showed us an extension to the house, finally an indoor toilet and water that flowed from the taps. We wouldn't have to go to the pump anymore. Daddy showed us the washing machine they got for Mary, and Mary said she was delighted with it as it gave her time to do the farm work outside, which she preferred to laundry any day.

'You see,' Daddy said. 'We've even managed to corrupt Mary.'

Little Jimmy ran around and my brothers took him out for a game of football. Ignatius refused the invitation and never left Seán's side. He followed Mary and Seán and Ignatius into the kitchen. I went to follow, but Eileen put her hand on my arm.

'Baby,' she said firmly. 'Stay with us here. You're a young woman now.'

'What does that mean?' I brushed her off and followed Mary.

I was looking for stories she might be telling but instead she was sitting in her chair and Seán was at the table. They didn't see me enter.

'I can't take much more of St Joseph's. It's a living hell on Earth.'

'And you've put poor Ignatius right into the thick of things?'

'I didn't know what either of us were getting into. Seamus and Sheila didn't want him and Fr Gilligan places children in schools at the drop of a hat. He scours the country with the Cruelty Men looking for wee ones to be taken away, so it would have been done anyway. This way, I'll keep my eye on him. I can protect him. But

I need to get out of there. Maybe Fr Lavin can place him with wee Jimmy's foster parents after the summer. Jimmy seems to be a fine young lad and doing well. Unless you can take him?'

'I'm not in a position to do that. This is not my house.'

'This is your house,' I blurted out. 'Whose house is, it if it's not yours?'

Seán smiled at me and Mary got up and Ignatius sat in her chair.

'Would you jump into my grave as quick?' she said to him. He looked at her horrified, and I laughed.

'She always said that when we took her chair,' I told him. Ignatius looked blankly at me again.

'Does he speak English?' I asked Seán.

'Yes. His mammy Sheila wouldn't allow Irish in the house. They all speak English. Though at the school all the lessons were through Irish. Unfortunately he can't read. Can you give him a few lessons over the next few days? I can teach maths, but I'm not sure how to start with the reading.'

'Mammy's the teacher. But I can try,' I said.

Ignatius made me a teacher. Over the next two weeks I had him reading. He stayed with Seán and Jimmy up at Fr Lavin's house, but came every day to me. Bright and quick, but never smiled or looked me in the eye. He never said thank you and never wanted to give anything of himself. He was hard to warm to. This was a direct contrast to Jimmy who was only a year older, and a light-hearted, eager-to-please child.

One day Jimmy ran in crying.

'Ignatius took a stick to me.' He had criss-cross marks on his arms. Seán and Fr Lavin were out for a walk and Seán was mortified when he came back. He was so angry with Ignatius that Ignatius stayed outside in the field rather than come near the house.

'I worry about him. There's a streak in him alright,' Seán said to Mary. 'He's hard-hearted.'

'Many's a ragged colt made a fine stallion,' Mary said. But Fr Lavin was livid with Ignatius and my mother was even angrier when she found out that he had taken her stallion out of the stable to ride it bareback. Mammy was the only one who could handle that horse, even Mary never went near it. We saw him in a flash, galloping over the top of the field holding onto the mane.

'He's like the Devil himself riding that yoke!' Fr Lavin said with his arm around Jimmy.

Seán snorted. 'And I've news for you: he wants to join the Christian Brothers.'

'That makes sense for the little savage.' Fr Lavin burst out laughing. 'He'd be perfect. You on the other hand should have been a Jesuit. I always told you that.'

Ignatius

What Would Genghis Khan Have Done?

At first I thought the Lyonses were a pack of snobs who thought their piss was port wine, but after that shower of savages at St Joseph's with them brothers who would eat the head off you for so much as looking in their direction I had a good time and began to take it cushy. The day after Christmas we went out on the wren. The lads took me, Joseph and James. We were all dressed in funny clothes and went door to door and caused mischief and sang songs.

Uncle Seán wanted to bring me to visit Mammy and Daddy. He drove the car and told me stories about history. I wanted to know about Attila the Hun and he told me how if he had won against the Gauls, Christianity might have been lost. He told me that after a great battle the river ran with blood and guts and those parched injured soldiers were crawling to the side of it to drink.

'A river of blood. Would you credit that? That's deadly,' I said. History was never like this in school.

'Who else would you like to hear about?' he asked as we bombed down the lanes. For a priest, he was a queer fast driver. And then he told me about a fellah called Genghis Khan. And how he came to a city and laid siege and when his soldiers battered their way in, they went mad killing everyone. A woman pleaded for her life and said she had pearls for the soldiers if they spared her. They took her to Genghis Khan and he asked her where the pearls were and she said she had eaten them. Immediately, he cut her open and took the pearls out of her stomach and then ordered his men to slice open all the dead and living for more plunder. And so they did.

Uncle Seán laughed when he saw how much I loved this story. When he was my age, Genghis Khan was abandoned by his tribe and left alone on the steppes with his family. They had a tough time even surviving; sure he wasn't born a king at all. He had an older brother, that annoyed him, and when he caught a fish the brother took it off him and told his mammy that he had caught it. So Genghis Khan killed his shite hawk brother and his mother was disgusted with him for that. Said he was a savage. It took him a long time to become a leader and unite all the Mongols but he did.

I wanted more, especially of this mad yoke Genghis Khan. Uncle Seán said that there was a secret history and it was all in Chinese and even when he died they killed those who knew where he was buried.

When we got to our house, my da wouldn't look at me and my ma narrowed her eyes. I was glad they didn't leave me alone with me brothers, for I was thinking of killing them like Genghis Khan. I wish I lived on the steppes of Mongolia way back then. You could just go haring off and grab a bride, like. Life had got all shrunk up and dried out to be sure. We didn't stay long, as all they did was complain and moan. I thought that was all anyone did until Seán had taken me away. I told them I was happy to stay away, and Ma and Da looked at each other in relief. They didn't want me back. So off I went from the house of the Devil to the house of the demon.

When we drove away, I told Seán that I never wanted to go back to that horrible house where I was raised. I was done with them.

He sighed and rubbed my hair and I cringed. I couldn't get used to everyone touching me as if there was nothing to it.

Baby

He Should Have Run Off to Hollywood

Mammy and Daddy, as tolerant as they were, were not at ease around the dark little creature of a boy. His knees were permanently scabbed and scrawny, but his body was stocky. He had a crooked look to his face and grey eyes that revealed nothing. Poor Jimmy, who thought he'd have a playmate, stuck to me like glue just to avoid him. I thought Ignatius would be embarrassed to get reading lessons with Jimmy around but this wasn't the case. Ignatius felt no shame in himself and was greedy for knowledge and information in an almost frightening way. He soaked it all up.

'Why had you not learnt to read?' I kept asking him. He finally opened up on the day he was due to go back with Seán to St Joseph's.

'You're the first one who tried to teach me.'

'Why didn't the master at your school in Rathcairn teach you?'

'I didn't go there very much and he'd had all my brothers before me and hated us all. Everyone hated my family in Rathcairn. The school was all in Irish and we spoke English at home. I kept using the wrong hand so had my hand tied to the table all the time so I'd use the other one. They only untied me at break, I couldn't be bothered with it.'

'How is Fr Lavin's house?' I asked him.

'Nice.'

'Are you happy to go back to the school?'

'No. I hate it there. But everyone leaves me alone because of Uncle Seán.'

'I know the feeling. I hate going back to boarding school myself.'

'Why does Uncle Seán sleep with the light on?'

'Sure how would I know?'

'Why is a priest afraid of the dark?'

'Why don't you ask him?'

'He won't tell me anything. He just keeps lecturing me about stuff.'

'That's a big word, Ignatius. A big word indeed.'

'They all said I was thick as two short planks, but since Uncle Seán came and got me, I can see I'm not.'

'Why? Because you've learnt so much and been around so many different kinds of people since you left the farm?'

He smiled slyly. 'Yes. And I know most of youse people are not so smart yourselves.' With that he plonked a shilling on the table and said. 'That's for the lessons.'

'I don't want your money. You keep that.' I gave the money back to him and he quickly pocketed it.

Eileen was going back to Dublin and I told her about him trying to pay me. She was watching my brothers outside the window having a last game of football.

'Joseph and James said money went missing from their room. I bet it was that little beggar.'

'He's odd alright.'

Eileen pulled herself up and said, 'There's a term for him.'

'I'm sure you've a term for everything.'

'He's a sociopath.'

'I'm not even going to ask what that is. I kind of like him. In a funny way. He's not normal but he's interesting.'

'I kind of like his uncle.' Eileen nodded towards Seán who was leaning against the wall smiling while the lads playing football, but not joining in. 'Such a waste.'

'Why?'

'Him a priest. He should have run off to Hollywood and become a film star.'

I burst out laughing. She joined in with me.

'I'm not messing. I swear even up in Dublin, I don't see the likes of him. Look at him. Men with faces like that and that lovely blond hair are as scarce as hen's teeth. If he wasn't a priest I'd have him myself!'

'You're an awful woman, Eileen.' I found myself blushing at her crudeness. Seán turned as if he sensed us observing him and gave a wave. We both started to laugh. He looked puzzled and shrugged.

Ignatius

He Had a Head on Him Like a Lump of Wet Turf (1963)

I was standing in front of Da and I felt a touch off my cheek with his phantom limb. But my daddy had never so much as touched me, except to scalp me, so I woke up with a jolt and found myself back in the big dormitory with all the boys and I'd wet the feckin bed. I swear I'd never done that in me life. I knew I'd be done for in the morning. So I took the sheets off while kneeling down so no one would see and I snuck off to the toilets with them. There was a window up at the top over the sinks and I flung the sheet out into the night. But then I lay on my bare bed and realized that it would have fallen into the yard and my number 100332 was on it and now I was lying on a bare thin mattress. I'd be in for it. I'd have to get to Uncle Seán before they got to me.

The usual routine started about 5 am. Everyone who had wet the bed had to line up with their sheets. They made them wrap them around their heads and parade around in the yard outside. I lay shivering on my mattress hoping and praying. To distract myself I pretended I was Genghis Khan. I would explain it all to Uncle Seán this afternoon. Uncle Seán was getting more and more quiet but I still went to him for private lessons.

During the day I was called out of the machine shop and there was Brother Boyle waiting for me. Brother Boyle was a living dread. He was a short fat little man with eyes very close together over a smashed nose. He had a head on him like a lump of wet turf. The boys said that he was in charge of the little boys' dormitory, the wee ones who were under eight years. He drugged them in the evenings and they said you could see him carrying the limp bodies off to his room in the middle of the night. I was going to tell Uncle Seán this but I never did.

'Follow me,' Brother Boyle said in his raspy voice that put the heart across me. I began to shake and feel sick as I followed him. He brought me to his room. He showed me the sheet.

'This is yours?'

'Yes, Brother.'

'Know where I found it?'

'No, Brother.'

'I found it on the ground outside.' He flexed his hands and I backed away. 'Only I know about this.' He tried to smile at me. 'I'm going to protect you. I can come to you at night and check if you've wet the bed.' He locked his door. He offered me a silver mint and I took it. I turned it about in my hand, as if it was the moon, fallen out of the sky and dried and shrunken. My knees shook. I'd heard about the badness from the other boys. Suddenly, there was a loud knock on the door. Brother Boyle winced and went rigid. I swallowed the silver mint whole.

'Brother Boyle. It's Brother O Conaill.'

He unlocked his door and Uncle Seán was standing there. The two of them stood facing each other.

'I need to give the extra lessons to my nephew to catch him up,' he said. I darted out and stood behind him.

We went to his room and he gave me some biscuits. He had rings under his eyes. I went to explain but he only shushed me.

'Brother Boyle isn't the worst of them. He was all right to me when I arrived. Showed me around and warned me who to steer clear of.'

I just looked at him and said nothing. It was always safer to say nothing.

'Do you know how Attila the Hun died?' Uncle Seán asked.

'No.' I didn't care now how Attila the Hun died. I was only thinking of how I'd get me sheet back.

'Guess?'

'Eh, in battle, Uncle Seán? Against Constantinople? Maybe he had another go at them since he couldn't get in the first time.'

'He was given a new bride. She was a young girl, no older than yourself. They had a party. A big celebration. They all drank and sang and he retreated to his hut with the girl. In the morning they thought he was having a lie in. They didn't disturb him but when they finally went in the young girl was weeping and terrified.'

'Had she killed him, Uncle?' Now I was interested. I still hadn't forgotten the sheet. I could kill Brother Boyle.

'No. He had choked in his own blood. Some kind of haemorrhage. Kind of ironic don't you think? He died of a nosebleed.'

'What's ironic?'

Uncle Seán was pacing up and down. I didn't know what this had to do with anything.

'I can't stay here another day,' he blurted out.

'Neither can I, Uncle Seán.'

'But I can't get you out. Your father and mother have said they thought you looked fine. They said you've learnt to read and you should stay.'

'I hate it here. Can't we join the Jesuits, like Fr Lavin says?'

Uncle Seán snorted. He almost laughed. But he had stopped laughing these last weeks.

'They've done it all through the schools and courts and Fr Gilligan. You are now property of St Joseph's.'

Uncle Seán sat on his bed and wept.

I wondered what Genghis Khan would have done.

435

And Make Her Like a Wilderness (1963)

'You'll end up like your mother,' they said, but I didn't know who she was or why she let them get me. I closed my eyes at night and imagined a beautiful, rich woman in a fur coat coming to the nuns. She would take me in her arms and carry me to a big car with a driver. I had a name but I forgot it now, 435 was sewn on my facecloth and my towel and written in my books. Some of the other girls told me their names, but I couldn't remember mine. This was a big place and my number seemed low, so I figured out I'd been here many years. We didn't go outside. We worked here. There was so much work to be done, so there was.

I was taken away from the babies after I killed that one. They had me scrub the toilets and wash the corridors. The long long long wooden corridors. There were tunnels to the church. We walked in through the tunnels and sat in the wooden pews in the church. We sat separate so we didn't mix with the laundry women, or with the girls from outside who went to the nuns' school. I could sometimes see the laundry women. Some of them had shaved heads and I thought it was because they had curly hair like me, and they were harlots. I didn't know what a harlot was but it was dirty, so it was. The priest was on the altar speaking to us:

Plead with your mother, plead for she is not my wife, and I am not her husband – that she put away her whoring from her face, and her adultery from between her breasts, or I will strip her naked and expose her as in the day she was born, and make her like a wilderness, and turn her into parched land, and kill her with thirst. Upon her children also I will have no pity, because they are the children of whoredom. For their mother has played the whore; she who conceived them has acted shamefully.

Sister Michael looked at us when he was saying this and she was breathing deeply and I didn't know what it meant but I knew it was bad for us after. Then there was the part where the other priest came in and talked about Jesus and Jesus said, 'Love is the greatest gift of all,' and called us 'my children'. But I didn't know what this love was or what it meant. I didn't dare to ask. I'd never talk to a nun, we relied on the girls who had been outside to tell us things.

Some of them came from families, and some had sisters in with them. I made a friend, 890, who said there was too many of them in her family and so the two middle ones were sent to here by the Cruelty Man. He wore a brown shirt and came doing inspections. She said all the childer hid when he came cos he would take them away if they had rickets, or their tummies were sticking out. 890 had her little sister in with her and they looked out for each other. 890 was eight like me and told me it broke her heart when the nuns got her five-year-old sister for wetting the bed or for slurping her soup or for talking at meals. Her sister, 891, was giddy, she skipped, and talked a lot or at least did when she first came in but was learning now, so she was. 890 said she would rather they beat her instead and that settled it, this I thought was love. I tried to concentrate on what I felt when the nuns grabbed the others out of the line and took the cane to them. I could feel it in the front of my bottom, I got a pain there even when I saw a girl fall and cut herself, I felt it too and I wondered was this love. Would Jesus feel it in the front of his bottom? I wondered if his bottom was like mine. But this girl, 890, knew an awful lot about the outside, she told me that Jesus was a man and his bottom was different that he had a thing hanging out of it. That's the first I heard that there was a thing called a man, and the priest was one of them and outside the world was mainly men and the nuns were afraid of them. I thought men must be really really good if Jesus was one and the nuns were afraid of them.

And the priest, he always asked us the question, 'Why did the Devil tempt the woman Eve with the apple and not the man Adam? Why? Why?' That question was like a hammer coming down on us.

Ignatius

The Clearing
(1963)

Autumn days came quickly, like the running of the hound on the moor. It was coming up to a year I'd been here and I had changed. I'd got rid of me culchie ways and accent, and there was no way I was talking like the other Dublin boys so I made sure I talked more like my uncle Seán: soft and educated. I was also the best in my class at Irish and history and maths, and Seán said I'd go to secondary school unlike all the other boys here who got stuck into learning trades or got shoved out onto the farm as labourers and then at sixteen pushed out into the world starved, broken, buggered, to become servants on farms and get paid fuck all by men like me da, my father I should say. He had me in his room every evening and he shared food with me so I would be strong, and I think he was avoiding the other Brothers as much as he was keeping me away from them or them from me. It felt like druid and child there in that little cell of a room he had, surrounded by books, for he was mad for writing them letters, mad for it. He corresponded with people as far away as China. But he taught me so much, about stuff in the time even before St Patrick was brought as a slave to this cold little island. St Patrick, the foreigner who brought us his Roman religion. He made me learn it all off by heart and by God I did.

I, Patrick, a sinner, a most simple countryman, the least of all the faithful and most contemptible to many, had for father the deacon Calpunius, son of the late Potitus, a priest, of the settlement of Bannavem Taburniae; he had a small villa nearby where I was taken captive. I was at that time about sixteen years of age. I did not, indeed, know the true God; and I was taken into captivity in Ireland with many thousands of people according to our deserts, for quite drawn away from God, we did not keep his precepts, nor were we obedient to our priests who sued to remind us of our salvation.

Uncle Seán would close his eyes when I'd recite it back to him: the confession of St Patrick.

And Uncle Seán would tell me that the soul was known even before Patrick came to Ireland. That the ancients living here knew well of soul and honour and God. He told me about an Irish traditional custom and it was called 'The Clearing from Guilt'. He would read to me from a book by Oscar Wilde's mother, Lady Francesca Speranza Wilde.

To prove innocence of a crime an ancient ritual is performed which the people have great respect for. They call it 'The Clearing'. It is a fearful ordeal and instances are known of men who have died of fear and trembling from having passed through the terrors of the trial, even if innocent. And it is equally terrible for the accuser as well as the accused.

On a certain day fixed for the ordeal the accused goes to the churchyard and carries away a skull. Then wrapped in a white sheet, and bearing the skull in his hand, he proceeds to the house of the accuser, where a great crowd has assembled; for the news of The Clearing spreads like wildfire, and all the people gather together as witnesses of the ceremony. There, before the house of his accuser, he kneels down on his bare knees, makes the sign of the cross on his face, kisses the skull, and prays for some time in silence. The people also wait in silence, filled with awe and dread, not knowing what the result might be.

Then the accuser, pale and trembling comes forward and stands beside the kneeling man; and with uplifted hands adjures him to speak the truth. On which the accused, still kneeling and holding the skull in his hand, utters the most fearful imprecations known in the Irish language; almost as terrible as that curse of the druids, which is so awful that it never yet was put into English words.

The accused prays that if he fail to speak the truth all the sins of the man whose skull he holds may be laid upon his soul, and all the sins of his forefathers back to Adam and all the punishment due to them for the evil of their lives, and all their weakness and sorrow both of body and soul be laid on him both in this life and in the life to come. But if the accuser has accused falsely and out of malice, then may all the evil rest on his head through this life forever, and may his soul perish everlastingly.

It would be impossible to describe adequately the awe with which the assembled people listen to these terrible words and the dreadful silence of the crowd as they wait to see the result. If nothing happens, the man rises from his knees after an interval and is pronounced innocent by the judgment of the people, and no word is ever again uttered against him, nor is he shunned or slighted by the neighbours.

But the accuser is looked on with fear and dislike, he is considered unlucky, and seeing that his life is often made so miserable by the coldness and suspicion of the people, many would rather suffer wrong than force the accused person to undergo so terrible a trial as The Clearing.

'But Uncle Seán,' I said. 'What if they who you accused were so bad that they didn't care and could brazen out Hell itself? I can think of some Brothers here ...'

'Hold your whisht. Don't accuse unless you are ready to take the consequences.'

'I don't accuse, Uncle Seán, because no one would care what I say.'

Uncle Seán busied himself finding another book on the shelf.

'Is it like this in all the schools? Or did they just send all the bad priests here?'

'Not all the priests here are bad.'

'But good ones don't say anything.'

Uncle Seán's face was twisted, and he looked almost horrible, which was strange because he was the most handsome person, man or woman, I'd ever laid eyes on in my life. He walked through that school, taller and purer than a mortal being. We lads worshipped him, and he had a reputation for kindness, he never beat a boy once, he had a pocket full of jam sandwiches, which he gave out secretly to any boy he found on his own. And bits of cheese. In fact Auntie Mary used to make him tiny packages of cheese herself and wrap them up for him so he could give pieces out to the children on the sly.

It was only in his Irish and maths classes that we actually learnt anything, and he taught without the strap or the stick. Once the fear was taken out of the class, we could actually start learning something. It didn't take much cop on to realize he was hated by the other Brothers. I'd say they put him under pressure to get out of here but I knew he was staying on account of me.

I didn't like to think he was wasting his life for my sake but then I was terrified of what would happen if he left. I lived the whole day for those hours of study in his room.

'If you hadn't taken me here, me ma and da would have just got Fr Gilligan to put me somewhere else just as bad,' I told him, to gauge his reaction.

'My mother and father, not me ma and da, Ignatius. Have you thought about your future? I can get you transferred to secondary school once you are twelve. I've been making enquiries.'

'I want to stay with you.'

'You will be alright without me. I'm set to go to the missions. To travel to the Far East.'

'You're only going there to stick your nose in them other religions,' I said. There were many books on his shelf that weren't Christian. He had lots of philosophy, Spinoza, Nietzsche, Kant, Hegel, poetry books, books on Hinduism, Buddhism, and novels by Christopher Isherwood. He let me read anything I wanted as long as I didn't take it out of the room and let on he had such a library.

There was a knock on the door and we both jumped. We weren't used to being disturbed.

In the frame of the door stood Brother Boyle, with the big belly on him and the leer and his eyes spinning around his head with the madness. He and the principal, Brother Peter, were the most hated and feared, and the bollix of a Brother who did the band. No one wanted to be caught alone by them.

'Good evening, Brother O Conaill.' His eyes settled for a moment on me and then did a twirl in their sockets and his hands clasped together. 'I see you have your young prodigy with you as usual. I hear he's making great strides.'

'All he needed was a bit of encouragement,' Uncle Seán said, still not standing aside to let him into the room. 'Sure he was raised like a weed. We're just putting a bit of civilization into him.'

'Is that what you call it, Brother O Conaill, and who is this we? I was under the impression that you keep him all to yourself here in your wee room. It's most,' he paused, and his tongue licked his thin upper lip, 'unorthodox.'

'What can I do for you Brother Boyle?' Uncle Seán's voice was steady as his face went deeply red. I saw his right hand twitch, and he put it in his pocket.

'There has been some talk about you.' Brother Boyle craned his neck into the room and I saw the folds of it stretch, red-ringed, and then resettle into rings of fat.

'What kind of talk?'

'If you make any further complaints to Brother Peter. I can always bring this unsavoury situation to attention.'

'What situation?'

'Well wouldn't you say you are compromising yourself every evening and weekends by showing such favouritism to your young nephew?'

'I'm tutoring him. When he came here he was nine years old and couldn't read or write. Now he is top of the class in all subjects. I don't see what I have done wrong.'

Brother Boyle looked me up and down with his rasping eyes.

'Brother Peter said you are to once more join all of us Brothers for tea in the evenings at the long table in the dining room. You've been absent for quite a few weeks.'

'I will, Brother Boyle. I've been studying and researching. I'll join you all tonight.'

'Ye must be doing great things in here altogether. As they say, be good to the child and he will come to you tomorrow.'

'I'll see you at tea so, Brother Boyle.'

Uncle Seán closed the door. I was taken aback at Uncle Seán's demeanour. I thought he didn't give a fiddler's fuck about the other Brothers and was so beautiful a creature that they let him wander about their midst untouched. He was their prize, a cut above them all and they knew it, he only kept himself here on account of me and they knew this too.

'Uncle Seán,' I whispered. 'He's the priest that uses the bullet.'

'The bullet?'

'The lads say he has a stick with a bullet on the end of it and he uses it on the boys.'

'I've made several reports, Ignatius. Let them deal with it now. Don't push it. You'll put yourself in danger. There's huge power at stake here. The reputation of something much bigger than either of us.'

'We should have a Clearing. I'd love to see that fucker kneeling down with a skull.'

'And who would do the accusing?'

'I'm not afraid. But no one would listen to me.'

'It is sometimes more dangerous to be the accuser.'

Then I saw him shaking and his feet twitching.

'Go on now, run along Ignatius. He won't touch you. You're safe here. Don't be worrying about things that you can't fix.'

'Did they get you, Uncle Seán?'

'I beg your pardon?'

'Did they get you when you were in the training school? Is that why you sleep with the light on? Is that why you are afraid of them still?'

Uncle Seán was clutching a book and his knuckles went white.

'Get out, Ignatius. GET OUT.'

And before I could say Jack Robinson I found myself at the other side of the door. I knew. When he'd been a young fellah, Uncle Seán had been got to.

I saw that slimeball Brother Boyle at the end of the corridor looking back at me. He had heard the shouting.

He beckoned to me but I turned on my heels and ran out of there as fast as shite from a goose. I had the run of the place and, as I entered the dining room, I could feel the green eyes of the other poor crayturs on me and I knew they'd all love to have a go at me and put me in my place. But I was Brother O Conaill's nephew, his family, his blood, and they were forced to respect me as much as they hated me. It was Brother Boyle's shift on dining room tonight. I balked at the slop of watery soup, with bits of tripe and guts in it and nothing else, at the tins of watery hot cocoa that was lukewarm and dirty looking. Each one of us got a hunk of bread that was so hard you could use it in the machine shop to hammer nails. The poor lads were starving as they dipped it into the soup to soften it, and I saw the fellah beside me, scrawny runt that he was and his gums were bleeding into the bread until it was soaked as much with red blood as it was with the grey slop of soup. I thought of Brother Boyle's saying, 'Be good to the child and he will come to you tomorrow' and I twisted it about in me head.

Be good to the child *or* he will come to you tomorrow. He'll come and get you. For the first time I hated Uncle Seán. I hated him for once being a child like these children, weak and with no kin of any worth. That they would have taken him off to dark corners and turned him inside out and made him into a coward.

435

890 Watching Out for 891
(1964)

The nuns had me cleaning most of the time so I hadn't been put in school. I wished I could read the Bible and find more out about Jesus but I liked to listen to the priest read the gospel every morning at Mass and I tried not to look at the bald women from the laundry. Once one of them came close to 890 and said she was finding out if her child was among us. The child's name would be Fionnula and she had a brother, and she would have curly blonde or red hair, 890 told me, thinking that might be my mother. I said my mother was a harlot and was long gone, so she was. Or, I said, my mammy is now given up her whoring. She was rich and wore fur. The nuns would be having a conniption but, she'd be so posh and would sweep in here and take me off in her lovely car. 890 said that the laundry women were repentant harlots and here to do penance for their sins, so she could be my mother. I didn't want to think that one of those awful women with their sack clothes was my mother and I hated my curly hair more than ever.

There were spies everywhere among the children, and if you told on someone sometimes the nuns gave you bread and jam, so they did. The nuns heard that 890 was talking to the laundry women and that was strictly forbidden. As low as we were, as spawn of Satan, they were Satan, so they were.

They made 890 strip and they beat her over her bed in front of all of us. Two Sisters tied her wrists to the bed. 890's little sister screamed and screamed. The little girl was so brave and fierce she ran and kicked the nun who was beating her sister, and they put both of them in the coal shed for the night. 890 said she was glad to be in the dark with her sister because they were able to hug each other all night. Normally they weren't allowed to go near one another. And I thought that this must be love. And one day I'd know for sure what it was, just to know like, because it was what the priest said Jesus kept saying, and I knew I wanted it.

I wanted to be a nun and marry Jesus like the Sisters. Sister Michael heard from one of the girls that I said I wanted to be a nun. She came to me and asked me about it. I was trembling all over and thinking of the rats in the coal shed. I hated the way they ran over my hands and feet when I spent nights there.

'Don't you be getting above your station,' she said. 'You're a skivvy, 435. That's all you'll ever be good for. You can't even read and write. What makes you think you'll become a nun? You are illegitimate. Do you know what that means? You'll end up in the laundry if you go around talking like that.'

I didn't understand illegitimate except it meant I was ill and sick in some way. I felt sick, so I could see that part, so I could. I was ashamed of myself. I'm not sure why, except I was born bad. Over and over again, they said, 'Ye are born bad, from the very rubbish of this country.'

Our mothers were dirty and we were dirty for coming from them. No one wanted us, so the nuns were the only people willing to keep us alive, they never let us forget who we were.

I took a scissors and I cut my curls off, and my hair was close to my head so no one could see that I was a daughter of a harlot. Every day in Mass the laundry women tried to look at us thinking maybe we were their children. I never had a curl on my hair again. I never looked over but made sure I stood next to Sister Michael and they would never look near the nuns because they took beatings too. We could see their bruised arms and legs.

The inspectors didn't seem to ever see the bruises. When 890 took that almighty beating that time for talking to one of them, the inspector came the next day and the nuns lined us up but hid her. The inspector always asked us questions, pushing her glasses up her nose.

'Are you happy here?'

'Do you like the food?'

'Do you go to school?'

Janey Mack if it wasn't the same three questions every time. And Sister Michael stood beside the inspector lady when she asked the questions. What did she expect us to say? I hated when she came. I didn't know who she was inspecting for and the nuns would put meat in our food that evening and put out the nice cups and plates.

There was no stopping them nuns, so there wasn't. They were a law unto themselves.

'Where did you get those bruises?' the specky-four-eyes inspector asked 891. She started snivelling and blubbering and her voice rose. There'd be ructions now, I thought, and was glad of it, so I was.

'The nuns hurt me because my sister was bold and they beat her so bad we haven't seen her since.'

Sister Joseph inhaled sharply and we all held our breaths. I was hoping she'd hit 891 there and then so the inspector could see what they done to us.

'Yes, sometimes we have to use moderate force when the children are really misbehaving. It sends a message. This child has been mentally unbalanced since she came here. Her father and mother are both drunks. She actually kicked me in front of the other children. Now what message does that send out? How are we to put manners on them all?'

We all held our breath in the line and looked at the inspector. The inspector nodded thoughtfully and patted 891 on the head.

'You shouldn't kick poor Sister Joseph,' the inspector said. 'She and her sisters are all you have. They take good care of you. And look how lovely and clean the school is. I could eat my dinner off the floors.'

But it was us who had to scrub and scrub the floors when the nuns said the inspectors were arriving. And they always gave notice. So with that, without so much as a by your leave, the inspector sauntered off with Sister Joseph. Their two well-fed, fat arses disappearing out of sight.

'She's an auld wagon so she is,' I fumed. Even at eight I was livid because it was not fair.

We gathered around 891, and told her she was in for it. She bunched down on the ground and started screaming until she fainted. She was a chubby little girl unlike the rest of us, her drunk parents must have fed her. Her little hands were flat pressing on the floor and she still had dimples, like a baby. Sister Paul came running in and grabbed her by the scruff and dragged her off. We waited for the inspector to come back to us but she didn't. When 890 came back from the sick ward a few weeks later she could still barely walk and her arm was in a brace, so it was. We told her about her little sister. She asked the nuns about her over and over but none of us ever saw the little one with the dimples again. They said she was moved to a more suitable place. She was too disruptive to mind here. 890 cried every night for years and years. She was always the one who got the most beatings. The nuns had straps. Some of them kept their leather straps in the fridges so they'd be frozen and do more damage. They'd beat us with hairbrushes, chair legs, anything that was handy. They'd strip us naked so it would be worse in front of everyone.

There was no stopping them.

I remember because 890 had the bed beside me. I knew now what was meant by love, because I felt a pain inside my chest listening to her crying. I felt her tears travel through the air in small sadness bubbles and instantly burst off of me because I had no love. But I didn't know if I wanted love anymore, because it hurt so much. And no one could hurt me if I loved no one. But all the same, it gave me something to pray about, because I never had anything to pray for myself. I prayed every night that the Blessed Virgin would find her little sister and bring them together once more. So 890 could watch out for 891.

Ignatius

Sick as a Small Hospital
(1964)

I woke up sick as a small hospital. Could not get out of the bed for the life of me, the thirst on me was something terrible, and my arms and legs were burning and my stomach churning with the cold shivers. Brother O'Brian yelled at me to get out of the bed. I swam out of it towards him, the air like sea, and the high ceiling the water surface. I gasped for air and his face changed. He dragged me to the infirmary and they called Uncle Seán away from his first maths class to my bedside.

That weekend Uncle Seán drove me to Kilbride. I lay on the sofa in Fr Lavin's house and Mary fed me some rancid dandelion concoction and I was truly frightened. The real doctor came and I said to him,

'No wonder they burnt all those auld witches.'

'I beg your pardon?'

'They missed some though,' I said, wondering if he was on their side. But he appeared neutral, and talked in low tones to the two priests in the hall. Fr Lavin had a young priest staying with him, a Fr Sullivan who was a distant relative of his who had just been ordained, and was as tall as Uncle Seán but had dark eyes and dark hair and a way of drinking his tea like a woman. How had I found meself in a house with three daft priests and a visiting witch feeding me potions?

Fr Lavin had people come in and out all day. They waited in the hall for him on chairs, under the ticking of the grandfather clock, and the picture of the Sacred Heart, and the portrait of de Valera on one side and John F. Kennedy on the other. He talked to them all, I never seen him turn anyone away. He seemed to have to take care of a lot of people.

Many of them were women in a right state. Some just beaten. Some just sad for reasons I couldn't fathom. They all loved Fr Lavin, not really loved. Revered. He had a gentle kind listening way about him and that was what Uncle Seán needed from him as well. And he was fierce fond of my Uncle Seán. Uncle Seán said he was his mentor because he was a really good priest and a good man. And he was, I suppose.

Uncle Seán would sometimes come and sit looking at me and praying for me and I would see some terrible guilt in his eyes. And often he'd be in his dressing gown and fingering the tie of it. I stayed on there when he went back to the school, if you could call that place a school. I told Fr Lavin and Fr Sullivan about the Brothers and the badness they did to the boys, and I didn't care if they thought I was mad. I told them that Brother Boyle had a stick with a real bullet on the end of it.

But sure it all fell on deaf ears. They patted my head as if I was raving and said, 'Haven't you come on a great deal since going to that school? And the Brothers do their best for the poor unfortunate orphan boys. They've their work cut out for them.'

'But most of them boys aren't orphans.' I protested.

'Some of them are truants or in trouble with the law,' Fr Sullivan sniffed.

'There were young lads there four years old,' I pleaded. 'Their crime's being poor as far as I can see.'

And so Fr Lavin got fed up of me and sent me to Mary's house as much as he could when Uncle Seán was up at St Joseph's during the week.

Uncle Seán was wary of me. He didn't like being alone with me anymore. I felt I had seen through him. He wasn't my hero anymore. I'd seen the rabbit under the table. All his books and his fancy letters to fancy people in China, Japan, India, and all around the world. But look at the state of his life. Did he ever get to those places? He never went anywhere except St Joseph's in Dublin, and then Kilbride in Meath, to sit with his sister Mary by her fire and play draughts with her and she would look at the trouble in his eyes and he would say every time, 'I should teach you chess, Mary. It's a better game.'

'I don't have the education for all that, Seán, draughts will do me.'

'You weren't ruined by education, Mary, that's all there is to it.'

'That's a fine thing to be saying. I never so much as darkened a door of a school.'

'Arra, they gave us some education to be sure, but not enough.'

'You were such a happy child, Seán. Now I look at you sometimes and you look hag-ridden.'

'Remember, Mary, when I was little? Things were simple then out on the farm and you were in charge, not Seamus.'

'You forget. I was killed keeping the Cruelty Man away from all of ye. He'd have come and taken us all to them schools. You used to sit on the fairy ring out on the hill and keep watch for him. I used to take turns putting you all on guard. Do you forget that, Seán? I sometimes wonder about all that education,' Mary said.

'There was little enough of it. It was more of a brainwashing. The rest I had to find out for myself. I have a man in Dublin who gets me all the books. Most of them are banned, Mary.'

'Well maybe they're banned for a reason. I'm not sure all those extra books have done you any good.'

'Do you still believe in the fairies, Mary?'

'I wouldn't be crossing them.' Mary stared hard at him.

Fr Lavin came in to the kitchen through the back door, rubbing his hands from the cold and in his usual jolly mood that cheered everyone up. 'Listen to that, Ignatius. Did ye ever hear the like? The day an O Conaill gives up believing in the fairies is not a good day for Ireland.'

Mary got up immediately and took his coat and hat. She busied herself getting him tea and her hot scones, and homemade butter and jam.

She had all her potatoes that had odd shapes on the window and she put sticks into them and little bits of coloured beads and buttons for eyes. I would pick them up and she would say I could have them to play with if I wanted but I'd snort at her.

'I'm only lookin,' I'd snap and put them down.

'Do ye want a story, Ignatius?'

Her medicines were vile, but the stories she told were something else. Her stories were the real medicine, and the best of all of them was the one from Kerry about a woman who married a bull.

When she was telling them even Mrs Lyons would come and listen in the kitchen. Mrs Lyons was somebody who I steered clear of. I was an O Conaill, so I knew to stay in the kitchen with Mary. Mrs Lyons was gentle and soft spoken and mannerly to me but I could see I was a bad smell in the house and on weekends, when Seán came, I'd go back to Fr Lavin.

It went on like this for a month until I was better. It was by far the best month of my entire life.

I was helping Mary feed her two pigs. She used to pet and talk to them.

'I don't know how you eat them when you know them,' I said to her as she scratched behind their ears.

'Arra, it's better than eating pigs I don't know.' She shrugged.

I scratched the back of the big one's ears to see what it felt like.

'Pigs can see the wind,' she said. Just like that.

'It's her certainty that rattles me.' Uncle Seán smiled when I told him what she had said. 'She's not afraid.'

But he was afraid. And only Mary and I could see he was going a wee bit mad with it.

One Saturday night, Fr Lavin, Uncle Seán and Fr Sullivan were up talking. I was sitting behind them playing solitaire with a deck of cards Uncle Seán had brought me. As far as I could see, Fr Sullivan couldn't take his eyes of my Uncle Seán. He was under the same spell I had been. To see the tall blond thin man with so much in him and his eyes like grey-blue speckled stones in streams flowing through his head. There was something I couldn't put my finger on. A mystery to him.

'He doesn't belong in this world,' was something everyone said about him.

I wanted to tell them that he had been got at. He was damaged. He shouldn't be a priest at all.

One night, I was sent to bed and Fr Sullivan went to bed also. But I got up again and sat outside the sitting room door in the hall to hear if Fr Lavin and Uncle Seán were talking about me. Uncle Seán had just gone to see my father on the farm in Rathcairn and I knew I'd be discussed. As much as I hated the school, there was no way I was going back to that boghole of a farm now.

'I've questioned my vocation, Patrick,' Uncle Seán said. I jolted to hear Fr Lavin had a name of his own like any of us, I couldn't imagine him as a child, and just as I was thinking that Uncle Seán said, 'You're a natural priest. You were born a priest. Everyone likes you. People come to you for help all the time and you are able to help them. They respect your authority. You have authority. You sing beautifully in Mass. I'm doubting that I'm cut out for it; I certainly don't want to stay at St Joseph's anymore. I'm only there on account of the lad.'

'Is that worth it?' Fr Lavin said. The fecker.

'He's a brilliant boy, Patrick. I know you don't always see it but you only have to tell him something once and he's got it. He's a bit rough, but that was his upbringing. He's different, left-handed. All they did before in school was tie his hand to the table.'

Fr Lavin shook his head, 'What odds does it make what hand you are writing with? It's what you're writing that they should care about.'

'My plan is that when he goes to secondary school this year I'm going to pay for that and I can just about afford it, but then I'm off.'

'Good, good,' Fr Lavin said. 'I told you from the beginning you don't belong there.'

'You were right. I want to go and live my life. Live out my vocation. I made a mistake going to work in the school. I should have listened to you. I thought I could make a difference. But there's no stopping them. The only thing is I don't think I can bear to wait around even another day, just for this boy.'

'Then you must go now or you'll grow to hate him.'

'I'd never hate him, he's my own nephew,' Uncle Seán said. 'I wish that when I was his age I would have had me at this age to protect me. If I can help one lad then that would have made my time worth it.'

'He's not you. You're not him. That's not what family is.'

'But isn't that what humanity is? Don't you have to recognize the other as you?'

'If you think too much you'll never ...' Fr Lavin began.

'I'll never get to God?' Uncle Seán said.

'No, no. Just that you should just trust and obey right now. Not do too much thinking if you can help it, you have your whole life ahead of you. My cousin there, Fr Sullivan, he's a young priest and he adores you. You could be a great leader one day. You could go up the ranks and then you can make the decisions and that's when you can really improve things.'

'I can't leave Ignatius, but I can't be there. Maybe my calling was to protect him.'

'Ignatius is a tough nut. He's a survivor. He'll be grand. Your calling was for God.'

'Then where is God? Where have we put him?'

'Seán, Seán. Everyone comes to me with their problems and their confessions. Wayward children, cruel husbands, unwanted pregnancies, land disputes. But none of them have problems like you. None are grappling with God himself. I've been working on my sermon for Sunday. Do you want to hear the gist of it? Embrace this time. We live in a world that is so different from our fathers' primitive world. Diseases are being wiped out. Great new medicines. Soon we'll all live as long as we want. And the motorcar has given us the freedom to drive all over this country where we used to have to go by horse and cart.

I'm getting a telephone here next week. I can talk to people miles away in an instant. Remember Genesis 1.28: '*And God blessed them, and God said to them, Be fruitful and multiply, and fill the earth and subdue it; and have dominion over the fish of the sea and over the birds of the air and over every living thing that moves upon the earth.*' Well, if it isn't happening in our own lifetime. What a time we live in. We have the dominion. So what do you think?'

Fr Lavin was pouring out the whiskey now for himself, he was clearly enjoying the whole conversation. Giddy with the challenge.

'Patrick, I think I have to become an infidel to get close to God. I'm beginning to think religion is a crutch getting in my way.'

'You can't run from your problems, Seán, with this mysticism. They'll follow you. We all question our vocation at times. You're just in the wrong place. That's so utterly obvious. Even to Ignatius.'

'What has the boy been saying?'

'The poor lad was raving, but if half of what he was raving about is true then maybe we should have another word with the Bishop about certain Brothers there.'

'It's not certain Brothers. It's the whole set-up. I did complain and the Bishop bounced it right back to Brother Peter and it didn't do me any favours. I even swore I'd go to the guards but sure one of the mammies went to the guards and the guards brought it back to the Bishop and the Bishop bounced it back to us. Trouble is we're a dumping ground for bad priests. The kids are poor so no one cares.'

'I'm more worried about you, Seán. Mary is fierce worried about you as well. She's always asking me to talk to you. Don't be going bothering the Bishop anymore, ye hear? You need allies and you don't need to make enemies. If we find a place for you you'll be fine. You need to protect your own career and you could go very far.'

'I didn't think it was meant to be a career. I thought it was meant to be more than that.'

Fr Lavin laughed, 'By God, young Fr Sullivan was right about you; if I'm a natural priest then you're a true one.'

I imagined Uncle Seán blushing and it made me blush. When were they going to mention me again?

'I don't know if I should have been a priest. I was so young and it was a way to get off the farm. Mary was so dead set that I'd get off that farm.'

'Wasn't she right? You've a college education now, don't you? How many from around here have that privilege? And Mary was up cleaning the church and working every hour outside of her hours at the Lyonses to put you through.'

'I'm thirty, I'm no longer a young man. I need to make some decisions. I don't like the city but I'm not sure I can come home; I don't know how you stand it here. When I think of the way I was raised here. If you scratch the surface here in the country Christianity has barely an innings. Look at my sister Mary. They're all pagans. For Mary the old Irish legends are the Old Testament. For Mary, Jesus is really just one of many.'

'They don't care much for Jesus here,' Fr Lavin was laughing in agreement. 'It's the Virgin Mary they go to to light their candles. Your Mary is a great woman. Sure there's people coming from far and wide at this stage for her cures. I don't know what I'd do without her. She's kept me good and fed. Too well. I'm getting fat. You need to relax. I just do what I can for the people who come to me for help, and I try to help, and for the rest I follow orders. You are the cause of your own problems. It doesn't have to be that complicated. Get Ignatius into secondary school and get out of there.'

'How will I ever get him out of St Joseph's? It was a mistake to go back to his father, I know it now. I talked to Seamus today and he wants Ignatius to learn a trade in the school. None of his boys went on to secondary school and neither did he so he's dead set against Ignatius doing it.'

'He's the father, Seán,' Fr Lavin said. 'You know you can't go against him. Ignatius is not your son.'

'Don't I know it? But Seamus doesn't understand Iggy.'

'And you do?'

'I think I do. I see something in him.'

It was the first time in my life I heard things about me that were good.

'If his father insists he stay on at the school I will have to stay to protect him because it's my fault he's there. It's not just the boy and the school that are getting to me, Patrick. I've had feelings ...'

There was more whiskey being poured. I could swear even Uncle Seán took some.

'We've all had those, we are men. They are there to test us.'

'Did you ever?' Uncle Seán sounded surprised

'We are mortals, Seán, don't be too hard on yourself, just pray and you will get the strength, at least you are surrounded by boys and men, you don't have the temptation of all the lovely ladies dressed up in their Sunday best.' Fr Lavin laughed. I could hear the clanking of the whiskey bottle on the Waterford crystal. Then Fr Sullivan himself was standing over me and saying, 'Well well what have we here? A wee spy?' He nudged me with his slipper and was about to open the living-room door.

I bolted up to my bedroom and he went in to join the others and I wondered would he tell them that I'd been listening.

In the morning Fr Sullivan was looking for Uncle Seán at breakfast. Fr Lavin was shuffling around in his dressing gown rubbing his stubble and drinking cup of tea after cup of tea. He held up a banana and an orange.

'Look at these. Can you remember the first time we saw an orange and a banana? I can. Once all we ate was made within a mile of here. And now every house in Ireland can have their food brought in from out foreign and your friend Fr O Conaill thinks we haven't made great progress.'

'Where is he?' Fr Sullivan was looking around. He was young and shaven and very fastidiously dressed, unlike his older cousin who looked like the wreck of the Hesperus, pouring out the last remains of the ashtrays and wincing as he rinsed the whiskey bottle.

'He's off for his morning walk, Frankie boy.' Fr Lavin coughed and rubbed his ample pot belly that you could only see when he was in his pyjamas and not dressed like a priest. 'He's a great one for the walking. He's probably all the way in Trim and he took Dagda with him for the walk.'

Dagda was Fr Lavin's new Irish wolfhound that one of his parishioners couldn't afford to feed anymore.

'He's going back today isn't he?' Fr Sullivan asked. 'I'll go join him. Can I take your car to catch up with him?'

'You can indeed. You've taken a shine to him.' Fr Lavin smiled. 'He's a good lad but don't be listening to a word he says or he'll have you gone all mystical as well on us. Take Iggy, he's getting better and could do with a spin.' He pointed at me. Fr Sullivan looked crestfallen.

We drove to Trim and walked along by the Boyne River. Uncle Seán was always going for ferociously long walks that I never saw the point of. We saw Dagda first, coming out of the Boyne and then racing up to the distant figure in black. Fr Sullivan perked up to have found him so easily despite the fact that I told him I knew the places he'd be. We quickened our pace to catch up.

Ahead of us the tall black figure with golden hair walked towards the cathedral ruins flanked by Dagda the wolfhound.

I couldn't believe it. We both stopped in our tracks. Uncle Seán started spinning. He was in the field by the stone ruins of the Jealous Man and Woman and he was spinning. With his arms wide open.

Dagda must have thought it was great fun and was running around barking. I was ashamed and embarrassed. He whirled and whirled. Fr Sullivan looked very shocked, his lip quivering.

I picked up a rock and legged it down by the river. Fr Sullivan began to race after me but he ran like a girl with his elbows and arse sticking out. I ran fast, and when I got up to Uncle Seán I flung the rock at him, aiming for his head. I really wanted to kill him. It struck him in the back and Dagda came at me growling as if to devour me. Uncle Seán, recovering from the rock, grabbed Dagda by the scruff of the neck as the dog had knocked me over and was about to eat my face.

Fr Sullivan caught up and was shrieking in a high voice. Uncle Seán was holding Dagda, and seemed bewildered as if woken from a trance. I'm sure his back hurt, it was a big rock and I'd put all my might into the throw.

'You're a fucking eejit,' I blubbered and began to cry. 'A right fucking eejit.'

'Ignatius,' Fr Sullivan said angrily. But he looked reproachingly at Uncle Seán. 'Seán what were you doing whirling like a dervish?' His silly Cork accent rising far too high at the end of every sentence. 'In broad daylight? Anyone in the town can see you?'

'I was just playing with Dagda,' Uncle Seán said his hand reaching for the place on his back where the rock hit.

'You're a feckin headcase.' I wiped my snot, backing away from the dog and the two daft priests, one as mad as the other. I turned and ran into the ruins. There was an old woman standing with her back to me in the roofless centre of the collapsed Cathedral of St Paul. She had her grey hair down her back and no scarf on her head and a blackthorn stick in her hand. I ran right up to her and she never moved. I gave a big yelp and she turned around and looked dead into my eyes.

'Don't bother your arse trying to pray to me, darling. I am deafened by the sirens of history.'

'Wha?' I took a few steps back from her.

'And don't even think of loving me. It's not your kiss I am after. I only wanted ye to love each other.' She wagged her stick at me.

I looked behind me and Seán was standing, still holding a growling Dagda by the broken wall of the ruin. Fr Sullivan was talking a mile a minute to him but he wasn't listening. I ran back to them but when Dagda barred her teeth at me, I slowed down

The mad old woman was yelling after me. 'I will shake you off to live. I can take care of myself. You were so briefly here, ten lifespans of an oak tree.'

Seán was not listening to Fr Sullivan blather on. He was looking straight over my shoulder at the woman.

'Was it her you came to see?' I gasped when I reached them, standing just out of Dagda's reach.

'See who?' Fr Sullivan said in a high-pitched voice. Uncle Seán smiled at me and reached his long, slender Viking arm out and brushed the back of his hand off my flushed cheeks.

Baby

More Nuns!
(1964)

Out of the frying pan and into the fire. The 6A bus brought me to Blackrock and I entered the gates of Carysfort Teacher Training College. I walked up the long drive, quaking at the sight of another formidable building. Another institution. More nuns. Would I ever be free of them? To my horror we were in dormitories. At least in the last two years of school I had a room of my own, with my own sink.

That night, as I lay in a strange new bed, I knew deep down in my heart of hearts that it was the wrong place for me. I got up in the frosty morning and went to the head nun, Mother Peter.

She was a grey old creature and it looked as if someone had got a tube and sucked all the moisture out of her. There was no softness in her, each line in her face deepened with anger when I said I was leaving.

'Fine, Miss Lyons. But you won't get a penny back from this institution. Have you thought of how many young women would love to be offered a place here? And what your parents will say when you tell them you wasted their money? And what about your future? Go back to your dormitory and wait for the bell.'

And I turned and went back to my room and waited for the bell.

After doing so well in my Leaving Cert and being the brightest in my class, here I was, crying into my pillow, once more imprisoned.

The academic standard was so low, I was bored for the two years. We had to learn to sing, I couldn't sing. We had to learn to sew, I couldn't thread a needle. The history teacher was a nasty old fellah who took the line of the Catholic Church against the Land Leagues. When I wrote my history essay for the end-of-year exam he failed me for defending the Land Leagues. He claimed they were communist organizations bent on anarchy, instead of land reform and justice. The Church had been pro-landlord of course. We were kept in all week and on Saturday we were let out at 12.30, but had a four o'clock curfew.

We could barely get down to Blackrock town where there was nothing to do except walk along the cold, choppy, grey sea and maybe stop in for a scone and jam.

Ignatius

Bleeding Gums
(1964)

Uncle Seán drove me back to St Joseph's. When we turned the corner into Dublin the night dropped down and he looked like a drowned man. I said a few things to him but he didn't hear me.

As we were driving he looked at the stale grey slate of a day and said, 'Do you ever think light is too slow?'

He was talking so softly I had to lean in to hear him.

'By the time it gets to us from the sun it is four years old. Stale.'

He was moving slowly. It could have been his sore back where I had thrown the rock, or I wondered was he getting my sickness. Even to see that drab old giant school was like going back into a prison. Just the smell of it, the Jeyes Fluid mixed with cabbage. Or the sounds, the screams of the boys at night mixed with the thwack of a leather belt on naked skin.

We walked side by side into the building and it was only when he was to go his own way to his room that he appeared to see me. He put his arm on my shoulder but couldn't say a word. Then as if mustering all his strength, 'Ignatius. Your father thinks you should stay where you are and learn a trade. But there's a scholarship exam coming up in January for a good school in the country. Fr Lavin has said it is a good school. You'll be grand there. I'll keep talking to Seamus. I went and saw Patsey and told him to go work on your mammy and see if she will soften. You are to come back to my room on Tuesdays and Thursdays and I'll coach you for the exam. Even if you don't get it, Mary and I between us can pay the fees.'

'I hate me da. Why should he decide? They got rid of me.'

'My father, not 'me da'. Seamus said to me that a handful of skill is better than a bagful of gold, and maybe he's right. All I know was my life was simpler when I was out with Mary on the farm and not thinking all the time.'

'I want to go to secondary school,' I stated coldly. Now I wanted it more than anything else because I could see the choice was to be taken away from me.

'I'll see what I can do for you. I'm responsible for bringing you here in the first place. I'll never forget that. Run along now.'

I half expected him to ruffle my hair, but this time he didn't, so I turned and skulked off. I don't know why but I hated the idea of owing him and Mary anything. I hated the idea of another big school. I thought of running away and hopping on a boat to England and working over there on the buildings.

It put me in a bad mood and there I was in the corridor and the small boy with the bleeding gums was standing by himself shivering. If I had to see him bleeding into his bread one more teatime I'd lose it for sure. As I walked by him, I pushed him into the wall.

That night, I was afraid I'd wet the bed so I got up and went to the toilets for a piss. On my way back by the stairs, I heard sounds from upstairs and two shadows on the stairs above. Quietly, I backed against the wall so no one would see me. There were two priests up there and they were with a young boy. Cowering, I had seen enough badness here to not want to see any more, so I slid along the wall to get away. Shadows were projected on the green walls. The wee boy shadow was whimpering and one priest had him by the shoulders. Big loud sobs came rattling from the boy. Two long-black-robed shadow priests were growling at him. The shadows clumped together in one solid mass until a shape rushed past me, then fell. The boy had gone over the banisters. I leaned out a little as he dropped down the middle of the stairs. I felt him brush off me. I heard the thump of him.

I ran back to my bed and lay there trembling. I heard Brothers coming down the stairs, and panic noises. Once he was no longer a shadow, I knew who the boy was. I'd seen him lying like a splatted spider in the dark. He was a brother of the bleeding gums one. A little brother with curly hair. I didn't see him next morning and I made an excuse to go to the infirmary. I had the run of the place at the time. He wasn't there. The Brother who worked there whooshed me off.

I took it on myself to go to the boy with the bleeding gums and muscled him into a corner.

'Where's your little brother?'

'Padser?'

'What was his number?'

'50239.'

'That's him. Where is he?'

Bleeding Gums shook his head.

'Did you see something?' he asked in terror.

'I didn't say anything I just want to know where he is.'

'I haven't seen him in days.'

'That's cos he's dead.' I said, suprising myself.

'Wha?'

'The Brothers killed him.'

'Fuck off willya? Ye'r sick in da head.' The little shit was sneering at me.

I began to punch the little lad. I punched him and kicked him and pulled him across the corridor by his hair, digging my nails into his sunken cheeks. I wanted to throw him down the stairs too, so

I'd never have to see his gums bleed again. Starved and stunted as he was, light as a feather.

Uncle Seán came running. He dragged me off him, and he was in a blind rage. Our rage matched, we fought and scuffled and kicked and punched. But he was stronger than me. His strength surprised me.

'Ignatius, Ignatius, what has got into you?' He held me at arm's length as I tried to swipe him. 'I was told you were bullying boys but I didn't believe it, how could you?'

'He does. He bullies us all, Brother O Conaill,' Bleeding Gums blurted, as he slid up the wall to standing, wiping his snot on his sleeve.

'Get away from me you bastard,' I shouted at my uncle, 'get away from me, you ... you, there's something wrong with you, there's something wrong with you, you're not a man at all.'

'Ignatius!' He tried to grab me but at his touch I kicked out and got him right in those useless balls of his. He staggered, hunched over and I grabbed him by both ears and tried to pull them off his head.

'What are you doing here? Do ya think ye can rescue yourself by saving us? I'm sick of you blaming me for your being here when you do nothing. Why did you come here? You didn't help any of them. Ye didn't stop anything happening. Why are you here?'

I swear to fuck he lost it, like I'd never seen before, and he walloped me straight in the face with a closed fist. At this point there was a crowd of boys around and a few Brothers. My ears were ringing from the wallop and I looked at all the Brothers who gathered and I growled like a beast, 'Murderers, murderers, where have you put him? I seen it, I seen what you done. There must be a body somewhere,' I pointed to my uncle. 'And you, yer a coward that's what you are! Yer afraid of yer own shite!'

Uncle Seán gave me another swift punch in the gut. Then he held his own hand as if he had broken it, and I was on the ground. He turned and slithered off like the coward he was, before I could get up and punch him back. The other Brothers, seeing this, landed on top of me, twisted me to the ground face first, and pulled at my arms so hard I heard one come from its socket with a pop. My collar bone cracked under my skin as they slammed me again and again into the floor.

There was no stopping them.

Dragged off, blubbering and bloody, I was put into solitary in the boiler house. They had never dared do that to me before. I waited all night, sure that Uncle Seán would calm down and come and get me out. The pain in my front shoulder was worse and worse and I couldn't move it. My arm was dangling loose from me like a puppet's. I heard a noise outside and I thought it was him.

A boy crept up to the boiler house. Shite, it was only Bleeding Gums, I recognized his soft girly voice. 'What do ya know bout Padser?'

'Who the fuck is Padser?'

'Remember? He's me brudder.'

'I saw him fall from the stairs down a few floors. There were two Brothers up there with him. Ask them what happened. Go to the guards.'

He was real quiet, I thought he had gone, but then he spoke in a tiny voice. 'They won't care what you saw. Sure who'd believe us anyway?'

'Tell my uncle. Tell Brother O Conaill. I've a feeling he'll do something finally. The way he snapped. I just have a feeling.'

'But he's one of them.'

'No he's not. He's different. He came here to stop all the badness.'

'Not anymore. You know what the boy who serves the Brothers saw?'

I grunted from behind the door.

'I don't tink he'll help. When Brother Seán went to tea tonight he looked as if he seen a bleedin ghost an when he came into de room all de Brudders got up and started clapping. Dey clapped an clapped, an some slapped his back and dey were fierce pleased at what he done. You're in for it now, boy. He's one of them.'

'They all stood up and clapped?'

'He just sat an didn't eat. He just sat an looked shook. He wouldn't look at anyone. I tink he hurt his hand, the boy serving said he just kept looking down at his hand. And there was purple on de knuckles where he bashed ya.'

'Ya gobdaw that means he's sorry. I know me uncle. They think he's one of them now but he isn't. No way. He's the nicest man ever. Everyone knows he's special.'

'There's a few of them that are nice to us but they don't stop anyting, do dey? I have ta run or I'll be battered for talking ta ya. Will ye help me find me brudder?'

'Your brother is dead. And I want to see all those fucking Brothers in jail where they belong.'

'No one cares. Our famblies put us in here first then the Brudders got us. Is it dark in there?'

'As black as the inside of a cow with its tail down and its eyes shut.'

I could hear Bleeding Gums giggle, and he scurried off and left me to the dark and the rats scratching their pink-tipped nails on the cement floor. I bunched meself into a ball to keep warm though the pain was something fierce.

Brother Boyle let me out of the boiler house in the morning and I ran before he could get me, but when I turned and sneaked a look from a safe distance, he was just smirking after me. Then he gave me a little girly wave with his hand held up and his fingers fluttering. Creep.

I ran up the stairs, passed the landing where I had stood and felt the boy whoosh to his death. I wanted to tell Uncle Seán what I seen. I had his name and number, Padser, 50239. I wanted him to know what I meant when I said they were murderers. I didn't mean him. He couldn't have known. I wanted to know what they had done with the boy. I thought together we could go to the guards. They'd put it in the papers and close the shitehole of a school down. And then I'd live with Mary or Fr Lavin, or they'd put me with the old couple that they put that fellow Jimmy in Cootehill, until the exam, and I'd go to the school they wanted me to go to. It couldn't be worse than here, and I'd never come back here. I'd make a name for myself like Genghis Khan. They'd put all the Brothers in prison and all the wee boys could be placed in foster families instead. Uncle Seán could go off to India or China to the missions and turn all them heathens into Catholics. I might even follow him out there when I finished school to see what the craic was. I had it all planned because I hadn't slept a wink with the agony in my shoulder.

I knocked at his door wincing with the pain. He didn't answer. It was early so he could still be sleeping. I didn't want Brother Boyle snooping around so I opened the door and jumped inside. Groping for the light switch my good hand brushing the wall, flipped it on. Uncle Seán wasn't in bed.

He was hanging by his neck from the curtain rail. Hanging by the cord of his dressing gown.

The world was very still and very small. Though my legs shook and wobbled, I walked over and touched him. The universe shrunk to the size of the cell. He was still warm so I thought I had caught him in time. I lifted his legs to take the pressure off his neck. I had to lift with just one arm because my collarbone was broken. It took all I had in me to get my arm working again. I heaved him up with all my strength.

Tomorrow was to be my twelfth birthday. He had given me a book on each of my birthdays there. I was sure he had a present for me. As I held him, I looked around for a second in case I saw my present. I made sure to keep him upright so his neck wouldn't choke more. If help came now we could cut him down and he would live. His pyjamas were all piss. Wincing with the pain coming from my collarbone, I kept pushing him up and up, my Uncle Seán. I was here to save him.

I howled until the Brothers came. I don't know what I was shouting. Oh Crom Cruach spit him out, I shouted. Idol of Trim please help me. I will restore you. I'll go to you in poxy Trim to the broken Yellow Steeple; I'll walk barefoot in winter to you. One more miracle and I will restore you.

Baby

She Took Me to the 4 Ps
(1964)

I lived for Sunday. We were let out of the teacher training college at 12-30 and could stay out till seven in the evening. My older sister, Eileen, was twenty-five and in an awful panic because she hadn't got married yet. We met every Sunday and she took me to the 4 Ps as we called it, the Four Provinces on Harcourt Street. They had afternoon dances. No rock and roll allowed but plenty of Pat Boone and Frank Sinatra. Eileen was mad to get a man. Convinced she was heading into spinsterhood, she thought any fellah would have loved to have such a laying hen as her as she was earning good money. I secretly thought it was her bossiness that put them off.

'But if you get married you're made to give up your job. You've worked so hard to be a nurse. You're in charge of the intensive care.'

'I'm not in charge. You have to be a nun to be in charge of anything. I don't care, Baby. I'll be as bitter as one of them old nuns if I don't,' she whinged.

'I don't want to get married,' I said emphatically.

'Baby, you just want to fight the whole world. Well I don't.' With that, she smoothed her dress as the music started. 'You were ruined by Mary to think you were the Queen of Sheba. You aren't. You're just like the rest of us.'

I stuck my tongue out at her and she stuck hers out back at me and we giggled.

I checked my watch to make sure I didn't go past the time.

'What will happen if you don't get back before seven?'

'They won't let me out at all next weekend. I don't think I could survive that.'

'Janey Mack, you wouldn't would you? You're new here so they'll all be asking you up. But watch it; some of them are right gougers, all Roman hands and Russian fingers.'

A man came up to take me to dance. I gestured towards my sister and he shrugged and took her by the arm. Eileen was pretty but she had that stern nurse streak in her that could put a fellah off. She knew that and I could see her try to laugh and be light but it came off a little shrill. Really Eileen should have been running the country, not pretending to be something she wasn't.

Suddenly, I saw a man who, from the back, looked like Seán, Mary's little brother. That happened a lot. He turned around and I could see he wasn't as beautiful and really looked nothing like him. He caught me staring at him and he winked. I threw my eyes up to Heaven and gave him daggers. As I walked into the toilets to avoid him I thought of the time, over a year ago, when I came home for Seán's funeral. In the toilets at the dance, I splashed water on my face, and it made my mascara run. I stood in front of the yellowed mirror wiping the black smudged lines out from my eyes before I went back onto the dance floor. As awful as they were I lived for these dances. They were the only release.

Fr Lavin had been whispering as we stood around the dismal reception back in our living room. It was a poor show, the funeral; a priest who committed suicide is a great shame and most stayed away for fear of being contaminated with the bad luck of it. Suicide was a mortal sin so poor Fr Lavin couldn't let his best friend be buried in consecrated ground. It was the only time I saw Mary sit in a chair in the living room. In all honesty, she really didn't know where she was. Where were they? All those people who beat a path to the door looking for her cures and she never charged one of them. Decent to the core, Patsey was the only person who turned up from Rathcairn. He had the rosary beads clutched in his hands and he didn't have any blessings when he entered. My brother Joseph had left the bank this year and announced to us all that he had got the vocation so he was going to Maynooth to train to be a priest at the grand old age of twenty-six. He wasn't given permission to go the funeral. That would be hard for Mary to take. I'm not sure my father and mother were thrilled either, but they accepted it.

Fr Lavin had taken me aside. 'Congratulations on your Leaving Cert. I heard you got third in all Ireland. And that you even got honours maths though you had to teach yourself the curriculum.'

I wasn't really listening to him until he said, 'A scholarship to Cambridge is a great honour for the family but you made the right decision. England is no place for a girl.'

'What scholarship? I never got that.' I was gobsmacked.

My brother James was there, he had a good job in the bank and a wife and son. I took him into the kitchen and beckoned to Mammy.

I closed the kitchen door.

'What's this about a scholarship from Cambridge?'

Mammy looked helplessly at James. She, who had been crying all morning, sat into Mary's chair by the stove. I almost tore her out of it. 'Don't sit in her chair!'

James broadened his shoulders and said, 'This is not the time and place for this discussion.'

'And were you ever going to have this discussion, only Fr Lavin let it slip?'

'The letter came when you were up in Dublin with Eileen.'

'A scholarship to Cambridge?' I was stunned.

'Mammy, Daddy, Joseph and I had a meeting,' James said carefully and slowly. 'We couldn't have you going off to England by yourself, Baby. You had the place in Carysfort and a whole life ahead of you as a national school teacher. England is no place for a girl on her own. We thought it was for the best.'

'Did Mary know?'

'No.' Mammy shook her head.

'She would have told me. Wouldn't she?'

'We were afraid she might, so we didn't tell her.'

'Don't make a scene today,' James urged. 'For Mary's sake. She needs you here now more than ever. Imagine if you had been in England for this awful thing?'

'Imagine.' I smouldered. Of course I didn't make a scene for Mary's sake. I glared at my mother.

'Get out of her chair,' I growled. She looked shocked but James was stern.

'Baby. There's no need. It was for your own good.'

'Don't Baby me.' I left the kitchen and went back and sat down in front of Mary. I took both her hands and we wept at each other. I'm not even sure what I was crying for at that point.

After the death of Seán and the news about my missed scholarship I wasn't sure what to think about my life. The annual school dance in Cleary's was coming up. I needed the distraction. It was the biggest dance of the year. Even if the nuns did pay to have the bar closed. I was invited by my friend's brother Michael, but he was a great one for the dancing, and I had two left feet so we split off from each other soon enough.

Paddy MacInespie from Tyrone couldn't dance either. We were at the same table and began to talk to each other. He could talk the hind leg off a donkey, but at least he was a diversion, better yet he offered me a drink of his bottle.

Because it was known that the bar would be closed, all the men brought flat bottles of whiskey that fit their inside pockets. The irony was that normally the women might have one Babycham or something light, but at this dance we were all supping the men's whiskey. Everyone got flootered, so it geared up to be a wild night.

Paddy and I sat and drank. He told me he had studied history and literature in UCD. Now he was getting a master's degree in history. At first I found him awful pompous; he talked to me as if he expected that I wouldn't understand what he was talking about.

'I'm not a communist. Especially after what happened in Stalin's Russia. But I'm a socialist. The difference is ...'

'I'm eighteen years old. I got an A in history in the Leaving Cert. I know what the difference between socialism and communism is,' I said haughtily. He looked at me and then smiled shyly.

'Sorry! Am I being boring?'

'At least you care about more than hurling and football, which is all my brothers talk about.'

I told him about failing history on account of my support for the Land Leagues and he got excited. He began to talk about Brehon Laws. The last time I had heard of the Brehon Laws was from Seán, who had once said on a country lane many years back, that we should have adopted them when we got independence.

'That's an interesting idea,' Paddy enthused. 'We should have become a socialist country after the 1916 rebellion. James Connolly was the only one thinking of the poor.'

'And the Brits shot him tied to a chair so he could sit straight,' I said, 'and then we became a theocracy.'

'Yes, yes,' he said, looking at me as if I was suddenly the greatest mind in the world, only because I was agreeing with him.

I told him about those days when the sun shone, and we picked blackberries along the country lanes and Mary pretended to scold Seán for all his ideas, and Seán talking about Buddhism one minute and Brehon Law the next.

'Those days when I was young and the world was young. In all the stories about ancient Ireland our ancestors fostered their children. And I had been that for Mary: her foster child. Loved more than her own child if she had had any.'

'You're only eighteen now, Teresa,' he said. 'I'm writing a paper on Brehon Law at the moment.'

'I'd like to read that.'

'Really, you would?' He was shocked, he looked around at all the young women and men dancing and talking. It was later he said that's when he fell in love with me: When I sat there in my turquoise taffeta ball dress with my high heels flipped off and earnestly asked to read a paper on Brehon Law.

For my part I looked at him closely; he was tall and had nice blue eyes and dark hair. He smiled easily and he was listening to me.

'Call me Baby,' I said. 'That's what everyone who knows me properly calls me.'

'I'd like to know you properly, Baby.' He said it in such a deep voice, I burst out laughing.

'Would ye now?' And everyone who was at the table overheard the last bit and we were all laughing until he turned bright red but he stood his ground and pushed his hand back through his black hair. I liked the way he didn't have a head full of grease like half the eejits there. When he went to the toilet, I wrote him a poem on the back of the menu. He folded it up and pocketed it. 'I'll read this later,' he said. 'When I'm not full of whiskey and there's quiet.' It was the first and last poem I ever wrote in my life, but Paddy would keep it forever between the pages of a book.

Mary, Seán and myself:
Barefoot in the lane,
Blackberry picking,
When was the last time I took off my shoes
And walked?
The sky was tuned to a blue key,

With a staccato of clouds,
And the fields were a noise of green.
The unseen world sang,
And we could hear the music then.

435

The Wild History of Their Past Has Faded from Their Minds (1965)

The head nun of the laundry was called the Superioress. Sister Paul brought me under the tunnel into the church, and when I came out there was no Mass going on. We walked through sections of the church I would not normally have been allowed into. We genuflected when we crossed the centre aisle. She opened a door and brought me down another tunnel and I entered the laundries, so I did. The air was full of steam and the ground was so wet that I felt faint and lost my bearings for a minute.

'This is where you'll go for now,' Sister Paul said.

'But I'm fifteen now. I can be out soon?' I asked.

'We'll see how you are doing. I'll take you to the Superioress. She'll tell you how to behave here and then you'll get your training and start work.'

All I ever done is work. She took me to a room and gave me new clothes to wear. I had always cut my curls off, but now they shaved my head. When we reached the office of the Superioress, I stood in my new laundry uniform and hat. The Superioress put out her hand and I had to kiss her ring.

'What have I done?' I asked, confused.

'How do you mean, child?'

'Why am I to leave the orphanage part and come to this part? Am I being punished?'

'We need someone to do the ironing and they said you were a good worker.'

A good worker? They'd never told me that. I'd worked for years as a skivvy for these nuns and nothing satisfied them. Now they were putting me in with the laundry women, the Magdalenes, the lowest of the low.

'Hard labour is the cure for the sexually charged mind, my dear.'

'Wha?'

'You will work with the other women from after Mass at 7 am till 7 pm at night. Sunday is a day of prayer. You will not talk to the others during work hours. What's her name?'

'She's 435,' Sister Paul said.

'We don't go by numbers. We'll put her down as Bridget.' The Superioress made a note of that. 'Do you know who Bridget is, child?'

I wondered was that my name when I had come in as a wee baby or was she just making that up on the spot. I shook my head. 'Was she St Patrick's best friend?'

'She's one of the foremost patron saints of Ireland. When her father the king wanted to marry her off to a pagan, she tore her own eye out to make herself ugly and became a nun. The very well where she threw her eye out is now a sacred place of healing.'

'And next year I'm finished, right? I'm not a Magdalene.'

'We all have to pay for the sins of Eve,' she said frostily, looking me up and down.

Sister Paul was behind me and I'd never seen the woman smile but, as I turned to look at her, she was almost smiling.

'Sister Paul will take you to the laundry room and you can get started. We will review your case in a year when you reach your sixteenth birthday.'

'Then can I go free?'

'You are not imprisoned here,' she snapped. 'Sister Paul, warn her to be careful among these women, be on her guard against their wiles.'

Sister Paul had known me since I was a baby. Now, she took my arm roughly and led me back to the laundry.

'It's the young ones you need to look out for,' she said. 'Don't fraternize with them on any account or you'll find yourself here for life.' She pointed to a few older women who worked quietly mending in a room. 'If that's what you want.'

'The older ones are subdued. The wild history of their past has faded from their minds.'

'Are they ever going to get out?' I asked.

Sister Paul shook her head. 'The wish and the intention of the good Sisters is that their inmates should remain with them for life, we know that very few of these who have lost their good name, and have contracted bad habits will be able to resist temptation if let out into the world again. It's for their own good.'

I was set to ironing the day of my fifteenth birthday, and that's how I ended up among the Magdalenes.

That evening we had to eat in silence. It was the same awful, watery food served to me all me life. The other women kept glancing at me, so they did.

'What did you do?' one young one asked. 'Did the Cruelty Man get you?'

'I'm from the home,' I said. 'I didn't do anything. They said they needed an ironer.'

'What's your name?'

'Bridget. They told me to go by Bridget.'

They all groaned.

'We've too many Bridgets here. The nuns call us all Bridget or Mary or Teresa.'

'Let's call her Bridey.'

'She was there at the beginning of the world, Bride, she brought it all in,' Teresa said. 'Some called her Bright, some Bride, some Bridget. It's where the word bride comes from, like when a woman marries.'

'Was Bridget not a saint who knew St Patrick? Is she the same as Bride?' I asked.

'That was later,' Teresa said. As if certain people can live forever. 'She brought life to the earth, she was the first to hear its song and know what it was longing for. She went back to the gods and convinced them to come. They couldn't get the song out of their head and agreed to follow her to the Earth. That's how all life on Earth started.'

I'd never heard talk the like of that except from the priest reading stuff at Mass. Teresa seemed to shine when she talked, she was smiling at me the whole time. I'd always hated the laundry women as we were told they were a bad lot. The others seemed to enjoy my shock and they nudged each other.

'Our Teresa has loads of stories, so she does,' one said proudly.

'Did she tell ye ye had to atone for the sins of Eve?' another one of them said, and the young ones snickered.

'Do yer one about Eve, Teresa.'

The one called Teresa slapped her chest.

'It's an old one so you can see it's always been this way.'

'Just do it,' one of them urged looking around in case the nuns were listening.

'I am Eve, great Adam's wife,
I that wrought my children's loss,
I that wronged Jesus of life,
By right 'tis I had borne the cross.'

'That sounds nice,' I said. No one had ever paid me much mind and now all these women were looking at me.

'It's not nice. Them nuns are blue in the face telling us about Eve taking the apple. That's where it all started for all of us. Eve's horrible mistake.'

The others pointed at Teresa proudly. 'On Sundays she tells us stories. The nuns don't mind it.'

'It's not really nice at all,' Teresa said. 'Are ye listening?'

'Yer lucky all they have ye doing is ironing,' one said. 'The sheets from the hospitals come in every morning. There's maggots and blood and shite in them. The newest girls usually get stuck with them.'

'I'm not a Magdalene,' I said softly. 'I'm just here for the year.'

'Keep telling yourself that, child of grace,' one said.

'Can't ye see why you're here? Why them auld nuns, the bitches, stuck you in with us?'

I shook my head. 'I thought youse lot were short of someone.'

'You're pretty,' Teresa sighed. 'Even if they've skinned your head. You're in here because you're pretty.'

I put my hand up to me head. I was glad they shaved it because otherwise it was curly red, and I'd got hell for that hair all my born days.

Another nodded. 'Too pretty for them to let you out.'

They all laughed at me. Teresa was staring real hard.

'Tell her the rest of it,' the woman beside her nudged her.

Teresa looked right into me:

'*I that brought the winter in*
And the windy glistening sky,
I that brought terror and sin,
Hell and pain and sorrow.'

'The sins of Eve,' one said, wagging her finger and narrowing her eyes in imitation of the nuns. 'We're all to pay for them.'

But I was thinking of something else. That was the first time in my life anyone had ever told me I was pretty.

'Bright!' Teresa said. 'Let's call her Bright. That's what I used to call my sister.' And she gave me the most beautiful smile. The only times them nuns smiled was as if to say, there now, we told you so. Punishment smiles. This was a real smile Teresa gave me. And now I had a name too. I never had one up to now. And no one had ever smiled just for me before. Maybe it wouldn't be so bad here.

Baby

The Burning of the Books (1968)

Fr Lavin got me a job teaching in Cootehill, Co. Cavan. I had a wee room in the Central Café at the top of a house on Market Street. Paddy drove up all the time and stopped on his way to Tyrone to see his family. He took me with him some weekends. The Troubles were brewing in Northern Ireland and Paddy was trying hard to stick with his socialism and not give in to his nationalism. The British were making that very hard.

I hated teaching. I was put standing in front of a class with a tuning fork and expected to have them singing when I was tone deaf. I had the Junior Infants' class and spent more time wiping their noses than imparting any knowledge. I had no feeling for little children and begged to be put into a higher class. Paddy had bought me a smuggled copy of James Joyce's *Ulysses* and one of the other teachers reported me to the priest for reading it. The priest walked into my class and asked for it. I told him it was at home. As he stood there before me, I felt my legs shaking, I thought my job was gone.

He came to the boarding house that night and I handed it over. Without ceremony, and without even flicking through the pages, there in the kitchen with my widow landlady, Kitty, and her twin sister, Molly, looking on, he opened the stove door and threw it into the fire. Molly and Kitty actually let out a gasp. My eyes filled with tears and I pinched my thigh hard so I wouldn't start crying. He looked at me in my miniskirt and leather boots and asked me to say a prayer with him.

'Sister Paul is pleased with you, says you are a good girl from a good family. And Fr Lavin and I were in the seminary together. He's a fine priest. Much loved over there in Kilbride. We'll say no more about this.'

While we watched the book burn we said an Our Father. My landlady stepped out while we prayed. I thought I'd be asked to leave for having such a book in the house but when he had gone they just smiled and poured me some tea in a china cup. Molly poked the burnt book with a poker. The book was so thick it was still in shape though quickly turned to a mush of ash.

'Give the priest his own side of the road,' Kitty sighed.

Her sister Molly said, 'Although there was nobody present but the priest and the friar, still have I lost my own property.'

They had made apple tarts, the priest had taken one on the way out, and the two good women gave me an extra big slice and we sat there and talked about other things. All their children but one had left the country and we three talked about the wonders of New York though none of us had ever been out of the country. When we finished, I opened the stove door, and taking the poker, I bashed the book to final ash.

Kitty and Molly gave me a stack of their Mills & Boon romance books to read if I was stuck. Molly had taken the time to write a solid 'NO' on the pages she thought I was too innocent to read. I lay in my bed that night flicking through the books reading those ones. It wasn't James Joyce.

I was fit to be tied when Paddy came that weekend. We were sitting in the White Horse Hotel and I told him everything, down to the last detail of the apple tarts.

'Will you marry me?' he said, and then looked away.

I drained my gin and tonic. I swirled the ice around the glass while he squirmed and fidgeted.

'I will, Patrick MacInespie, if you come back next weekend with a new copy of *Ulysses*.'

'What? But where am I going to get it? My brother took that one in the bottom of the suitcase from New York. It had a cover on it that said 'Jerusalem the Bible'.'

'Then I won't marry you so.'

'You're an awful woman. Did you even understand any of it?'

'I was getting the gist of it,' I sniffed haughtily.

'It was all gist to me, I'm afraid,' Paddy took my hand. 'Give me Steinbeck, Orwell or Hemingway any day. And you can just march into a shop in Dublin and buy them. You drive a hard bargain, Mrs MacInespie.'

'I'm not Mrs MacInespie yet.' I took my hand away.

'You know the Censorship Board used to be called the Evil Literature Board.'

'They're a shower of shites,' I bristled. 'Who are they to dictate what I read?'

'Oh they're only trying to protect the maidens of Ireland from evil influences. Not to have us all polluted.'

'Then they wonder why half the country is polluted with drink.' I drained my drink and ordered another.

'In 1952 one member of the censorship board reviewed seventy books and banned them all.'

'You're a great man for the facts, Paddy MacInespie.' I mock yawned. He looked hurt but I elbowed him just to let on I was messing.

I don't know how, but Paddy came the next weekend with a battered, second-hand copy of *Ulysses*, covered in brown paper. We got engaged on the spot. He told me that it actually wasn't officially illegal, but since everything else was banned they never tried to bring it openly into the country. I took no chances. This time I kept it hidden in my room in my empty jewellery box, under the picture of Mary appearing to Bernadette.

Ignatius

Now a Free Man
(1968)

My deep hatred for them grew and grew like a big swell over the grey giant prison of St Joseph's School, and my huge hate would raise into the air and go from horizon to horizon and fill the world with my hate, my hate, my hate. Most of all, I hated Uncle Seán for killing himself and leaving me at their mercy. They who didn't know the meaning of the word. I hated myself for murdering him. I had boxed Bleeding Gums and my uncle was so disgusted he boxed me and we all were lost, for the smell of blood and cabbage drove us all mad.

After the Brothers found me holding my uncle, for a moment I thought they would do me for murder. When Brother Boyle was cutting him down, I found two books on the dressing table. One was his Spinoza book, but on top of it was a slim volume with a yellow cover entitled *Zozimus*. Inside Uncle Seán had written, 'Happy Birthday, my dear Ignatius.'

I wanted something more. To know why he had he hit me, and fled, leaving the others to light on me. I took both books. I kept reading the books for signs but I never found any. I had to wonder sometimes how much I really meant to him if this was all I was left with.

And they tried to teach me to be a cobbler but they used the stick on me so much my hands were broken and useless in the end, two big curled paws sticking out of my filthy coat, so after two years they had put me on their farm. The irony was I had been rescued from my bastard father's farm for this?

When my Uncle Seán had topped himself, I was not sad for Mary, I was not sad for Fr Lavin, I was not sad for Baby, or anyone who loved him. I was sad because I knew I would not go to secondary school. I was sad because I knew I would be learning a trade at St Joseph's or out on the farm. I knew I would be stripped and beaten just like the others. I knew that I would be starved and worked here till I was fifteen and then turfed out on the streets without a penny for all the years labour I done for the Brothers. I was sad because I knew that I would be got by Brother Boyle and the stick he had with a bullet on it, that he would put it into me, he would twist and pull out my lower bowel and I would lie for a week in the infirmary unable to move from the pain, and the nurse there would say nothing, and I'd say nothing, and the doctor that came from the outside would say nothing. And the boys would be satisfied that I'd no more protection and would descend on me like locusts for all the bullying I did to them when my uncle was alive. That's why the fuck I was sad.

Finally, my time was done, they could no longer hold me. The Brothers had offered to place me down the country where I could work as a slave for auld farmers like me da, but I ran onto the streets of Dublin, and even when I'd walk by a church or see a priest I'd feel the sick rising in my mouth. I was this full of hate, I walked out of St Joseph's Industrial School in 1968. They thought I was sixteen but I was barely fifteen and I wasn't going to correct them.

Now a free man, I lay down beside the canal with the hate oozing out of me. When winter came, I slept with the other tramps around city fires we lit in cans, huddled in the pram sheds in the flats. Sometimes we crept onto the buses that were parked at night and slept on the grey seats and smoked the butt ends left under them. There were a legion of us and we all could find each other, men from Daingan, Letterfrack, there were St Joseph's Industrial Schools all over Ireland, and the prisons were full of the children they had broken.

Baby

Live Horse, and You Will Get Grass (1968)

My parents and Mary were shocked when I got engaged.

'You're only twenty-two,' Mary said. 'Would you not live your life a bit? He's the first serious boyfriend you've had. You don't have to marry your first boyfriend these days.'

'Eileen won't be happy you beat her to it,' Mammy said, and Mary nodded.

But Paddy's intelligent earnestness charmed them all, and James and Daddy liked him and approved.

'I thought you were meant to come to me first,' Daddy teased him. Paddy blushed and looked at me.

'He's only messing with you,' I said. 'If you had gone to him first I'd have never spoken to you again. I'm not anyone's property.'

'Baby!' Mammy shook her head, but she was amused.

Fr Lavin clapped his hands. 'You two are well suited. She's as full of opinions as you are. As long as socialists raise their children as good Catholics I suppose we'll survive you lot too.'

'We'd love to meet your family. You're from Tyrone?'

'I know people in Tyrone.' Fr Lavin squinted his eyes to think of names.

'He's going to grill you until he finds that he knows someone who knows your people.'

'Remember the traditional Irish proposal.' My father smiled. '"Do you want to be buried with my people?"'

'Lovely, Daddy,' I said. 'They might not want to meet you.'

They all looked at me, Paddy most of all.

'Sure aren't they Protestant?'

There was a silence at the table. Mary let out a little bit of air that got caught in a whistle; she put her hand to her mouth as if to squash it.

'She's joking,' Paddy said quickly.

'OH!' Fr Lavin burst out laughing. 'You're not a black Protestant are you?'

'No,' Paddy blushed and kicked me hard under the table. My parents rolled their eyes.

'I'm glad you're taking her on.' Daddy sighed.

'We'd like to get married next month,' I said. They all looked at me as if to say something but none of them did. I wasn't pregnant, just impatient.

'I don't see the point in a long engagement,' my mother said quickly.

'We'll book the church for you,' Fr Lavin said.

'I'd love if you could do the ceremony,' I said to him and he beamed.

'Well go after to the hotel in Trim.'

'No you won't,' Mary said. 'I'd like to cook for Baby's wedding.'

'No, no,' I said. 'I want you to enjoy my wedding. The hotel in Trim would be grand.'

'There's one other person I'd like to tell,' I said, as Mary took our plates and disappeared into the kitchen. 'Sister Assumption.'

'Of course.' Mammy smiled.

Daddy brightened up and said, 'We were awful worried about you up there in that place.'

'You'd have got less for armed robbery,' I said.

'It wasn't as bad as the boys' schools, at least ye never got bet!' Daddy said.

'*Mair, a chapaill, agus gheobhaidh tú féar*.' Mary walked in with her homemade cake and sherry on the tray. 'That's what your favourite nun Sister Assumption told you when you would come crying to her. And I'd tell you the same.'

'What does that mean?' Paddy said. He bristled when the odd bit of Irish was spoken in our house. He associated Irish with the church and de Valera, and all the fascists, as he called them. He saw the language as an oppressive tool of the state. It was not the language of the poor and working classes anymore. 'Live horse, and you will get grass,' my mother said, softly looking over at me with pride.

'And so you did. I have the special decanter out to celebrate your good news, Baby.' Mary poured sherry into the tiny crystal glasses. She called them Protestant glasses, on account of them being so small.

'MacInespie,' Fr Lavin said. 'What kind of name is that at all?'

'It means son of a bishop,' Mary said.

We all laughed.

'Do you know that until the thirteenth century in Ireland priests and monks could marry and have children?' Paddy said.

'He loves his facts,' I said. 'Sure they only brought in the rule of celibacy so they could keep all the acquired land in the hands of the church and thereby increase its wealth. Not have the women and children get in the way.'

Mary nodded. 'That makes sense. I'm sure them nuns never wanted to marry. Marriage is good for men but not so good for women.'

Fr Lavin placed both hands on the table and shook his head. 'The things I hear in this house!' he declared. 'And from yourself Mary, I'm surprised.'

'Sure Mary is a pagan at heart,' Daddy said. 'She doesn't belong to your flock at all at all.'

'And these are only the things they say when you're present.' My mother laughed. 'Imagine what it's like when you walk out that door.'

Fr Lavin looked around the table and began to smile, but he looked slightly uneasy.

Paddy and I drove up to my boarding school the next day and I sat in the parlour and the nuns looked at my ring without much interest and served me tea and sandwiches. I kept looking around for Sister Assumption but she never came. I asked how she was and they said she was well. I asked did she know I was here and they said that she did.

The following week I got a letter from Sister Assumption who said that she was so sad to have missed me and the nuns told her my good news, she congratulated me. She said she really wanted to come and see me, but I would have had to ask for her directly for her to be allowed to come to the parlour. I hadn't even thought of that. I wrote her a letter of apology saying I would come back and ask for her directly, but I never did.

I wasn't pregnant when I married but I did get pregnant on the honeymoon, in a B&B in Co. Kerry. I remember that B&B, with the narky beán an tí and the sign over the sink in the bathroom down the hall '*ná usáid an uisce te*': don't use the hot water. But sure we didn't care, Paddy and I were that happy.

We sought out Mary's village Cill Rialaig on Bolus Head, in the Barony of Iveragh. It was exactly as she had always described it. We got out of our little Morris Minor and walked through the ruins of the houses. We climbed the hill behind the houses, our feet sinking into the boggy earth. A hare bounded by. There was no one around but us and we lay in the long grasses under some standing stones.

'The setting is wonderful. We really are on the last road in Ireland.' Paddy stood and looked out at the Atlantic and the islands just off the shore.

'But her village is just a bunch of ruined houses full of stupid-looking sheep,' I said. 'We can't tell Mary we came here and what has become of it.'

'It has an awful sad feeling about it,' Paddy agreed.

When we stood there above the fallen slate houses we decided that it was better that it fall into the sea, for places like that were full of hard memories of desperate, hungry days. Paddy reached out for me as I leaned against the stones.

435

The Mountains Are Not Dead (1969)

Mass was at five in the morning, then we went without eating to the laundry and we hand-washed, dried and ironed clothes that came from the orphanage, the church, the prisons and hotels. The worst ones of all were the hospital sheets. Breakfast was stale bread and watery porridge. We were never paid for any of this work and we were told that the scrubbing was intended to wash away our sins. What chance had I to commit sins? But I was a woman, and daughter of Eve, and every month we all got the sickness and it reminded us of our dirty insides. They never stopped telling us that however much we washed, we would be dirty.

We were forbidden to talk to each other when the nuns were around, and mostly did not during the week, but on Sunday we were allowed to whisper a bit after Mass and confessions. We all loved Teresa's stories. She had a great store of them and the one we all craved was 'The Children of Lir'. The others said Teresa had come straight from the big house in Mullingar, which was an asylum, or a loony bin as they called it. I knew she was a bit mad, but she had a light spirit to her that most of us didn't. That I couldn't find in meself anyway.

Even Teresa said it to me: I was like the lone house at the end of the lane that never got hooked to the electricity. She said that with sadness though, and not to hurt me like when the nuns said things. I was attracted to her light. She knew how to read and she would sometimes take her time with meself and any of them young ones to show us the reading if the nuns didn't catch us and flay her for it. She got the most beatings out of any of us. I never got the beatings anymore because I just learnt from being a wee one never to even have a thought go on in my head when them nuns were around.

One Sunday we were gathered whispering in the dormitories and Teresa was giving out to me because I had my period again. I called it 'the curse', because that's what we girls always called it. The nuns called it 'the sickness', and some of the girls from inner-city Dublin called it 'your others'.

'Don't worry about the mess it makes,' Teresa said. She was old and kept her hair almost shaved like most of us. I was shocked when she said she still got hers.

'Of course I still get mine,' she sniffed. 'You young wans thinks the world revolves around ye. What do youse know?'

'She doesn't know nothing.' One of them laughed at me. 'She came straight from the orphanage and into here. Sure she hasn't ever seen a fellah that's not a priest.'

That was not true.

'I seen the gardener, Jimmy,' I protested, and they all broke their shite laughing at me.

'Much good he'd do ya! He's ancient.'

'My lovely Bright,' Teresa said. 'I know I look like an old hag but if I got out of here I could still have a baby.'

'Jaysus tonight, sure isn't that what got you into here?' one said.

'I was put in here because I was writing poetry,' a little one said. She was new in, fourteen. 'I was walking by the Dodder River in me bare feet, an I liked to dip me feet into the water and write poetry. Me ma said, 'If youse don't stop that I'll send ye to the sisters.' She found me by the river saying the poems out loud and she went and got the Cruelty Man. He and the priest took me here.'

'What's a Cruelty Man?' one asked.

'They're meant to be there to protect the children,' Teresa said. 'To save them from cruelty. But they just shove everyone into these places. My sister used to send my brother out to the fairy ring on the hill to keep an eye out for them. Who were you saying the poems out loud to?' Teresa asked the new girl.

She shrugged and they smiled at each other. I felt a jealous pang. I had been the one Teresa looked out for until now.

'Well Teresa is in here because she had not one bastard but two.'

Teresa shrugged. 'They were twins. I couldn't help it. But then I was down as a repeat offender. So my goose was cooked.'

'How do you get out of here?' the little poet asked scratching at her baldy scalp that had just been shaved.

'You have to be claimed by a relation,' Teresa said. 'Actually you have to be signed out by two men.'

'Then I'm done for.' She put her head down and big tears plopped onto her knees. 'All I did was write poetry by the river.'

'You're pretty,' I said to her. I knew by now why they ended up here.

'And with that queer behaviour your family thought you'd be dragging their name through the mud in any time at all,' Teresa said. 'Better to get rid of ya. Even if the family comes, the nuns have us all under different names and they just say we moved away. They're raking it in here. Why would they let us go?'

The little poet stared at her in fright.

'Don't be scaring the poor mouse,' one said.

'All I started saying was that we should not call your monthly period a curse. It's the only colour we get in our lives and it comes from us.'

'She was in the loony bin before here,' another one winked at the little poet, tapping her head with her finger.

'Look around you, grey and grey and grey and white walls, and even the church is dark. There's a bit of puke green on the walls but no real colour anywhere. Then once a month I get it. I know it's hard to keep washing it out but next time look at the colour of the blood. That red is so beautiful. It starts out bright and at the end of the week it gets darker but it's still lovely. Once I got outside into the garden and sat on the grass and let it leak into the ground. It was a lovely feeling. Ye should try it. Good for the plants too.'

We were all sniggering at her, and she looked annoyed and turned to the wall as if to sleep, so someone said quickly, so we wouldn't lose our Sunday story, 'Tell the little poet about the Children of Lir.' Her name was Dympna, but that became her name from then on, Little Poet.

'I know that story.' Little Poet lit up.

'She tells it so well,' one said, and lay back in waiting. We all settled. Even the nuns didn't mind the stories. They saw no harm in them, I suppose.

Teresa told of the story of the four children who were turned into swans: Fionnuala, Aodh, Fiachra and Conn. As she was telling it, I watched her eyes come alive with the spirit in her and I loved to watch her face with a wild look in it, I don't know why. She did seem to be special among us. As if everything hadn't been scrubbed and steamed and ironed out of her. Teresa had tried to escape three times since even I'd been there. She had got as far as the street the last time and the guards had picked her up when the nuns called them. They had taken her back and the nuns had stripped her in front of all of us and they done mortification on her, as they called it. But we were secretly glad to get Teresa back because she was the only untamed one amongst us and we didn't know who could tell the stories like her.

Teresa was coming to the part where the wee children who had been turned into swans had done three hundred years by the lake, and three hundred years by the rough freezing Sea of Moyle. Then they got to the Western Sea and found it to be colder and more terrible than the Moyle, so they suffered greatly and were happy after the nine hundred years was up, and they could go back home to where they had once lived with their father, Lir. This was the part where we all secretly cried to ourselves. Not just me. I got a lump in my throat and then I'd shake with sobs and Little Poet looked around in astonishment at us all having our weep.

The swans looked at the hills they had known, and every hill and mountain they could see was dark and sorrowful: not one had a star-heart of light, not one had a flame-crown, not one had music pulsing through it like a great breath.

'O Aodh, and Conn and Fiachra,' said Fionnuala, 'Beauty is gone from the earth; we have no home now.'

The Little Poet began to rub her eyes herself as Teresa continued:

The people of the Goddess of Dana were gone from the land, and a different people now dwelt there, who were not as shining and special. A man came to them and said he was Aibric, he was seeking for Tír na nÓg, *the land of eternal youth that they had seen.*

'The mountains are dead,' Conn said.

'The mountains are not dead,' said Aibric. 'They are dark and silent, but they are not dead. I know. I have cried to them in the night and laid my forehead against theirs and felt the beating of their mighty hearts. They are wiser than the wisest druid, more tender than the tenderest mother. It is they who will keep the world alive.'

'O,' said Fionnuala, 'if the mountains are indeed alive let us go to them; let us tell them our sorrowful story. They will pity us and we shall not be utterly desolate.'

But when they flew to the mountain, it looked dark and sombre against the fading sky and the sight of it, discrowned and silent, struck chill to the hearts of the wild swans.

But Aibric stretched his hand out to the mountain and cried out, 'O beautiful glorious mountain, pity us, Tír na nÓg *is no more, welcome the children of Lir, for we have nothing left but you and the earth of Ireland.'*

'Girls,' Sister Paul came in, clapping her hands noisily as if to shoo the swans from the room. 'It's time for bed. Seven on the dot. You have work tomorrow.'

We all groaned as she shut out the light and sat at her place, taking out her rosary and beginning to say the prayers loudly. They had nuns do shifts as we slept to keep us under guard though it was only really Teresa who would have bolted. Many's a time I thought of running away, but since I'd never so much as even seen the outside world or talked to anyone who wasn't a nun or one of their captives I didn't know what would happen to me if I ever got out. I had never even really seen money, let alone how to get it to get food. Teresa whispered to Little Poet,

'I was raised on a mountain you know, in Bolus Head, Cill Rialaig, Ballinskelligs, in the Barony of Iveragh in Co. Kerry. I grew up on a farm in Meath, then I was cursed, three hundred years in the mother and baby home, three hundred years in the big house in Mullingar, and now three hundred years as a Magdalene. My time is almost up. I can feel that it is coming to an end. This ordeal is over. Come with me next time, Little Poet. Do ya want to become like Bright over there? She's been here so long, walked through a tunnel from the orphanage, through the church, and a tunnel to this laundry, she wouldn't know what to do with no walls around her, with no doors locking her in. I'm going to go next week when the trucks come in the back from the hospitals. I'm going to get in them, hide, and go with them.'

I was jealous she was talking to Little Poet. For when I first came, she had taken me under her wing, and I felt like she was our big sister. So this is what it was like to be on the Sea of Moyle under Fionnuala's wing. She had asked me to come with her many times but I was too scared.

I was the girl at the end of the dormitory, lying here without so much as the chance of a dream to come to me in the night, for what could I dream of but the washing coming in with blood and shite on it? What dreams come into the dark house at the end of the lane, with broken windows and a smokeless chimney? They called me Bright but my lights were out, so they were.

I that brought the winter in.

The next night Little Poet was crying in her bed and Teresa snuck into the bed beside her and I heard her whisper, 'My auld segotia, my great wee gersha. You're the best girl in the whole wide world.' She stopped and said, 'That's what my sister Mary used to say to me when my daddy left us and never came back.'

So help me God, I was so frightened that she'd take Little Poet with her and never come back to me, that I told the nuns of her escape plan the next morning. Didn't she get a beating for it that made us all weep and cry and made me get sick again so they'd stop? The nuns told her it was me who ratted her out, so she never spoke to me again after that. But I could still listen to her stories, so I could. And they watched her like hawks when the laundry trucks came and went and she, still standing with the Little Poet, lost behind the steam and the beauty that was never in me would be taken out of them both in the laundries, and their fires put out and their lights cut off, till we all slept on our beds, under guard, like a whole row of dark empty houses forgotten by the electricity. But maybe I knew what love is, love is what I done to her, only I could never tell her that was why I done it.

And knowing I had made sure Teresa would never leave me, I began to close my eyes at night and was finally able to dream. I dreamt of the big wooden door unlocking and swinging open. I dreamt I left these pale green walls. I came out and floated into the cool air and saw a green country beneath me, with shining green fields, and tall green trees, and I saw the Cruelty Men in brown shirts, like insects teaming through the country, their heads darting left and right, and all the children burrowing underground to hide. I was nothing, so I was. And they did not see me.

Ignatius

All We Have Is Love
(1969)

I lifted a pile of old clothes in a laneway and found Bleeding Gums himself, poor craytur. He was clutching a bottle and trying to get a night's kip. We watched each other's back for a while until he went off to London, probably to drink himself to death. His brother had never reappeared and God knows how many unmarked graves there were out there in the fields beside the school. And it wasn't just us lads who had suffered, the women selling their flaps up around the squares were from the girls' schools, the Sisters of Mercy, the so-called orphanages, the laundries.

All I had was the rumpled, crumpled stained books that my Uncle Seán left for me on his dressing table. So I said I was Zozimus' great-grandson, the slum poet and storyteller, and I stood and recited my poems and stories on Essex Bridge, like he did a century before me, in a big ragged coat. Hate, always hate, grizzled and worn inside of me like an old dead thing, until she found me.

She found me on Essex Bridge and gave me money and asked

for the story of the Bull Bhalbhae, of course I knew who she was. Of course I knew it was Baby. And, to be sure, I knew the story.

'Bejaysus, but that's an awful long one, you'd need a full night for that one,' I winked at her.

'But you know it?'

'I do.'

'How does it end?'

'With the sad sigh of all the endings.'

'And what's that when it's at home?'

This is my story. If there is a lie in it let it be so. It was not I who composed it. I got no reward but butter boots and paper stockings. The white-legged hound came, and ate the boots from my feet, and tore my paper stockings!

She laughed, a laugh like light on water, 'Ignatius, Mary sent me. She's been looking for years. Even Patsey and Fr Lavin were looking for you. They all were.'

'I'm Zozimus.'

'Come on out of that, Ignatius.'

I declared, 'I'm Zozimus, great-grandson of THE Zozimus. The bard of the streets. I can tell you a story. I can read you a poem. I can tell you the story of Genghis Khan from the secret history that has yet to be translated into any Latin language. I can tell you about the fairy world.'

'Go on then.' She seemed game, in anyways she wasn't moving away.

I put my hand out and she ceremoniously gave me a shilling. I bowed graciously and began.

There is a difference between this world and the world of the faery, but it is not immediately perceptible. Everything that is here is there, but the things that are there are better than those that are here. All things that are bright are there brighter. There is more gold in the sun and more silver in the moon of that land. Everything in the faeryland is better by this one wonderful degree.

'Yeah right, I've heard that one many's a time from Mary. I was rared on those stories before you were born. It *is* you, Ignatius; sure I'd know that divil's look in your eyes anywhere. I remember the time you rode my mother's horse bareback and dressed up for the wren with my brothers, and wasn't it I who taught you to read? And you learnt fast. Seán used to tell us you'd a photographic memory. We've been looking for you, come on with me. I'll get you a cup of tea and some soup somewhere.'

I shook my head, 'Missis, I have no idea who you are.'

Baby, Baby the beloved, the luck-child. The family pet. Mary's pride and joy. Shining eyes, glossy hair piled high in a beehive, lovely long legs in a tiny miniskirt. White teeth.

And my teeth like cavity sins, all but rotted out of my cadaver mouth. Bleeding Gums where are you now? Come back from London. We could have a competition.

'Where did you learn that story? 'The Bull Bhalbhae'. You might be the great-grandson of Zozimus, but you have the O Conaill knack of storytelling.'

I jolted at that name. Seán O Conaill, from Bolus head, Cill Rialaig, Ballinskelligs, in the Barony of Iveragh in Co. Kerry, never been there but that's where my people were from. And who told me that? Not my father. Not my father who put his hand in the reaper and fed it to the land and his foot into the pig shite and lost that too.

Drochubh, drochéan.

A bad egg, a bad bird.

Uncle Seán. He told me, that's who. He had poured out everything to me. Shared so many secrets. So many poems he taught me. That I got pennies for now. So I could have my whiskey. So I could warm up the scattered bits of me. Sure I went meself to the park when short on cash. I was brought there a while ago, and taught how to get paid. I stuck myself into many a desperate furtive man in the bushes. Grief is a place where everything is the same as in this world but one degree darker. A world serviced by a blind chilly sun. And I guessed the story of the other priest, though no word was ever said. Was I the only one not blind? The natural priest Fr Lavin, and his Cootehill son, Jimmy, the living spit of him. Lies lies. The power leaking out of the mad Brothers, into me, till I was seeping with it. How I hated watching the starving children sucking at their bread, while I was fed and a special wee man. Better than them. Better than those with their piss sheets wrapped around their heads. Better than the drugged children, limbs flopping, like demented pietàs in the arms of Brother Boyle. For in the end it was more of a relief to be one of them. To no longer be special. Truth is I'd rather get the beating myself than watch the others being beaten.

What was the incantation that was so bad it could only belong in the Irish language? The fear in the land. The crops pulled out black with it. Oh we were in free Ireland now. Hadn't we got the Brits out? Of most of it anyway? And who had we let in? The fucking Romans. Bastard crucifier betrayers, pacts with Hitler, sided with Mussolini. Right behind Franco. Blue Shirts making the trains run on time. Threw a hissy fit when poor Noël Browne tried to bring in the Mother and Child scheme. This must be the only country where a man who eradicated TB and tried to stop infant mortality, the highest in the Western world, could bring down a government. Because our spiritual leaders wouldn't have it. We gave them the children of the poor. Human sacrifices. Bog bodies. The hag that hungered for us. Her craggy hand reaching down the chimney. Each time. Tearing us off our mother's breast. Throwing us into the river. The land offered to us. Our promise broken to it. Our language lost. What does the land think of us? The hag of Ireland? So many scooped up and locked away. So many buggered children abandoned. So much beauty wrung out in the laundries.

'Are you still with us, Ignatius?' Baby asked. 'You look like you're in a trance.' I held onto the bridge and she came closer to me. She touched my arm and I wanted to kill her.

'What are you seeing now?' she asked. 'Look at those mad eyes of yours?'

'There for a long time I lived in the shape of a hawk, so that I outlived all those races that invaded Ireland,' I whispered into her ear, she could have recoiled at the smell of me but she didn't. 'I was a river salmon, known by every fisherman in every pool, scarred from the claws of hungry birds, exhausted and caught and taken to a woman who was stuck in a miserable cabin and fed into her and I remember the time that I was in her womb, and what each one said to her in the house and what was done in Ireland during that time. I knew all that was being done in Ireland, and I was a seer and a name was given to me, Ignatius O Conaill, cursed while taking shape from devoured fish into unloved rotten boy, born the sixth unwanted son of Sheila O'Reilly from Oldcastle and Seamus O Conaill from Bolus Head, Cill Rialaig, Ballinskelligs in the Barony of Iveragh, Co. Kerry.'

Baby shook her head and her clear eyes were lit, 'I knew it was you. I just knew it. What have they done to you, at all, at all?'

I took both her hands as if to dance, and we spun in a slow circle on that bridge over the river Liffey. 'Oh Baby! The Summer of Love has been and gone. Somewhere it really was the summer of love. We are on the march. Crying freedom, freedom. But they shot the Kennedy brothers, and Martin Luther King. And the wee boys in the Artane Boys Band kissing the ring of Archbishop McQuaid on the GAA pitch before a game. Our own Wild West, in the Barony of Iveragh. Driven with pikes from our land to the edge of the world. Then starved out of it a few hundred years later. Swollen with the stories, fit to burst with them. I was hawk and salmon, I shifted into barefoot baby boy terrified of my father's stick. Dragged off the farm,' I ranted and raved as we spun, then I let her go and waved my arms to keep her at bay, but she just got her balance and stood there bemused, one hand on her hips and the other dangling an enormous blue handbag.

'What are ye like?'

'And you, Baby Lyons, step from the Ireland of blackberry picking and glowing turf that your own daddy cut out of the prehistoric earth, for to keep you twentieth-century warm. You are unbeaten, no one raised a hand to you.'

'Oh I had the nuns, you forget that.' Baby swung her handbag in mock battle with me. I ducked.

'Them nuns kept you horrid pure,' I leered. 'Baby, Baby, be my Baby! What a beautiful young woman you have become. I have so much shame inside to stand before you. Go away from me.'

'What's with all this Zozimus stuff, Ignatius?' Baby asked.

'I am Zozimus,' I bowed. 'Second rate, borrowed man, threshold beast. Like the Bull, fenced in. Poor, poor craytur. Not the full shilling.'

'You're too much, so you are,' she smiled.

'Too much for the world, but not enough for myself.'

'Today is the anniversary,' she said somberly. A cloud passed over the sun. In a second the city was one degree darker. The Liffey water under the bridge shifting from glittering green to a smelly streel of grey.

'Excuse me mam. I have to go and talk to a man about a dog.' I began to back away over the rough edges of the city, don't come close, she'd smell the canal ditches and dark pram sheds on me.

'It's five years since Seán died. That's why I came.' Baby stepped closer to me. 'I had heard it was you. Mary made Fr Lavin ask around even. He asked the Vincent de Paul in Dublin. We were sure you would come to us as soon as you left the school. We didn't realize they let you out a year early. Then we thought you might have gone to London. But we heard there was a man on the bridge telling the story of the Bull. It was Patsey's sister. She was up in Dublin and heard you on the bridge. Can you imagine that? Once Patsey heard he came to Mary. You know Patsey, he arrived saying, 'Mary, may you live to be one hundred years and one extra year to atone.'

I laughed, I could see the feckin eejit saying just that.

'That's when I had this feeling. It's his anniversary. Fr Lavin's saying a Mass but I couldn't go to it. I came here instead to see if I was right.'

The anniversary of Uncle Seán's death. 'They wouldn't bury him in consecrated ground, would you credit that?' I said to her. And I backed up and held onto the bridge railing. 'And him the holiest man I'd ever known, the gentlest animal. I saw him carry spiders on pieces of paper and place them outside the window, he never raised his hand in anger, except the once, and God did I deserve that beating. I had turned him into them. So much so, they gave him a standing ovation for battering me. He's in Hell now for sure.'

'You found him hanging, didn't you?' Baby's eyes were full of tears.

'That means it's my birthday tomorrow,' I said, the realization suddenly wrenching myself from my thoughts. 'I'll be sixteen.'

'So you will. Come on, Ignatius. Follow me. I won't bite you. You can tell me the story of the Bull and I know somewhere you can have a bed for a few nights for it.'

'I don't need any of youse lot.'

'It's not charity. As payment for the stories I know someone collecting them, a friend of ours at the university.'

I looked at her long legs, her skirt barely covering her pert little arse. I thought of putting my hand up there. Of finding her up there. I'd never had a woman but I dreamed about it. Her breasts were moving under her tight sweater. I could lick them. She was wearing an engagement ring, an emerald.

'*An áit a bhuil do chroí is ann a thabharfas do chosa thú,*' I said.

'What does that mean when it's at home?' she said and gestured for me to follow her, so lightly, so lovely.

'Aren't there hippies putting flowers in guns, Baby?' I began to circle her as she was standing. The circles getting closer and closer. 'Isn't the world changing? And the Beatles are bringing us Asia back with messages from the ashrams, singing all we need is love. But they're wrong, because we need so much more. All we have is love, that's what they should have sung. They got it so wrong.'

I was now standing right in front of her. We were face to face. I could feel her breath.

'All we have is love,' she said softly.

'I don't know if I can come,' I whispered and put my crooked hands on her shoulders.

'Ah now, come here to me, Ignatius, you have to.' She backed away and beckoned to me. I stuck my ugly claws into my coat and I followed her. I followed a few paces behind. We talked as we walked down the quays.

'Why didn't ye come and get me out of that place?' I said. 'Mary, Patsey, Fr Lavin, any of ye? I told everyone what it was like, what they done to us.'

Baby looked down at the ground. 'Mary couldn't have paid for your school. We thought at least you were getting schooled at St Joseph's. It took her a few years before she'd even say your name, or mention anything about it. She took it awful hard, Seán's death. She had heard the banshee the night it happened. I swear to God.'

'The feckin banshee. Weren't we so grand that she would come for us. So she blamed me for killing Uncle Seán?'

'No. No. She never said that. Mary doesn't have a bad bone in her body. I owe it to her to find you and we can look for her sister Maeve and her child. She never did anything but good for anyone and she got so little.'

'She got you, Baby,' I whispered words that scuttered over the ripples of the smelly Liffey river as it rolled under the bridge I stood on day after day after day telling my stories. Being someone else. Anyone else.

She laughed, light on water.

And I took my bottle of whiskey from my coat pocket and took a slug. And she, as bold as brass, took it off of me and took a wee sip herself.

'Love is all we have,' I sang.

We walked side by side through Merchant's Arch, through the old walls of Dublin that they built to keep the Irish out. And here we were, milling into the city, it was ours now. But I was vanquished alright. She would never love the likes of me.

'Did you ever hear tell of the Cruelty Men? All of us, legions of us, generations of us, poor children snatched away and made unlovable,' I seethed. 'That's what hurt the most, everyone said it, not the beatings, not the buggery. The boys and the girls, all of us said the same, that in all those years not one kind word, not one kind touch. That was the poison.'

'Oh God I'm so sorry, Ignatius.'

'If I reached out to touch you I would destroy you and it makes me want to kill myself.'

She bit her lip. And reached her lovely hand up and touched my arm.

'What are you thinking of Ignatius? You've a quare look on your face,' she said.

'Why did ye all forget about me?' I now had big stupid, girly tears welling up in my eyes.

'I'm here not for you. I know about Mary's life. She told me all the stories. Her story is my story. She made me, so she did. Mary gave me a shape. If I tell you a bit about Mary, you'll understand where she was coming from and where you come from too. And in exchange you come with me and tell my friend all your stories.'

'And where will I sleep tonight?' I leaned into her, where I could see the tiny hairs between her eyebrows.

'You can sleep in our flat tonight I suppose.'

I snatched her hand and looked at that emerald ring, there was a wedding ring below it. I shifted back into Zozimus to protect myself from her. To protect her from me. I would let her tell me my history, for what good that would do me. But she seemed to want to. And she had someone to collect my stories, had she? Oh I was a quare one alright, the genuine article, and I'd play my part, and keep her in my life.

I walked beside her over cobbled streets chanting stories and songs.

Baby smiled all the way, familiar as she was with the stories that Mary had told Seán and herself, and Seán had told me and I was telling them back.

'You said we didn't come looking for you,' Baby said. 'I'm so sorry we didn't. But there's one thing I can't understand. You've been out of that place for a year, why didn't you come looking for us?'

We were on Dame Street in front of the iron gates of Trinity College. I stopped, suddenly weary, took a swig from my flask, and asked her: 'When have the well fed ever understood the hungry?'

*

That is my story. And if there's a lie in it let it be so. It was not I who composed it. I got no reward but butter boots and paper stockings. The white-legged hound came, and ate the boots from my feet, and tore my paper stockings.

Acknowledgments

More people supported me while writing *The Cruelty Men* than there are characters in it, and that's a lot. I wrote this book in a studio on Eleanor and Paddy O'Sullivan's farm in County Meath. I felt sustained as an artist in their house and sometimes that is key to keeping going. At first, like my characters, I resisted the flatness of Meath but the land has a way of revealing its poised allure. I thank my generous big-hearted parents, Eamonn and Marguerite, who helped raise my two daughters, Jasmine and Jade, and continue to raise me as a very late developer. Life was bearable and even rich thanks to my sister Ciara Martin and her husband Kieran Fulcher and my nieces Aisling, Roisin and Clodagh, whom I watched become formidable women. To my brother Daragh, who doesn't do small talk but immediately opens up with discussions of emperors, schisms and the Neolithic world; his best friend Daithí swapped folktales with me, one of which I borrowed for this book.

The community of Drumree in County Meath welcomed me. Mairead and Padraig Brady, who had me over every Friday, and included me in so many family events. Paula and Johnny Leonard, whose door was always open; I'd give one swift knock and come right on in to put on the kettle. Caitriona Curran, who taught my kids and became my great and lasting friend. Aisling McCabe, who made me endless cups of tea in her kitchen while our kids went feral. Christ, there were so many kitchens. In Dublin, Beth Quinn's energy and sharp mind helped me through that time both practically and mentally. To Alison Crosbie, who became a force in my life and a recurring figure in my dreams; we tore around Dublin manys a night and sat up into the wee hours dismantling the world, sometimes forgetting to put it back together.

Alison Crosbie, Linda Quinn and June Caldwell were first readers of the early raw draft and they gave me the support to carry it through all the doubts and doubters. Irvine Welsh's feedback and belief in the value and seriousness of the work kept me going. Cliona Hannon, my hero, tirelessly works for education of disadvantaged students and brought me into the Trinity Access Programme as a teacher. Judith Mok and Michael O Loughlin's penthouse apartment perched over the Royal Canal became a haven and meeting place for so many artists and performers. Their commitment to their own work was an inspiration. Michael's initial editing of the hunk of raw marble that became the book helped it take a shape. Philip Casey was an advocate for the work and had a fathomless knowledge of historical elements.

Noelle Campbell Sharpe opened a portal when she sent me off to Cill Rialaig's magic mountain with an imperious sweep of her hand with orders to respond to Sean O Conaills' folktales. Ger O Connell, an artist and a man with his foot in both worlds, was the guide on the other side of the door.

All the Banshees – Helena Mulkerns, Imelda O Reilly, Caitríona O Leary, Elizabeth White and Darrah Carr whose twenty-year anniversary is this year; we're still all miraculously working as artists.

Anna Van Lenten and Maria Behan were stalwart editors of various drafts; their professionalism and rigor was a guiding force.

The poet Kevin Williamson frequently lured me to Scotland to perform in Neu Reekie and his faith in my work over the years has sustained and nourished me. Our hunt for Síle ná Gig's has led to many nefarious adventures and travels.

Seán Farrell became the final editor; his perception and attention to detail and nuance and voice were invaluable. Afshin, Jasmine and Jade put up with the vagaries, uncertainties and indigence of living with a writer, and nightly walks with Valerie Sabbag, my neighbour and friend, kept me sane. Donna Collins and Rick Williams whose family became family. Finally, thanks to the filmmaker Alka Raghuram, with whom I hatched a plan as we bought matching silver shoes to take us across the threshold and through the door.

I read many books while researching this book. The key ones were: Kieran Hickey's fascinating *Wolves in Ireland: A natural and cultural history* (2013) and the illuminating and thought-provoking *Origins of the Magdalene Laundries: An Analytical History* (2009) by Rebecca Lea McCarthy. Hanna Greally's heartbreaking *Bird's Nest Soup* (1971) allowed me to imagine what life inside the asylum was like. I remain in awe of Mary Raftery and Eoin O'Sullivan's seminal *Suffer the Little Children: The Inside Story of Ireland's Industrial School* (1999), an example of research with heart. I will be forever haunted by *The Ryan Report Commission to Inquire into Child Abuse* published on 20 May 2009 and by *The Murphy Report Commission of Investigation into the Catholic Archdiocese of Dublin* of November 2009. The bravery and endurance of the people caught up in this hideous system was both moving and devastating. None of the trails my fictional characters endured are exaggerations. The system was brutal. Their courage in telling their stories changed Ireland forever.

Especial thanks to Sarah-Anne Buckley, who wrote *The cruelty man*: *Child welfare, the NSPCC and the State in Ireland, 1889-1956* (2013). I discovered this book after I finished my own but it provided much information that I could check my work against.

The ancient folktales included in the book are in italics because one of the aspects of folktales is that they get passed down word by word unchanged. Many of those recording the folktales took them directly from the storytellers: Lady Gregory, *A Book of Saints and Wonders* (1908), James Stephens, *Irish Fairy Tales* (1920), Lady Francesca Speranza Wilde, *Ancient Legends, Mystic Charms, and Superstitions of Ireland* (1887). Ella Young's *Celtic Wonder Tales* (1910) was particularly beautifully written. Her version of 'The Children of Lir' was the one read out as a child over and over again until it became part of me.

Finally, I am indebted to the storyteller Seán Ó Conaill and to his editor Seamus O Duilearga, who came to Bolus Head to gather all that ancient wealth of lore into Seán *Ó Conaill's Book: Stories and Traditions from Iveragh* (1981). Without this meeting, all of these stories would have been lost forever. Thank you to all the storytellers who keep them alive.